WITH LOVE
FROM
HARLEM

ALSO BY RESHONDA TATE

The Queen of Sugar Hill
Miss Pearly's Girls
A Little Bit of Karma
The Stolen Daughter
The Book in Room 316
Seeking Sarah
The Perfect Mistress
Mama's Boy
Finding Amos (with Bernice L. McFadden and J. D. Mason)
What's Done in the Dark
A Family Affair
The Secret She Kept
Say Amen, Again
A Good Man Is Hard to Find
Holy Rollers
The Devil Is a Lie
Can I Get a Witness?
The Pastor's Wife
Everybody Say Amen
I Know I've Been Changed
Let the Church Say Amen
My Brother's Keeper

With Victoria Christopher Murray

Saints & Sinners
Friends & Foes
Fortune & Fame
Pay Day
It Should've Been Me
A Blessing & a Curse
If Only for One Night

Anthologies
The Motherhood Diaries 2
The Motherhood Diaries
Have a Little Faith
Four Degrees of Heat
Proverbs for the People

Nonfiction
Help! I've Turned into My Mother

Poetry
Something to Say

Teen Fiction
Eye Candy
Boy Trouble
Truth or Dare
Real As It Gets
You Don't Know Me Like That
Rumor Central
Drama Queens
Caught Up in the Drama
Friends 'Til the End
Fair-Weather Friends
Getting Even
With Friends Like These
Blessings in Disguise
Nothing But Drama

WITH LOVE FROM HARLEM

A Novel of Hazel Scott

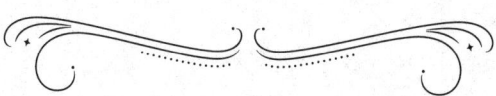

ReShonda Tate

WILLIAM MORROW

An Imprint of HarperCollins*Publishers*

This book is a work of fiction. References to real people, events, establishments, organizations, or locales are intended only to provide a sense of authenticity, and are used fictitiously. All other characters, and all incidents and dialogue, are drawn from the author's imagination and are not to be construed as real.

hc.com

FIRST EDITION

Interior text design by Diahann Sturge-Campbell

Library of Congress Cataloging-in-Publication Data

Names: Tate, ReShonda author
Title: With love from Harlem : a novel / ReShonda Tate.
Description: First edition. | New York, NY : William Morrow, 2026. | Includes biographical information.
Identifiers: LCCN 2025015780 | ISBN 9780063421189 paperback | ISBN 9780063421202 ebook
Subjects: LCSH: Scott, Hazel—Fiction | Pianists—United States—Fiction | Jazz musicians—United States—Fiction | African American women musicians—Fiction | Harlem (New York, N.Y.)—Fiction | LCGFT: Biographical fiction | Fiction | Novels
Classification: LCC PS3602.I445 W58 2026
LC record available at https://lccn.loc.gov/2025015780

ISBN 978-0-06-342118-9

Printed in the United States of America

26 27 28 29 30 LBC 8 7 6 5 4

For every woman who has ever felt unseen—
whose brilliance was overlooked,
whose voice was silenced,
whose story was never told.
This is for you.
And for my sister, Tanisha Tate—
who fights hard, loves fiercely,
and makes sure our voices are heard.
Thank you for seeing me—and all of us.

PART
I

CHAPTER 1

March 1943
Manhattan, New York

S he'd played to packed houses all over the country, but only New York knew how to love her like this.

The "Hazel Scott Returns to Cafe Society" sign pulsed in sync with the energetic crowd. As Hazel peeked out from behind the velvet partition, a surge of electricity coursed through her and danced along the edges of her nerves.

She'd expected a full house—every one of the fifty tables in the club was crammed with patrons, and at least two dozen more spectators lined the walls. Jewel-toned swing dresses, wide-legged trousers, and checkered zoot suits were on full display.

Hazel inhaled the anticipation. These people were ready for a show. And she was ready to give them one.

The announcer's voice cut through the chatter like a brass horn. ". . . She's back from making history as the first Negro woman to have her own show in Las Vegas, from touring all over the world, and capturing our hearts in movies. Here for one night only before she heads back out to change the world with music. Ladies, gents, and drunks, put your hands together for America's biggest jazz star, the incomparable Hazel Scott!"

The applause exploded as Hazel slipped from behind the partition. The spotlight beamed on her shimmering off-the-shoulder gold floor-length gown, the fabric cascading like liquid light against her golden-brown skin as she glided into the center of the room. Each step felt like a homecoming, a return to the place where her heart and soul had always belonged.

"Welcome home, Hazel. We love you!" a voice rang out from the back of the room.

Hazel pressed her hands together in gratitude, relishing the familiar faces and adoration that filled the U-shaped space around her. Cafe Society was as she remembered—elegant, intimate, decadent. The art deco murals shimmered under the soft chandelier light. Cigarette smoke curled lazily in the air. A beautiful tapestry of faces, white and colored, sat side by side, drawn together by the one thing that transcended the world: music.

"New York, how is everyone doing tonight?" Hazel purred into the microphone.

As the crowd roared in response, her attention landed on a table directly in front of her where a handsome man sat wearing a pin-striped suit that made him look like he had just stepped out of a Langston Hughes poem—smooth, confident, and full of purpose. Hazel recognized him as the Harlem representative for the New York City Council, Adam Clayton Powell Jr. A petite, fair-skinned woman with soft curls pinned neatly in place sat next to him, dressed conservatively in a navy knee-length dress and a single strand of pearls. She eased her hand on Adam's arm when he didn't take his eyes off Hazel.

"We missed you!" someone shouted.

"I missed you, too." Hazel extended her arms to the crowd. "All of you."

She glanced at Adam again. He stared at her with an intensity that made her shiver.

Hazel took a breath and turned her attention back to the enthusiastic crowd. "You ready for a show?" she asked before making her way to the grand piano in the center of the room.

"Yeah!"

"For sure!"

A chorus of enthusiastic replies filled the room as she took her seat. For many artists, facing this crowd of ritzy, integrated folks might be intimidating, but not for Hazel. From the moment she first stepped in front of the Cafe Society crowd, Hazel had felt an inexplicable connection with this place and its patrons.

Hazel's fingers hovered over the keys, and as the first note escaped the piano, it was like oxygen to her soul. Now, she was alone . . . just her and the music.

"Swing those classics, Hazel!" someone shouted, and she obliged, beginning with Chopin before seamlessly transitioning into a jazz improvisation. Her hands obeyed no script, turning centuries of classical precision into something raw and unique. This was her signature, what had made her a star. Hazel let herself indulge in the sight of the men swaying along, the women snapping their fingers, and everyone tapping their feet. But then, her eyes, like magnets, were pulled back to Adam.

He took a long, slow drag of his cigar, the red ember glowing, then fading. The music surrounded him, but he didn't move, didn't crack a smile. It was as though he were dissecting her with his gaze, peeling back the layers of her performance to see what lay underneath.

"That's how you do it, baby!" another voice called from the back, and Hazel answered with a cascade of faster, wilder notes. She wasn't the first to jazz up the classics, but she was the first to do it like this—to blend them so seamlessly that you couldn't tell where the classical ended and the jazz began.

Just as the crowd seemed to settle, two men rolled out another piano to the right of Hazel. Confused chatter rippled through the room as Hazel continued playing Fletcher Henderson's "Sugar Foot Stomp" with her right hand, while her left hand launched into Beethoven's *Moonlight* Sonata on the new piano. The simultaneous melodies set the crowd on fire.

"That's the cat's meow!" someone yelled.

Hazel performed a few more pieces, each song a story, each note a word, weaving tales of love, loss, and the indomitable spirit of New York. As she played her final refrain, a hush settled over the room before thunderous applause broke out. Hazel rose from the bench, stepped forward, soaked in the moment, then took a deep bow. As she straightened, her gaze locked on to Adam.

He was still sitting, still watching her, yet his posture had softened. His lips curved into a smile, and Hazel felt something electric and unsettling shift deep in her spine. Despite the woman by his side, whose lips were pressed in a tight, irritated line, Adam's eyes never wavered from Hazel. And for a brief moment, her pulse quickened, as though they were the only people in the room.

"Another round of applause for Hazel Scott," the announcer's voice boomed.

The audience roared again as the house music kicked in and patrons jumped to their feet, all rushing to surround Hazel. She basked in the love.

"Hazel, you just get better every time I see you!" Her friend Langston Hughes pulled her into a hug, snapping her attention away from Adam.

"Nothing matches the warmth of familiar walls," she replied. "You know I love being able to feel the heat of the room."

Hazel glided through the tables, greeting strangers and hugging old friends. A young woman with wide, hopeful eyes and a mouth painted in Victory Red lipstick sidled up to Hazel. She looked barely out of her teens as she clutched a small beaded purse that glittered under the club lights. "Miss Scott, I just wanted to say thank you," she said. "I hope to play the piano as well as you one day. Thank you for opening doors. It's like you're making it possible for the rest of us to dream."

Hazel's expression softened as she took the young woman's hands in hers. "That's exactly why I'm here," she whispered. "You just keep dreaming, keep working, and you'll get there. And when you do, promise me you'll do the same for the next girl. What's your name?"

"Eunice Kathleen Waymon," the young woman said, her voice filled with a nervous energy. "But my stage name is Nina Simone. I mean, I haven't been onstage yet, but I'm sixteen, just six years younger than you. So I'm praying one day I can be a star like you."

"Well, Nina Simone, I look forward to that day." Hazel gave her hand a reassuring squeeze before moving further into the audience, exchanging pleasantries and laughter as she worked her way toward the dressing room. But as she neared the door, a large, warm hand closed around hers, halting her steps.

She turned and found herself face-to-face with Councilman Powell. Up close, he was even more magnetic. As his gaze cut through the dimness, she could feel the strength of his hand enveloping her own. The words on the edge of her tongue scattered like startled birds.

"Hazel Scott." Adam lifted her hand to his lips, and just as she thought he was about to kiss her fingers, he turned her hand over and kissed the center of her palm. "Well done."

She opened her mouth, intending to thank him, but all that came out was a quiet, flustered "O-okay."

Adam's smile widened, as though he'd sensed the effect he had on her. His thumb traced slow circles against her fingertips as he continued talking. "The crowd loved you tonight. But not more than I did."

Adam moved even closer, and Hazel felt heat rise in her cheeks as the scent of his Acqua di Parma Colonia mingled with the lingering aroma of cigar smoke.

"You are an exceptional artist and magnetic presence," he said.

"Thank you, Councilman Powell," Hazel said, finally finding her voice.

"Adam," he corrected her with a charming smile. "Please, call me Adam."

"Adam," she echoed, the name rolling off her tongue with a surprising familiarity. She'd seen him around Harlem—always in motion—but never this close. He was undeniably striking. It wasn't just the sharp cheekbones that cut lines across his fair skin or the piercing eyes beneath that halo of perfectly coiled black hair. It was his commanding presence. At six foot four, he towered over her by a foot.

"I've been hearing amazing things about you," Adam said. "I can't believe this is the first time I've been able to make it down to see you perform."

She straightened her shoulders and lifted her chin, instinctively squaring herself. "Thank you for coming. I'm scheduled to go back out on my concert tour soon, so it was amazing to be able to squeeze this performance in," she said, finally able to fully form a sentence.

"Would it be possible for us to meet to discuss your career prior to your departure? I would love to interview you for *The People's Voice*."

Hazel arched an eyebrow, surprised. She was a regular reader of the newspaper Adam had founded last year, a platform he used to tackle police brutality, housing discrimination, and other civil rights issues. But since when did he cover entertainers?

She tried to pull her hand away. His grasp tightened, and she didn't resist. That is, until she noticed the petite woman who had been sitting next to him, her dark eyes glaring over Adam's shoulder. This woman shooting daggers their way was no doubt his wife.

"I appreciate your kind words. Perhaps when I return I can call your office to set something up," Hazel said, finally managing to slip her hand from his.

"Or you could call me."

There was something about the way he looked at her that touched her in a way applause never could. "Enjoy the rest of your evening, Reverend Powell," she said, in an effort to remind herself that the man making her insides flutter was a man of God. Hazel summoned all her strength to guide her away.

The smell of his cologne was still with her as she entered her dressing room, where her mother greeted her the second she walked in.

"Sweetheart, you made your mother proud!"

It had been a long night, and Alma Long Scott was her usual pristine self. Her silver-streaked hair was styled in soft waves and she wore her favorite floral dress, the one with the high collar and pearl buttons. Her mother was always proper, always poised—like a refined Trinidian belle, though Harlem had sharpened her edges.

Her mother tilted her head slightly, observing Hazel. "Love that double piano move. You didn't share that little trick with me."

The large dressing room was overflowing with bouquets and telegrams—well-wishes ranging from Frank Sinatra to First Lady Eleanor Roosevelt, who often had Hazel speak at social justice rallies.

"That last note was a little too tight," her mother continued, instantly dissolving the lingering euphoria Hazel felt from her encounter with Adam. That was Alma—she wouldn't be herself if she didn't find something Hazel could improve upon. It was the music teacher in her mother, and with Hazel as her only student for the past ten years, she took her job more seriously than anyone else ever could.

Before Hazel could respond, Barney Josephson strode into the room, his leather shoes clattering on the linoleum. "Now, Alma," he said, "you know Hazel was phenomenal." His voice was warm, a little raspy, but full of pride. As the owner and visionary of Cafe Society, the only integrated nightclub in the city, Barney wore his convictions as comfortably as the slightly rumpled suit he favored.

"My darling is always phenomenal, though." He handed Hazel her signature martini in a frosted glass—the one she enjoyed after every show. "What twenty-two-year-old can light up a crowd like that?"

"I don't disagree," Alma said, folding her arms. "But there's always room for improvement."

"Well, considering there's a line of folks outside who couldn't get in the building because there wasn't a seat left to spare, I'd say tonight was a huge success," Barney countered with a grin, brushing his hand through his thin hair as he did whenever he was excited. "I will be forever grateful to Billie for the introduction."

The memory brought a smile to Hazel's face. Billie Holiday, who was like a big sister to her, used to be Barney's star at Cafe Society. Then, one night, she feigned illness to give Hazel a shot at replacing her when she left to go on tour. Hazel had taken the stage that night and had stayed onstage for three years, until she, too, left to tour and make movies.

Hazel glanced at Barney, his pasty face flushed pink from excitement, his wispy blond hair more disheveled than usual, and she felt overwhelming gratitude. He'd always been there for her, cheering her on with unwavering loyalty and pride.

"You're the best thing this city has, Hazel," Barney said.

"Well, I'm glad you're happy." Hazel clicked the rim of her glass against Barney's with a soft *ting*. The gin was cold and crisp as it touched her lips, the olive brine sitting on her tongue.

Hazel was four years old when her father, R. Thomas Scott, a West African scholar from Liverpool who had emigrated to Trinidad to teach English at St. Mary's College, moved to New York alone with the promise to send for them one day. That day never came. Still, in 1924, her mother and grandmother had packed up their belongings and moved to Harlem. Though they'd moved just seven blocks from her father, they might as well have been thousands of miles apart. The sharp sting of rejection had lingered, shaping her in ways she didn't fully understand even now.

For all her father's absence, for all the complicated feelings she harbored about him, Barney's steadfastness made up for it.

"Well," Alma finally said. "There's no denying it. You were spectacular, my love." She stepped forward, adjusting the strap of Hazel's gown, as though she were still her little girl. "But don't let it go to your head."

Hazel laughed softly. "Wouldn't dream of it, Mama."

Just then, the door swung open. "Haze!"

Hazel's smile faltered. The air shifted as Billie entered, using the nickname she'd given Hazel when they first met ten years ago when Alma brought Billie to their house for a jam session. From that moment, Billie had taken Hazel under her wing and become her self-declared big sister.

Billie's hair was a disheveled mess, her makeup smudged, and her eyes glazed. A heavy waft of perfume laced with something more illicit drifted into the room with her, and she swayed on her feet.

This was a woman worn down by her own battles.

"That show was spec-tacular!" Billie slurred, her words tumbling out slowly. "I been tellin' people how talented you are."

Alma stopped mid-scoop as she gathered Hazel's belongings and flinched at Billie's careless grammar. Billie didn't notice—or didn't care. She staggered to the chaise and toppled over, right onto Hazel's mink coat.

"Billie, are you high? Drunk? Insane?" Alma said.

Billie let out a low, throaty laugh, hitching her dress over her knees. "All of the above," she said with a shrug.

"Did anyone see you like this?"

"Oh, I'm guessin' everyone did."

"Come on, Billie," Hazel snapped, unable to hide her frustration. Privately, Billie had been battling drug addiction for years. Lately, though, she'd been careless about hiding her vice. "You know if the newspapers get wind of this, you'll never live it down."

Billie waved a dismissive hand. "Ain't nobody got the right to judge me."

Barney moved quickly, taking Billie by the arm. "Let me take you home."

She tried to swat him away, but it was only a slight slap. "I'm fine," Billie mumbled. She tried to stand and almost toppled over again. "Okay, maybe I'm not," she cackled.

"You need to go home and rest," Hazel said.

When Billie looked at her, the old fire had returned to her eyes, a spark of the fierce woman Hazel had once idolized. But just as quickly, it faded, replaced by resignation.

"Yeah, okay," Billie murmured as she let Barney guide her toward the door. "But not 'cause you told me to. You not my mama." She turned to Alma, her head wobbling as if she was having trouble keeping it upright. "And neither are you."

Alma's eyes locked on Hazel as Barney led her friend out. Alma and Billie had become friends on the musical circuit, and at one time, her mother had been closer to Billie than Hazel was. But Alma had little tolerance for Billie's troubled side.

"What?" Hazel said after they were gone and silence filled the room.

Alma studied her for a moment before saying, "I know you want to help. But she's not your sin, and you're not her savior. One day, you'll look up and realize you've poured yourself out for everyone else—and there's nothing left for you." She paused. "You say you want to be the biggest entertainer in the country. You're almost there, baby girl. And hitching your wagon to Billie will derail you both."

CHAPTER 2

April 1943
White Plains, New York

S pring was in full bloom in White Plains. A blend of bright leaves and budding flowers blanketed the town in color. Warm breezes rustled the freshly cut bushes, and the sunlight spilled through the large bay window of Hazel's new home.

She let her hand rest on the gleaming windowsill, her fingers grazing the wood as if to reassure herself that this place was real. It had taken months of planning and relentless effort to find the perfect house: four bedrooms, a spacious kitchen where her mother could cook up her favorite West Indian dishes, and a backyard big enough for long afternoons of gardening.

Hazel had mixed feelings about being only the second colored woman to live in this neighborhood just forty-five minutes from Harlem, but when the real estate agent didn't want to sell because of her skin color, Hazel was even more determined to close the deal.

"Blessed assurance . . . Jesus is mine . . ." her mother sang from the kitchen where she was unpacking dishes. The faint clink of porcelain mixed with the melodic sound of her mother's favorite hymn, brought a smile to Hazel's lips. This woman had been her anchor through so much, struggling to make ends meet and then watching Hazel grow from a precocious child into a celebrated pianist. She'd

tried her hand at love when Hazel was in middle school—but ultimately, her love for her daughter took precedence over everything else.

Though they kept their Harlem apartment—her aunt was staying in it—White Plains was their new home. Leaving Harlem had been bittersweet. Every corner of that neighborhood carried memories, but her mother longed for a garden, a yard, space. This house provided all of that. The minute Hazel found out her last album had sold over one hundred thousand copies—making her the highest selling artist for her label, Decca—she'd begun saving for this home. Or rather, she had her mother save, since Hazel didn't concern herself with money matters. And now that they'd found their dream home, everything felt right. It was peaceful. Stable. And stability was something she desperately wanted for her mother, even if their relationship was a never-ending Ping-Pong game of sharp words and reconciliations.

Hazel surveyed the living room, still half swallowed by boxes. The sunlight spilling across the hardwood floors highlighted the framed photographs she'd already set up on the mantel: her first job at Mabel Laws Horsey's dance studio, her debut with Count Basie when she was fifteen, and one from her high school prom with her boyfriend, Lee, looking boyishly handsome.

Her mother's voice floated in from the kitchen. "Hazel! Come and see if this set should go in the china cabinet or the buffet!"

"I'm coming, Mama!" Hazel caught a glimpse of herself in the mirror and smiled as she adjusted her headwrap. The barefaced reflection staring back would've startled her fans, who were used to seeing her draped in glamorous gowns and furs and dripping in jewels. But offstage, away from the spotlight, Hazel reverted to her girlish comforts: ankle socks and Oxford loafers, long skirts that swayed at the calves and a face free of makeup.

As she entered the kitchen, Hazel caught her mother holding up two mismatched teacups like they were national treasures. Alma frowned at them with all the intensity of an art appraiser.

"Are we curating a museum or just having tea?" Hazel said.

"Don't tease," Alma replied, her lips twitching into a smile. "This is important. If we're going to live in a house with a real dining room, we're going to do it right."

"Fair enough. Let's put them in the buffet."

Before Alma could respond, the front door opened, and Lee entered, carrying a small brown bag from the hardware store. His denim overalls were slightly smudged with something Hazel couldn't identify but suspected was dried blood since he'd come straight here from his job at the slaughterhouse. His grin was as wide and unbothered as a lazy summer afternoon.

"Got those screws for your bed frame," he announced, holding up the bag like it was filled with precious gems. "I'm gonna finish it up before I head home. Shouldn't take long."

"Thanks, Lee," Hazel said. For all his simplicity, he was steady and kind, two qualities she found increasingly rare.

Lee kissed her cheek—a brief, almost shy gesture even though they'd known each other since they were twelve—then nodded to Alma. "Miss Alma, this house is somethin' else. You picked a good one."

Alma beamed. "That's Hazel's doing. She's got fine taste."

"Don't I know it," Lee replied, adjusting his overall strap, his smile wide with pride. "I'll be in the bedroom if you need me."

As he disappeared down the hall, Hazel called after him, "And don't forget, you promised to sweep up the sawdust when you're done!"

His cheerful "Yes, ma'am!" echoed back. Hazel shook her head, smiling despite herself.

"He's so sweet," Alma said.

"He is," Hazel admitted, then let out a whispered sigh. "But I don't know how many more conversations about butchered pigs I can handle before I lose my mind."

Alma laughed and resumed unpacking and humming. Outside, a robin perched on the low stone wall by the garden, its chirping song weaving into the hum of Alma's hymn. Hazel stood for a moment and took in the beauty.

"Hey, daydreamer," her mother said, pointing to the empty boxes strewn across the room. "You want to finish up here?"

Hazel chuckled as she picked up an empty box and moved it to the corner. Thankfully, they'd made substantial progress and should be finished within the hour. Since the TV had been set up, Hazel turned it on. A movie called *Affectionately Yours* filled the screen.

Hazel frowned as Butterfly McQueen's character whined, "*Who dat say who dat when I say who dat?*"

"Do you hear this, Mama? What does that even mean? This is nearly as bad as when they had Louis Armstrong dressed in leopard skin, playing a savage," Hazel said with disgust.

"Why do you let those movies rile you up so much?" her mother answered.

"It's infuriating." Hazel threw up her hands. "Hollywood doesn't believe we're talented enough to be anything but the maid."

"You didn't play a maid in any of your three movies."

"And I never will." Hazel was always cast as a pianist. Her last role, in a movie called *Casablanca,* had been canceled at the last minute. The studio had decided to give the role to Dooley Wilson instead because they wanted a man. But Hazel loved acting and would have loved the chance to be more than a pianist.

Her mother placed the last of the china into the buffet. "Don't knock those artists, sweetheart. That's all they're given. You have choices, but Hollywood isn't ready to see those actors in other roles yet."

"I won't wear a uniform or those degrading costumes," Hazel huffed as she changed the channel to the five-o'clock news. "No, thank you. I will not pander or perform for their comfort."

A tap on the door halted her tirade. Hazel answered to see Barney standing with a stack of stapled papers, flashing his signature smile.

"Barney"—she motioned to the chaos around them—"welcome to the mess."

"Looks like progress to me." He kissed her cheek before stepping inside. "And I come bearing gifts—two new movie role offers."

"If they're for singing maids, forget it." Hazel took the papers. "I'll stay right here in New York rather than humiliate myself in Hollywood."

"What about her concert tour?" her mother asked.

"She'll be wrapped with the tour by the time filming starts," Barney said. "She will need to complete the next album, but we can find a studio in Los Angeles for her to do that."

He waited, watching as Hazel skimmed the page. Her eyes widened. "'Artist will be compensated four thousand dollars per week to play herself in *The Heat's On* and *Rhapsody in Blue*,'" she read. "Is this for real?"

"It sure is."

"Four thousand?" she exclaimed. "Hattie McDaniel only got four hundred and fifty dollars for playing Mammy."

"Exactly!" Barney said, pride flashing in his eyes. He didn't take a commission on her film earnings, using her appearances as leverage for her work at Cafe Society instead.

Hazel continued reading, her smile spreading with every word. *Artist shall receive same pay as her white counterparts.* "This is wonderful. But I still want final approval over all music I perform. And if the wardrobe isn't flattering, I'll wear my own."

Barney chuckled, pulling out a notebook to jot on. "I told them you'd want music approval, and they agreed. I'm sure they'll be fine with the wardrobe too."

"I'm in." She handed the contract to her mother, who had started reading over her shoulder.

"Told you I'd fight for you." Barney looked pleased. "But I'm bringing in a film agent, Isa Kloukowsky, because, Hazel, I think this is just the beginning. I'll keep handling the music side, and she'll take care of film and TV."

"TV?" her mother asked.

"Yes," Barney exclaimed. "Hazel said she wanted to be the biggest star in the country. That means we need to have her in front of every audience—TV, film, clubs, newspapers, everywhere—and Isa can help us make that happen."

"I'm impressed," Hazel said as all the dreams she'd had since she was eight years old and accepted to Juilliard, started to materialize in her mind. If she could make it in film *and* TV, in addition to her music, it would make her high school instructors who called her work "popular junk" and the other members of the all-female band she was a part of at fourteen all see her for her talent. Growing up, Hazel had created an imaginary world where she no longer possessed the childhood feeling that failure would cause her to lose her mother's favor. In that world, her story had a happy ending, and now she was positioned for it all to come true.

They talked a little more, until a voice drew Hazel's attention back to the television. It was a preacher's rhythm that made every sentence sound like prophecy, and the minute she saw Adam Clayton Powell Jr. on her screen, her body stilled.

". . . It is my hope that the people of Harlem will elect me to be their first Negro congressman."

Hazel instinctively leaned forward.

"Congressman? Wasn't he just elected to the city council?" her mother asked.

"Seems he wants something bigger." Barney glanced from the screen to Hazel. "And judging by his interest in you, that's not all he wants."

Hazel blinked and stood up fast. "Shush," she said, her voice low. "Lee's in there."

Before Barney could reply, Lee reappeared, wiping his hands on his overalls. "All done! Bed's sturdy as a rock now." He waved at Barney. "Hey there, Mr. Josephson."

"Lee," Barney greeted smoothly, watching as the young man adjusted his straps.

"I better get home and bathe," Lee said. "Slaughtered a whole ox today and didn't get a chance to change. Hazel, maybe we can grab some soda pops later?"

Hazel forced a polite smile. "We'll see."

Lee exited, whistling a jaunty tune, and Barney waited until the door closed before leaning in conspiratorially. "You're the darling of Cafe Society and he's offering you soda pops. I can see why you're struggling to keep your eyes off Adam."

Hazel opened her mouth, but nothing came out at first. Then: "You're reading too much into things. Adam isn't interested in me like that."

Barney tilted his head. "He asked about you. A lot. And during your set? I've never seen a man look at a woman like that in a room full of people."

Hazel waved a dismissive hand. "I gave a show. He enjoyed it."

A pause. "That's all." Her gaze returned to the screen, as reporters hurled questions. "Plus, he's married."

"Mm-hmm." Barney let the silence stretch when she didn't take her eyes off the television.

She lifted her chin, more certain this time. "Doesn't matter anyway. My dreams don't have room for a man." Hazel took the papers her mother had handed back to her, flipped to the back page, and signed with a flourish.

"I have love for my family, friends, career . . . and Harlem. And that's more than enough."

CHAPTER 3

May 1943
Harlem, New York

Harlemites were packed shoulder to shoulder in the basement of
Mother AME Zion Church. There had to be at least two hundred
people here for this community forum. Folding chairs scraped against
the scuffed linoleum floor as the crowd waited for the program to begin.

On the small, raised platform at the front of the room, four local
leaders sat beneath a banner that read "Justice for Harlem's Working
Class." "Buy Where You Can Work" and "Support Local Artists"
posters lined the walls.

The stage was cramped and uneven; a simple wooden table and
mismatched chairs did little to lend authority to the figures seated
there. Newsman George Schuyler sat stiffly in his gray suit, flanked by
labor organizer Louise Thompson Patterson, Reverend Shelton Hale
Bishop, the rector at St. Phillips Church, and Adam.

Hazel's breath caught the moment her eyes landed on him. They'd
only crossed paths once since that night at Cafe Society—last week,
when he showed up unannounced at her concert in New Jersey. The
very concert she'd walked out of before playing a single note, refusing to perform once she learned the audience was segregated.

Adam had been waiting backstage when she exited to disgruntled
patrons shouting their displeasure. He had looked at her with admi-

ration when he said, *A woman with conviction is a woman after my own heart.* Then he'd turned up the heat on his flirtation.

Hazel had found his charm both undeniable and inconvenient. She was not about to lower her standards to involve herself with a married man. And yet, every time he looked at her, something inside her stirred.

Now, sitting onstage, Adam wore that same flirtatious smile when he spotted her walking in. Hazel nodded cordially and quickly turned toward the crowd in search of a seat.

She saw her friend Josephine Cogdell Schuyler, George's wife, sitting in the fifth row. Of course, she'd be here. Jody, as Hazel affectionately called her, was a white Southern belle turned Harlem Renaissance icon. Born in Texas, she had fled the constraints of Jim Crow, immersing herself in Harlem's vibrant intellectual life. She had written articles championing progressive ideals and interracial harmony before meeting George, a controversial journalist and staunch critic of segregation. They were one of the first interracial couples in Harlem.

"Hey, Jody," Hazel slid into the wooden chair next to her. Josephine's blond hair was styled in soft victory rolls, the glossy waves cascading into a neat curl at the nape of her neck. An ivory scarf draped at her throat. She was dressed far more conservatively than Hazel, wearing a navy blue suit and white gloves. Hazel, on the other hand, had opted for a deep emerald-green belted dress that swayed just above her calves.

"Evening," Josephine said.

Hazel smiled at her friend's Texas drawl. Jody had been in Harlem sixteen years but couldn't shake that twang. "How are you?" Hazel said.

"Nervous." Josephine twisted her gloves in her lap. Her face was pale, her shoulders tense as her eyes darted from George to the crowd.

The moderator finally took the podium and, after an introduction, began asking questions to each of the panelists. When he reached George, Hazel felt Josephine tense beside her.

"Mr. Schuyler," the moderator began, "many in Harlem believe that art, literature, and music are essential to defining and advancing the Negro identity in America. Do you see value in a distinct Negro cultural movement, or do you believe there's a different path forward for racial progress?"

As if anticipating the answer, murmurs immediately spread throughout the crowd.

George leaned into the microphone, the light catching the sheen of his salt and pepper hair. He adjusted his collar with a sharp tug and cleared his throat, a futile attempt to command attention.

"I wish he hadn't agreed to speak," Josephine muttered. "It's only getting harder for him in this community."

Hazel was sympathetic but unsurprised. Once, George's sharp words had been a rallying cry for Harlem; his poetic prose as a columnist for *The Pittsburgh Courier* had been electrifying. But his recent pivot toward conservative ideals had alienated many who once admired him.

"Why do we bellow for Negro art, Negro literature, Negro music?" He paused, letting the question hang in the air. "We are not a separate and different group. We don't need to distinguish ourselves from Americans as a whole. This whole call for racial solidarity is a farce. Negroes should focus on individual advancement, not collective action. It's time to stop focusing on racial struggles."

The rumbles swelled into a wave of agitation. Onstage, Adam shifted in his seat, a bemused smile curling his lips. He leaned forward, and pulled the microphone closer to him.

"You're just loud and wrong, George." Adam's voice cut through the noise like a well-tuned horn. The murmur in the crowd simmered, all eyes shifting to him. "You ask why we are here, bellowing for Negro art, Negro literature, Negro music? Because for centuries, we have been erased, dismissed, and told that our voices don't matter. Because when America talks about its great writers, it doesn't mention Langston Hughes or Zora Neale Hurston. When it sings of its musical legacy, it ignores the spirituals that birthed jazz, the rhythms that shaped swing, and the voices that carried the blues from the cotton fields to the concert halls.

"We do not separate ourselves, George—America separated us," Adam continued. "We were auctioned off, segregated, redlined, and denied the very rights you now say we should seek as individuals. You speak of advancement as though the playing field is level, as though a single Negro rising through the ranks of white society is a victory for us all. But tell me, what does individual success mean when the masses are still scraping for scraps? What good is one Negro man in a tailored suit when thousands are still breaking their backs for a pittance, locked out of schools, housing, and fair wages?"

Adam's pastoral skills were on full display now. "This call for racial solidarity isn't a farce—it's a necessity. It's how we built schools when they denied our children an education. It's how we formed unions when they shut us out of fair labor. It's how Harlem became a haven when landlords wouldn't rent to us anywhere else. We are not asking for handouts, George. We are building power. And if you can't see that, then you are not just wrong—you are willfully blind."

Applause erupted as Adam sat back, his expression cool, waiting for George's rebuttal. Hazel felt a surge of pride, even though she could feel the tension from Josephine. It felt like Adam was seeing inside her heart. Negroes had to fight—together. And those who could had to be the voice for those who couldn't.

George's eyes flashed with irritation. "Self-help," he retorted, raising his voice over the chatter of the crowd. "That's where we ought to focus. Not these endless protests, meetings, and boycotts. Progress doesn't come from holding out our hands. The Negro needs to stand on his own two feet, not lean on grievances."

The room exploded in dissent—boos, hisses, and shouts reverberated off the walls. Some attendees stood, fists raised, while others jeered from their seats.

"Get him off the stage!" someone shouted.

"That Uncle Tom thinks he's white like his wife!" another person yelled.

Josephine's face paled, her hands trembling as she fumbled with her gloves like they were a security blanket.

"I can't stay here," she muttered as Reverend Bishop joined Adam in admonishing George. The side door was just a few steps away. Josephine bolted out, and Hazel quickly followed.

In the quiet of the hallway, Josephine stopped abruptly, pressing her hands to her face. Hazel guided her to a bench near the wall, sitting beside her as the muffled roar of the crowd persisted beyond the oak doors.

"I don't know who he is anymore, Hazel," Josephine whispered. "I married a man who set Harlem ablaze with his ideas, his passion. But now his rhetoric is so divisive, and he criticizes everything every colored leader does. I don't even recognize him."

"Jody," Hazel said softly, taking her friend's trembling hands. "I know how much he's changed, but this doesn't change who you are. Everything you've done for Harlem—it matters."

Josephine's laugh was bitter. "Do you know in Texas, my father and brother had colored mistresses and children they wouldn't acknowledge? I'm the only who will even admit a love for Negroes, but it doesn't matter. Now, it's only going to be worse as they lump me in with my husband."

"Jody, you're part of this community."

"But that's just it!" Josephine's voice rose, and she caught herself, glancing around before continuing in a fierce whisper. "Even here, I'm 'that white woman married to George Schuyler.' I want to be seen as more than that. I want to be part of this fight. This isn't just a hobby for me."

That much, Hazel knew. She'd met Josephine when her mother had started piano lessons with Josephine's daughter, Philippa, five years ago. Though Josephine was twenty-three years older than Hazel, the two of them bonded over art and activism.

Josephine shook her head. "I can't speak against him, Hazel. I won't. But I can't keep defending someone who's abandoned everything we fought for."

Before Hazel could reply, the sharp sound of heels echoed through the hall. Hazel turned to see Eslanda Robeson approaching. She moved with measured grace. Her gaze fixed on Josephine like an arrow aimed and released. As the wife of the influential actor Paul Robeson, whose voice thundered through the movement, Eslanda wielded her status like a crown, the self-declared guardian of Harlem's soul.

Draped in a perfectly tailored suit the color of Bordeaux, Eslanda wore power as naturally as she did her perfume.

"Mrs. Schuyler," she said, her diction immaculate. "Your husband is out of touch with how deep the color line runs in this country. Perhaps the two of you would feel more at home back in Greenwich Village . . . Harlem belongs to its people, the people who know its soul. The *real* Negroes. Not outsiders who play at our struggles, only to abandon us when it's convenient."

Josephine's complexion turned ashen. But Eslanda wasn't finished.

"I don't care how much you might 'want' to be part of this community," Eslanda added, her voice laced with disdain. "You and your husband don't belong here. George has shown his true color.

And it matches yours." She motioned toward Josephine's face. "And no matter how many shades of bronzer you use on your skin, you are still pasty white. Go back to Texas, or San Francisco, or wherever it is you're from."

Then she turned her sharp gaze to Hazel. "And you. You stand up for your people, then turn around and throw in your lot with Miss Anne?" Her lips curled when she spat out the name many gave to the white women who lived in Harlem and worked for colored rights. "That makes you no better than her."

"Good thing I don't care what you think," Hazel said, her hands going to her hips.

Eslanda huffed, then turned, her heels clicking sharply against the floor as she strode out the front door.

Hazel had never been a fan of women like Eslanda, toity know-it-alls who looked down on others. "Don't worry about her, Jody," Hazel said as they watched her disappear.

Josephine bit her lip, her expression a mixture of shame and sadness. "Maybe she's right. I came here, married George, thinking I could become part of Harlem's struggle. I love him, but I also loved what I thought we could accomplish together. But I am and always will be an outsider." She swallowed, looking at Hazel with a bleak smile. "My husband's a Yankee through and through. And in many ways, I'll always be a Southerner, complete with the warranted disdain of my racist ancestors, even though I want nothing to do with them." A mist filled her eyes. "I've poured everything into this community. Not just fighting for interracial issues, but civil rights."

"And you've made a difference." Hazel stepped in front of Josephine, forcing her friend to meet her eyes. "And trust me, Harlem knows what you've done."

Hazel stopped talking when George came stomping past them.

"Let's go," he muttered to his wife without stopping. He didn't wait for her as he burst through the church doors.

Josephine hung back for a moment, inhaled, then, with a nod, straightened her coat and followed her husband outside.

"Trouble in paradise?" Adam's voice broke through as Hazel watched her friend. His tone was light, teasing.

"Don't start," she said. "You're too smart to pretend you don't know the difference between debate and disruption."

"I didn't say a single thing that wasn't true."

"That may be, but sometimes the truth can afford a little tact," Hazel countered. She crossed her arms, fixing him with a pointed look.

"Tact doesn't get people moving." His smirk widened. "Passion does. Fire does. And Harlem's fire has been dimming lately. Somebody needs to stir the embers."

Hazel sighed, unable to fully argue with him. "Just don't burn the whole house down in the process."

He studied her. "Has anyone ever told you how absolutely beautiful you are?"

Hazel's spine straightened. She was used to men fawning over her—how they romanticized her sleek features and her svelte figure. But she'd worked too hard to be reduced to just another pretty thing. And she'd learned early that flattery was often the first note in a tired, predictable tune. Still, there was something in Adam's voice that unnerved her.

"Is the forum over?" she asked, ignoring his compliment.

He gave a careless shrug. "Just about. I stepped out because I had something important to tend to."

"Oh?"

Adam's grin was easy. "Catching up with you."

She let out a dry chuckle. "You don't give up, do you?"

"Not when I see something I want."

She tilted her head, amused in spite of herself. "And what do you want, Councilman?"

He stepped closer and slowly ran a single finger along her bare arm. "You."

Hazel's heart skipped—a quick, rebellious rhythm against her better judgment. But before she could respond, Adam leaned back with a knowing smile.

"The interview."

Warmth instantly rose in Hazel's cheeks. Adam Clayton Powell Jr. was many things—charming, infuriating, brilliant—but subtle wasn't one of them. She should have walked away, should have shut this down before it even started. But she thought about the way his words moved her during the forum and she found herself saying, "All right, Councilman. You'll get your interview. But on one condition."

"And what's that?" he asked, his face now full of intrigue.

"You behave yourself." Hazel tilted her head and narrowed her eyes. "No stirring the embers, no fanning the flames. Just a good, honest conversation."

His smile lit up, and for a moment, the heat in his eyes was replaced by something more sincere. "Scout's honor."

Hazel couldn't help but laugh. "Something tells me you were never a Scout."

"True," he admitted, "but I'll be on my best behavior. You have my word."

"Good." She stepped back and adjusted her coat. "Because I leave for Los Angeles in two weeks, and I do not have time for any nonsense."

"Two weeks is all I need," he said.

CHAPTER 4

May 1943
Manhattan, New York

Hazel had never been to Le Café Chambord before, but she knew
its reputation. Tucked discreetly along Third Avenue in Manhattan, it was the kind of place where celebrities slipped in to escape
the flashbulbs—where deals were whispered over cognac and no one
dared to stare too long.

She stood outside the French restaurant, taking in how different
it was here from Harlem. The block hummed with a quieter kind
of New York energy. There were no children darting up stoops, no
saxophones spilling down from open windows. The sidewalks were
clean, lined with tailored pedestrians and polished storefronts. A de-
livery boy pedaled past on a bicycle, dodging a parked cab. Across
the street, the glow of a neon sign flickered to life in the window of
a corner bookstore.

Hazel's heart skipped when the sleek black Cadillac convertible
pulled into an empty spot in front of the restaurant. Adam stepped
out the car looking like he'd been conjured from the silver screen. He
wore a sharp tailored gray suit—broad in the shoulders, tapered at
the waist, no thread out of place. His tie was knotted clean between
perfectly pressed lapels. The setting sun bounced off the windshield,
catching his profile, like the moment had been staged.

Their eyes locked, and his mouth curved into that maddeningly confident smile.

"You look stunning, Hazel." His eyes swept over her. She'd taken extra time picking out the sapphire-blue crepe dress. The color made her skin glow, and the hem skimmed her calves just enough to hint without revealing. "Hope I didn't keep you waiting long."

"Thank you." She lifted her chin just enough to recenter herself. "You did not keep me waiting. I believe in punctuality. My driver is close by. I'm surprised you're driving yourself."

He gave a small shrug. "Some nights I like to take the wheel, especially on important dates."

"Interview," she corrected. "This is an interview."

He chuckled, offering his arm. "Right. Might I escort my *interviewee* inside?"

She hesitated but then took his arm and let him lead her inside. The warmth of his body next to hers eased the tension she'd been carrying all day.

The restaurant inside had a rustic, understated elegance that made it easy to understand why celebrities came here to disappear. Le Café Chambord exuded old-world charm—lace-trimmed windows, polished wood beams across the ceiling, soft amber sconces flickering along exposed brick walls, and white-linen tablecloths lit by the glow of candlelight. A glass partition offered a glimpse into the bustling kitchen, where copper pots hung in neat rows and white-jacketed chefs worked with quiet precision. The scent of garlic, butter, and herbs wafted through the air.

"*Bonsoir,*" the waiter said, handing them menus after they'd been seated. He quickly flashed an apologetic smile. "Apologies. I just moved here from France, and it's hard to break the French habit. So, let me begin again. Good evening, what can I get for you?"

Hazel smiled at him. *"Apportez-moi votre meilleur vin rouge, s'il vous plaît?"*

The waiter's mouth opened in surprise. *"Oui, madame.* A bottle of our best red wine coming right up."

Adam watched her with an amused smile, clearly impressed. "Miss Scott, is there anything you're not good at?" he teased.

Hazel was not one to be bashful, but his compliments sent a fresh wave of nervous energy through her. "I speak seven languages, but I don't cook." She wiggled her fingers. "My hands are insured with Lloyds of London, so I'm not allowed near the stove."

Adam tilted his head slightly. "Oh, I bet for the right man, you'd learn to be a regular Xavier Marcel Boulestin."

Normally, arrogance was a surefire way to lose her interest—but with Adam it didn't land that way.

"I'm not so sure about that," she said. "Anyway, I thought this was supposed to be an interview. Where's your notepad?"

"Don't need it." He tapped his forehead. "I store everything up here."

Adam leaned in and gently ran a finger over the top of her hand. "So let's begin. Who is Hazel Scott? And not the résumé. I know the headlines—the all-female band you were in as a teen, all the movies, Broadway, sell-out concert venues."

"Someone's been doing their homework," she said, trying to sound unaffected.

"I want to know things that no one else does."

They talked about everything and nothing—her childhood, philosophy, politics, war, and the weight of expectations.

When they turned to books, Adam revealed that he primarily read nonfiction, which surprised her. She'd always thought of him as a man with stories running through his veins. They found common ground despite their different tastes, especially in their admiration for Harlem Renaissance literature—Langston Hughes's sharp wit, Zora Neale Hurston's folklore, and Claude McKay's unflinching poetry about Negro identity and resistance.

But it was music that truly drew them in. While they dined, they swapped stories about the first time they heard Duke Ellington's orchestra swell through a ballroom and how Bessie Smith's voice carried the history of the blues in every note. Adam confessed his admiration for Big Joe Turner's booming vocals and the rollicking swing of Count Basie, while Hazel spoke of the way Art Tatum's fingers danced across the piano keys like magic and her love for music composed by pianist Blind Tom Wiggins.

"Are you a Fats Waller fan?" Adam asked, leaning in slightly.

"Who isn't? That man could make a piano laugh. Both he and Art are family friends and taught me how to let the music feel me."

Adam chuckled. "You definitely know the difference between just playing music and living it."

"I'd like to think that I do." Hazel sipped her wine. "Let me ask you a question. Is it true that A. Philip Randolph was going to announce he was running for Congress and you usurped his announcement?"

Adam didn't answer right away. That slow, devious grin of his stretched across his face like he enjoyed answering that question. He leaned back in his chair, fingertips tapping the base of his wineglass.

"That's a mighty sharp word—*usurped*," he said finally.

Hazel raised an eyebrow. "Am I wrong?"

He chuckled low in his throat. "Let's just say this: in politics, as in chess, *he who moves first, controls the board.* Randolph was thinking. I acted."

She laughed, more impressed than scandalized. "So you just . . . beat him to the punch?"

Adam shrugged, eyes twinkling. "I knew the people were ready. Harlem was ready. Randolph's a brilliant man—he's spent years building labor power across the country. But I've been in these streets, in these churches, talking to folks who can't pay their rent and can't ride a streetcar without a fight. Timing matters."

Hazel tilted her head, studying him. "And ego?"

He smirked. "That, too."

As the waiter set their desserts before them, Hazel eyed the île flottante with a satisfied smile. The poached meringue floated atop a pool of silky crème anglaise. Across from her, Adam had wasted no time digging into his tarte tatin, the caramelized apples glistening over the buttery pastry.

Hazel tapped her spoon against her plate. "You strike me as more of a chocolate mousse man."

Adam gave a slow, deliberate smile, chewing thoughtfully. "And you strike me as a woman who enjoys proving people wrong."

She scooped a bit of the meringue, letting it melt on her tongue before shrugging. "Maybe. Or maybe I just like the lightness of mousse. Something soft and sweet to balance the weight of the world."

Adam rested his chin on his hand. "That's what I like about you, Miss Scott. You think of everything as a composition—balancing flavors, sounds, even life."

Hazel chuckled, stirring her spoon through the vanilla custard. "Don't romanticize it. Sometimes a dessert is just a dessert."

Adam gestured to his half-eaten tarte. "Maybe. But this? This is more than just a dessert. This is indulgence, Miss Scott. This is rebellion against war rations and the world's troubles. And I believe in indulging . . . when it's worth it."

Hazel shook her head. "And let me guess—you consider yourself an indulgence?"

Adam grinned. "Wouldn't you?"

She took another bite, savoring the sweetness on her tongue before finally meeting his gaze. "We'll see."

After the waiter had taken their dessert plates and refilled their wineglasses, Hazel turned serious. "Another question."

"Ah, the interviewee has become the interviewer." He set his wineglass down to give her his undivided attention. "The floor is yours."

"Do you normally ask women out . . . for interviews?"

A flash of distress crossed his face.

"Just wondering about your situation," she added.

He leaned back, thinking before he spoke. "Honestly, I wouldn't be here with you if things were going well at home," he admitted. "My wife . . . Isabel and I . . . we've been drifting apart for years. She knows I'm unhappy."

"I'm sorry to hear that," Hazel said. "No one should be unhappy."

"It wasn't always that way." A wistful smile touched his lips. "I met Isabel during my junior year at Colgate University. She and her sister, Fredi Washington, were two of the most talented women I'd ever seen."

"Fredi Washington? The actress who played Peola in *Imitation of Life*?" Hazel asked, intrigued.

He nodded. "Yes, that's her. Isabel was the star of *Harlem*, one of the most successful dramas on Broadway. She had everything—talent, beauty, grace. I had no intention of marrying her, and I don't think she had any intention of marrying me."

"Then why did you?"

He laughed softly, though without joy. "Probably because my parents were so against it. I was young. They didn't like the idea of me marrying an actress, especially one who was older than me, albeit by only six months. But she had already been married, and had a child. I think their resistance made me want her even more."

"And now?"

He sighed, then picked up his glass and took another sip. "Now I realize I was selfish. Isabel gave up everything for me—her career, her passion. She was offered the lead in *Showboat*, a transcontinental tour, a Broadway revival. She gave it all up to be my wife. And I let her."

His words hung in the air, and Hazel felt a pang of sympathy for Isabel. She couldn't imagine giving up her music.

Before she could respond, two elderly women approached their table. "Reverend Powell, I just had to come over and say thank you. My son worked at the hospital when you got them to give the colored folks equal pay."

The second woman leaned in, her eyes bright with pride. "And my husband was one of the drivers hired by the city after your bus boycott. We will always be grateful to you."

"Please, call me Adam," he replied. "And that's what I'm here for. What's your name?"

"Vera Miller. And this is my friend, Barbara Jean Brown. We don't usually come to places this fancy, but it's my seventieth birthday."

Adam stood and shook both of their hands. "Well, happy birthday. It is a pleasure to meet you, and if you ever have any issues, you call my office and tell them I said to always patch you right through."

Both women giggled like schoolgirls. "Thank you so much, Reverend. I mean Adam," Barbara Jean said.

Vera turned to Hazel. "And, Miss Scott, I just love your music."

"Thank you very much," Hazel replied.

"Well, we know you two are cooking up big things for Harlem," Vera said. "So, we'll let you be."

As the women walked off, a flush of discomfort rose to Hazel's cheeks. She glanced around, suddenly aware of how exposed they were despite the intimacy of the restaurant. This was exactly the kind of speculation she didn't need.

Adam returned to his seat and leaned forward. "What are we cooking up, Miss Scott?"

Hazel's expression was flat as she said, "Let me make something clear. I think you are remarkable. But my focus is on my career, and when it's not, I'm seeing someone. So regardless of whatever situation you say you're in, the fact remains—you're married."

Adam gave a nonchalant shrug. "Who knows what the future holds?"

When Adam walked her to her car two hours later, Hazel once again felt completely at ease. As Jimmy, Hazel's driver, held the door open, Adam took her hand and let it linger in his.

"Tonight was wonderful. Thank you."

She smiled. "Thank you for dinner."

"Good night, Hazel," he said softly. "Best of luck in Hollywood. Hopefully, I can see you when you get back."

"Good night, Adam," she replied, not addressing the latter part of his comment.

CHAPTER 5

July 1943
Hollywood, California

The smell of gardenias and tulips greeted Hazel as she entered her dressing room. She paused in the doorway and let the sweet, fresh scent flood her senses as her gaze fell on a bouquet on the coffee table. She stepped closer, inhaling the fragrance before plucking a card from the arrangement.

With the note between her fingers, she read the elegant scrawl: *Can't wait for you to light up the screen. Take care, ACP.* A smile tugged at her lips despite herself. Adam had written her twice during her time in California and despite how expensive it was and the wartime excise taxes, called her long-distance three times. Now he was sending flowers.

Hazel tucked the card into her handbag, feeling both charmed and unsettled.

Today was the final day of production for *The Heat's On,* a Mae West musical. They'd been filming for eight weeks, and everyone was ready to wrap. The industry had been in overdrive, producing movies to boost wartime morale. In this film, Hazel was, of course, playing herself, and performing a patriotic number, "The Caissons Go Rolling Along." Watching the Negro soldiers dancing with their sweethearts during rehearsals had brought her genuine joy and briefly transported her away from the realities of the war being waged for the past two years.

"Miss Scott, you're on in five," a young production assistant called from the doorway.

"Tell Gregory I'm coming," she said, referring to the director, Gregory Ratoff.

"Oh, he's out sick. David Lichine is taking over."

Hazel loved working with Gregory. He was the one who discovered her, secretly filming her while she worked at Cafe Society years ago, and he worked tirelessly to make sure she was happy on set. But she'd worked with Mr. Lichine before and was confident he'd finish out the project with class. "Well, tell him I'll be there shortly," she said.

Hazel dabbed on the last bit of rouge, giving herself a final once-over in the mirror. Her reflection stared back: hair perfectly coifed under a Women's Army Corps service hat, her two-piece khaki uniform making her feel as if she really were part of the US military.

As she headed to the set, the usual buzz of activity surrounded her. Extras rushed about, stagehands adjusted lights and microphones, and Mr. Lichine was at the center of it all, barking orders like an overzealous sergeant.

"These aprons are too clean!" Hazel heard him shout, sending everyone on set scurrying in different directions. "Spray some oil and dirt on them. These women are supposed to be seeing their husbands off to war, not hosting a blasted tea party."

Hazel frowned, her gaze landing on eight Negro actresses standing together, looking confused and scared. They wore A-line dresses with crisp white aprons tied neatly at their waists, waiting for their moment on-screen. Hazel's stomach clenched as she watched the costuming crew smear dirt on the aprons, making the women look like they had just come from the fields.

Unable to stay silent, Hazel snapped, "Mr. Lichine!"

He turned, annoyance flickering across his face before softening slightly when he saw her. "Hazel," he said, trying to sound placating. "We're just getting the costumes ready for the scene."

"Why are you dirtying their aprons?" Hazel gestured to the actresses. "No colored woman would wear a filthy apron while seeing her man off to war. It's an insult."

Mr. Lichine blinked, as if she had spoken another language. His face hardened. "Hazel, we're aiming for realism here. War is dirty."

"These women aren't at battle, though. They're seeing their men off," Hazel argued. "They would take pride in their appearance, see them off with dignity. They would not come out like they've been working in the fields."

Mr. Lichine pursed and unpursed his lips as if that was his way of calming himself before he stepped closer. "What's it to you? You're beautifully dressed. And you're here to perform," he said, his tone dripping with condescension. "So just play your scene. The costumes are not your concern."

Hazel squared her shoulders, refusing to back down. "The portrayal of Negroes is very much my concern. Have you ever even seen any Negroes other than your own servants? I won't perform if those women are dressed like that."

The room went silent. Crew members stopped what they were doing, casting glances toward the exchange. The actresses looked on in fear.

Mr. Lichine's jaw clenched, and he took a deep breath. "Might I remind you that you have a contract, Miss Scott? Are you really going to hold up production over a few dirty aprons?"

"Yes. I refuse to perpetuate another harmful stereotype."

After a tense pause, Mr. Lichine muttered something under his breath and stormed off toward the production office. Hazel turned to the actresses, offering a reassuring smile. "I'm sorry. But this isn't right. You ladies deserve better."

One of the women spoke up, her voice low. "Miss Scott, we don't want you getting into trouble on our behalf."

"It'll be okay," she replied, then stepped closer. The women swarmed around her. "But look, when they finally shoot this scene, with or without me, I want every single one of you fresh from the hairdresser, looking your absolute best," Hazel replied. They nodded like they were ready to take marching orders.

Hazel returned to her dressing room. She took a seat at her vanity and tried to still her trembling fingers.

She opened the top drawer and carefully pulled out the letter Adam had sent just a week ago. The paper, worn soft at the folds, still carried the faint scent of his cologne. Though she'd read the letter at least fifteen times, her eyes scanned the words again.

Hazel, you should've seen it. More than 20,000 people packed into Madison Square Garden for the Negro Freedom Rally. Twenty thousand! The energy was like nothing I've ever felt before. There were white folks standing shoulder to shoulder with us, chanting for change as I spoke. We're shifting the ground beneath our feet, and, baby, I swear we're making it quake.

The way his fire leaped from the page was so inspiring. She held the letter to her chest for a moment, then continued reading.

I know your schedule is grueling and Hollywood can chip away at you until you forget you're carved from stone. You've got a fire that they can't dim. So when it gets hard—and I know it will— shine anyway.

Adam had been concerned about her because she'd started performing at the Mocambo nightclub on the weekends, in addition to trying to finish her album and do the movie. He thought she was overdoing it. That was no doubt what he was talking about, but little did he know those words were coming in right on time for what she was dealing with now.

"Shine anyway," she whispered, folding the letter back with care. She was much calmer when the production assistant knocked on her door again. "Miss Scott, someone's on the telephone for you."

Hazel inhaled, bracing herself, and made her way down the hall to the commons area to take the call.

"Hello," Hazel said.

"Hazel, what's going on?" Barney's voice boomed through the receiver. "David Lichine just called and said you walked off set."

"I didn't walk off," she replied. "They put the women in filthy aprons. I told them I wouldn't perform until they were changed."

Barney groaned. "Hazel, this isn't a fight we want to pick. You're going to get yourself blacklisted."

"I don't care," she snapped. "Nothing changes until we make it change. This was an opportunity to portray beautiful Negro women with dignity, and they want them looking like vagabonds. It matters how the world sees us, Barney."

Silence stretched on the line. Hazel knew Barney was weighing his options. He had always been cautious, but she wasn't. She couldn't afford to be.

Finally, Barney released a heavy sigh. "All right. I'll see what I can do, but don't expect miracles."

"I never do," Hazel said before hanging up.

For the next three days, Hazel's standoff held. She refused to return to the set, practicing piano at the apartment she was renting, running scales and rehearsing notes while the phone rang incessantly with calls from Mr. Lichine, Barney, her mother, and studio heads, all urging her to reconsider. But she stood firm.

On the third day, as Hazel sat at the piano, the phone rang again. She answered, preparing herself for the news that she was being replaced.

It was Mr. Lichine, his voice resigned. "We've changed the aprons. They'll wear floral dresses. Satisfied?"

A small smile tugged at her lips. "Thank you, Mr. Lichine. I'll be there in the morning."

Though she felt a small victory over this battle, everything inside her said the war was just beginning.

HAZEL WAS GREETED on set by all eight actresses, looking radiant in floral-print dresses, hair immaculately styled. The aprons were gone altogether. Their eyes flickered between gratitude and uncertainty. One of them, a young woman with squared shoulders and doe eyes, stepped cautiously toward her, as if she'd been appointed the group's spokesperson.

"Miss Scott," she said in a soft whisper. "I'm Beverly. Thank you . . . for everything. You didn't have to stand up for us, but you did. You are an inspiration to so many young women."

Hazel glanced at the other women, who nodded in appreciation, pride filling their expressions. Beverly's words warmed Hazel, though the feeling was bittersweet. This fight for respect shouldn't have been necessary in the first place.

"I'm happy it worked out," she replied.

"Can we get to work now, or is there some other cause you all need to fight for?" Mr. Lichine barked from his chair. He didn't bother hiding his irritation.

Hazel squeezed Beverly's hand and whispered, "Let's make a

movie," before stepping back into her role. As the scene commenced, she noticed Mr. Lichine's scowl, but after just one take, the begrudging acknowledgment in his eyes revealed that he could see the improvement. The scene looked better, more polished, and pride radiated from everyone involved.

Hazel headed to her dressing room, eager for a moment of solitude. But when she opened the door, she froze. Harry Cohn, the notorious head of Columbia Pictures, sat in her chair, feet propped on the vanity as though he owned the place—which, technically, he did. Light flickered over his bald spot, and the glint in his eye made it clear this wasn't a social visit. His lips were pressed into a thin line of barely contained fury.

"Mr. Cohn," Hazel said, keeping her voice level. "How are you?"

He stared at her with cold, calculating eyes, then slowly lowered his feet to the floor and stood, towering over her. Mr. Cohn was known around Hollywood as "King Cohn" and was infamous for his dictatorial, bullying demeanor and his crude, vulgar language.

His eyes narrowed, studying her like an adversary.

"Miss Scott, I need a word with you."

"What can I do for you?"

His voice was a snarl masked as civility. "What you did this week cost me. You know that, don't you?"

"I did what was necessary. Those women deserve respect."

He thrust a crinkled piece of paper toward her. "This little stunt of yours? Cost me $31,640. You have any idea what that means?"

She didn't take the paper. "It wouldn't have cost you a dime if Mr. Lichine had listened to me from the start."

Mr. Cohn's face hardened, and he moved within inches of her. "You're nothing but hired help here. You think you can walk in and make demands?"

In her mind, Hazel heard her mother's voice: *A spoonful of honey will catch more flies than a gallon of vinegar.* She took a breath. "Mr. Cohn, I understand your frustration. But once you see the scene, you'll agree—the women look better. The film looks better. And your Negro audience will appreciate it."

A sneer spread across Mr. Cohn's face. "I didn't claw my way to the top of this industry to have an uppity Negro tell me how to run my studio. You might be a star in your little world, but here, you're nothing."

He continued, each word dripping with disdain. "I've run this studio since me, my brother and Joe founded it in 1918. I've been in the film industry since 1908. How many films have you produced? What are your credentials?"

She responded without missing a beat. "I don't need to have produced a single film to know that Negro women wouldn't send their husbands off to war in tattered and dirty clothes."

Mr. Cohn's face was inches from hers now, his voice a low, menacing whisper. "The only reason you're even still here is because it'd be too inconvenient to replace you at the last minute. And yes, it may look like you've won, but let me tell you something, Hazel Scott—you'll never set foot on another movie studio lot as long as I live."

His words hung in the air before he scoffed and stormed out of the room.

As Hazel gathered her belongings, a pang of loss washed over her. Though music was her world, she'd allowed herself to dream of a future in Hollywood. But now that future was slipping away.

Hazel had just finished packing when the actresses gathered at her door. Beverly, eyes wet with unshed tears, took a step forward. "Miss Scott, is everything okay?" she asked. "We saw Mr. Cohn, and he was terribly upset. We'd all be devastated if you got in trouble on our behalf."

Hazel flashed a comforting smile. "Don't worry about me. You ladies will be beautiful for all the world to see. That's what matters."

They shared a moment of solidarity before Hazel closed her suitcase and prepared to leave California behind.

At the train station, she boarded, settling into her seat as the engine lurched forward. The rhythmic chug soothed her as she gazed out the window, watching the scenery blur past. Her heart felt heavy, but her spirit remained undiminished. She might be blacklisted, but she wasn't broken.

CHAPTER 6

July 1943
Manhattan, New York

Jazz music and lively chatter filtered through the walls of Cafe Society as Hazel stepped inside her old dressing room.

Billie sat in front of the mirror, adjusting the white flower in her hair. Their eyes met in her reflection, and she turned with a smile that lit up her entire face.

"Haze! It's so good to see you," Billie exclaimed.

Hazel leaned down and hugged her friend. "It's good to be back. Nothing beats being home." She pulled back to look Billie in the eyes. "I know Barney is thrilled to have you return for a performance."

"I'm not just here for him. A girl's gotta eat." She flashed that once-over look that she often did when she was trying to assess Hazel. "Are you all right for real? I heard about what happened on the set of your movie. You really went on strike?"

"I sure did. The whole fiasco will probably leave me blacklisted, but if that happens, so be it." Hazel shrugged.

"I taught you well." Billie nodded in admiration. "But on the level, you're brave, girl. It takes guts to stand up like that. When did you get in from California?"

Hazel eased down onto the sofa, weariness from the long train ride setting in. "This afternoon. I haven't even unpacked. I have to go in the studio in the morning, but Mama said you were performing tonight, so I changed and came on. I just needed to hear some 'Strange Fruit.'"

"You and everyone else in the club." Billie grabbed a cigarette, then leaned back, her expression sobering as Hazel picked up a framed photograph of the first night Billie performed "Strange Fruit" on Cafe Society's stage. Billie always displayed the picture in her dressing room when she performed, calling it her inspiration.

"You know I love 'Strange Fruit,' but it's draining," Billie murmured. "Abel poured his heart into it, and I have to pour my soul into it every time I sing it."

Hazel nodded, understanding the toll it took on her friend. "But you know how powerful it is. What did you say in that *Life* article? It's a call to arms."

"I just don't want people to see the song as begging for pity." Billie sighed.

Their conversation drifted to lighter topics as they caught up. Billie shared her problems with her husband, Jimmy Monroe, while Hazel mentioned that she had recently discovered her posters were all the rage among soldiers.

"Hazel Scott, the pinup girl for servicemen." Billie laughed.

The door opened slightly, and Barney peeked in. "Excuse me, ladies. Hazel, Councilman Powell is here, and he's asking about you."

Billie frowned, immediately going into protective big sister mode. "He needs to be asking about his wife. And how is he trying to run for Congress while sniffing behind another woman?"

Barney shrugged, a sly smile playing on his face. "He's unhappily married, I heard."

"Unhappily married is still married," Billie said.

Hazel dismissed his words with a flick of the hand. "He's just a friend."

"So, he didn't write you while you were in Los Angeles?" Billie asked.

Hazel's eyes widened. She combed through her memory, trying to recall who she could have possibly told about Adam's letters.

"Who told you about that?" she asked.

Billie let out a rich, knowing laugh. "You just did, sugar."

Hazel exhaled sharply, shaking her head at her own slipup, but Billie's amusement faded as her expression turned serious. "Just be careful, Haze. You're a beautiful young woman, sittin' on top of the world right now. Men are gonna come sniffin' around, lookin' to catch a little shine off you."

Hazel waved off the concern with an easy shrug. "You don't have to worry about me, Billie. I know how to handle myself."

Billie studied her for a beat, then shook her head. "I'm just telling you how it is. Some men got a way of pulling you into their web, and before you know it, your life is turned upside down." She glanced toward the exit, as if Adam were waiting just beyond the door. "And Adam Clayton Powell Jr. is one of those men."

"He's a beloved minister," Hazel pointed out. "A *married* minister."

"A snake comes in many forms, and I got a feeling you're his next prey."

"And I know me." Hazel stood up defiantly. "I don't give a hoot about Mr. Powell. And besides, does anything about me say 'First Lady'?" She placed her hands on her hips and gave a little shimmy.

Billie relaxed, her smile returning. "The thing about you, Hazel, is anything you want to be, you will, including a First Lady."

"Well, trust me, I have no desire to be a First Lady of anything, except jazz," Hazel replied.

Billie looked at her, as if trying to figure out if Hazel was serious or simply naive.

Finally, Billie stood and smoothed out her dress, taking a deep breath. "It's been great catching up, but it's time for Lady to take the floor."

Hazel followed Billie out of the dressing room and watched as she made her way through the bustling backstage area. Hazel slipped out the side curtain into the club. The place was packed, and the audience eagerly awaited Billie's performance.

Hazel scanned the crowd, looking for a seat. She spotted Adam at a back table. As if he'd been waiting for her, his smile lit up when he saw her. He gestured to the empty seat next to him, and, after a brief hesitation, Hazel moved toward him.

"Hello, beautiful." Adam stood and greeted her. He was immaculately dressed in a tailored charcoal-gray pin-striped suit. "I was hoping you'd come out and enjoy the show with me."

She wondered if he'd truly kept the seat open just for her in the crowded club. In her last letter, she'd told him that she was coming home and shared her telephone number, but she hadn't told him that she'd be here tonight.

"Hello, Adam," Hazel said, sitting down. His cologne, a blend of orange, jasmine, lavender, and musk, drifted through the air. "It's nice to see you."

"The pleasure's all mine," he replied, taking her hand and kissing her palm like he'd done before.

Why did she find that so doggone sexy? "How did you even know I'd be here?" she asked.

"I didn't. I came to see Billie."

Hazel's cheeks were flushed with embarrassment. "Oh, sorry."

His smile made her relax a bit, especially when he added, "Okay, you got me. I remembered you'd be returning today, so I called your house and Miss Alma told me you were going to be here."

The lights dimmed, and a hush fell over the crowd. Billie moved to the center of the room, her presence drawing every gaze like a siren's call. She pulled the microphone to her and immediately started singing "No Regrets," then drifted into "God Bless the Child." Each note seemed to weave a spell that left the audience mesmerized.

Adam swayed to the music, his fingers drumming softly on the table, his eyes flickering between Billie and Hazel. She felt the heat of his gaze, and her pulse quickened with each darting glance.

Then came the haunting strains of "Strange Fruit." Billie's voice took on a tremor, one that sent chills through the room as she closed her eyes, letting the lyrics pour out from some well of pain and resolve. Adam leaned in, his lips brushing the sensitive skin behind her ear, his breath warm against her neck.

"I want you, Hazel Scott," he whispered.

"*Southern trees bear a strange fruit . . .*" Billie sang as Hazel tensed.

"My marriage is over, so you don't need to be concerned about that . . ."

"*Blood on the leaves and blood at the root.*"

"The music and the movement . . . together we could move mountains . . ."

"*Black bodies swinging in the Southern breeze . . .*"

The sorrow in Billie's voice mixed with the hushed heat of Adam's words, and Hazel felt herself pulled in two directions—between the pain of the past in Billie's song and the possibilities of the present.

"*Strange fruit hanging from the poplar trees . . .*"

Hazel sat captivated by Billie's final, fading note, the room plunging into blackness as it ended. A breathless silence filled the room, and when the lights returned, Billie had disappeared from the stage and the fight within Hazel faded.

The applause erupted around them, but Hazel barely heard it. Her chest felt tight, her heart pounding in a rhythm that had nothing to do with the music. Adam was close—too close—but she didn't move. His hand rested on the back of her chair. The raw sincerity in his eyes pierced through her defenses. He wasn't just charming her. He wasn't playing games. He meant every word.

"I've spent my life fighting battles," she finally said, her voice trembling slightly as she turned to meet his gaze. "For respect, for dignity, for my voice to be heard. I've fought for everyone and everything . . ."

Adam reached for her hand, his fingers brushing hers with a gentleness that sent a slow, unexpected warmth curling through her chest.

"It's time you let someone fight for you." His voice was low, steady, and filled with conviction. "You don't have to do it alone anymore."

Her breath hitched. Adam Clayton Powell Jr., the man who had made a name for himself for being bold, brash, and relentless, now looked at her with a tenderness that threatened to unravel her completely.

"What do you want from me?"

"No, it's what I want to *give.* My heart."

"That's not easy . . . especially, considering everything."

"I'm working on that," he promised.

She exhaled, a shaky but resolute sound, and nodded. "Let's see where this goes."

The corners of his mouth curved up slow and triumphant, but there was no arrogance in it—only relief and joy.

As the crowd began to settle back into the hum of conversation, the lights dimmed again, and the house band began playing a new soft and romantic melody. Adam stood and held out his hand. "Dance with me," he said, his tone more a plea than a command. As if he sensed her apprehension, he said, "It's dark. No one is paying us any attention."

Hazel hesitated before sliding her hand into his. He guided her to the center of the couples who had gathered on the dance floor, his arm slipping around her waist as they began to sway to the music. She could have pulled away. She should have. But instead, she let her body rest against his, absorbing the warmth, the comfort, the quiet danger of being this close to him.

"Adam . . . this isn't a good idea," she mumbled, though she made no effort to stop swaying.

His thumb traced the small of her back. "Maybe not," he whispered in her ear. "But tell me you don't feel it, too."

The young singer in the house band belted out the sultry strains of Ella Fitzgerald's "I'm Making Believe," and the words wrapped around them like a secret.

Hazel wanted to tell Adam she was immune to his charm. But she felt the words slipping from her grasp.

Adam tightened his hold ever so slightly, his fingers pressing gently against the curve of her waist as though anchoring her there, keeping her from running.

She exhaled, her resolve wavering.

Maybe she should fight it. Maybe she should let go.

Maybe it was already too late.

Because as the music swelled around them, Hazel knew—some truths were impossible to deny.

CHAPTER 7

August 1943
Harlem, New York

The last month with Adam had felt like a fever dream—intoxicating yet impossible to resist. They hadn't crossed every line, but they'd come so close it was hard to imagine where one ended and the other began. He made her feel seen in ways she hadn't felt in years. Their connection was undeniable, electric, but it wasn't just physical. They talked for hours about everything—the movement, music, faith, and Harlem itself. He made her laugh when she thought she'd forgotten how, and when he looked at her, it was as if he believed she could move mountains. It was such a contrast from what she had with Lee.

She shook away thoughts of Lee and Adam and returned to the mission at hand—checking on Billie. Her dear friend James Baldwin had called her this morning in a panic.

Billie needs you. That was all James had said before telling her he'd meet them as soon as he could. But he didn't need to say much more. Hazel had learned to read between the lines when it came to Billie. Whatever was happening, it wasn't good.

Hazel had tried to call Billie's husband, Jimmy Monroe, but of course he was nowhere to be found. So here she was, heading to the Braddock Hotel, where James said Billie had been spotted. Hazel felt guilty about the fact that she hadn't seen Billie in a month—she'd let herself forget everything else whenever she was with Adam and hadn't made much time for anything else.

Now, approaching the hotel at 126th and 8th Avenue, Hazel couldn't help but feel the weight of reality crashing down. She thought of Billie—the woman who could command a room with a single note but whose private battles were often louder than her music. She had seen Billie at her best and worst, but this time felt different. James didn't have many details, but his tone had been panicked. Hazel didn't know what she would find, nor what she would do, but she had to try to help her friend.

As Hazel stepped into the lobby, a sharp voice cut through the air.

"I want all my money back! Even the tip I gave that lazy bellhop!" A woman in a faded floral dress slapped her handbag on the check-in counter. Behind the desk, the clerk threw up his hands, clearly exasperated.

"Ma'am, I told you—we don't refund tips," the clerk said.

A uniformed officer standing nearby stepped in. "All right, miss, you heard the man."

"I ain't going nowhere till I get every dime of my money!" The woman paused when she recognized Hazel. "Miss Scott! Miss Scott!"

Hazel moved toward the woman. She didn't have time for this, but maybe she could help calm the woman down. "Is everything okay?"

"No," the woman cried. "Do you see how they're treating me? Tell all your fans this place is a dump!"

The officer jerked Hazel's arm to push her out of the way. "Move it along, gal."

"*Gal?*" Hazel said.

"That's Hazel Scott," the woman shouted.

"I don't care if she's Jesus Christ. Move it along, gal," he repeated.

Hazel took a deep breath. She probably had jewelry worth more than this man made in five years and yet he still felt like he could disrespect her. She was about to step toward him, but a young soldier stepped in to try and defuse the situation, reminding Hazel that she was there for Billie.

"I don't have time for this," she muttered as she turned and headed down the hallway while the arguing continued. She read the weathered numbers on the doors: 102 . . . 103 . . . 104.

Hazel knocked once.

Then again, louder.

She pressed her ear to the door, listening for any sign of life. Nothing.

"Billie, it's me," she called softly, leaning closer. Her voice echoed faintly in the hallway, but still there was no response.

She tried the knob—it turned. Hazel's breath caught as the door creaked open, revealing the dim, smoky haze of the room. The sharp smell of sweat and something bitter made her stomach twist. A weak yellow lamp barely lit the room. Billie lay sprawled on the bed. The sight of her arm dangling off the side, a needle still embedded in her skin, stopped Hazel's heart.

"Billie!" Hazel raced to her side.

Billie lay motionless, her usually vibrant presence dimmed to a shadow.

"Billie, it's me," she said again, louder this time, her voice trembling. "It's Hazel."

No response.

She looked down and gasped at the sight of Billie's bruised, punctured feet, signs of desperation that turned Hazel's stomach. "Billie." Her voice rose in pitch, as she lightly shook her friend.

Slowly, Billie's eyes flickered open and her lips curled into a dazed smile. "Hey, Haze . . . what're you doing here?"

Relief danced along the edges of anger. "I came because I heard you were killing yourself in this place."

Billie's smile faded as her eyelids drooped. Her skin felt clammy when Hazel touched her hand, carefully pulling the needle from her arm and tossing it onto the cluttered nightstand where a glass of amber liquid and a full ashtray bore testament to Billie's spiral.

"Oh, Billie." Hazel hurried to the bathroom and wet a towel with cold water. She returned and began dabbing her friend's face, desperate to pull her out of her stupor. "You're not going out like this, do you hear me? Snap out of it!"

Billie shivered at the touch of the cold water, swatting weakly at Hazel's hand. "What the hell, Hazel?" she murmured, wiping her damp face with a shaky hand. Her pupils were tiny, lost in the dim light. "How'd you even know I was here?"

"Harlem is small, Billie. You know that. Somebody called James, and he called me."

"So am I gonna be the tragic heroine in the next great James Baldwin novel?" Billie moaned.

A sudden crash from down the hall caused Hazel to whip her head toward the cracked door. Muffled shouts and footsteps filled the hallway. Hazel's heart lurched as she listened intently.

"What's going on out there?" Billie slurred.

"I don't know. I'll go check."

Hazel moved to the door, cautiously peeking out into the hallway. There was some kind of commotion coming from the lobby. Hazel eased toward the noise. She rounded the corner, and her mouth dropped open in horror. Blood stained the linoleum floor, and the soldier who had stepped in earlier lay motionless, his half-open eyes staring blankly. The woman who was arguing earlier was handcuffed and hysterical as several officers surrounded her.

"What happened?" Hazel whispered to a maid standing nearby.

The woman's voice was thick with a West Indian accent, her face streaked with tears. "That poor soldier. All he was trying to do was help, and they shot him." Her voice trembled as she spoke, her gaze darting toward the doors. "Somebody ran out and told folks, and now—look."

Hazel followed her pointing finger. The street outside, which had been eerily still just thirty minutes ago, now churned with movement. Dozens of people stood in front of the hotel, their voices rising in anger. Several police officers had gathered as well.

"Ma'am," the maid said, her voice trembling, "you should go back to your room. Things are about to get dangerous out here."

Hazel nodded, but just as she turned to leave—

CRASH.

A brick slammed through the lobby window, shattering the thick glass into a thousand sharp daggers. Screams rang out as shards sprayed across the floor. Hazel ducked instinctively, her arms flying over her head.

"Get back! Get back!" officers barked, their guns drawn, their voices cracking with tension as the crowd roared louder.

Hazel's heart pounded. The room had turned into a frenzy of movement—hotel guests scrambling, police shouting, the front doors rattling as the pressure outside built.

With her breath coming in short gasps, Hazel scuttled down the hall, forcing her legs to move faster. She reached Billie's door and slipped inside, slamming it shut behind her. Leaning against the wood, she pressed a hand to her chest, trying to steady her racing pulse.

Billie was sitting up now, her head tilted back against the headboard, eyes half closed as she looked over at Hazel with a distant curiosity. "What in God's creation is going on out there?" she asked, her voice heavy.

Hazel dropped into a chair beside the bed, her legs weak. "It's hell out there."

Billie chuckled softly, a bitter, broken sound. "Then I'm home," she muttered, her eyes slipping closed as she sank back into her haze.

ONE HUNDRED AND twenty-fifth street was choking in smoke. Hazel watched the city she loved from the windows of James's apartment. The acrid scent filled the room as the sounds of chaos outside intensified. Shattering glass and angry voices clashed with police whistles and sounds of anguish. Harlem wasn't just in flames; it was burning with rage.

"Get away from that window, Hazel," James said, his voice heavy with fatigue. He'd been writing in the midst of this madness since he showed up at the Braddock and helped Hazel and Billie sneak out the back. Even now, his pen furiously scribbled across the paper like he was battling the world with words.

Reluctantly, Hazel tore her gaze from outside and stepped away from the window.

James sat hunched over his cluttered desk, his head bent low as he poured himself onto the page. Hard lines were etched in his brow, and his lips were pursed in a thin, tight line. He appeared much older than his nineteen years. When he finally looked up, his eyes were clouded with exhaustion.

"What are you even writing?" Hazel asked.

He'd been writing since high school, where they'd met when he served as the school magazine editor and interviewed her about her Broadway debut in "Sing Out the News." His dream was to one day be published.

James leaned back, loosening his grip on the pen as he rubbed the bridge of his nose and sighed.

"The best stories," he murmured as he crossed his legs, "are born of tragedy."

Hazel longed to embrace him, to soothe away the sorrow clinging to him like a shadow. He'd just returned from burying his father when the riots erupted and had just made it to the hotel before all hell broke loose. They'd sought cover in Billie's room until sunrise, when they'd been able to sneak out a back door and retreat to James's apartment a few blocks over. Now they were exiles trapped by the flames of fury consuming their streets.

"Is it ever going to end?" Hazel whispered, half to herself, half to him.

"Hopefully soon. And hopefully, something new can rise from the ashes," he replied.

She sat down across from him, folding her arms over the table. "Do you ever wish you could just escape it all?"

His gaze softened, something tender flickering as he studied her face. "Escape? I dream about it every day. Thinking about going to Paris. Maybe things are better for a Negro over there."

"Maybe so, my friend. Maybe so."

After a quick phone call to her mother to ease her nerves, Hazel coaxed Billie to wake up and eat before she drifted back to sleep. Hours passed, but Hazel grew restless. Glancing outside, she noted the crowds thinning, the smoke smoldering, and for the first time in the last forty-eight hours, she started to feel like maybe this was coming to an end. She turned up the small TV just as a reporter began detailing the riots.

". . . and it appears the mayhem is tapering off. So far, there have been reports of six deaths, over a thousand arrested and injured, and property damages estimated at five million dollars," the newscaster said. "Members of Abyssinian Church will host a community meeting at six P.M. to discuss the matter."

Hazel sat straight up. "We need to go." She hadn't been able to make contact with Adam, but her mother said both he and Lee had called to make sure she was okay.

James didn't look up from his writing. "I don't know if going out is wise."

"Sitting here isn't an option. Doing nothing isn't an option." Hazel glanced at the clock. It was 5:35.

She grabbed her pocketbook. "I'm going to the meeting."

James finally looked up. "You're really going out there?"

"I have to."

He sighed. "Then I'm coming with you."

"No, you stay here with Billie."

"Billie's been out for six hours. She'll be okay. I can't tell the world I let Hazel Scott go out into an uprising in Harlem by herself." He huffed, then scribbled on a piece of paper. "I'll leave a note for Billie if she wakes up."

Outside, the aftermath was heartbreaking. Storefronts were shattered, and debris littered the streets.

"Get out the way!" some woman yelled as she dragged a sack of flour, no doubt from a looted market. A group of men across the street heaved crates of canned goods into a waiting car.

James shook his head. "Survival and defiance wrapped in one volatile scene."

They moved down the street, keeping their heads low, passing stationed soldiers with rifles slung across their chests.

They stepped around broken glass and charred debris still smoking at the edges. The sharp scent of tear gas lingered in the air. Sirens wailed in the distance.

At 7th and 126th, a police wagon blocked the intersection, its lights pulsing red against the darkening sky. The moment they approached, a white officer leaped from the vehicle, his boots hitting the pavement with a heavy thud. His pistol was already drawn, pointed low but unmistakably ready.

He was broad and red-faced, with a jaw so clenched Hazel could see the muscle twitching beneath his skin. Sweat streaked down his temple, cutting through the grime on his face. His uniform looked like it had been worn for hours. His eyes were erratic.

"Where are you headed?" he barked.

Hazel instinctively moved half a step behind James. Her heart pounded so loud she was sure the officer could hear it. One wrong move, one wrong word, and the night could end with blood on the sidewalk.

James raised his hands slightly—not high enough to seem like surrender, but just enough to signal calm. "We live in the neighborhood. We're going to a community meeting at the church."

The officer didn't lower his weapon. The sound of glass shattering caused all three of them to look toward the building in front of them. A group of teenage boys scrambled up the fire escape on top of the deli. The officer took off toward them, and James and Hazel quickly pressed forward.

Just a few weeks ago, riots had claimed lives in Detroit. Texas, California—all across the country, colored communities were rising up, and now Harlem was no exception.

By the time they reached Abyssinian, the sanctuary was filled to capacity. Men, women, even a few children sat on the wooden pews, their faces tight with worry and exhaustion, looking like they were desperate to stop the bleeding in their community.

"Welcome." An older woman greeted them at the door with a warm but weathered smile. Her skin, a deep ebony, was lined with years of struggle, and her wiry gray hair peeked out from beneath a wide-brimmed hat decorated with a single silk flower.

"I'm Olphelia, a member here," she said, her voice tinged with a prideful Harlem lilt. She extended a folded flyer. "If you want to help in the cause, join us next Thursday for a meeting. We're going to change things, one step at a time."

Hazel took the flyer, her eyes scanning its blocky text printed on cheap paper. Across the top, in bold black letters, it read *A CALL TO ARMS: HELP ADAM CLAYTON POWELL JR. HELP HARLEM!* Beneath it, a grainy photograph of Adam with his fist raised high was flanked by bullet points listing ways to get involved: attending rallies, volunteering at food drives, and spreading the word about voter registration.

"Thank you," Hazel murmured, clutching the flyer as she and James eased into seats near the back.

Adam was already in the pulpit. Dressed in a dark brown suit with his tie slightly loosened, he looked every bit the man who had spent the day grappling with Harlem's fury.

"The mayor wants us to believe that the biggest problem in Harlem tonight is broken windows and stolen food," he bellowed. "But those shattered windows are nothing compared to the broken lives we've been forced to live. This is a protest against empty stomachs, over-crowded tenements, filthy sanitation, rotten food, and unscrupulous landlords. This isn't a riot! It's a reckoning!"

The audience erupted in applause.

"Mayor La Guardia says Harlem needs to be controlled, con-tained," Adam continued. "But what he doesn't understand—what none of them understand—is that Harlem isn't just a neighborhood. It's a people. The La Guardia's of the world have never dined on bones sucked dry by stranger's mouths, bread soaked in juices of a garbage can. The people of Harlem are hungry, not just for food, but for justice."

"Amen!" someone shouted.

"Hallelujah!" others chimed in.

Hazel felt herself drawn to Adam like never before, as his words called out the harsh realities of their lives.

"This is about dignity," he roared. "Harlem is misunderstood, but it's a world of its own, fighting for survival while the rest of the country watches us burn. They call us angry. Well, we are angry—because we've been ignored for too long."

Hazel pounced to her feet, applauding like everyone else as Adam continued, the fiery preacher on full display.

"They think we're ready to riot," Adam's voice boomed, "but we're ready to lead."

A storm of cheers rolled through the air. Adam's words had her ready to work. James stood next to Hazel, applauding as well. "Reverend Powell is pretty good," he said.

Hazel nodded, her eyes locked on Adam. In that moment, she understood the magnetic pull he held over people, the power he wielded to make them believe in something better. One thing she knew for sure, Adam Clayton Powell Jr. was going to change Harlem, and she wanted nothing more than to be a part of the transformation.

CHAPTER 8

September 1943

Olphelia Harrison's apartment felt more like a battleground than a gathering of women working for a cause—electing Adam to Congress. The space was warm and hazy, filled with the clatter of porcelain teacups and the chatter of women jockeying to be heard. The faint scent of perfumes mingled in the air, the fragrances blending with the heady clash of personalities filling the room. Hazel sat at a small round table, stuffing envelopes to be mailed out. Josephine was assisting, though she seemed more uncomfortable than usual. The noise from the street below filtered in through the open window, but inside the atmosphere was all business.

"You okay?" Hazel whispered.

Josephine shrugged. "Just feeling a little unwelcomed."

"Everyone appreciates your help," Hazel replied. "They're just focused."

The apartment, cluttered with art and books, was as lively as Olphelia herself. She moved between tables, her gray hair pulled back into a no-nonsense bun, a cigarette dangling from her lips, trailing smoke like an afterthought. She seemed like a different woman than the one from the church who had invited Hazel to this meeting.

Olphelia nodded approvingly at the women around her, scribbling notes, sorting through campaign materials, and exchanging whispered strategies. These women were the backbone of Abyssinian—sharp-tongued, iron-willed, and fiercely loyal. They handed out literature, registered voters, and made sure every corner of Harlem knew Adam Clayton Powell Jr.'s name. Adam's name was spoken with reverence that made Hazel's skin prickle. Admiration, longing, and a barely contained affection lingered in their eyes whenever they spoke of him. They loved him. Perhaps more than they should.

"If you're going to be out helping us"—Olphelia's voice cut through the room—"can you tone down the Hollywood?" She directed her words squarely at Hazel. Her tone was casual, but the words landed like a slap.

Hazel paused mid-stuff, glancing around. Surely, Olphelia wasn't talking to her. "Excuse me?" she said.

Olphelia didn't retreat. "The mink stole and all that extraness. It's not necessary. It's cold, but not cold enough for a *mink*," Olphelia continued. "No one needs to try to be seen. Plus, Pastor only has eyes for his wife."

There it was, the sting following the slap. The women around them paused, their eyes darting between Olphelia and Hazel, waiting for her reaction. But Hazel had met her share of catty women who threw barbs, so she knew how to keep her composure.

"I'm here for the cause," she said, meeting Olphelia's gaze head-on, "not a husband. Unlike some, I don't need a man to make me whole. I make my own way."

A palpable tension filled the space.

"Maybe you should go tend to your junkie friend," someone muttered from across the room. "And take Miss Anne with you," she added.

The offensive remark was as sharp as a knife and caused Josephine to gather her belongings.

"We don't need to leave," Hazel said.

Josephine gave a terse smile. "It's okay."

"Well, wait. I'll come with you."

Josephine squeezed her hand, a mist covering her eyes. "No. Stay. Really." She lowered her voice. "I'm used to this." Then she scurried out the door.

Hazel debated taking off after her, but she needed to say a few things to these ladies.

She spun toward the woman who'd last spoken, a middle-aged matron with too-tight pin curls, wearing a perfectly pressed suit and a thin line of disapproval etched across her face. Hazel recognized her from when she used to hang around the musicians on the party scene. "You could only wish you were half the woman Billie Holiday is," Hazel said, her voice low but steady, "even when she's high."

A few gasps rippled through the room, as Hazel continued. "And Josephine was working in Harlem back when you were working the brothel—you know, back before you got right with the Lord."

The women's eyes bulged in horror but Hazel didn't care. These sanctified folks got on her nerves.

Before the tension could settle, Hattie Freeman, Adam's personal secretary, stepped in. Her voice was sugary sweet, but there was an edge beneath it. "Ladies, we're here to work on our lord and master's behalf," she said, smiling tightly.

Hazel froze. *Lord and master?* Was that really how they saw Adam? She glanced around, searching for any sign that Hattie was joking, but instead, she found nods of agreement. Hattie stood with a smug expression, and Hazel suddenly felt out of place—an outsider in a room full of devotees.

Another woman rose to give her report, breaking the uncomfortable silence. "We can't let the devil sidetrack us. We need to get back to business." She looked down at some notes in her hand. "The deacons have pledged ten thousand dollars to Pastor's campaign, and the Negro Labor Victory Committee, representing three hundred thousand workers, gave their endorsement along with a fifteen-thousand-dollar pledge."

Excitement buzzed through the room as they discussed the pledges and endorsements and the money flowing into Adam's campaign. Their devotion to him was feverish. Yes, Adam was charismatic and inspiring. But what made these women work themselves to the bone for him?

Then the door swung open, and there he was—Adam, in all his glory. He strode into the room as though he owned it, wearing a smile that could make people forget their own names. The women immediately flocked to him, their voices rising in pitch, their movements quickening as they rushed to hand him papers and offer him tea. It was like watching bees swarm around their queen.

"Hello, ladies," Adam said warmly. "Just wanted to drop in and see how things were going." He gave each woman a smile, a touch on the arm, a moment of his attention. They practically melted at his feet.

Hazel watched them scramble for his approval, for even a sliver of his attention, and it was more than she could take. She slipped out the door.

She had barely made it down the steps when his voice sounded behind her. "Leaving so soon?"

Hazel paused and slowly turned around. "I came to help your campaign and your cause, but it looks like you don't need any help. Your little harem will make sure you're well taken care of." She tried and failed to temper her disgust at the entire afternoon. "And do you know they call you lord and master? That's utterly ridiculous."

He released an easy laugh. "I do have some die-hard members. They don't mean it literally. There's only one God, but they see me as one of His disciples," he admitted, stepping closer. "Really, they just want to see me and the church succeed."

She crossed her arms. "I think those women want more than that."

Amusement glinted in his eyes as he closed the distance between them. "Do I detect jealousy?"

She waved his words away but didn't respond.

"All that matters," he said softly, "is what I want. And I want you."

"I don't compete, Mr. Powell."

"I would never ask you to."

His declaration made her breath hitch, but then just as quickly, she caught herself. "I'll let you get back before tongues start wagging." She turned and sashayed down the sidewalk as his laughter floated behind her.

CHAPTER 9

October 1943

The scent of smoked ribs and cornbread filled the air as Hazel stepped into Mom Holiday's Restaurant. The door swung shut behind her, muffling the busy sounds of Ninety-Ninth Street and Central Park West. Inside, the clatter of utensils and bubbling pots softened the atmosphere, adding a homey warmth. Behind the counter, Billie's mother, Sadie, worked, slicing ribs with quick, practiced movements as she chatted with a customer while the jukebox played Billie's songs on rotation. Her caramel-toned face shone with the heat from the stove, but her smile stayed constant.

Hazel watched as Sadie piled a plate high with food—ribs dripping with sauce, collard greens, and black-eyed peas—and handed it to a man in tattered clothes and worn shoes. He murmured a quiet thanks before heading to a corner table and diving into the meal as if it was the first he'd had in days.

"Miss Sadie, how are you doing today?" Hazel said, glancing around the room at the mix of neighborhood folks, musicians, and down-and-out wanderers.

Sadie looked up, her warm brown eyes twinkling as her hands moved on to prepare the next plate. "Blessed to be a blessing to others," she replied, nodding toward a sign on the wall: "No one goes hungry. God Bless the Child."

"Don't you look beautiful." Sadie pointed to Hazel's wine-colored silk dress.

"Thank you." Hazel paused. Sadie had probably heard about Billie's near overdose, but since Hazel wasn't sure, she just said, "How's she doing?"

The way Sadie's shoulders drooped said she had heard the news. "Same. Acting like she don't have a problem when everybody in Harlem knows she does." She shook her head. "That husband of hers ain't helping none. But she's up there."

Hazel's eyes darted toward the stairs at the back of the restaurant that led up to Billie's apartment. She made her way up the stairs and was greeted by the sight of Billie curling her hair in front of a small mirror propped on the kitchen counter. A can of Sterno heated the curling iron as smoke wafted in lazy circles around the room. Billie's black leather bag sat nearby, its telltale syringe barely concealed beneath the folds.

"Billie, we're supposed to be at Uptown House by seven," Hazel said, leaning against the doorframe. "It's six forty-five. Let's move it."

Billie's eyes met Hazel's in the mirror, one brow arched as she dragged the curling iron through a lock of hair. "Almost ready, doll. Can't go out half done. You know that." She released the curl, letting it spring back, then took a slow drag from her cigarette.

Hazel's gaze flicked toward the hidden syringe, but she decided not to bring it up—not here, not now. She tried a different approach. "Your mother's downstairs working herself to the bone. She's not too fond of Jimmy, by the way."

Billie's laughter was sharp and bitter. "Mama doesn't like anyone who might take a piece of her pie. But Jimmy? He's a footnote, honey. Won't be around much longer."

Hazel tilted her head. "Are you serious? What's the plan now?"

Billie shrugged, picking up her lipstick and expertly applying it in a single stroke. "I've got Joe Guy waiting in the wings. Man can blow a trumpet like nobody's business. And he's a lot more fun than Jimmy ever was."

Hazel frowned. "You're trading one mess for another, Billie. That's not exactly progress."

Billie stood, smoothing her sleek black dress over her hips. "Progress is boring, sweetheart. I walk the tightrope for fun." She grabbed her pocketbook and gestured toward the stairs. "Now, let's scram."

Together, they descended the creaking stairs and stepped into the warm, bustling atmosphere of the restaurant. Sadie glanced up from the counter, her face lighting up briefly when she saw Billie, only to cloud over in an instant.

She slid a steaming plate in front of a waiting customer, wiped her hands on her apron, and made a beeline for her daughter.

"Billie, let me talk to you," Sadie said, gripping her arm and pulling her toward the corner, out of earshot of the patrons.

Billie sighed, and Hazel sensed where this was headed. "What is it now, Mama?"

"I need some money." Sadie's tone was hushed but firm. "The fridge is on the fritz, and I've got bills piling up. You know I'm barely keepin' this place afloat."

Billie stiffened. "I don't have it," she replied flatly, crossing her arms. "Not this time."

Sadie's eyes narrowed. "So you can't give your mama no money?"

Billie's jaw tightened. "You're not gonna be happy till you bleed me dry, are you?"

"At least I'm asking for money to keep this place afloat. Unlike that husband of yours, who just wants it to stick a needle in his arm."

Billie's face flushed with anger. "Don't you worry about what Jimmy's doin'."

Sadie snapped, "You've got no problem callin' me out, but you'll defend him to the grave, even when he's draggin' you down."

Their voices rose, drawing a few glances from the customers, but neither seemed to care.

Sadie finally threw her hands up, exasperated. "You think you're better than me, don't you? Just 'cause you got outta here for a little while?"

Billie let out a bitter laugh, shaking her head. "No, Mama. I think we're both drowning, and you're too proud to admit it."

The two women stared at each other, the weight of unspoken pain and years of resentment hanging heavy in the air. Finally, Sadie broke the silence, her voice quieter, but no less sharp. "Well, have fun tonight. I love you, girl. Be careful."

Billie's face lost its edge, though her guard remained up. "Yeah, I love you too." Her tone was laced with a complicated mix of affection and frustration. Without another word, she turned and walked toward the door, her back straight, her steps deliberate.

Hazel, who had been standing near the doorway trying to remain inconspicuous, touched Billie's arm as they stepped outside. The cool evening air was instant relief from the heat and tension inside.

Hazel's black Packard was idling at the curb, her driver already out and holding the door open. Billie slid into the back seat first. Hazel followed, and the door shut with a solid thunk. The car pulled away from Central Park West and eased north onto Manhattan Avenue. Hazel waited a moment, then glanced sideways at Billie. "So, you and Sadie still at each other's throats?"

"That's how she shows her love," Billie said, pulling out a cigarette with fingers that trembled just slightly. She struck a match, the flare lighting her face for a brief second before vanishing into smoke. "I wouldn't know how to act if she said something kind for once."

She took a long drag and let the smoke out slow, her eyes focused on the blur of storefronts and bus stops sliding past. "But hey, at least she's here. That's more than I can say for most of my life."

Hazel stayed quiet, letting the hum of the engine and the rhythm of the city fill the silence. She knew Billie had spent years trying to patch the cracks between her and Sadie—sending money and scribbled notes from the road, asking her to come to shows—but Sadie's love always came laced with judgment.

Hazel nodded, choosing her words carefully. "She's trying, Billie. You both are. It's messy, but it's something."

"Yeah," Billie said, her voice barely audible. "It's something."

They turned onto 134th Street, the Packard slowing as they approached Uptown House. The marquee glowed faintly in the Harlem night. Hazel looked at Billie, her voice gentle as she said, "She's worried about you. We all are."

Billie scoffed, flicking ash out the window. "She needs to be worried about herself. Diabetes is killing her. What is she worried about me for?"

The car rolled to a stop in front of the club. The door opened, but neither of them moved just yet.

Finally, Hazel said, "Because she's your mother. Not to mention the overdose a few months ago."

Billie waved her off as she stepped out the car. "That was nothing," she said, her tone dismissive. "Just a bad night. Don't make it a big deal."

"Billie, you could've died," Hazel said, following her out. "Took dang near three days to come out of your haze. That's not nothing."

Billie stopped walking and faced Hazel. "I thrive on the edge. Been doing it a long time. I know how to handle myself. Don't you worry about me."

Hazel's heart ached at the mix of defiance and vulnerability in Billie's voice. "I just don't want to see you fall."

Billie's smile was brittle. "Falling's part of the act, Hazel. It's the getting back up that counts."

Hazel wanted to push further, to break through Billie's armor, but she knew better. Billie only let people in on her terms, and tonight wasn't one of those nights.

The last traces of daylight slipped behind the jagged Harlem skyline as they walked toward the entrance. A group of men in wide-brimmed hats and double-breasted zoot suits leaned against the brick outside the club, laughter spilling from their mouths.

"Ay, Red! That walk should be illegal," one called out to Hazel, his voice slick with mischief.

"Tell your friend she can smile too—it won't hurt," another added, aiming at Billie, who didn't flinch.

They ignored the catcalls and entered the smoky club. Billie headed to the bar, ordered a whiskey neat, then turned to Hazel. "I'm meeting Joe here," she admitted.

"Billie," Hazel warned. "Don't go inviting trouble. That isn't smart." Billie's brother-in-law owned Uptown House, so he would no doubt see Billie and Joe together.

Billie laughed, tossing back the whiskey. "Where's the fun in smart?"

Before Hazel could respond, Billie nudged her arm with a knowing smirk. "Speaking of trouble." She nodded toward the far end of the room.

Hazel followed her gaze, and her pulse quickened the moment her eyes landed on Adam. He had told her he was going out with friends, but she didn't know they'd end up at the same place. He sat with a group of men, leaning back in his chair with ease. Adam's eyes locked with hers, and both of their smiles were instant.

Hazel felt her cheeks warm, and she quickly turned back to the bar, hoping the dim lighting might hide the telltale flush.

Billie, of course, caught it all. She let out a low, teasing laugh. "Oh, honey, you two suck at secrets. Anyone with eyes can tell you two got more heat than a Harlem summer."

Hazel opened her mouth to deny it, but before she could form the words, Adam had already eased up to them.

"Ladies," he said, his smooth baritone cutting through the air. "A pleasure to see you both."

Billie leaned back against the bar with a devilish glint in her eye. "Adam, darling. You buying the next round of drinks?"

Adam chuckled, but his eyes remained locked on Hazel. "It would be my pleasure. Two whiskey sours?"

"Make mine a double," Billie said.

"Be right back," he finally said, breaking his gaze, and made his way to the end of the bar.

Amused, Billie leaned closer to Hazel, her voice low and dripping with mock sincerity. "I gotta say, he's a lot different from Lee. Powerful, charming, dangerous. I can see why you two are fooling around."

Hazel feigned shock. "Billie! There's nothing going on. You're imagining things."

Billie's eyebrow arched. "I'm going to need you to work on your lying." Before Hazel could stammer out another excuse, Billie straightened and gave her a pointed look. "At least now you can't judge me." She tossed back the rest of her drink and then added, with a wry smirk, "Guess we're both making bad decisions these days."

Billie's words hit harder than she expected. But before Hazel could respond, Joe Guy entered.

"There's my man." Billie's lips parted in a reckless grin as Adam approached with their new drinks. "Thank you kindly," she said, taking the glass. To Hazel, she said, "Don't wait up, sugar. I'll be fine."

"Billie, wait," Hazel started, but Billie was already sauntering toward Joe, her hips swaying in time with the band's rhythm.

Hazel sighed, turning back to Adam, who now stood beside her.

"She's something else," he said, watching Billie with amusement.

"She's just looking for love," Hazel replied quietly, the words heavier than she intended.

Adam tilted his head, studying her for a moment before speaking. "Aren't we all?"

CHAPTER 10

Moonlight spilled into the ballroom of the Hotel Theresa, casting a silver sheen across a black and gold banner draped above the stage. At its center, the seal of Alpha Phi Alpha Fraternity gleamed with quiet authority.

Hazel hadn't planned to come. But as Jimmy pulled into Harlem after their four-hour drive from Baltimore—where she'd played an afternoon concert—she'd found herself saying, *Take me to the Hotel Theresa.*

Now she stood near the back of the room, half concealed behind a potted ficus, watching without being watched. Her beige dress felt out of place among the sea of pink-and-green satin gowns, but no one seemed to notice. Every eye was fixed on the stage—on Adam, commanding the room as only he could.

He stepped to the microphone, confident and composed, his voice filling the ballroom with ease.

"Ladies and gentlemen—brothers of my esteemed fraternity, our sisters of Alpha Kappa Alpha, honored guests . . ."

The crowd stilled as his voice took hold. Hazel's eyes fixed on him. She tried telling herself it was just his charm that she found attractive, but deep down, she knew better. It was more than that. It was the way he carried himself, the way the room bent to his will as if he'd always been meant to lead it. He was the man her father had dreamed of being. Hazel knew that was why her father had failed her. Armed with a college degree and endless ambition, he had moved from Trinidad to Harlem with high hopes, only to be crushed by a world that refused to see his worth. The weight of his disillusionment had suffocated his dreams—and eventually his love for her. Adam would never let anything stop his dreams, and she loved that about him.

". . . As you know, I'm ready to be your United States congressman from Harlem!" Adam's voice rang out, followed by raucous applause. Cheers filled the air like a gospel choir reaching its crescendo.

Adam talked about the work the fraternity was doing, then painted Harlem's future in bold strokes—better schools, safer streets, real jobs that paid more than scraps. He spoke of power, of dignity, of a world where Negroes weren't just scraping by but thriving. The crowd swayed with him, their elegance bending beneath the pull of his vision. It was easy to get caught up in his rhythm, in the certainty of his voice.

When he finished, the cheers roared, sweeping over him as he waded into the crowd. He moved through the people like he was born for this moment—handshakes, back pats, a flash of teeth at the right moment.

When he saw her, his smile stretched wide. Anticipation and apprehension tangled inside her.

"So," he said, his voice slipping into a smooth, teasing lilt. "Are you going to vote for me, Miss Scott?"

The formality was for the crowd's benefit, but the sparkle in his eyes? That was for her.

She arched a brow. "I'll have to see where you stand on the issues."

His smile deepened. "How about I tell you over a glass of wine?"

She hesitated, just for a beat, then without words, allowed him to guide her away from the noise and into a quiet corner in the Hotel Theresa's private lounge. He leaned in as they settled into their seats, and the warmth of his presence curled around her.

"I'm hoping I can convince the people of Harlem," Adam said as they waited for their drinks. "There's only one Negro congressman in the country, and William Dawson . . . Well, he doesn't want to rock the ship. Our people don't need safe. They need a fighter."

She met his gaze. "Then I look forward to helping get you elected."

Something in his expression flickered at that—satisfaction, maybe.

They sipped the smooth vintage, and the wine settled in her chest. Then, before she could overthink it, she asked, "Why don't you have children, Adam?"

He stilled, the question catching him off guard. A rare moment where his polish cracked. "Isabel has a son, Preston. I adopted him, and I love him as if he were my own. But I've always wanted—" He exhaled, rolling his glass between his hands. "I've always wanted a son of my own. A legacy."

The way he said it—low, quiet—felt like a confession. His mind had drifted somewhere distant, a place she wasn't sure she was welcome.

Hazel had spent her life chasing music. She'd never questioned whether she wanted children. Never had the time. But now, for the first time, she wondered—when the music stopped, when the curtain fell for the last time—what would be left of her?

She set her glass down. "Adam," she said, her voice softer now, "what about Isabel?"

His jaw tightened.

Hazel pressed on, because she had to. "How can you talk about wanting to be with me when you haven't ended things with her? Or . . . do you really intend to?" She forced herself to say the next part, even though it lodged like glass in her throat. "I need to be clear. I can't be the reason you leave. I won't be responsible for breaking up another woman's marriage."

He took a measured breath. "My marriage is over," he said, but the words felt heavy. "But my relationship with Isabel . . . it's complicated. We built a life. Untangling it isn't easy."

Hazel studied him, searching for truth in the spaces between his words.

"I probably would've stayed," he admitted, his voice rougher now, "and just been miserable. But you—" He exhaled sharply, shaking his head. "I feel alive with you. You've made me want more." His eyes locked on hers. "I want the things I dream of, Hazel. All of them."

An approaching waiter halted their conversation. Adam ordered more wine, but when Hazel looked up and said, "Do you have any Green River? Neat, if it's not too dusty," the air between them shifted.

Adam stilled. His fingers, draped loosely over his glass, went quiet.

"Green River?" he echoed, his voice softer now. "Haven't heard anyone ask for that in a long time."

Hazel tilted her head. "Too bold for a lady?"

A smile tugged at his mouth, but it didn't reach his eyes. "Not at all. It's just . . . my sister, Blanche, used to drink that. Swore by it. Wouldn't touch anything else."

Hazel's teasing smirk faded. "I didn't mean to—"

"No," he said quickly, shaking his head with a quiet breath. "It's . . . nice. I haven't heard that name out loud since . . . well. You surprised me."

She watched him closely, her voice gentler now. "Good surprise or bad?"

Adam glanced at her then, the smile returning—smaller this

time, but real. "The kind that makes you remember something worth remembering."

"I didn't know you had a sister, though. For some reason I thought you were an only child."

Adam smiled faintly. "She was older than me, the light of my parents' lives. My mother adored her. She was everything I wanted to be—smart, driven, kind. She made me believe I could be more than a preacher's kid tagging along in her shadow."

A glimmer of grief passed over him. Hazel could see the memories swirling behind his eyes. The distance between them seemed to shrink as she reached out, lightly resting her hand on the edge of the table, not quite touching his, but close enough to let him feel her presence.

"What happened to her?" Hazel asked.

"She died in 1926 when I was a freshman at City College. Ruptured appendix. Just . . . like that." He snapped his fingers, the sound sharp in the quiet space between them. "It hit her fast. They couldn't save her. She was gone before they even realized how bad it was. It was . . . umm, it was bad for me after that. I turned my back on God. Felt like the church was a fraud, my father the lead perpetrator, my mother a rubber stamp. Blanche was everything to me. I don't think I'd ever felt so low as after losing her."

His words hung in the air. Hazel pursed her lips then, before she could stop herself, she offered, "I, umm. I had a little brother . . . He died when he was a baby." Hazel had never told anyone—not even Lee—about her brother. She continued. "The doctor . . . his scalpel was dirty, and it infected my brother. I was too young to understand, but the grief . . . it stayed with my mother. I've always tried to make her proud as a way to, I don't know, compensate for her loss and lifetime of what-ifs."

For a moment, silence stretched between them. But it wasn't

uncomfortable. He understood her buried grief. They didn't need to say more.

Adam cleared his throat, breaking the tension. "You know, I don't talk about Blanche. Ever. But with you . . ." His words trailed off. "Talking to you feels easy. Natural."

She smiled because she felt the exact same way.

Adam paused as the waiter set their drinks down. As Hazel reached for her whiskey, he reached across the table, his hand covering hers. "Hazel, I want you."

She eased her hand away. Though no one seemed to be paying them any attention, they were still in public.

"You've made that clear," she replied, trying to keep her tone light.

Adam shook his head as he reached in his pocket and removed a hotel room key and set it on the table. "No. I want you in *every* way. Now."

Adam eased his chair back, stood, left some money on the table, then looked at her with his eyes filled with hunger, and Hazel felt the walls she'd built around herself begin to crack. "Room three twelve."

As he walked away, Hazel's pulse raced; her mind screamed at her to stop, to think, to remember Lee and the complications of Adam's life. But her heart didn't seem to care about rules or reputations.

She wanted this. She wanted him.

Hazel eased the key into her hand, clutched it to her chest, and then stood. Could she risk stepping into the fire, knowing the burn it might leave behind? Her footsteps moving toward his room, seemingly with a mind of their own, answered that question for her.

When she entered room 312, Adam stood watching the door as if he'd been unsure whether she would come. Then he stepped toward her, his hand cupping her cheek as he whispered, "You don't have to be afraid, Hazel. You are the only woman I want."

And just like that, the final wall came down. Hazel closed the distance between them, her lips meeting his in a kiss that felt like he was memorizing the taste of her. Her hands slid up his chest, careful and certain, and when she pulled him toward the bed, it was without hesitation.

They moved together like they'd done this dance a hundred times—but tonight, it was something else.

There was no going back now.

CHAPTER 11

December 1943

Daylight streamed through the slit in the heavy curtains of the hotel room, casting long stripes across the rumpled bed. Hazel stood in front of the mirror. She fastened the top button of her coat with deliberate care, then smoothed her scarf.

Behind her, Hazel watched as Adam moved slowly, slipping one arm and then the other into his sport coat, his eyes never leaving her reflection. His expression was soft. Untroubled. "You ready?" Adam asked.

She gave a small nod but said nothing. The words were stuck somewhere between her chest and her conscience. Last night had been magical. But daylight had a way of draining the color from dreams. The guilt she'd managed to silence had returned with the sunrise.

They had agreed to drive to Lindy's for breakfast. It had seemed harmless. A way to stretch their time together before slipping back into the separate compartments of their lives. Adam had wanted to walk to Frank's a few blocks away, but Hazel wanted to get away from Harlem's prying eyes.

"I am starving and cannot wait to dig into those Lindy's pancakes," Adam said as they exited the room.

She said nothing as they stepped onto the elevator. Adam hummed—off-key and cheerful—completely at ease. Hazel stood stiff beside him, her gloved hands clenching the strap of her handbag. Her mind was a spiral of thoughts: She still had on her dress from last night. What if someone saw them? What if it made the papers? What if Isabel found out?

The elevator doors opened and the sight of the bustling lobby snapped her back. Businessmen in crisp suits scurried past, a bellhop wheeling a tower of matching luggage, a woman in a fur stole laughing too loudly at something her companion said. The world outside their room was wide awake.

Hazel froze for a split second. Then said, "Walk ahead of me a little."

Adam paused, frowning. "What?"

Her gaze darted toward the front desk, then to a couple seated in velvet chairs, both reading a newspaper. Panic fluttered in her chest. "It's nine in the morning. I don't want anyone seeing us coming out together. Can you pick me up around the corner or something?"

He stared at her like he was just noticing how uncomfortable she was. "That's ridiculous, Hazel."

She finally looked at him, guilt etched into every line of her face. "Please," she whispered. "Just humor me."

Adam didn't argue. He studied her for a long moment, his expression softening, understanding settling behind his eyes.

"Fine," he said gently. "I'll drive up two blocks and pick you up by the newspaper stand on One Hundred Twenty-Fifth and Lenox."

He nodded and turned, slipping into the flow of the lobby like he belonged there. Hazel, however, lingered, pretending to look for something in her bag until he turned the corner. Then she slipped out, head down, sunglasses on, heart pounding like she was doing something criminal. Outside, Harlem moved around her with weekend energy—men shouting for taxis, women in gloves and hats darting in and out of stores.

Hazel kept her eyes forward until she reached the newsstand, where Adam's black Jaguar waited, purring like it had nothing to hide.

He leaned across the passenger seat and pushed the door open. "You happy now?" he asked, a teasing warmth in his voice.

"I'd just rather not have tongues wagging," she muttered as she slid in.

Adam smiled, one hand on the wheel, the other already guiding them up Lenox Avenue. "Let them wag. I'm not ashamed of you."

Hazel didn't respond right away. She stared out the window as the neighborhoods shifted—barbershops, jazz lounges, bakeries with fresh rolls in the windows, and stacked brownstones. The guilt sat in her chest, even as the wind from the open window lifted the edge of her scarf.

Adam turned onto Broadway, easing the Jaguar through traffic, and Hazel finally exhaled for the remainder of the drive.

They parked a half block down from the restaurant. Hazel stepped out, draping her arm through Adam's as she scanned. That's when she saw the building across the street, a simple brick structure, its window glowing with yellow light. The words *Garrison Packing House* were stenciled across the glass. And inside, moving between the slabs of meat hanging from hooks, was Lee. He was staring out the window, obviously enamoured with the Jag.

"Adam," Hazel said quickly, reaching for his arm. "Let's go around the back—"

But it was too late. Lee spotted her.

Their eyes met across Broadway. His face shifted from admiration to confusion to something sharper—recognition, disbelief. He darted out the door and across the street, dodging a cab as he picked up speed.

"Hazel!"

Hazel turned slowly, her pulse roaring in her ears. Adam followed her gaze and straightened as Lee reached the curb.

His voice was rough as he struggled to catch his breath. "Hazel, I thought that was you."

The faint, coppery smell of raw meat reached her first. His butcher's apron was smeared with blood.

"Lee." Hazel's voice was tight as she eased her arm away from Adam's.

Adam's eyebrows rose slightly as his eyes volleyed between the two. He stepped forward and extended a hand. "Adam Clayton Powell Jr.," he said smoothly. "Nice to meet you."

Lee limply shook his hand, but he didn't take his eyes off of Hazel. "What's going on?" Hurt crept along the edges of his voice. "When did you get back in town?"

"Ummm, yesterday." Hazel tried to appear casual. "Just had a meeting with the councilman," she said lightly, though she could feel the awkward tension hanging between them.

"Meeting," Lee repeated, his tone flat. He looked at Adam, then back at her.

Adam's lips twitched in a faint smile. He stood tall, composed, as if the whole situation amused him. Hazel hated that it made her feel small, hated that she was embarrassed. "You should probably get back to work," she said softly to Lee.

Lee's face fell, his shoulders sagging slightly. "Right." He looked at her again, as if trying to find an explanation she wasn't offering. "We'll talk later?"

"Yes. Come by after work," Hazel said, her voice breaking slightly on the words. Why hadn't she broken things off with Lee? He was a friend above all else and deserved that. She watched as he turned and walked back across the street, dragging his feet like a wounded puppy.

Adam waited until Lee disappeared before speaking. "Is that your ex-suitor?" he asked, his tone casual, as if they'd just passed someone she barely knew.

"No." Hazel hesitated, feeling the shame creep up her neck. "I mean, he's still . . . we kind of are courting."

A glimmer of amusement flickered through his eyes. "No," he said confidently. "As of today, that's your ex." He offered a warm, teasing smile. Hazel didn't return it. She fully intended to break things off with Lee, but she needed to make sure Adam was clear.

"Just so you know, I don't get an ex until you have an ex." With that, she turned and continued making her way to Lindy's.

HAZEL SAT AT the kitchen table, tracing the rim of her teacup with her finger. Lee had called as soon as he got off from work, asking if he could come by. Hazel wished she didn't have to do this, but Lee deserved an explanation. He had stood by her side when she was being picked on in junior high school. He helped her stay on top of her studies while she balanced music with academics in high school. Above all else, she didn't want to cause him any pain.

The light tapping made Hazel inhale sharply before opening the door. Lee stood there, looking cleaner and more put together than she'd seen him in months. Gone were his usual work clothes; in their place was a neatly pressed button-down and slacks. His hair was combed, his jaw smooth. He'd made an effort—and the sight of it twisted the guilt in her chest.

"Lee." She stepped aside and gestured to the kitchen table. They sat down across from each other. The silence between them stretched until Lee finally spoke.

"So," he began, "are you seeing Reverend Powell?"

Hazel flinched, his directness catching her off guard. "No," she said quickly. "It's not like that. Adam and I are friends." She paused, the lie heavy on her tongue. She was usually bold, brutally honest. But the look on Lee's face pushed the truth back down inside her.

"Are we over?" he asked, his voice quieter now, as if he knew he couldn't compete against Adam Clayton Powell, Jr.

She opened her mouth, but the words caught in her throat. Finally, she managed, "You deserve more than what I can give, Lee." She meant it, but she hated how small the words felt compared to everything between them.

Lee shook his head in disbelief. "You didn't even give me a chance to understand what was going on," he said, his voice cracking slightly. "One day, I'm thinking we're in love, and the next, it's just over. Just like that. How do you expect me to be okay with that, Hazel?"

Her chest ached, and she looked down at her hands, her voice barely above a whisper. "I didn't mean to hurt you, Lee. You've been such a dear friend. But things changed. I changed." She hesitated, forcing herself to meet his piercing eyes. Their youthful friendship couldn't exist in her have-it-all world. She should've told him that long before now.

Lee stared at her, his eyes searching hers for something—an explanation, a reason, anything that could make sense of the pain she was causing him. "Then what's it about?" he asked, his voice thick with emotion. "What did I do wrong?"

"You didn't do anything wrong," she said. "It's me. I've always had these dreams, these ambitions that are bigger than this—bigger than us. And I can't keep holding on to something that I know in my heart isn't right. It's not fair to you."

Lee ran his hands across his face, his expression a mix of pain and frustration. Finally, he sat upright. "So what happens now? Do I just walk away and pretend the last few years of my life didn't mean anything?"

"No," Hazel said, forcefully. "You meant everything to me, Lee. You held me steady when everything else was falling apart. You'll always have a place in my heart. But I can't keep pretending we're headed in the same direction."

Lee let out a heavy sigh, pushing back his chair. He stood, and she followed, her heart breaking at the sadness that seemed to permeate his body. "I guess there's nothing left to say, then," he said quietly.

"Lee . . ." Hazel tried to take his hand, but he shook his head as he stepped out of her reach.

"Take care of yourself, Hazel." His voice was thick as he walked away.

The sound of the door closing echoed through the room, leaving Hazel standing there fighting the sea of emotions threatening to overtake her.

Her mother appeared in the doorway, her expression saying she'd heard everything. "Sowing is easy. Reaping is hard," she said, taking her daughter into her arms.

CHAPTER 12

May 1944

Hazel adjusted the cuffs of her silk blouse, offering a composed smile as the *Time* magazine reporter scribbled furiously in his notepad. They were seated in the grand lobby of the Hotel Cecil. The reporter, a fast-talking young white man with slicked-back red hair, leaned forward eagerly, as if they hadn't already been talking for thirty minutes.

"How does it feel to be the biggest, classiest jazz pianist in the country?" he declared, his voice tinged with admiration. "Bigger than Billie."

Hazel kept her smile. Why must people continue to try and pit colored women against each other, as if there wasn't room enough for more than one star? "Billie is Billie. And there will never be another."

The reporter smirked, undeterred. "But surely you see yourself in a different league—more refined, more—"

Hazel cut him off with a graceful tilt of her head. "I see myself as a musician. A Negro woman in this industry who's had to fight for every opportunity. Just like Billie."

Before he could press further, her eyes flickered toward the entrance. The appearance of her friend Miles Davis, entering the revolving doors, his slim frame clad in a rumpled dark suit, trumpet case in hand, gave her the opportunity to exit.

"I appreciate your time," Hazel said smoothly, standing and extending her hand. "But I have to go."

The reporter looked momentarily stunned, as if he'd expected to sit and chat with her for hours. But he recovered quickly, shaking her hand. "Thank you for meeting with me. I know you're on the road a lot, so I'm glad we could work this out."

She offered a final nod before gliding toward Miles. He was young, not yet twenty, but carried himself with the quiet confidence of a man destined for greatness.

"Miles, what are you doing here?" she asked.

His boyish face was alight with excitement. "Hazel, what a pleasant surprise. I'm heading to Minton's," he replied, hugging her. "The fellas are all there tonight."

Minton's Playhouse, nestled in the corner of the Hotel Cecil, had become the epicenter of the jazz revolution. Miles eyed her gloves, which she was slipping on. "You heading out?"

"Just finished an interview."

"Why don't you come hang out with us for a bit," Miles said.

Hazel looked at her wristwatch. On cue, someone came out the club door, and the music wafted through the hotel, like it was extending a personal invitation.

"Okay, for a little while."

Together, they walked into the smoke-filled room. Though it was an intimate setting, tables were crowded with men in wide-brimmed hats and women in sleek dresses. Every one of the twenty or so seats were taken. It was a mostly colored crowd, save for a white man who sat in the corner, bopping his head to the tunes.

"You all right?" Miles asked, anxious to get to the stage.

"Yes, go do your thing," she said, looking around. Minton's was no ordinary club. For the last four years, musicians who'd grown bored with the constraints of big-band swing came to the tiny Harlem venue after hours, letting loose, breaking rules, and bending notes into shapes no one had imagined before. Legends like Charlie Christian and Kenny Clarke had laid the groundwork, and now Charlie Parker, Dizzy Gillespie, and Thelonious Monk were pushing the boundaries even further. The new world of bebop was chaotic and unpredictable—everything her own meticulously crafted performances were not. As she listened, she couldn't help but feel like this music was jazz turned inside out—frenetic, angular, and unapologetically bold. It wasn't for the faint of heart, and Hazel was all in. The sharp, syncopated rhythms crashed against the walls. This was no ordinary jazz—it was a rebellion.

Thelonious stood over the piano at the front of the room, while Dizzy blew his horn with a wild abandon that made Hazel's breath catch.

She spotted Billie, languid at the bar, a half-empty glass in hand. She swayed slightly, her eyes half closed as she took in the music.

"Well, look what the cat dragged in," Billie drawled when she noticed Hazel. "What brings you to the lion's den?"

Hazel slid onto the barstool beside her friend. "I had an interview in the hotel and saw Miles." She pointed toward the band, where Miles had already scurried over to set up. "He told me to stop in. What about you?"

Billie lifted her glass toward the bandstand. "Watching Joe play." She motioned toward Joe Guy, who was blowing his trumpet next to Dizzy. Billie smirked. "Didn't think I'd see you here, though. You haven't been out much since Adam put you on a leash."

Hazel bristled but kept her voice light. "I'm not paying you any mind, Billie. I just wanted to check out this bebop."

Billie raised an eyebrow. "And?"

"And it's . . . different. But different can be good."

Before Billie could respond, Dizzy bounced over, his horn-rimmed glasses resting on his nose. "Hazel Scott, as I live and breathe!" He grabbed Hazel's hands, spinning her around playfully. "What's a straitlaced virtuoso like you doing in a place like this?"

Hazel laughed, swatting him away. "I'm not that straitlaced."

"Oh, yes you are," Dizzy teased. "But stick around—we might corrupt you yet."

"Let's get her up here!"

Hazel looked across the room at the voice that had just called out. It was Thelonious.

"Don't get any ideas," Hazel warned, though the idea thrilled her. She turned to Dizzy. "How'd this all start, anyway? This bebop thing?"

Dizzy's grin widened. "Bebop isn't a thing, baby girl—it's a movement. We got tired of playing the same old tunes for dancers, so we started experimenting. You can't be the only one to change things up."

"I hear you," Hazel said. The way Dizzy's eyes danced when he spoke pulled at her heart.

"Faster tempos, new chord changes, solos that go wherever the hell they want. It's freedom, Hazel. Pure freedom," Dizzy said.

Hazel nodded slowly, taking it all in. Freedom. That word stuck with her. She'd spent her career walking a tightrope—pushing boundaries in classical and jazz while still maintaining an air of respectability. But here at Minton's, respectability seemed irrelevant. It was about the untamed music. The patrons erupted into applause as Charlie finished his solo, and Thelonious struck the opening chords of the next tune.

Billie was watching her with a knowing smile. "You're itching to play, aren't you?"

"I don't know bebop," Hazel replied.

"Just let the music drive you." Dizzy nudged her toward the piano. "Go on." He grinned. "Show 'em what you got."

"Well, well, looks like we've got royalty in the house," Thelonius announced as Hazel eased toward the stage. He stood to let Hazel take his place at the piano. "All yours, Your Highness."

Hazel slid into the seat. She didn't even think about it as her fingers went to work. This was different from her regular performances. The stakes felt higher—not because the audience expected perfection, but because they demanded authenticity. She launched into a jazzy intro, her left hand laying down a steady rhythm while her right hand danced over the keys. The band picked up on her energy, Dizzy and Thelonius traded phrases as Miles leaned back, nodding in approval. The music swelled, filling the tiny club with a sound so big it seemed impossible. Hazel felt herself let go, the constraints of her classical training falling away. This was even beyond jazzing up the classics. This was flying in the wind. She wasn't just playing anymore—she was speaking, laughing, crying through the piano. When the song ended, the room exploded in applause.

"Damn, Hazel," Dizzy said, wiping his brow. "You've got more fire in you than I thought."

"I had good inspiration," she replied, a satisfied smile on her face.

"Sing something!" someone shouted from the back of the room. Hazel hesitated again. She was a pianist first. But the crowd was insistent, and she couldn't resist their enthusiasm. Dizzy handed her the microphone, and she closed her eyes, searching for the right song. She settled on "Embraceable You," and the band began playing with a soft, velvety tone that grew richer with each phrase. By the time she hit the final note, the room was silent, every face turned toward her in awe.

"I thought you were just a pianist," someone yelled when she finished. "Why don't you sing more?"

Hazel smiled. "Maybe I should."

"Get her on TV!" another voice called out.

Hazel laughed. "I sure hope God's listening."

After the set, Hazel returned to the bar, where the white man who had been sitting in the corner stood next to Billie. He was in his early forties. His blond hair was immaculately groomed, and he wore a tailored suit that spoke of old money, but his demeanor was warm and approachable.

"I'm Richard Rodgers," he said, extending a hand. "Composer."

Hazel's eyes widened. "Richard Rodgers of Rodgers and Hammerstein?"

"That's me."

"I absolutely loved *Oklahoma!* It's an honor."

He was visibly impressed. "The honor is mine. I came just to hear some music and had no idea the treat that was in store. That was extraordinary."

"Thank you, Mr. Rodgers," Hazel said, feeling a blush creep up her neck.

"Call me Richard," he insisted. "And let me say, if I had my way, you'd be on every stage in America."

Hazel chuckled. "That's quite the endorsement."

"It's the truth," Richard said. "You have something no one else does. A spark, a passion . . . Don't ever lose it." He downed the rest of his drink and set the glass on the bar. "Hopefully, I'll see you around."

CHAPTER 13

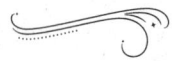

June 1944

The crowds along Seventh Avenue mirrored the electricity in the air. Adam wasn't just a candidate for Congress; he was a gravitational force drawing Harlem into his orbit.

"Adam Clayton Powell Jr. for Congress!" a newsboy shouted, hoisting a copy of *The People's Voice* with the same headline emblazoned across the front page.

"Miss! This hat would look perfect with your dress!" a vendor shouted, holding a yellow crocheted hat with a matching scarf out at Hazel as she navigated the crowded sidewalk.

"No, thank you," Hazel said, stepping aside as a squealing child ran in front of her, trying to escape the water streaming from an open fire hydrant.

Hazel smiled at the sight of Harlem in its element. A jazz quartet played on the corner, the music the perfect soundtrack to the day's events. The aroma of fried fish drifted into the air. She was just a few steps behind Adam, sunglasses and a scarf making sure the focus was on him and not them. Everywhere he went, people gravitated toward him—workers in dusty overalls, mothers balancing babies on their hips, and teens leaning out of shop windows, eager to catch a glimpse of him.

Adam strode up and down the street, his booming voice carrying over the noise with the help of a microphone hoisted atop a wagon. Ralph Cooper, the Apollo Theater's famed emcee, acted as his hype man.

"He's the man with the plan, he's no sap. He's the cat who will put Harlem on the map!" Ralph's voice rang through the loudspeaker, drawing laughter and cheers. Physically, with his pale skin and handsome looks, Ralph could've passed as Adam's brother. But with his charming personality, he could've been Adam himself. Ralph raised his arms theatrically, commanding attention with a showman's ease. "Folks, you all know him! We all love him! Make sure you cast your vote for our very own Adam Clayton Powell Jr.!"

The response was electric. Women waved handkerchiefs, men exchanged hearty slaps on the back, and even the vendors paused to join the applause.

Hazel stood at the edge of the crowd, watching him transform Harlem with his words. For weeks, she had been at his side, observing how he brought hope to the city. She admired how hard he worked, even though the polls showed him leading by a landslide in the Democratic, Republican, *and* American Labor Parties.

"You sure are spending a lot of time with him," Hazel's mother had said when she left the house last month.

"I'm helping him campaign. I believe in what he's doing." That was the explanation she gave everyone—her mother, Josephine, Billie, Barney. And it was true. But it was so much more than that as well.

They had bonded over their love of Harlem. By day, she immersed herself in his world—speaking at rallies with him, campaigning. She helped him garner the West Indian vote in Harlem. By night, he entered her world, accompanying her to her late-night sets and discovering a world of music that lit a fire underneath him.

Hazel had tried not to fall for him. But Adam had a way of disarming her defenses.

They'd carved out their own rhythm over the past few months. Dinner at Harlem's finest—Lafayette Grill, where the waiters knew their order by heart, or Frank's on 125th, where jazz floated through the air and the maître d' always winked when they walked in. Sometimes Adam walked her to her nightclub performances and waited backstage like a lovesick teenager, beaming whenever she stepped into the spotlight. He had moved out of the home he shared with Isabel and was living in the parsonage at Abyssinian. Hazel wasn't comfortable there, but they would spend quiet nights in hotel rooms or go back to her home in White Plains, always after her mother had gone to bed, of course.

Though they often appeared in public, which created rumors, Hazel was careful to confirm nothing. She had thought she was doing a good job of keeping their relationship a secret. But a few weeks ago, her mother was waiting right after Adam tiptoed out at sunrise.

"You're not going to keep sneaking that man into this house like a thief in the night," her mother declared. "If he wants to keep calling, he can come see me proper. Like a gentleman."

Hazel was speechless. She wasn't sure what unsettled her more: the fear of her mother's disapproval or how much Adam's reaction to the request would matter.

To her surprise, Adam didn't balk.

"I should've come sooner," he said. "I want her to know I'm serious. About you. About us."

That evening, as they headed to her place, Hazel gripped her gloves in her lap the entire ride. Adam, seated beside her, looked maddeningly at ease—legs crossed, humming low under his breath like they were heading to a Sunday picnic and not into a battlefield of judgment.

When they pulled up to the house, Hazel spotted her mother before the car had even stopped. She was standing in the doorway, apron still tied at the waist, arms crossed like a gatekeeper. Her mouth was drawn into a tight line sharp enough to slice through bone.

Adam stepped out first, a bouquet in hand. "Mrs. Scott," he said, with a small bow, offering the peonies like a peace treaty.

Alma took the flowers but didn't say a word. Just turned on her heel and walked back inside.

Hazel followed, her heart hammering.

The dining room table was already set—linen napkins folded crisply, the good china out. Hazel picked at her plate as her mother grilled Adam. But he was undeterred. He answered every question lobbed at him with a measured calm—talking about Harlem, the latest bill he was pushing, and all the changes he was trying to bring to Abyssinian. Hazel couldn't tell if her mother was listening or calculating.

Then something shifted.

It might've been when Adam gently asked about Hazel's father. Or maybe it was the way he leaned in—not just politely, but attentively—when she began talking about life in Trinidad.

By the time dessert was served, Alma had set down her fork, looked across the table, and said evenly, "Well, Adam, I suppose you'll want coffee."

That was just a few weeks ago. Today, Hazel and Adam had spent the afternoon fishing on the lake in White Plains—her mother's idea, no less.

"You should take the man outside," she'd said. "Let him do something other than sit in my parlor laying it on thick for me."

They moved to the backyard. Adam sat down beside her and, without a word, reached into his briefcase. He pulled out a package and placed it in her hands.

Hazel's curiosity was piqued. She unwrapped it carefully, revealing a rare first edition sheet music publication. The name Blind Tom Wiggins was scrawled in elegant script and a faded publisher's stamp said April 10, 1867. Her breath caught. This was one of Blind Tom's original compositions! A piece of history, a treasure from the nineteenth century. He was one of the best-known Negro performing pianists who had defied incredible odds. Hazel had only ever dreamed of owning such a thing, not just as a musician, but as a lover of all things art. Her eyes met Adam's. "How did you find this?" Her voice wavered with emotion.

Adam's smile was soft, but there was something deeper in his gaze—more vulnerable, more open. "I wanted to give you a meaningful gift. One that speaks to you."

Hazel's fingers caressed the paper, as though she might break it with the weight of her awe. "This is . . . incredible. I can't believe you found it."

"I remember you said how much you loved him." Adam shifted closer, turning toward her, his expression growing more serious. The playful demeanor he often wore was gone, replaced by something much more earnest. "I want more than this, Hazel," he said quietly. "More than just stolen moments. I want a life with you."

Hazel's heart skipped. The quiet night, the peaceful chirping of crickets—it all seemed to fade into the background.

"Adam, are you sure you want to do this?" she whispered, her voice trembling. They'd been involved for just over six months. Could she give herself fully to him without losing the dreams she had spent years building?

Adam reached for her hands, his gentle grip grounding her even as her thoughts swirled in chaos. He held them as though he were holding her heart. "I've never been more sure of anything. I love you, Hazel Scott."

The warmth of his words filled her heart, but the thought of losing herself in their love terrified her. She didn't want to be someone who sacrificed her dreams for love. She had worked too hard, given too much, to let her career become a shadow of what it could be.

And yet . . . with Adam, it felt different. It felt possible to have both—a life of love and purpose, of music and movement. They could change the world together.

The thought thrilled and terrified her in equal measure. Her heart ached with the possibility of what might be, but also with the fear of what it could cost. She traced her fingers over his before saying, "I love you, too."

Nothing more needed to be said.

CHAPTER 14

August 1944

The day had been quiet. Too quiet, almost. Adam sat at his desk in his office at Abyssinian, papers spread out before him like pieces of a puzzle he was determined to solve. Hazel ran a cloth gently over the framed photographs. Her fingertips traced a brass plaque before settling on the awards lined neatly on the shelf— testaments to a life lived in service of Harlem.

This was their rhythm now. No need for constant conversation. Their presence spoke volumes. They'd shared months of whispered mornings, laughter tucked between meetings and speeches, indulged in meals behind closed doors. They remained hidden from the world, tethered by a secret they both carried: Isabel's signature still missing from the divorce papers. Though Adam had asked for a divorce, Isabel wasn't ready to let go.

Hazel slid a book into place on the shelf and turned slightly, watching Adam. He hadn't noticed her looking. His brow was furrowed, lost in thought. She smiled, wrapped in the stillness they shared. For a moment, it felt like sanctuary.

Then, suddenly, the door burst open.

"Adam, we need to talk." The voice sliced through the silence. Hazel's hand froze on the spine of a book.

Isabel.

She looked thinner than the last time Hazel had seen her, that night she performed at Cafe Society. Her clothes hung loosely on her frame. Her weight loss sharpened her features, and her cheekbones jutted out like glass.

Adam looked up, seemingly startled but not entirely surprised. Hazel knew he had been dreading this moment. They both had. There was no way Isabel would walk away from her marriage without a fight.

"Isabel," Adam said, his voice measured. "What are you doing here?"

She walked in, cut her eyes at Hazel, then fixed her gaze on Adam. Hazel instinctively took a step back.

"Bunny," Isabel's voice quivered, "how do you wake up one morning after eleven years of marriage and just . . . stop loving your spouse?"

There it was, the plea beneath the fury. Her voice was so small, so vulnerable, that Hazel couldn't help but pity her.

"Isabel, please," Adam said, rubbing his temples as if trying to ease the tension mounting between them. "This is so unbecoming."

Isabel's face crumpled. "You're just going to throw me away like some stranger you never knew? After everything I've done for you, for this marriage, for the church?"

Her voice cracked on "church." Hazel silently watched the scene unfold.

Adam exhaled sharply. "Isabel, don't do this. Not here, not now."

Her eyes darkened as her pleas morphed into fury. "Oh, not here? Is this not the place?" She motioned wildly around the office. "Is it because you made love to me on that very desk? Or had me put all my dreams on hold and sit in that chair and help you realize yours?" Her voice rose. "Where would you prefer me to speak? In front of the congregation? Or maybe in the press? Is that how you plan to end it?"

"Hey, what's all this noise?" Reverend Powell's entrance interrupted her tirade. He stopped at the office door, looking from Isabel to Adam to Hazel.

"I'm fighting for my marriage." Isabel kept her eyes locked on Adam.

"Dad, I've got this under control."

Isabel let out a bitter laugh. "Under control? Oh, that's rich, Adam. You can't control anything! You've got your secretary inventorying every spoon, every piece of furniture in our apartment like I'm some guest you're tossing out. You've been staying here in the parsonage like I wouldn't hear about your little love nest, at the church no less. Then your lawyers are demanding that I go to Reno, of all places, for the divorce," she spat. "I'm the one who's supposed to file, huh? When you're the one who broke our vows?"

Adam stood abruptly, slamming his palms on the desk. "Enough, Isabel. This isn't the place for this."

Isabel spun toward her father-in-law. "And you, Old Man Powell, you approve of this? Your son throwing me out for her?" She jerked her head toward Hazel, finally acknowledging her presence.

"Isabel, you know I stay out of my son's affairs." He was visibly aggravated.

"Of course you don't care, considering your own past aggr—"

"Stop it!" Adam shouted.

Her eyes bored into Adam's. "After everything I've done for this godforsaken—"

The tension snapped, and Adam's face hardened as he cut her off. "Isabel, I think you should go."

But Isabel wasn't finished. She turned her glare on Hazel, lowering her voice to a near whisper. "This will not end well, Hazel Scott. Not for you, not for him." She jabbed a finger in Adam's direction. "I hope you're ready for the consequences. And I can only pray that I'm around to witness him do to you what he's done to me!"

Hazel felt frozen in place.

Adam reached for Isabel's arm. She didn't move her piercing glare as she yanked her arm away. "I hope you know what you've signed up for. Because this unholy alliance"—she gestured between them—"is doomed. God will never bless a mess."

With that, she turned and stormed out, the door slamming shut behind her.

CHAPTER 15

August 1944
White Plains, New York

The scent of sizzling bacon curled through the house, mingling with the sharp crack of eggs against a hot skillet. The familiar sounds should have been comforting, but as Hazel stirred from the haze of last night's wine, they felt like an alarm bell. A dull ache throbbed behind her eyes.

She groaned, rolling onto her back, her fingers grazing the silk of her robe as she slid from bed. The chill of the floor sent a shiver up her spine. Mama had risen. Of course she had. Alma Long Scott always rose with the sun, no matter how much the world threatened to tilt off its axis.

Hazel descended the stairs, each step slow and careful, bracing herself. The kitchen was warm, fragrant with butter melting into biscuits fresh from the oven. But there was something else in the air.

Mama didn't turn when Hazel entered, her back rigid, her wooden spoon moving with slow, deliberate strokes in a cast-iron skillet.

"Morning, Mama," Hazel said, her voice thick with sleep. She moved to the counter and skimmed through a neat stack of mail. Bill. Invitation. Flyer. And then—

The newspaper. With her and Adam's photo front and center.

Her mother lifted a slender finger, motioning for her to pick it up. "Read it."

Hazel hesitated, her heart kicking up a notch. Her fingers trembled as she lifted the paper. The bold headline leaped from the page:

PASTOR POWELL PREFERS HOTSPOT GAL, SAYS WIFE

Her stomach clenched. She read on, despite her hammering pulse.

> **Isabel Washington Powell has filed for separation in Supreme Court, charging that she has been supplanted in her husband's affections by a nightclub performer. Sources close to the couple allege that the Harlem councilman and the well-known pianist have been seen in compromising positions on numerous occasions.**

The words blurred, black ink smudging under her grip. Her hands shook.

"No," she whispered. "No, no, no."

Her mother scoffed, turning off the burner with a sharp flick of the wrist. She wiped her hands on her apron, then folded her arms, her eyes locked on Hazel.

"Well," she said, her voice cool. "This is the reaping part."

Hazel blinked. "The what?"

"The reaping." Her mother nodded toward the paper. "You made a mess, and now you have to clean it up."

A sharp sting of anger pricked Hazel's skin. "I'm not responsible for that garbage."

"No, but you gave them the story. You didn't think this would come out? That she'd fight back?"

"They're lies." Hazel's arms crossed, a shield against the weight pressing down on her. "It's not even that seriou—"

"Stop. Just stop, Hazel," her mother said evenly. "Stand in your dirt."

The words landed hard. Hazel stared at her mother, her breath caught somewhere between rage and shame.

Three weeks had passed since that catastrophe at the church. Long enough for Hazel to start breathing easy again. Long enough for Adam to assure her—over and over—that Isabel was now fine with the divorce. That she'd moved on. That there wouldn't be any drama.

Hazel had wanted to believe him. Long enough to let her guard down.

"Their marriage was over long before I came along," she said, but her voice lacked its usual snap. "She's fine with the divorce and everything."

Hazel glanced down at the paper again. Adam had been so certain—so calm—when he said Isabel had accepted it. Like it was already done.

Her mother sighed, stepping closer, her eyes full of something deeper than disapproval. "My dear child, you are still young, but keep living, and you will know her pain."

Hazel flinched. "Why would you wish that on me?"

"I'm not wishing anything." Her mother's voice was soft but firm. "I just think things should be done proper and in order. You said Isabel was fine with the divorce." She jabbed a finger at the newspaper again. "The woman in that article doesn't seem fine."

The back door creaked open. "Good morning." Adam stepped inside, brushing off his coat. He spotted the newspaper sprawled across the table and his jaw tensed. He exhaled through his nose, rubbing a hand over his chin.

"Well," he muttered, "that's why I'm here so early. I wanted to explain."

Her mother didn't bother with a greeting. "Did you leave her for my daughter?"

Adam stiffened, but his recovery was quick. He leaned against the counter, arms crossed. "Of course not. Isabel wanted me to live the cloistered life of a monk, so I had to leave her for the sake of my health and tranquility of mind."

Hazel stole a glance at her mother. Her expression didn't change, but Hazel knew her well enough to see the disapproval in her eyes. Her mother didn't believe him.

"You told me she was fine with the divorce." The edge in her voice was unmissable.

Adam flinched—barely, but Hazel caught it. He looked down, then straightened and met her eyes. "She said she understood," he replied, slower now. "But understanding and accepting aren't always the same. I wasn't trying to hide anything—" He stopped himself, shook his head. "I just don't want you to feel any way responsible."

"I don't care what you tell the papers." Her mother stepped toward him. "But I'll tell you this—anything you do, you need to do boldly and proudly. If it must be done in secret, it's not right."

She turned to Hazel, her voice softer but no less firm. "My daughter deserves better than to be a mistress."

Heat climbed up Hazel's neck. "Mama!"

Adam chuckled, low and amused, but there was an edge to it, something sharp under the humor. "Mistress? That's not what this is." He shook his head, a half smile playing at his lips. "I'm going to marry your daughter, Mrs. Alma. But first, I'm going to Congress. No one is ever going to call me Mr. Hazel Scott."

Ambition crackled around his declaration. He believed every word.

But Hazel was stuck on just one.

Marriage.

He had said that with conviction.

Her mother didn't smile. She didn't look impressed or amused. She leveled Adam with a stare so unwavering it could cut steel. "I hear what you're saying, Mr. Powell. But take care of the marriage you have right now."

She headed out of the kitchen, but turned and said over her shoulder, "Then you come to my daughter the right way."

CHAPTER 16

September 1944
Harlem, New York

Adam was making good on his promise to her mother. He was bringing his relationship with Hazel out into the open, and she had never been more scared.

"Hello, Olphelia. Hi, Deacon Jones." Adam stopped to greet every other person as they entered the sanctuary of Abyssinian. Hazel walked by his side, a polite smile plastered on her face. She shook the hands of those who greeted her and ignored the ones who didn't.

Hazel kept her posture unflinching as the grumblings followed her to the front pew. Adam leaned into her ear. "They'll come around," he whispered, motioning for her to sit beside his mother.

"Hi, sweetie," Mrs. Powell said, moving her purse for Hazel to sit down. She looked regal in a dark blue dress with a single strand of pearls. She squeezed Hazel's hand as she took a seat, and it brought instant relief. The Powells had welcomed Hazel to dinner last month. They'd been warm and cordial. Hazel had been worried that they were just being performative, but the smile on Mrs. Powell's face now showed her that the sincerity was genuine.

The service began, and Hazel tried to lose herself in the hymns and prayers, but her thoughts churned. Raised Catholic, she found the Baptist service lively and expressive—yet somehow more rigid in its expectations for its leaders and their families.

Though she no longer attended church regularly, Hazel didn't want to give up the faith she'd been raised with. But she knew stepping into Adam's world meant she'd have to do so completely.

Hazel settled into the rhythm of the service, the choir's harmonies soothing her. For a brief moment, she allowed herself to relax, her hands resting lightly in her lap.

The sermon concluded, and the congregation stood for the closing hymn. Even though she didn't know all the words, she hummed along. The tension she'd carried into the service faded and was replaced by a tentative sense of peace. But just as the benediction began, Reverend Powell stepped up to the pulpit. He'd turned the pastoral reins over to Adam six years ago, but he was still respected as the founder of Abyssinian.

He cleared his throat. "Before we close, my son would like a word." His tone was steady, but there was a gravity to it that made the congregation sit up straighter.

He stepped aside, and Adam returned to the pulpit. He adjusted the microphone and surveyed the congregation with a calm, collected expression. His voice, when he finally spoke, was steady but carried an undercurrent of emotion.

"By now," he began, "many of you have heard the rumors." He paused as noise rippled through the pews like a low tide. Hazel felt her entire body tense. *What is he doing?*

Adam continued, locking eyes with those in the front row before lifting his gaze to the balcony. "I wanted to address my church family directly, with honesty and transparency," he said. "Yes, it's true. Isabel and I have amicably agreed to divorce, and I am with Hazel Scott."

Murmurs swept through the congregation, followed by hushed

but intense whispers. Hazel felt their eyes on her, hundreds of them, drilling into her from every angle. She thought they were just making a formal appearance, not a speech.

Beside her, Mrs. Powell tightened her grip on Hazel's hand. The older woman's touch was firm, reassuring and protective, but it wasn't enough to drown out the swirl of emotions crashing over Hazel. Shame, fear, anger, and, somewhere buried beneath it all, a flicker of pride that Adam would claim her so boldly, in a space that meant so much to him.

He continued with a knowing smile. "Do not fault my parents. You all know me. They have always tried to guide their rebel son on the righteous path . . . and I always have my own plan."

"You sure do, Pastor," someone yelled as laughter filled the sanctuary.

"But matters of the heart don't always follow the path people want," Adam added.

Adam's eyes locked with Hazel's. "Hazel is a remarkable woman—a trailblazer, a fighter, and a source of inspiration for me and so many others. We've chosen to walk this path together, and I hope you'll support us as we do."

His words hung in the air, but the tension in the room didn't dissipate completely.

Hazel glanced at Mrs. Powell, whose expression remained serene, and then at Reverend Powell, whose stoicism gave nothing away. She wanted to speak for herself, tell these people that she hoped to win their approval but, if she didn't, that would be their loss.

Adam returned his attention to the congregation. "I know there will be questions, and perhaps even criticism. But I ask for your understanding and your prayers as Hazel and I step into this next chapter of our lives."

When the benediction finally came, Hazel barely registered it.

She rose with the rest of the members, then waited until Adam took her arm and led her out.

As they reached the doors, Reverend Powell placed a firm hand on Adam's shoulder and said quietly, "You've chosen your path. Now you'll have to walk it with conviction."

Adam gave his father a respectful nod before turning to her. His eyes were warm and steady, a stark contrast to the storm swirling inside her.

"Are you all right?" Adam whispered as they walked down the steps.

"I don't know," she admitted. Her mind was still reeling, her emotions raw. She felt exposed, as if the entire congregation had seen straight into her soul.

"You're stronger than you think, Hazel, and together our strength is unmatchable."

He lightly kissed her, and the words settled over her. They joined the crowd heading to the church cafeteria, and Hazel noticed a group of women assessing her with thinly veiled disdain. They huddled together in hushed conversations as they glanced her way.

Just as the whispers subsided, Mrs. Powell approached, her eyes twinkling with admiration. A slow, approving smile spread across her lips as she gave Hazel a subtle nod.

Mrs. Powell's voice was rich with quiet assurance as she said, "I think you're going to be just fine."

CHAPTER 17

October 1944
Harlem, New York

Winnette's dress shop exuded an air of elegance. Jazz played softly throughout the room. Crystal chandeliers hung like droplets of light, sprinkling a warm glow over racks of dresses in every imaginable shade. The faint scent of lavender and starch—freshly pressed fabric—filled the room. Large polished mirrors reflected Hazel's image from every angle.

Hazel faced the largest mirror, holding a mustard-colored flared dress against her body, twisting slowly to assess its fit.

"This is perfect." Her mother's eyes gleamed with approval as she measured the length of the dress.

Before Hazel could respond, Billie snorted from her sprawl across the chaise lounge, one leg draped over the arm and a smirk tugging at her lips. "Hell, no," she said, flicking her cigarette ash into a crystal dish she had pulled out of her pocketbook. "Can someone please explain why Hazel needs a whole new wardrobe? Don't you already have closets full of clothes, girl?"

"She has entertainer clothes," her mother replied, lifting Hazel's arm to test the fit of the sleeve. "She needs respectable church lady clothes now."

Billie raised an eyebrow, her lips parting in mock disbelief. "Respectable church lady? Is that the goal? Lord help us."

"I thought you weren't coming, anyway," her mother said.

"Had to get away from some drama."

Alma shook her head. "You're always in some drama these days, Billie."

"Who else would add spice to your life if I didn't?" She grinned.

Her mother shook her head as she continued to inspect the dress, adjusting the waistline to flatter Hazel's figure. "Hazel's entering a new world. She's going to be by Adam's side, and we need something that is understated yet elegant," she said, as if that settled everything. "She has to adapt."

The dress was way too plain for Hazel's taste. "Maybe Billie's right, Mama," Hazel said, turning to her reflection. The dress suddenly felt foreign. "Why can't they adapt to me? Why do I have to change?"

Her mother's fingers tightened on the fabric, and her voice lowered slightly. "Don't listen to Billie," she said, pulling another dress from the rack, this one a muted tan. "Try this one. It's more . . . subtle."

Hazel scrunched her nose as she took the dress, eyeing it like it was a punishment.

Billie's laugh filled the room. "That's perfect if you're planning to become a schoolmarm at St. Catherine's. Real subtle, Alma."

Hazel let out a heavy sigh and tossed the dress onto the bench and folded her arms. "She's right, Mama. I don't like any of these dresses. It's just church. I can wear something in my closet."

Her mother's expression softened just a bit, though her shoulders stayed tense. "I'm not trying to change who you are. I'm just trying to find you more appropriate clothing," she said. "You chose this life,

Hazel. Adam's world is different, and you're already coming in with eyes on you and tongues wagging."

Billie swung her legs off the chaise and sat up. "Let them talk, Hazel. They talked about Jesus, didn't they?"

"Billie, that's not helping," her mother snapped, her patience fraying. She turned toward Hazel. "We don't need to give those church folk any more ammunition than they already have."

Hazel turned back to the mirror, her reflection blurred by the swirl of emotions. A sudden cough interrupted the conversation, and they all turned. The timid shop clerk stood by the racks, her hand in a fist up to her mouth. "Excuse me, ma'am." Her eyes flicked to Billie's cigarette. "There's no smoking in the shop."

"I brought my own ashtray," Billie said as she took a deliberate, slow drag, blowing smoke out of the corner of her mouth. The clerk swallowed hard, her resolve fading. "Just . . . let me know if you need anything," she mumbled before scurrying away.

Billie flashed a victorious wink as she leaned back.

"You're impossible," Hazel said with a chuckle.

"And you're not some church lady." Billie flicked her cigarette into the dish with finality. "You're Hazel Scott. You're the one they copy, baby."

As her mother returned to the rack, Billie leaned back and said, "You know Isabel got the cottage in Martha's Vineyard."

"Why do you feel the need to update me on Adam's ex-wife?" Hazel asked in exasperation.

"First of all, she's not an ex yet. Secondly, all of Harlem knows," Billie replied with a shrug.

Just then, the door to the dress shop swung open with a loud clang.

"There you are!" a voice boomed.

Billie bolted from the chaise and ducked behind the counter as a lanky white man stormed toward them. Hazel and her mother froze in fear.

"I know you took my drugs!" he screamed, his eyes wild and bloodshot. His thin blond hair hung messily around his face.

"Get outta here with that foolishness, Specs. I don't know what you're talking about." Billie's voice trembled as she yelled back.

"You and your dope fiend boyfriend stole my stuff!"

Hazel had seen Tony Specs around Billie before but only knew him as a shady character from Texas. Judging by his disheveled clothes and rage-filled face, he wasn't someone she needed to personally know.

"Well, I didn't take your stuff," Billie called from behind the counter. "And Joe is on the road."

"I'm about to show you what happens to people who steal from me!" he snarled.

Before Hazel could process what was happening, Specs lunged across the counter, grabbed Billie by the hair, and dragged her around to the center of the floor. Hazel rushed to help Billie, who fought Specs like a cornered cat.

"Stop it!" Hazel shouted, grabbing his arm. Specs, who had surprising strength despite his small frame, released Billie. With a sudden force, he slapped Hazel across the face, sending her tumbling to the floor.

The sting spread through Hazel's skin as her mother yelled and rushed to her side.

"Get your hands off her!" Billie scrambled toward Hazel.

Specs spotted Billie's pocketbook on the chaise and dove for it.

"Get away from that!" Billie yelled, lunging forward.

Specs dumped the contents of the bag onto the chaise. He spotted a small foil packet. Billie managed to grab his arm, but he slapped her again, knocking her to the floor. "Dirty tramp," he spat.

"Screw you, Specs," Billie retorted weakly as she rubbed her jaw. "You know you owed us for shorting us last time."

"Look at you now, Lady Day. Just a stupid hype," he muttered, pocketing the drugs. He kicked her in the stomach, and she yelped in pain before he stormed out of the store.

The shop clerk scrambled from behind the counter and to the phone. "Hello, we need the police here now," she cried as Hazel raced to her friend's side.

"Billie, are you okay?"

"No," Billie whimpered. "He just took my stuff." Tears streaked her face as she struggled to sit up.

"Mama, help me," Hazel said as the two of them took an arm and guided Billie to the ottoman. Hazel grabbed a napkin and dabbed at Billie's bleeding lip. She paused when she noticed her mother looking at her, horrified.

"Hazel . . . your face."

Hazel glimpsed at her reflection in the mirror. Her skin was darkening from where Specs had hit her.

"How are you supposed to go to church tomorrow?"

Hazel ignored her mother and her own pain, focusing instead on Billie, who flinched as the napkin touched her lip. "Do we need to get you to a hospital?"

Billie shook her head, eyeing the scattered contents of her pocketbook. "I . . . I just need a cigarette."

The shop fell silent as the aftermath of the chaos hung in the air. The clerk, still visibly shaken, approached them cautiously. "The police are on the way," she said.

"Can we go? I don't want to deal with the coppers," Billie said.

Her mother stepped forward, her eyes warming slightly. "Hazel, let's take Billie home. We can find something in your closet for tomorrow."

Hazel nodded, grateful for her mother's understanding in that moment, though she knew the conversation was far from over.

CHAPTER 18

November 1944

The bruises had faded, but Hazel still examined herself with the precision of a woman who couldn't afford a single flaw. Every curl in place, every line of her makeup sharp enough to silence questions before they were asked. Her heart pounded as she stared at herself in the bathroom mirror. Tonight's pending performance didn't rattle her—she'd faced bigger crowds—but this evening felt different. It was Adam's official last campaign rally before the election on November 7, and while the room would be filled with his supporters, she knew every eye would also be on her.

Hazel smoothed the plum fabric against her hips. The dress was a rouched column gown. She leaned into the mirror and applied her lipstick—a bold red, her armor for the night. Her reflection stared back at her, replaying her mother's warning this morning.

Be sure, Hazel. Once you go public with this, there's no turning back. You'll be the villain in every wife's imagination. The press will circle like buzzards.

Hazel had dismissed her words at the time, but they clung to her now. Everyone had an opinion on how she needed to stay in the shadows until the divorce was finalized. But all of Harlem knew anyway, especially after the announcement at church. Hiding did nothing.

"Adam sent me in here to see if you had fallen into the toilet or something."

Hazel turned around to see Billie in the doorway, looking effort-lessly elegant in a black Kitty Foyle dress.

"Hey." She gave Billie a kiss on the cheek. Billie had been in iso-lation since that incident at Winnette's, so Hazel was happy to see her. "Glad you could make it."

"I head to Chicago tomorrow, but wanted to come check this shindig out." She leaned against the wall, her expression turning serious. "Haze, I know you don't want to hear this, but I don't have a good feeling about this. Powerful men don't usually like to share the limelight. Plus, you're stepping into a world where everything is on *his* terms. Don't think he'll be different with you. When a mistress becomes a wife, that means the mistress spot is now open."

Hazel was aghast.

"Sorry if that's too raw, but you know I'm going to tell it like it is," Billie said with a one-shoulder shrug.

"Isn't Joe Guy married?" Hazel snapped defensively.

"Yep, and so am I," Billie coolly countered. "But we teeter on danger. You're Harlem's darling, and I'm just telling you to be care-ful and wise."

A brief silence hung between them. Finally, Hazel said, "I'll be careful. I know what I'm doing."

"Just don't let him be your undoing."

And with that, she was gone. Hazel turned to the mirror, but the woman staring back now seemed fragile and uncertain. She straight-ened her shoulders and lifted her chin. Doubt had no place tonight.

Laughter greeted Hazel as she stepped into the narrow hallway. Her heart caught as she spotted Adam at the end of the hall, leaning casually against the wall, his smile smooth and devilish.

"I was beginning to wonder if you'd gotten cold feet," he said.

"Absolutely not."

He took her hand and together they stepped into the Golden Gate ballroom. Harlem's elite filled the space: politicians in tailored suits, newspaper editors with notepads tucked beneath their arms, activists in crisp trench coats, and women dressed in floor-length gowns and chinchilla wraps. Socialites with high cheekbones and higher opinions sipped champagne beside NAACP organizers and church leaders.

The flash of cameras burst across the room like tiny fireworks, capturing Hazel and Adam mid-stride. Chatter rippled through the crowd—some polite, some pointed. Hazel could feel it: the subtle shift of attention, the side-eyes and not-so-quiet whispers curling through the air.

So it's true?

Hazel Scott . . . with Adam?

What about his wife?

Adam's hand was steady against the open back of her dress, but the knot in her stomach remained. This was the price of being with a man like him.

"Tonight is ours," Adam whispered as they approached the stage. There had to be at least four thousand people packed into the space to hear Adam speak.

Hazel took her seat on the front row as Adam strode onto the stage. The crowd fell silent, all eyes turning to him like sunflowers following the light.

After his introduction, Adam launched into his campaign speech. His voice rolled through the room.

Hazel found herself mouthing along, since they'd practiced well into the night. "I will advocate for the passage of a national fair employment practices commission, and we will make lynching a federal crime," she whispered in unison.

Her gaze drifted over the applauding crowd. There were so many reasons to love Adam. The gifts he had showered her with this morning—flowers, a diamond bracelet, and an original signed copy of W.E.B. Du Bois's *The Souls of Black Folk*. The way he loved on her. But this—the power he held over people, to inspire them to fight for change—was what she admired most. It was intoxicating and made her want to be better.

". . . And we will do away with segregated transportation!" Adam continued. "I'm fighting for you, Harlem!"

The crowd exploded to its feet.

"Adam! Adam! Adam!" they began chanting.

In that all-consuming moment, she forgot all the reasons she and Adam shouldn't be together. She focused only on the fact that they *needed* to be together.

CHAPTER 19

January 1945
Washington, DC

"Where are the cherry blossoms?" Hazel asked their limosine driver as she searched through the bare trees for the cherry blossoms she'd heard so much about.

He glanced at her in the rearview mirror. "Oh, you'll have to come back in March. That's when they bloom. They're pretty bare the rest of the season."

She leaned back and rested her head on Adam's shoulder. She felt like a child embarking on a new adventure. Hazel had visited DC before, during her tours, but being here now, outside of work, beside Adam, cast the city in a different light.

"I'm really glad you cut your tour short to join me," Adam said. She'd only canceled three cities, something she rarely did, but she wouldn't have dreamed of missing this historic moment.

Hazel snuggled up to him, and they rode in a reflective silence until the car pulled up to the Capitol. Their driver raced out to open the door.

"Thank you so much," Adam said, stepping out. "What's your name?"

"Barry. And you're more than welcome, sir." Barry's smile widened. "I'm from Harlem, Mr. Powell. It's an honor to be able to drive you today. I'm actually in school here at Howard University, just working to pay the bills."

"Well, you keep the faith, baby," Adam replied, patting him on the back.

Barry nodded enthusiastically. "Yes, sir. And please know that everyone's pulling for you."

Adam extended his hand to Hazel, helping her out of the car. She pulled her coat tighter against the biting cold as she looked up at the Capitol. Its neoclassical architecture gleamed in the winter sunlight. They made their way up the walkway and entered the building, passing through grand corridors lined with marble columns and historical portraits. People stared as if a well-dressed Negro couple were some sort of anomoly, but Adam moved forward, undeterred.

They entered an elevator, followed by two white men. One of them, a stout man in a cowboy hat, glanced briefly at Adam. "Howdy," he said, before turning to his companion, who didn't bother to speak.

"I still can't believe they're letting another colored into our ranks," the other man muttered. "Dawson was bad enough—next thing you know, this place'll be overrun with them like rats in a sewer."

The man in the cowboy hat nodded. "At least Dawson knows his place. He needs to make sure he teaches that other darkie how to behave."

Hazel clenched her fists, anger flaring inside her. How could they speak like this in front of them? But Adam stood resolute, his face unreadable, gazing straight ahead as if their insults were nothing but noise. He tightened his hold on her hand—a gentle reminder to hold her tongue.

The elevator reached the third floor, and the two men exited, pausing to chat with a colleague as Adam and Hazel passed them. It took everything in her not to lash out, but she followed Adam down the corridor, where he moved with an air of quiet authority.

"Adam!" Congressman William Dawson approached as they reached the end of the hallway. He was dressed as sharply as Adam, his hand outstretched in greeting. "Welcome to Washington, my friend." Congressman Dawson was older than Adam by at least two decades, with skin the shade of polished mahogany and a carefully groomed mustache that gave him the air of a statesman from another era.

"Thank you. It's an honor to be here." Adam shook his hand with genuine appreciation.

Then Dawson turned to her. "And Hazel Scott, what a pleasure."

She offered her hand, impressed by the congressman's dignified bearing. He radiated the kind of quiet power that came from fighting battles most folks never saw.

"The pleasure's mine, Congressman," she said with a smile. "Your work has inspired so many of us."

He gave a slight nod, clearly pleased. "And your music, Miss Scott, has done the same." He motioned toward the chambers. "Well, let's not dally. You've got a date with history, Congressman."

As they walked down the hallway, Dawson spoke optimistically about the challenges ahead, recounting his own struggles in the year he'd been in Congress and the progress he had fought to make. When they reached a room at the end of the hallway, Dawson placed a firm hand on Adam's shoulder. "Remember, Adam, you're not just representing Harlem now. You're representing all of us."

"I won't forget."

The door opened, and Hazel noticed Adam's secretary, Hattie Freeman, standing nearby. It was no surprise that she'd be here since Adam said she would be moving to DC to be his congressional secretary. Hazel offered Hattie a brief nod, which was returned.

The House Chamber of the United States Capitol pulsed with energy. Hazel took her seat in the visitor gallery next to Reverend

Powell. He squeezed her hand as she sat, his eyes misting with pride. Mrs. Powell had been feeling ill lately, so she was unable to be here.

Hazel scanned the vast chamber below. Rows upon rows of suited men—more than four hundred of them, a few women—filled the floor in solemn formation.

After the invocation, the clerk began the roll call. "Alabama . . . Alaska . . . Arizona . . ."

It took time—more than twenty minutes—as each name was read aloud and answered with a firm "Present." Hazel shifted in her seat, not from impatience, but from the overwhelming magnitude of it all. Each name was a thread in the fabric of the nation, stitched together in this room. And Adam's presence meant a new thread was being added.

After the roll call and the election of Sam Rayburn as Speaker of the House, it was time.

"Ladies and gentlemen of the Seventy-Ninth Congress," Rayburn began. "Please rise to take the oath of office."

The entire chamber stood in unison. Hazel held her breath as Adam stood with the others, hands raised as they repeated in one collective voice: "I do solemnly swear . . . that I will support and defend the Constitution of the United States . . ."

When the oath concluded, applause broke out—tentative at first, then swelling into thunder. Some clapped politely. Others, especially the Negroes in the gallery, stood and cheered through tears.

Hazel didn't clap. She just stood there, smiling as if her body couldn't hold all the joy that surged within her.

CHAPTER 20

January 1945

It seemed all of Washington was on hand for the annual White House luncheon. Hazel marveled at the sheer opulence in the Mayflower Hotel: gilded columns reaching toward the painted ceiling, ornate tapestries lining the walls, and chandeliers overhead.

Adam moved with ease through the crowd, Hazel by his side. Every few steps, someone stopped him.

"Congressman Powell," came a warm voice from a cluster near the fireplace. Eleanor Roosevelt extended her hand.

"Mrs. Roosevelt," Adam said, bowing his head slightly as he shook her hand. "It's always an honor."

She turned to Hazel with curiosity and warmth in her eyes. "And if it isn't my favorite pianist. Hello, Miss Scott."

"It is wonderful to see you again," Hazel said, offering a gracious nod. Adam had told her no one would question her presence, and it appeared he was right. Everyone he spoke to greeted her as if she belonged by his side.

"May I steal Adam for a moment?" Congressman Dawson approached them and gestured toward a group across the room. "There are some people I'd love Adam to meet."

Hazel nodded. "Of course. I'll find our seats."

As Adam walked off with Congressman Dawson, Hazel made her way over to their assigned table. She froze when she saw the small cream placard in front of her seat. Written in elegant script, positioned just above a gleaming charger plate, was the name *Mrs. Powell.*

The title looked so official, so permanent. As if the real Mrs. Powell weren't sitting at home waiting for her divorce to be finalized. Hazel swallowed hard. Was she really supposed to slip into this name, into this life, like it had always belonged to her?

She eased into the chair with practiced grace, smoothing the ivory silk of her gown over her lap. The fabric clung in all the right places, its off-the-shoulder cut showcasing her collarbones and cinched waist. A matching white turban crowned her head, and diamonds shimmered at her ears, throat, and wrists—each one catching the light as if it were part of the performance.

A sharp voice sliced through the polite murmurs of the room.

"Well," said a woman with fiery red hair, her Southern accent thick as honey and just as sharp, "aren't *you* a vision. I thought I was at the Oscars for a moment. I suppose every luncheon needs a little drama—though I do hope the spotlight finds its way back to the congressman."

"Thank you," Hazel replied with a polite smile. "I'm sure Adam will seize all the shine he's due."

The woman glanced at the placard, her lips curving into a sly smile. "Mrs. Powell?"

Before Hazel could respond, Hattie leaned forward from the other side of the table. "Oh, no. Mrs. Powell isn't here," she said. "That's Hazel Scott, the jazz pianist."

Hattie reached across the table, snatched up the placard, crossed out *Mrs. Powell* in a single, bold stroke, and wrote *Hazel Scott* in its place. She set it back down with a firm tap. "There. Wouldn't want anyone to be confused."

Heat flushed Hazel's cheeks, but she held her composure. "Oh," the redhead said, her eyes gleaming with sudden understanding, "the boogie-woogie lady?"

"A congressman's . . . special friend," one of the other ladies said with a tight smile. "Playing jazz. What an interesting hobby."

The redhead nodded, clearly relishing Hazel's discomfort. "But, darling, don't you think it's time to find something more fitting? Or perhaps let all that go in order to support your . . . Well, is he your boyfriend?"

Their laughter cut into Hazel like shards of glass, but she held her head high. "Jazz is my career," she replied. She didn't even know who these women were. "I'm no one's shadow. I have my own light, unlike some." Her voice was defiantly calm.

The tension at the table grew thick, but Hazel remained cool. After a few moments, she excused herself and found Adam again, joining him as he moved through the crowd, greeting his new colleagues. Thankfully, he wanted to move and sit at the table with Congressman Dawson, so Hazel was able to enjoy the rest of the luncheon in peace.

Later, as they left, Adam's face glowed with the thrill of the evening. "We make a great team," he said.

Hazel wanted to tell him about the catty women, but she swallowed the burning irritation, refusing to let it overshadow the evening. This night was for him, for them. "Yes, we do," she replied.

Back at the hotel, Adam swept her into their suite with a quiet urgency. His eyes were soft and vulnerable, a stark contrast to the sharp, calculated public persona he wore so effortlessly. In this space, with her, he could shed the weight of the world. Before she could even slip out of her gown, he pulled her toward him. His smile was tender as he pressed a small velvet box into her palm.

She opened it, her breath catching in her throat as she saw the princess-cut diamond ring, gleaming with an understated elegance.

"I don't care what anyone thinks." Adam's voice was low and fervent as he dropped to one knee, his eyes locked with hers. "I want you. Always. *Veux-tu m'épouser?*"

Hazel's heart swelled, and tears pooled in the corners of her eyes. "Did you learn French for me?"

"For you. For this moment," Adam said.

The box trembled in her hand. "Oh, Adam. *Oui! Oui!* I will marry you!" The world outside, with its judgments and expectations, seemed to melt away. She extended her hand as Adam slid the ring onto her finger. "I want to be the wife you need, darling!"

That night, they lay together, tangled in soft sheets, the world outside forgotten. Hazel rested her head on Adam's chest, lulled by the steady, comforting beat of his heart, as if it was the only rhythm she needed to hear.

HAZEL STOOD ON the balcony of the Mayflower Hotel, replaying Adam's words. *A month off for us.* She couldn't help but feel apprehensive at the audacity of the idea. A month without music, without the piano that had been her constant companion since she was a child. A month without the thrill of performing. Could she do it?

She turned toward Adam, who was sitting on the edge of the bed, meticulously knotting his tie. The sharp lines of his suit only amplified the weight of his presence. This was the man who had fought his way to Congress, and yet here he was, asking her to prioritize *them*—to take the kind of leap she had never imagined herself taking.

"You're serious about this month off?" she said.

Adam looked up. "I am. After the wedding, we take a month for us," he replied. "Hazel, I've spent so much of my life trying to fix the world. And I'll keep doing it, but I need something for myself too. I need *you*. I don't want to look back one day and realize I let the best thing in my life slip away because I was too busy chasing everything else."

Hazel felt a tightness in her chest, a strange mixture of pride and vulnerability. She crossed the room and stood in front of him, her hands resting on his shoulders. "You know I've spent my whole life fighting for what I have," she said quietly. "For the respect, the platform, the chance to use my art to make a difference. The idea of walking away from it, even for a moment . . ."

"I'm not asking you to give anything up," he said. "I'd never ask you to do that. I just want us to carve out a little space for each other. To remind ourselves that we're not just what we do."

She studied him, the raw sincerity in his expression melting some of her hesitation. "You're a new congressman, Adam. A Negro congressman. You're already under scrutiny. What would they say if you disappeared for a month?"

"They'd say whatever they want," he replied, his voice firm. "And I wouldn't care, as long as I had you by my side."

Hazel's lips quirked into a half smile. "You really believe we can have it all, don't you?"

"I do," he said, leaning forward to kiss her palm. "Because I'm building a future, and it doesn't mean anything if you're not in it."

She stared down at him, her mind racing. For so long, she had told herself that love was secondary, something to be managed carefully so it didn't interfere with her ambitions. Slowly, she nodded, her voice catching as she spoke. "Okay. Let's do it. A month for us. But only if you plan the honeymoon."

Adam's smile was dazzling, his relief palpable. He stood, cupping her face in his hands as he kissed her deeply. When they finally pulled apart, his forehead rested against hers, his breath warm against her skin.

"I'll give you the honeymoon of a lifetime," he murmured. "And for the record, I've already been planning it."

Hazel laughed, shaking her head at his audacity. "Of course you have." She resumed dressing for their visit to the Lincoln Memorial.

Before Adam could respond, the phone rang. He answered, and within seconds, his jaw hardened. "Okay. I'll be there" was all he said before hanging up. A crease formed in his brow. "They've called a meeting today. Some senior congressmen want to discuss my stance on civil rights."

How were they supposed to take a month off when they couldn't even get a day? "Go, take care of your business," she said, forcing a smile.

"Are you sure?" The concern in his eyes was evident. "I want nothing more than to stay here with you."

"I'm sure," she replied, hoping this wasn't a sign of things to come. "I can show myself around."

He smiled gratefully. "Thank you, my love. And I'm glad we made the promise to one another."

CHAPTER 21

Hazel couldn't yet fully claim the name, but it filled her with joy to know that soon she would officially be Mrs. Adam Clayton Powell Jr.

Yesterday's visit with Adam's mother had left an unexpected imprint on her heart. Though Mrs. Powell was still unwell, she had offered them her full blessing.

You have something I didn't when I married into this family— self-awareness. Use it. Protect yourself. Love my son, yes, but never forget to love yourself more.

Hazel didn't know why the words Mrs. Powell spoke to her over tea hit so deeply. She was still thinking about them today as she made her way to Josephine's house.

Sugar Hill shimmered with the promise of prosperity and prestige. The neighborhood, perched on Harlem's highest ground, was a bastion of Negro excellence, where ambition met artistry and intellect. Stately brownstones and grand apartment buildings, their façades adorned with intricate ironwork and carved limestone, stood as monuments to the dreams of those who defied the odds.

Hazel hadn't been here since the Schuylers moved into the six-story building overlooking Colonial Park, a structure built in 1910 with high ceilings and crown molding so elaborate it seemed to lace the rooms with elegance. Wrought-iron fire escapes clung to the side of the limestone façade.

"Good afternoon." The doorman greeted her warmly as he swung open the heavy glass door, its brass handle gleaming from years of careful polishing.

"Good afternoon," Hazel replied, stepping inside. "I am a guest of Josephine Cogdell Schuyler."

"Yes, Miss Scott. Mrs. Schuyler is expecting you."

Inside, the lobby exuded quiet opulence. The parquet floors, a rich mahogany in a herringbone pattern, gleamed under the glow of art deco chandeliers with geometric tiers of frosted glass. A Persian rug, its intricate patterns woven in deep sapphire and crimson, cushioned the footfalls of residents who moved with the ease of those who belonged to Harlem's aristocracy.

Minutes later, Josephine greeted her at the door. She wore a tailored blue silk dress that clung to her slender frame, her blond hair pinned in loose waves. "Thank goodness you could find time to swing by," she said.

Hazel stepped into the apartment and was immediately struck by its vibrancy. The walls and an oversized piano were painted a cheerful apple green. Chairs upholstered in bright Hawaiian fabrics of orange and green sat against the window, and the bookcases—painted in alternating colors—overflowed with books and photographs. African masks and sculptures adorned the corners of the room, alongside stacks of phonograph records.

Philippa emerged from the back room, strikingly beautiful, yet dimmed by an unmistakable sadness. Fourteen and delicate as a porcelain figurine, she had Josephine's fair skin and George's strong, brooding eyes. Her long dark hair was pulled into an elegant chignon, but the effect was undone by the slump in her shoulders and her distant gaze.

"Hello, Philippa." Hazel greeted her gently. "Your mother told me you were practicing some new music."

Philippa sighed, her lips barely curving in a polite attempt at a smile. "Yes, though I don't see the point. No matter how well I play, there will always be those who see me as neither here nor there."

Josephine's face tightened, her fingers gripping the back of a chair. "That is precisely why this concert is so important, Philippa. You must show them your brilliance, make them see past their own ignorance."

Philippa groaned. "Fine. I'll be begin my lessons."

Josephine collapsed into a chair, brushing a stray curl from her forehead. "I've got George's essays to edit before the deadline for *The Pittsburgh Courier,* Philippa is struggling with belonging, like being of mixed race is a curse and not a blessing, and then . . ." She waved the sheet music. "Then she wants to add this to her recital program, but I can't decide if it's too modern for her audience."

Hazel took the pages and scanned the lines. "I don't think it's too modern at all." She studied her friend. "But, Jody. I'm concerned. When's the last time you breathed? Really breathed?"

Josephine laughed, but it sounded hollow. "Breathing is a luxury I can't afford. If I don't keep everything together, who will?"

Hazel's gaze swept the room. Sheet music was scattered across the dining room table. The faint tremble in Josephine's hands didn't match the composed way she sat.

Hazel leaned forward. "You're going to burn yourself out. What happened to your own writing? Remember when you came to Harlem, ready to take on the world?"

Josephine sighed as if she were mourning a version of herself she'd quietly let go. "My goals have shifted, Hazel. George's career, Philippa's music—that's where I'm needed."

Hazel frowned. "You shouldn't have to sacrifice yourself for everyone else. What about what you want?"

Josephine inhaled and exhaled slowly. "I'm preserving Philippa. Like a hothouse flower, she needs constant care. And George believes we're building something bigger than ourselves—an example, a future. That's my work now."

Hazel studied her friend, noting the shadows under her eyes, the faint tremble in her hands. She had once been all fire and purpose, but now she seemed like a candle burning too fast.

The front door opened, and George entered, loosening his tie with one hand and carrying a leather briefcase in the other.

"Afternoon," he said, scanning the room with a tired glance. "Is Philippa doing her music lessons?"

Before Josephine could answer, the gentle melody of a Chopin nocturne floated from the parlor. It was beautiful, momentarily soothing. Then came a sharp, discordant chord—followed by a chilling silence.

"I can't do this!" Philippa shouted as she stomped into the living room.

Josephine bolted upright. "Darling, you cannot afford to fall to pieces every time something isn't perfect."

Philippa's cheeks were flushed, eyes shining with unshed tears. "You mean every time *I'm* not perfect," she cried as she ran into her bedroom and slammed the door.

George stepped forward, pinching the bridge of his nose. "Josephine"—his voice was clipped—"you *have* to keep that girl in line. I've got work to do and no time for another one of her episodes."

Josephine stiffened, her hands smoothing her skirt out of habit. "She's just emotional—"

"She's a young lady, not a child," George interrupted. "And it's your responsibility to make sure she behaves accordingly. I'm preparing for a lecture. I don't have time for dramatics. I'll be in my study," he muttered before retreating down the hall without another glance.

When the door slammed, Hazel turned to a weary Josephine. "No wonder you can't get any work done. Is this what you've been enduring?"

"Every day." Josephine's eyes fluttered closed for a brief moment before she whispered, "My work no longer matters."

The resignation in Josephine's voice had said it all. The dreams once so vivid had been packed away, boxed beneath duty, wifehood, motherhood, the expectations of a race, a husband, and a daughter. Hazel could feel the cost of it pressing in from all sides.

She glanced down at the engagement ring on her finger. For the first time, it didn't look like a promise. It looked like surrender.

CHAPTER 22

July 1945

The bliss of their engagement had officially come to an end. It had been replaced with the weight of mourning. The death of President Roosevelt in April had cast a somber shadow across the country. Then, two weeks later, Mattie Powell took her last breath—and it was as if all of Harlem bowed its head in grief. Adam had buried himself in his work to cope with the loss of his mother, while Reverend Powell moved about in a daze, his once-commanding presence now dimmed by sorrow.

Hazel tried to honor their grief while still holding on to her own sense of purpose. Life had to go on, even when it hurt. The war had ended in Europe two months ago and Americans were feeling extremely patriotic. So, when she heard about the rally for the Double V Campaign, a movement to champion victory against fascism overseas and victory against racism and discrimination at home, she knew she needed to be there—not just for herself, but for the future they were all still fighting for. And after so much loss—Roosevelt, Mattie—it felt urgent to stand up for something that looked like hope.

The sweltering summer heat pressed against her skin as tightly as the diverse crowd packed into the 135th Street branch of the New York Public Library auditorium. From backstage, Hazel glanced through the narrow slit of the curtains and caught glimpses of the soldiers seated in the front row. Their pressed uniforms gleamed under the stage lights, their faces stoic yet alight with pride. These were men who had risked everything overseas, only to return to a country that didn't fully recognize their humanity.

"Miss Scott, you're up in two." A stagehand's voice caused her to close the curtain.

Hazel straightened her shoulders and smoothed the fabric of her fitted sweetheart neckline gown. The speaker onstage, a minister with a voice like rolling thunder, concluded his speech.

". . . And let us never forget the brave men of the Four Hundred Seventy-Seventh Bombardment Group, who stood tall not just against fascism abroad but against the tyranny of racism at home during the Freeman Field Mutiny," he said. "Your actions opened doors all across the land. Your courage paves the way for a better tomorrow. We owe you a debt greater than words can express."

The crowd applauded. That was her cue. Hazel stepped onto the stage, her heart pounding—not with stage fright but with the weight of what she knew she had to say.

As the noise ebbed, the minister's voice boomed again. "And now I present to you the one and only Hazel Scott, a woman whose music is a gift and whose voice speaks to the very soul of our fight for justice."

The room was a sea of expectant and eager faces as Hazel offered a warm smile and a graceful nod before sitting at the grand piano.

But she didn't play. Not yet.

"Thank you for that kind introduction," Hazel said pulling the microphone toward her. "Before I play, I feel compelled to say something. More than three million colored Americans registered for service during the war. Half a million saw action overseas, fighting for President Roosevelt's Four Freedoms—freedom of speech, freedom of worship, freedom from want, and freedom from fear. But when they returned, they found those freedoms still denied to them. How can we call this the land of the free when the very people defending it come home to violence, discrimination, and exclusion from the GI Bill's promises?"

The room was silent.

Hazel had expected some reaction, but this stillness—this sharp, suspended moment—made her pulse quicken. Usually, she reserved her activism for her music, using it to empower and challenge the status quo. But in the past months of entertaining soldiers, not to mention all the inspiration from Adam, she knew her voice was needed beyond the piano keys.

Hazel took a breath and steadied herself.

"I come before you this evening not just as an artist, but as a woman who believes that change is possible. These men"—she gestured to the 477th—"are proof that bravery isn't confined to the battlefield. It lives in every action we take to demand dignity and equality. I applaud you all—every soldier, every activist, every person here who refuses to settle for anything less than justice. Because the fight for freedom doesn't end with victory overseas. It begins at home."

The applause was thunderous—loud enough to drown out hesitation, powerful enough to ignite something deep inside her. A standing ovation before she'd even played a note.

Hazel let their energy guide her fingers and the first notes of *Rhapsody in Blue* filled the air.

When she finished, the crowd was on its feet again. Hazel rose, curtsied, and left the stage, her cheeks flushed from the heat of the lights and the adrenaline pulsing through her veins.

Backstage, the organizer of the event approached her, shaking his head with a rueful smile. "You went off script, Miss Scott."

Hazel dabbed at her brow with a handkerchief, still catching her breath. "I'm sorry," she said. "I couldn't help it. The moment—"

"Hazel."

She turned to see her agent, Isa, striding toward her with clipped, precise steps. The set of her jaw and the way she gripped her purse told Hazel everything before she even spoke.

"What were you thinking? Do you know what you just did?" Isa whispered, glancing around as if expecting someone to leap out and brand Hazel a radical. Her voice was filled with exasperation. "You're safe, Hazel. That's what America sees when they look at you—a sophisticated, talented Negro woman who plays jazz and classical music. Not a woman who makes speeches about rights. That makes people uncomfortable."

"Maybe they should be uncomfortable."

Isa sighed, rubbing her temple. "You said you wanted to move back to film. Or maybe even TV. This is not the path. We're just rebounding from the fiasco with the Mae West movie. America needs to see you as nonthreatening. They will let you in rooms because they think you'll stay in your place. Speeches like that . . . they see it as a disruption."

Hazel opened her mouth to argue, but another voice cut in. "Those types of things are exactly what we need."

Hazel turned.

Richard Rodgers.

He stood there in his crisp suit, hands in his pockets, watching her with an expression of deep interest. Hazel straightened, glancing briefly at Isa, whose eyes had widened when she recognized half of the famous Rodgers and Hammerstein duo.

"Richard." Hazel greeted him with a smile. "What a pleasure."

"I actually made it a point to come tonight once I heard you'd be performing," Richard said, stepping forward and shaking her hand.

"Your music speaks to people who might never attend a rally or read a speech. You have the power to reach them where they are: to inspire, educate, and even provoke change. The world needs artists like you." His eyes gleamed with enthusiasm.

She had been praised before, but this—this was different. Richard wasn't just admiring her. He was challenging her to step into something bigger.

"Thank you," she said finally.

Richard smiled, the kind of smile that suggested he was about to say something outrageous. "No, seriously. Why not let your art lead the charge for change? I feel I speak for Oscar when I say we want to create something magical with you."

"What are you thinking, Mr. Rodgers?" Isa interjected.

"This is my agent, Isa Kloukowsky," Hazel said.

"Pleased to meet you," Richard said. "Oscar Hammerstein and I have been discussing ways to innovate. And the lead in *Carousel* has fallen ill. We were looking for a white actress to replace her, but watching you perform at Minton's that night got me to thinking. Now is the time we've been waiting on. We have never had a Negro star in one of our performances, and I know Ethel Waters broke ground as the first on Broadway, but this is a role written for a white woman that you will take over. That's unprecedented."

Hazel's breath caught. "Are you serious?"

Richard nodded. "It's ambitious, but with you as the centerpiece, it could be groundbreaking. I came here to speak to you in person because, unfortunately, we'd need a decision soon. Rehearsals are already underway. The show debuts on July twenty-ninth."

"Oh, that is spectacular," Isa chimed in.

Hazel's heart soared.

Then it faltered.

Adam's divorce had been finalized last week, and they'd settled on their wedding date.

"I'm getting married August first," Hazel said, and Isa looked like she was ready to keel over.

Richard's face fell slightly, but his enthusiasm didn't waver. "Well, I'm hoping we can figure this out." He pulled a card from his pocket.

Isa reached out and quickly took it. "Oh, we will."

He smiled at Hazel. "I'll need an answer by the weekend."

Richard shook her hand again and then he was gone, disappearing into the sea of people backstage.

CHAPTER 23

July 1945

The parlor at Hazel's home smelled of freshly baked scones and jasmine tea, a comforting backdrop to her growing unease. Across from Hazel, Billie lounged on the couch, a teacup balanced in one hand and a silver flask in the other. Without hesitation, Billie tipped a generous splash of bourbon into her cup and stirred it with a finger.

"Billie, for Heaven's sake," Hazel chided, though her voice held a thread of laughter. "Do you ever drink tea the way it's meant to be drunk?"

Billie flashed a devilish grin, popping her finger into her mouth with exaggerated flair. "Darling, life's too short for anything boring, tea included."

Josephine, who was perched on a nearby armchair, raised an eyebrow but held her tongue. She always seemed to shrink when Billie was in the room. Hazel's laughter faded, and her fingers tightened around her teacup.

"I didn't ask you both here just to drink spiked tea," Hazel said, her voice quieter now, almost hesitant. "I need your advice."

Billie's teasing expression eased, and Josephine's dark eyes narrowed with concern. "Okay, Hazel. What's weighing on you?" Josephine asked.

Hazel set her teacup down, the porcelain clinking against the saucer as her hands trembled. She knew what her heart wanted, but she was hoping her friends could help her find some balance. "I've been offered the lead in a Broadway show," she finally said. "*Carousel* by Rodgers and Hammerstein."

Billie let out a low whistle, leaning back against the plush settee with amusement. "So is that why he was checking you out at Minton's?"

Hazel fidgeted with the hem of her skirt. "Well, that's where he first saw me," she admitted. "But the offer comes with . . . complications."

Josephine leaned forward. "What kind of complications?"

The reply felt heavy in her throat. "It would mean cutting my honeymoon short," she finally said. "Maybe even delaying the wedding altogether."

The weight of her confession settled over the room. Billie was the first to speak. "So? Honeymoons can wait. Hell, weddings can wait. Broadway opportunities don't."

Josephine looked horrified. "You can't be serious, Hazel. You and Adam have planned this wedding for months."

"Months?" Billie quipped. "They just met last week!"

"That's not funny," Josephine said. "Didn't you say Adam made it clear how important this time is to him—and to your marriage? That he wanted to take a whole month off for just the two of you?"

"This sounds like a discussion I need to be involved in."

Hazel turned to the voice that had interjected into their conversation. Her mother stood at the door's threshold, looking weary in a silk robe, even though it was the middle of the afternoon.

"Did we wake you?" Hazel asked after everyone exchanged greetings.

"No, this cough won't let me nap." Alma eased into the chair across from her daughter, the lines around her mouth tightening with fatigue.

"Let me pour you some tea," Josephine said, reaching for the teapot and cup at the center of the table.

"I wasn't trying to eavesdrop," her mother said as Josephine handed her a teacup, "but explain to me why you're trying to postpone the wedding?"

Hazel sighed, then filled her mother in, carefully choosing her words. Her mother had always been laser-focused on Hazel's career, so she knew her advice would be to take the Broadway gig.

When she finished detailing Richard's offer, her mother exhaled. "I know I've pushed you, but maybe it's time to think about more than just the stage. Maybe it's time to think about having a family, you know, shifting your priorities before it's too late."

Hazel's eyes widened in disbelief. "I'm twenty-five. Hardly a spinster. And neither Adam nor I have time for a child right now," she said, more defensively than she intended.

"There will never be a perfect time, sweetheart. If you're waiting for that, you'll wait forever." Her mother flashed a knowing smile. "The world will always demand something from you. But love? A family? Those things don't wait for you to be ready. They happen because you choose them."

The words landed like a stone in Hazel's chest. She looked down at her hands, at the engagement ring she had been twisting absentmindedly. If she took the role, she risked jeopardizing her future with Adam. If she didn't, she risked resentment—her own.

Billie sighed dramatically, breaking the moment's tension. "Now, I won't pretend to be the maternal type," she said, taking another sip of her tea. "But I just don't get it. Men don't shrink for us. Why should we shrink for them?"

"It's not about shrinking, Billie," Josephine countered. "It's about building something with someone who will be there when the curtains close."

A throbbing coursed through Hazel's temples. She wanted both. She wanted it all. But was that even possible?

She cleared her throat, shaking off the heaviness. She didn't want to keep talking about this in front of her mother. "I'll figure it out. Anyway," she said, "did you all hear there's a new magazine coming out later this year? They're calling it *Ebony* and it's supposed to be the colored *Life* magazine?"

"I'll be sure to read it, but changing the subject doesn't change the fact that you need to go and tell your man you're going to Broadway," Billie said.

Alma stood and stretched. "As much as I love having you ladies here to chat, Hazel, Billie is partially right. You should go talk to Adam so you can figure out what you're going to do."

THE PARSONAGE WAS quiet, wrapped in the warm hush of early evening. Hazel sat on the edge of the settee near the front window, the long phone cord stretched taut as she whispered into the receiver.

"Hazel, I'm thrilled," Isa said. "This role is the kind of thing that shifts the entire landscape. What did Adam say?"

Hazel glanced down the hallway. She had arrived at the parsonage with a quiet determination and had gone straight to the telephone to call Isa and tell her she was accepting the offer. "Well—technically, I haven't told Adam yet."

"What are you waiting for?"

Hazel winced, lowering her voice. "He's in the office, working. I know this decision is right for me, whether he sees it that way or not."

Isa paused. "Are you sure you don't want to talk to him first?"

"I'm sure. Get the contract." Hazel said her goodbyes and hung up. She stood, trying to still her trembling hands, then took a steadying breath as she moved through the hallway.

Framed photographs of past church leaders lined the walls, their sepia-toned gazes seeming to follow her as she walked. She paused in front of her favorite—a portrait of Reverend Powell in his clerical collar, standing beside a young Adam wearing a suit two sizes too big and shoes he had yet to grow into.

Adam had told her the photo was called *In My Father's Shoes*. The name had stayed with her—equal parts legacy and burden.

She moved toward his office, heels silent against the worn wooden floors. The parsonage, which was attached to the church, was beautiful—but it also carried ghosts. Isabel had once lived here too, until the new house was purchased. Hazel didn't know if she'd ever feel fully at home in these walls, no matter how many nights she stayed.

She found Adam at his desk, writing with deep concentration, brow furrowed as he scribbled in long strokes across a yellow legal pad. His glasses, slightly askew, had slipped halfway down his nose, and the furrow between his brows deepened as he worked.

Hazel lingered in the doorway, watching him—steady, focused, brilliant. She loved him, truly. But she loved herself, too. And tonight she had chosen *both*.

She knocked gently on the frame. "Good evening, darling."

He looked up, startled but smiling. "Hello, my love. Everything okay?"

Hazel stepped inside, her heart beating just a little too fast. "Yes. What are you working on?" she asked, stepping closer.

"Our vows," he said, glancing up briefly before returning to his work. "I want them to be perfect."

She peered over his shoulder and immediately frowned. "You're even writing my part?" she teased.

Adam chuckled. "Just trying to make it easier for you."

Hazel's eyes danced across the page, but then she stopped short. "'Love, honor, and *obey*'?" she read aloud, her brows shooting up.

He turned slightly in his chair to face her. "Yes. That's what vows include."

"I thought we'd use more modern words to make us equal," she said.

Adam sighed, setting his pen down. "Hazel, it's about trust. A wife should trust her husband to lead."

She let out a short laugh. "And here I thought we were to be equals."

"A man has a role in marriage, just like a woman does. There has to be Divine order."

Hazel loved his conviction, his sense of duty. But the idea of being expected to obey—even in the context of love—felt anti-quated, at odds with the independent spirit that had carried her this far. Still, she knew another conversation was coming, one that might test them even more. She exhaled slowly and nodded. "All right. If it means that much to you, we'll leave it in."

"It does."

A small silence settled between them before Adam asked, "How was Mrs. Alma?"

"Okay," Hazel replied, slipping off her jacket. "She has a cough she can't shake. I'll have to get her to the doctor when I can find some time."

Adam studied her. "Is everything all right? Why do you look like something heavy is on your mind?"

Hazel took a deep breath, her decision hanging on the edge of her tongue. She knew this conversation could change everything. "I have some news," she said carefully. "I've been offered a role in a Rodgers and Hammerstein show. It's a lead role. Broadway."

The excitement across his face was instantaneous. "That's incredible. What a wonderful wedding gift."

She hesitated, her smile faltering. "Actually . . . the show launches on the twenty-ninth."

Adam's smile thinned. "The twenty-ninth of what?"

"July."

"Three days before our wedding?"

Hazel nodded, and before the disappointment in his eyes could fully register, she pushed forward. "I know how this sounds. And I know this isn't what we planned. But rehearsals are already underway. It's moving fast, and they need me. I was hoping we could talk about pushing the wedding back."

Adam's brow furrowed, his expression a blend of disbelief and hurt. "You can't be serious."

"I am," Hazel replied, more firmly than she intended. "This isn't just some chorus part—I've never been offered anything like this. It's a Rodgers and Hammerstein lead. This could change everything for me, for other Black performers."

He cocked his head, trying to process her words. "Let me get this straight. You want to push back the wedding—where invitations have already gone out, where plans are already in motion—so you can sing and dance onstage?"

"This is the kind of opportunity people wait their whole lives for," she said, more defensively now, feeling the heat rise in her chest. "I've worked too hard to turn this down. I didn't ask for it to come at the same time as the wedding, but I can't ignore it either."

Adam's jaw clenched. "And we've been waiting our whole lives to find each other," he said, his voice rising before he took a long, steadying breath. "We made a promise. To take time for us. To prioritize *us*. And now you're asking me to put that on hold."

Hazel met his gaze, standing at the intersection of ambition and love, where neither road was easy. "I'm not asking you to put *us* on hold," she said. "I'm asking for a little flexibility. You're the one who says marriage is about compromise."

Adam shook his head. "This isn't compromise. This is you choosing your career over us."

"That's not fair. You told me yourself that you regretted how Isabel gave up her career for you."

"I'm not asking you to give up anything. You already have a thriving career. You're the biggest star in the country right now. When is enough enough?"

"It's not about 'enough.' It's about making the most of the opportunities I've worked so hard for."

"And what about us?" Adam snapped, his attempt at composure forgotten. "What happens to us if we keep letting everything else come first?"

Hazel looked away, tears stinging her eyes. This was exactly how she didn't want this conversation to go. "I don't know," she whispered.

"I can't do this if I'm going to come second," he muttered as he stood and stomped out of the room.

Hazel stumbled to their bedroom and sat on the edge of the bed, her head bowed and her hands clasped tightly in her lap. Adam's words hung stubbornly in the air. Her heart ached. She needed to make him understand that it wasn't about prioritizing her career over him. It was about not losing herself in the process of loving him.

When Adam returned, a glass of bourbon in hand, he stood silently in the doorway for a moment, watching her. Her eyes shimmered with tears threatening to spill over as they stared at each other.

"Why can't they postpone the show?" he asked. "If you're the star, you tell them when you want to do it."

"I'm taking someone's place. Everything is already planned out and underway."

"Kind of like our wedding?" He took a long swig of his drink, his eyes fixed on her.

"This is a dream I don't want to give up. I wouldn't ask that of you, and I can't let you ask it of me."

Adam rubbed the bridge of his nose, his frustration simmering. "It feels like you're asking me to bend until I break."

Hazel reached out, resting her hand on his. She tried to curl her fingers through his, but his fist remained closed. "I'm asking you to trust me. Trust that I'm not being reckless. I'm trying to figure this out—for both of us."

He didn't respond.

A heavy silence settled between them. Hazel stood and walked to the window, watching the night flicker outside. Her heart pounded in her chest, and she knew she couldn't hold it in anymore.

"I already said yes," she admitted, her voice barely above a whisper. "I took the role."

"You *what*?"

She faced him. "I accepted the offer a few hours ago. But I told them I'd only do opening night, then an understudy would have to take over that first week. I *did* think about us, Adam."

His expression hardened. "You made a decision about our future without even having the decency to talk with me first."

"I made a decision about *my* future. Because this opportunity— it's everything I've worked for. Everything I've fought for."

"And what about everything *we've* worked for?" Adam's voice rose slightly before dropping to disappointment.

"I'm not walking away from us. I'm asking you to meet me halfway. Isn't that what we promised too?"

Adam stared at her for a long moment, his jaw tight, his hands clenching and unclenching at his sides. "You don't get to rewrite the promise after you've already broken it."

Then he turned away, grabbed his keys off the dresser, and headed for the door.

"Adam—" she called after him.

But he was already gone, the door shutting behind him with finality.

CHAPTER 24

August 1945

Hazel stared at the clock on the wall of Bethel AME Church again. The hands inched closer to the hour, each second a cruel reminder of Adam's absence.

It was ten minutes before she was supposed to walk down the aisle. And Adam was nowhere to be found.

Hazel's hands shook as she traced invisible lines along the side of her wedding dress, as if that would still her spiraling thoughts. Adam had said he was over the hurt, the wedge her decision to take the Broadway role had driven between them. She believed him. After all, he'd shown up opening night. She replayed the moment, trying to figure out if there was a sign that she had missed.

Hazel had dived into her role as the best friend of carousel barker Billy Bigelow. Not only did she play the piano, but she got a chance to sing and act. Opening night, when the curtain fell and the roar of the audience washed over her, Hazel thought that was her greatest moment. Until she walked backstage to see Adam standing with a bouquet of red roses.

"I was wrong," he'd said, pressing the flowers into her arms. "I let my pride get ahead of your purpose. And that's not the man I want to be." He kissed her forehead. "You were magnificent. I understand now. And I'll always be there."

So where the hell was he now?

"He's coming," Josephine said as if reading her mind. Hazel turned toward her friend, who had spent the last hour trying to keep her calm. Josephine was a vision in pale lavender chiffon, a cluster of violets pinned just above her ear.

"Josephine's right," her mother said, though the tightness around her eyes showed she was more worried than she was letting on. "He's going to show, Hazel."

Hazel tuned them out. Maybe Adam was leaving her at the altar, payback for her Broadway decision.

Hazel shook her head, trying to block out the poisonous thought. No. Adam loved her. Surely he wouldn't humiliate her like this.

The lace sleeves of her gown itched as her pulse pounded beneath the fabric. She paced the length of the small room.

"Just try not to worry." Her mother's confidence felt like sand slipping through Hazel's fingers. Adam was now twenty-eight minutes late. He was always punctual, so that could only mean he wasn't coming.

Hazel turned back to the window, staring out at the front of the church, where rosebushes gleamed in the morning sun. The sight should have calmed her, but it only deepened her fear. Hazel forced a shaky breath, her chest tight with the effort.

Just then, the door burst open, and the wedding attendant stumbled in.

"He's here!" she gasped, visibly relieved. "He and Reverend Powell had a blowout near Greenwich, but a tollbooth attendant drove them here."

Hazel sagged against the window frame, her knees weak. He was here. He'd come.

"Hazel, sweetheart, I'm so sorry." Adam was breathless as he called out to her from down the hall.

The attendant panicked. "No, no! He can't see you yet—tradition!" She pulled the door to the room closed as she darted out to intercept him. The attendant's voice was muffled as she spoke to Adam. "You must get dressed at once."

"I'll see you soon, my love," Adam called out, and Hazel wanted to cry tears of relief.

Just before eleven a.m., the hum of the organ filled the church, signaling the start of the ceremony. Hazel took a deep breath and gathered her bouquet of gardenias and orchids.

"You look gorgeous, my love." Her mother's eyes glistened as she adjusted the Chantilly lace draped over Hazel's head and trailing down her back like a veil of dreams.

"So do you, Mama." "Regal" would have been a better word to describe her mother, who wore a cream lace dress and a matching chapeau.

"I love you." Alma pressed a kiss to Hazel's cheek before slipping into the church.

Nervous energy tingled at Hazel's fingertips as she waited in the vestibule. It was just Adam and her today—no prying eyes, no whispers of scandal. It was why she'd insisted they marry here and not at Abyssinian. The pews were nearly empty. Billie had a concert in Detroit, so only Reverend Powell, Bethel AME minister Reverend George Turner Sims Jr., her mother, and Josephine were there.

The organ swelled, a rich, triumphant sound that echoed off the vaulted ceilings of the church as Hazel stepped into the center aisle. She walked slowly toward Adam, who stood at the altar in morning attire—a black double-breasted jacket and gray pin-striped trousers. His black-and-white tie was perfectly knotted, his boutonniere a single white bloom, as fresh as if plucked seconds ago. But it was his face that undid her—softened with a smile so warm and full of affection, it made her feel foolish for ever doubting him.

His eyes never left hers. And yet, even as relief rose in her chest, a whisper of doubt still lingered at the edges.

But then she reached him, and something inside her anchored.

"Dearly beloved . . ."

Reverend Powell's voice rang out, cutting through the swirl of emotions rising in Hazel's chest. Joy. Gratitude. Fear. Hope. Love. It was all there, jostling for space in her rib cage.

When the time came to recite her vows, she drew a breath. Her voice didn't waver.

"I promise to love, honor, and . . ." She paused, the word catching on her tongue. "Obey . . ."

Adam's grin widened, and Hazel matched his smile. They were all in. For better or for worse.

A MASSIVE CROWD awaited them at Cafe Society Uptown. Barney had insisted on going all out, his "fatherly duty," he'd said. Hazel thought the two thousand guests he'd invited was exorbitant, and she was sure they wouldn't all show up.

"With the nation still at war, this wedding gives people something to look forward to," Barney had told her. And obviously, looking at all the people that had doubled his expectations, he was right.

"Wow," Adam's driver, Clarence, murmured as he navigated the limousine through the crowd. "This is madness."

"This is love," Adam replied, as if he expected nothing less.

Camera bulbs popped the moment the car door opened—sharp bursts of white light, like fireworks in rapid succession. The cheers came next, loud and rolling, rising from the crowd that had spilled into the street. Police strained to hold the barricades, but the excitement was too big to contain.

Adam stepped out first. He gave a short wave, then turned to help Hazel out of the car. Her lace veil fluttered behind her. She still held her bouquet but her grip was tight, her knuckles pale. The crowd chanted their names.

Inside Cafe Society, candlelight shimmered across mirrored walls, casting soft reflections that danced between the guests. Crystal vases towered from each table, bursting with white gladiolas that reached for the ceiling. Emerald velvet curtains framed the room like stage drapes.

In the corner, Gene Fields sat hunched over his guitar, pulling warm, gliding notes from its strings. Waiters in white jackets moved like clockwork, balancing trays of oysters, champagne, and éclairs too pretty to eat.

Hazel glanced around, taking in the scene. This was what Barney had promised. Glamour, elegance, and New York's finest all under one roof.

"Presenting Mr. and Mrs. Powell!" Barney's voice thundered above the music. He stood near the front in a white tuxedo jacket, arms flung wide.

Manhattan's elite were out in full force as they moved slowly through the throng of well-wishers, pausing every few steps as someone reached out to clasp their hands or offer congratulations. Hazel's bouquet had shifted under her arm, petals brushing against her lace sleeve as she leaned in for hugs, air kisses, and more than a few whispered blessings.

"Hazel!" Langston held out his arms. He was dressed in a sharp navy suit with a boutonniere of his own. "You float in like a lyric."

Beside him, James grinned wide, a champagne coupe in one hand.

"You're practically glowing. I just want to know why we couldn't come to the nuptials."

"Because we wanted a little intimacy before all of this." Hazel laughed as she motioned around the room.

"There you are, Mrs. Powell," Adam said, wrapping his arms around her from behind. "How about we cut a rug before Barney starts demanding more photo ops?"

Hazel smiled as she looked at her husband. "How can I say no to that?"

Adam welcomed congratulatory remarks from Langston and James, then led her to the dance floor. The Gene Fields Trio eased into a lively swing as Adam swept Hazel into his arms. His confident twirls pulled a genuine laugh from her lips. She felt as though the entire room had dissolved, leaving just the two of them spinning in a world of their own.

As the music faded into a hush, the crowd erupted into warm applause, the kind that ripples through a room when no one wants the moment to end. Hazel, still catching her breath from the last spin across the dance floor, tucked a curl behind her ear as Adam took her hand and led her to the center of the room.

"Everyone, please grab your glasses," Adam announced. "Thank you all for being here. Hazel and I are grateful to have our loved ones surrounding us on this incredible day."

Hazel stood still in the soft glow of the chandeliers, her fingers curling around the stem of her champagne flute.

"I'd like to propose a special toast," he continued. Hazel's cheeks flushed as she lifted her glass, certain she knew what was coming.

"To my heart," Adam said. Hazel's smile widened. "To Harlem!" Adam finished with a triumphant expression.

There was a brief silence before the room erupted in laughter and cheers. Hazel blinked, caught off guard, then chuckled despite herself. She leaned in close to Adam, her voice soft but teasing.

"I'll give you that one, Congressman. But next time, I get the toast."

Adam wrapped an arm around her waist, his voice low and amused. "Darling, Harlem *is* my heart. But you, Mrs. Powell— you're the melody that keeps it beating."

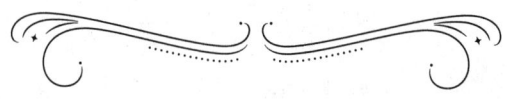

PART
II

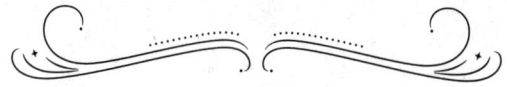

CHAPTER 25

September 1945
Washington, DC

The Broadway run had been everything Hazel had hoped. Yes, their promised time together had been buried under packed schedules and mounting obligations, but all that was over now, and Hazel was ready to see her husband.

She wanted nothing more than to rekindle the connection that had felt increasingly stretched thin in the weeks since they said "I do." Between Broadway performances, working on her album, and late-night cast dinners, Hazel's visits to DC had been few and fleeting. But that was over now, and she was looking forward to collapsing in her husband's arms and savoring the quiet spaces between his words.

Jimmy navigated the limo off Constitution Avenue and rolled to a stop outside Adam's building—a stately apartment nestled on a quiet tree-lined street just blocks from the Capitol. The night air was brisk, hovering around fifty degrees, but Hazel hardly noticed. She was focused on imagining Adam's surprise that she had come to DC earlier than expected.

The doorman greeted her with a nod, and she breezed past him with a practiced smile. As she rode the elevator up to the fourth floor, she adjusted the feathered tilt of her hat. Everything about her was polished, elegant.

The key turned smoothly in the lock. Hazel pushed open the door, a soft smile blooming across her lips—until it faltered.

Adam's apartment was warm but chaotic, an elegant bachelor's den. Books spilled from shelves. A decanter of scotch sat half full on the sideboard. The deep-brown leather sofa was covered with newspapers. It was masculine and lived-in.

At the small kitchen table near the bay window, Adam stood bent over a scatter of papers, gesturing animatedly. His sleeves were rolled up, tie loose, the intensity in his voice unmistakable. Across from him sat Hattie, her posture poised, her chin tilted upward as she listened closely, nodding at his every word.

Neither of them noticed her until she cleared her throat.

"Hazel!" Adam exclaimed, straightening. "I thought you weren't arriving until tomorrow."

Hazel's gaze shifted from Adam to Hattie, then to the papers between them. "I wrapped early," she replied evenly, setting her traveling case down. "Working late, I see."

Adam walked over to her and kissed her cheek. "Yes, my love. Trying to get everything in order to support this bill."

"It's almost midnight. Shouldn't you call it a day?"

He massaged his temples. "You're probably right." He turned to Hattie. "Let's pick this up tomorrow."

"Of course," she said.

"Good night," Hazel offered, giving Hattie her most charming smile.

Hattie gathered her things with a nod, but instead of heading left to the front door, she turned right and walked down the hall. Hazel's smile morphed into confusion.

"Excuse me, where are you going?" Hazel asked, her voice sharper than intended.

Hattie looked back over her shoulder, bewildered. "Um, to my room."

Hazel's eyes darted to Adam. Surely, she must have misheard. But Adam's expression remained a mask of indifference that only fueled her disbelief.

"Your room?" She looked back and forth between the two of them. "What is she talking about?"

Adam sighed, rubbing the back of his neck. "Hazel, come on now. Nothing is going on with Hattie. She's my secretary. She lives here because there's plenty of space, and I'm rarely home."

"Lives here?" Hazel was incredulous. Though their calls had not been consistent, when they did speak, he never mentioned that, nor had he sent her a telegram informing her that his secretary was his roommate.

"Good night. I'm going to turn in," Hattie said.

"You're living with your secretary, and you didn't think I deserved to know?" she demanded as soon as Harrie disappeared.

Adam wasn't a dumb man, so why he was standing there looking like a man who realized he'd bet his last dollar on a losing horse was a mystery. "Hattie left her family in Harlem to work here in DC," Adam explained, his tone pleading for understanding. "I didn't want her in some rundown boarding house. This arrangement is for her safety and convenience and efficiency in my job. And it's not like you've exactly been around for me to talk to."

"You're just as busy. And that's not the point," Hazel snapped. "You have a woman living with you. Everyone in Harlem knows that woman is infatuated with you!" The words burst out before Hazel could stop herself. The exhaustion, the late hour, and the frustration of finding her husband living with another woman all collided.

"So?" he shot back, his voice rising to match hers. "I told you." He lowered his voice and tried to compose himself. "I'm not interested in Hattie."

"And yet you're living with her." Hazel struggled to stay composed. "And you didn't think it was something worthy of telling your wife? And I'm supposed to sleep here with that woman right down the hall?"

"You're overreacting."

"Overreacting?" Hazel felt the blood rush to her cheeks. They'd sparred before, but this fight—their first fight as a married couple—was exasperating. "So I suppose you'd be fine if I moved in with one of the men in my band?"

"That wouldn't happen," he replied coldly, then sighed in exasperation. "Sweetheart, you need to trust me. Have I given you any reason not to?"

Adam was right. He'd been devoted to her, accepting of her taking the Broadway gig, and the last thing she wanted was to have their reunion marred by arguing. "I do trust you, Adam. But that doesn't mean I want another woman living in your apartment."

They faced one another, a heavy silence hanging between them. The joy of their anticipated reunion had dissolved, replaced by a frigid distance.

Adam pulled him to her. "Sweetheart, I promise you nothing is going on with Virgin Hattie. I do not desire her. I only have eyes for you." He pressed his lips to hers—slowly at first, as if seeking permission, then deeper, as if reminding her of every promise they had ever made. "Now." He pulled back and stared into her eyes. "I hope that you are not too exhausted for me to show you just how much I missed you."

He kissed her, then led her into the bedroom.

The next morning, Adam was already gone by the time she awoke. A note on the bedside table invited her to join him for lunch at the Capitol. Just a casual request, as if everything were perfectly fine. Perhaps he thought it was because of the way he had worshiped her body, the way they had melted into each other, tangled in sheets until exhaustion claimed them both.

Hazel crumpled the note in her hand. The thought of salvaging their time together outweighed her frustration, and she dressed quickly.

At the US Capitol, she forced a smile as Adam greeted her in his office. He looked dashing in a navy pin-striped suit, appearing every inch the distinguished congressman.

"I hope you're not still upset with me," he said, planting a kiss on her cheek. "I just want to spend time with my wife."

The sincerity in his voice softened her. "It's fine. We'll talk later. I'm starved," she replied, trying to sound lighthearted. "Where are we going? I heard about this new place called the Florida Avenue Grill. They say the owners are struggling, so much so, they fry two chickens at a time, sell them and use the money to go buy two more. I'd love to go support them."

"Oh, we're eating here in the House cafeteria," Adam replied casually, motioning for her to follow him.

Stunned, she hesitated before trailing after him. The House cafeteria? He had to be joking. But as they walked downstairs, she was even more perplexed when she saw Hattie and four other Negro men, all dressed in suits and visibly anxious, standing outside the cafeteria.

Adam greeted them with a broad smile. "Everyone ready?" he asked, receiving nods in unison.

Before Hazel could ask what was happening, Adam led them into the cafeteria. She hesitated at the entrance, feeling swept into a moment she hadn't anticipated. The timid, white-haired man behind the counter glanced up as Adam approached.

"Congressman Powell, sir, we c-can't—" the man stammered, but Adam interrupted.

"Good afternoon, Ronald. We'll take a table for seven, please."

"Sir, you know Negroes can't—"

"We'll take that table right over there," Adam declared, pointing to a spot by the window. He strode confidently, his entourage following, while Hazel stood frozen, trying to grasp the gravity of the moment. She noticed a photographer lurking near the entrance.

"Sir—" Ronald attempted again, but Adam cut him off, his tone commanding.

"Speak loudly so the reporter from *Newsweek* can be sure to get all your words."

Ronald paled, stammering, before scurrying off as Adam and the others took their seats, Moments later, Congressman Sam Rayburn approached. Hazel recognized him from the inauguration, where she had watched him be elected as the Speaker of the House.

"Powell, what are you doing?" Rayburn's face was etched with frustration. "I told you, as a freshman congressman, you need to take things slow. People already think you're down here with a bomb in each hand."

"I just want a bite to eat," Adam replied smoothly. He gestured toward Hazel. "My lovely wife is in town, and she's famished."

Hazel, however, felt more furious than hungry. She had expected a private moment with her husband, only to find herself part of his public demonstration. While she supported desegregation, Adam should have given her a choice as to whether she wanted to participate in this act of resistance. Now she felt like a pawn in his game. She wouldn't embarrass him here, though.

"I know you've never had a colored man lunch on the House's famous bean soup, but it's time, don't you think?" Adam remarked, tapping the menu.

Congressman Rayburn sighed, rubbing the back of his neck like he was trying to ease the tension. "Why can't you be like Dawson? He brings his lunch each day and eats it in his office."

"I want to eat where everyone else eats," Adam replied, loud enough for all to hear, and motioned to the *Newsweek* photographer. "Make sure you get a good shot of my wife." He pointed to Hazel. "She's a world-renowned jazz pianist."

Hazel's anger simmered, her own needs and emotions sidelined. Adam, with his unyielding determination, was making a stand. This moment would be remembered.

"This is not the way," Congressman Rayburn said, shaking his head in exasperation as he stomped off.

"Are you okay?" Adam asked quietly, leaning toward her.

Hazel met his gaze, searching for understanding, but saw only resolve. His cause, his mission—it was everything to him.

"I'm fine," she said through a forced smile.

Adam nodded like that was the answer he needed to hear. He waved to Ronald. "Now can we get seven lunch specials and a round of sweet tea?"

CHAPTER 26

September 1945
Harlem, New York

Hazel sat in the front pew clutching her Bible in her lap. Sunday service at Abyssinian Baptist Church pulsed with life. She struggled to blend into the rhythm, to let the spirit move her.

Adam sat in the pulpit, his eyes closed as if lost in a trance from the gospel music. This church was his heart, his anchor, and yet Hazel still felt like an outsider. She recognized some of that was her fault. While Adam came home every weekend for church, she'd only made a few services. It also didn't help that the whole church knew about Hattie living in DC with him. She'd heard some members gossiping about how inappropriate it was in the ladies' room this morning. One of the women had even said that "Hattie wasn't the woman Hazel needed to be concerned about, there were plenty others." Hazel had almost said something to the woman, but she didn't want to give anyone the satisfaction of feeding into gossip.

But the side glances, the whispered comments behind raised fans, were exhausting and endless. Some of the women had warmed to her, occasionally asking about her latest recordings or complimenting her dresses. Others, though, still saw her as a jazz performer from smoky clubs, not the First Lady they wanted.

"I was thinking," Hazel said when she and Adam had met in

his office after the service. "Maybe if I invited some of the deacons and their wives to a performance, let them get to know me, they might . . . warm up a little more."

Adam chuckled, a dry sound that showed little amusement. "They're set in their ways. They'll come around when they're ready."

Hazel's jaw tightened. She picked at a thread on her skirt, then let her hand drop with a sharp sigh. "*I'm* trying," she said, her voice tight. "I show up, I smile, I make conversation. But no matter what I do, all they see is some lounge act who doesn't belong."

"Well, you *do* sing in a nightclub."

Hazel cocked her head, and Adam immediately held up his hands.

"Kidding, my love. But honestly, many of the members feel slighted that their First Lady misses so many services."

"I have to work. Just because these biddies are happy being housewives—"

Adam pulled her into an embrace before she could go off on her tangent. "Sweetheart, just give it time. Do not invite these people to a nightclub."

She blew out a sharp breath. "It's just something to consider, that's all."

Adam shook his head as he released her. "Fine, it's not like you'll listen to me anyway." He kissed her on the forehead and returned to his desk. "But don't say I didn't warn you."

Hazel sighed, adjusting her gloves. "I am going to try and drop in Rose's this afternoon to get my hair washed. She opens on Sundays for a select few clients, and I'm meeting Billie there."

"Why are you wasting money at a beauty shop? You're beautiful just as you are," Adam said as he pulled out a folder and started reviewing papers.

"You're my husband. You're supposed to say that." She blew him a kiss and headed out.

The Rose Meta House of Beauty was a staple in Sugar Hill, its doors usually buzzing with the energy of women who filled it with gossip and laughter. But since it was Sunday, only about five women were there in various stages of getting their hair done. The familiar scent of pressing oil and singed hair greeted Hazel as soon as she stepped inside. But so did silence.

It was subtle at first—just a beat. Then it spread. Conversation dwindled. Rollers paused mid-set.

Hazel had felt eyes on her before. But this was a full-on freeze. And then she saw why.

Perched in Rose's chair, hair in uncombed pin curls, a full cape draped across her shoulders, sat Isabel. Even half done, Adam's ex-wife looked immaculate. Her deep plum lips pressed together. She was holding *The Manhattan Whisperer,* open just enough for everyone to see. On the front page, a grainy black-and-white photo rested beneath the bold headline:

ADAM CLAYTON POWELL JR. SEEN WITH SOCIALITE IN LATE-NIGHT OUTING

Knots filled Hazel's stomach. Margie Thompson, one of the church deacons' wives, sat in the chair next to Isabel. She lightly tapped Isabel and motioned toward the front door.

Isabel's gaze lifted slowly, locking eyes with Hazel from across the salon. Without a word, she folded the newspaper with precise care, smoothing the crease with one graceful finger. Then she stood, removed her cape with quiet poise, and laid the paper face-up on the counter.

She didn't raise her voice. Didn't rush. Just calmly looked around the room and said, "Rose, I think I'll tend to the rest of my hair at home."

She gave the newspaper a pat. "I'll leave this here in case anyone else is behind on the news."

With that, Isabel gathered her purse, slid on her gloves, and glided out the front door.

A hush hung in the air, until Billie shifted beneath her dryer hood and muttered loud enough for everyone to hear, "Lord have mercy . . . she's got more self-control than me."

She stood and sauntered over to Hazel, who was still frozen in place.

"I'm just sayin'," Billie added, half under her breath, half not, "*I* might've had to knock you clean into next week."

The room erupted with nervous laughter. The tension broke like a dropped glass. Stylists went back to their clients, women resumed their chatter.

But Hazel didn't laugh. Her chest felt tight, her cheeks warm with shame.

Billie plucked the newspaper off the counter and tossed it in the trash with a practiced flick of her wrist. Then she laid a hand gently on Hazel's arm, her voice softer now, barely above a whisper.

"You all right, baby?"

Hazel didn't answer right away. Just gave a faint nod, eyes fixed on the floor, wishing it would open up and swallow her whole.

CHAPTER 27

Hazel's fingers lingered on the keys as she finished the final note of "Willow Weep for Me." Her gaze swept over the smoky, dimly lit room of Cafe Society Uptown, settling on a corner where three couples sat, their discomfort practically palpable. These were church deacons and their wives—Adam's people, his congregation, and by marriage, now hers. She had invited them, perhaps naively, hoping that witnessing her music firsthand might temper their judgments. When Rose had set her at the dryer next to Margie Thompson after that nightmare in the salon last week, Hazel took the opportunity to invite the deacons' wives and their husbands out despite Adam's warning.

But now, as the room buzzed with a mix of regular patrons, jazz aficionados, and the occasional new face, the deacons and their wives sat stiff-backed and tense, their lips pressed into tight lines of disapproval.

"We love you, Hazel!" someone called out from the audience, but her attention remained on those she'd invited. She'd hoped that bringing them here—showing them the artistry, joy, and passion in her music—might shift their views, might help them to respect her place as both an artist and Adam's wife. As she approached them after her set, the music flowed through the club's speakers.

Hazel groaned. Tonight of all nights, they would play Bessie Smith's "I Need a Little Sugar in My Bowl" during the break between sets.

The sultry song drifted through the air, and Hazel saw the horror ripple through Mrs. Thompson's face.

"I need a little sugar in my bowl. I need a little hot dog on my roll . . ."

A gasp slipped from Mrs. Thompson's lips, her grip on her husband's arm tightening. The other church folk stiffened, their eyes darting toward the stage as the song's bawdy undertones settled over the room like a velvet cloak of sin.

Mrs. Thompson inhaled. "This place . . . It's not godly. We won't be back." And with that, she and the others stormed out.

As Bessie bellowed lyrics demanding sexual satisfaction, Hazel felt the weight of their condemnation settle like stones in her chest. The room still pulsed with laughter and conversation, but all she could hear was Mrs. Thompson's echoing judgment. *This place isn't godly.*

Before she could fully absorb the sting of their rejection, a hand landed on her shoulder. A glass appeared in front of her, its contents a familiar milky frost.

"Drink."

Hazel turned to find Barney holding out one of his signature frosted martinis. She took the glass but didn't drink, just ran a finger along its chilled rim. "You saw that, didn't you?"

"Saw it? I felt it from across the room. Those people were wound so tight I thought their collars might strangle 'em on the spot." He leaned against the bar beside her, shaking his head. "Hazel, let me tell you something for the hundredth time—stop trying to make folks love you." He motioned toward the door where the deacons and their wives had disappeared. "If they can't see you for the wonder you are, screw 'em."

Hazel let out a breathy laugh. "That's your advice? Just screw 'em?"

"Hell, yes. But if you want a classier version, how about 'Hazel, my dear, you are a brilliant, talented, breathtaking woman, and it is not your job to drag the fearful and the foolish into the light'?" He took a sip of his own martini. "But 'screw 'em' sounds so much better."

Hazel finally took a sip. The gin slid cool and smooth down her throat, taking the edge off the hurt. "Maybe I should've listened to Adam. It's just—" She set the glass down. She had been a little distant with Adam because of *The Manhattan Whisperer* gossip column, which of course, he'd dismissed as lies. So they really hadn't talked any more about her decision to invite the church members. Though now it seemed like he'd been right all along. "I thought if they saw me, really saw me, they'd understand," Hazel continued. "Maybe even respect me."

Barney sighed. "Hazel, those people came here already knowing what they wanted to see. Didn't matter what you played, how beautifully you played it. They came to confirm their own fears, and that's exactly what they did." He nudged her lightly. "Now, I'm not saying it doesn't hurt, but you don't need their respect to be who you are. You don't need their approval to be brilliant."

Hazel stared into her glass. "It's not just them. It's Adam's whole world. I walk into church, and half of them look at me like I'm not worthy."

Barney chuckled, shaking his head. "You think Jesus would've turned his nose up at 'Willow Weep for Me'? Please. He was out there breaking bread with tax collectors and fishermen. You think he'd clutch his pearls at a little jazz?" He snorted. "Some of these so-called righteous folks wouldn't know holiness if it sat down and ordered a drink next to 'em."

Hazel laughed then—really laughed, full and rich.

"There she is," Barney said, smiling. "Now, finish that drink and get back out there. You've got a whole room of people who *do* see you, who *do* love you. And I guarantee they tip better than the ones who just left."

Hazel took another sip, feeling the weight on her chest ease just a little. "Thanks, Barney."

"Always, kid." He lifted his glass to her, then winked. "Go give 'em something to pray about."

When she finally made it home that night, Adam was waiting, leaning against the couch with his arms crossed, his eyes filled with both fatigue and questions.

Hazel set her handbag down. "So I guess you heard it didn't go well. Maybe if you'd been there . . ."

Adam's brow furrowed. "I had a meeting with the Harlem developers, you know that." He sighed, running his fingers through his hair. "But I told you it wasn't a good idea. You insisted, Hazel. You never listen." His tone sharpened as irritation flickered in his gaze.

"I thought it was important for them to see what I do. This is part of me, Adam. You met me in a nightclub. I've built my career in clubs."

"You shouldn't be performing in places where whiskey is sold, Hazel." His defensiveness heightened as he began pacing, though the irony wasn't lost on her—he enjoyed a glass of whiskey himself several times a week. "You're not just a performer anymore. You're a preacher's wife, and they need to see you as—"

"As what?" Hazel cut him off, her voice rising. "As some silent, obedient woman sitting in the front pew, waiting for you to finish your sermon? That's not me, Adam. You knew who I was when you married me."

"I was hoping that you'd come to this conclusion on your own." He looked at her, his eyes pleading now. "It's different, Hazel. They're my congregation, my community. Their opinions matter. They need to see that I have a supportive wife, not one who's . . . parading around in nightclubs."

"Parading?" Hazel echoed, incredulous. "I'm playing music. I'm doing what you loved about me in the first place. Why do you suddenly care so much about what they think?"

"It's not sudden!" he retorted, his voice cracking under his frustration. "I've always cared. This isn't just about you or me—it's about respect. It's about building a community that trusts me, that trusts us. You don't understand the weight I'm carrying, Hazel. All of Harlem, hell, the country is depending on me."

"And you don't understand the weight of what you're asking," she shot back.

"Things are different. I'm a congressman now. The stakes are higher."

She was incredulous. "Do you hear yourself, Adam? You're asking me to disappear."

He took a deep breath, stepped closer, and took her hands in his. "I'm not asking you to disappear. Just . . . I don't know, maybe leave the nightclubs. Have Isa book you more film, even some more Broadway stuff. You can still do concerts, just more . . . respectable things. We can find a compromise."

A bitter laugh escaped her. "Respectable? Anywhere I perform is respectable. You want me to trade everything I've built because you're afraid of a few whispers in the pews?"

They stood in silence, both refusing to bend.

Finally, he stroked her cheek. "You told me you wanted to be the wife I need. I need this. I love and respect your work, Hazel. I just want us to find a compromise," Adam continued. "You know you're bigger than nightclubs. It's why you left Cafe Society in the first place."

She considered his words. Maybe she could give a little on this. "Fine, I'll leave the nightclub circuit." The words felt like sandpaper in her throat. "I'll focus on concert halls. But the church . . . they don't get to dictate my life. My career."

Adam's relief was instant. "Thank you." He pulled her into a hug. "I know this isn't easy for you."

"It's not." She allowed herself to sink into his embrace. "But I love you, Adam. I'll make this compromise."

As they lay in bed, Hazel watched her husband peacefully sleeping. How long could they keep up this fragile balancing act— between her music and his ministry, between her independence and his expectations?

Less than two months into their marriage, and it already felt like they were in trouble.

CHAPTER 28

October 1945

L adies and gentlemen, thank you for coming." Adam's voice was smooth and authoritative, and the crowd before them instantly quieted. They were outside the *People's Voice* office, and Hazel felt like a prop as she waited for her moment to speak. She tugged at the hem of her jacket, then adjusted her hat, the veil's edge grazing her cheeks. Adam had insisted on the veil.

"We need them to focus on your decision, not your beauty," he had said.

"Miss Scott, can you explain your decision to permanently leave Cafe Society?" a reporter yelled out before Adam could even call for questions.

Hazel's eyes swept the small crowd gathered in front of the office. Women in pillbox hats and men in fedoras crowded together on the sidewalk, their faces plastered with curiosity. The press jostled for positions, their camera bulbs flashing.

Behind them, the streets of Harlem buzzed with their usual symphony of life—a jazz melody spilled out of a nearby record shop mixed with joyful shouts of children skipping rope on the corner.

She glanced at Adam standing beside her, his broad smile and carefully orchestrated gestures in such contrast to her turmoil, as he took a step back and motioned for her to come forward.

"Thank you for the question," she began, her voice steady, though each word felt like a pebble in her mouth. "Cafe Society was my home for many years, and Barney Josephson gave me opportunities I will always be grateful for. However . . ." She paused, gripping the edges of the lectern tightly as the world blurred for a moment. "However, I believe it's time for me to explore new horizons as . . ." Her words trailed off when she spotted Barney in the crowd. She'd delivered the news to him last night. The hurt on his face then was the same pain he carried now.

"She's been ready for a change," Adam interjected, his hand resting lightly on her back as he moved in front of her at the microphone. "For too long, Hazel has been confined to nightclubs when she deserves concert halls, theaters, places where her brilliance can truly shine. Did you catch her on Broadway? She was magnificent."

Cameras flashed, capturing Hazel's forced smile.

"So my wife is shifting course, that's all. No more nightclubs, but she's far from done. You'll be seeing her brilliance in other venues."

The reporters nodded, their pens flying across their notebooks, recording Adam's version of events as truth.

"Would you say Cafe Society made you a star?"

The question shouted over the crowd gave Hazel pause, especially when she saw it was Barney who had asked it.

Adam didn't give her a chance to reply. "Hazel made herself a star," he said with a dismissive laugh.

Another reporter pressed on. "Do you have any regrets, Hazel? Your time at Cafe Society is legendary."

Before she could respond, Adam spoke again. "Regret? Hazel is moving forward. Cafe Society limited her scope. What Hazel deserves is a stage that matches her talent."

Hazel opened her mouth to protest, but the sight of Barney disappearing into the crowd stopped her.

Finally, she spoke, "I will always cherish Cafe Society." She glanced at Adam, daring him to interrupt again. "But sometimes, we have to make sacrifices for something bigger."

Adam's hand tightened ever so slightly, a reminder of who was really directing the show. He turned back to the crowd, dropping his bombshell. "That's why I've secured an unprecedented solo appearance at Constitution Hall in Washington, DC," he announced.

Gasps filled the audience, and Hazel froze. Constitution Hall? The same venue owned by the Daughters of the American Revolution that had refused Marian Anderson in 1939? They'd made an exception two years ago and allowed Marian to perform with others in a concert to benefit war relief, but no Negro had ever performed there alone.

"More details to come," Adam said. "But for now, thank you for coming."

Hazel felt a tightness in her throat as she stared at Adam. Her emotions churned—shock, anger, fear—but he only gave her that triumphant smile, like his surprise was one she'd be eternally grateful for. She knew what he was thinking: headlines, history-making moments. But this wasn't his history; it was hers.

A photographer called out, "Hazel, over here! One more shot of the happy couple!"

She straightened, grateful for the veil that concealed the storm in her eyes. Cameras flashed, reporters scribbled, and all Hazel could think about was how her story was being written without her voice.

Once they were in the car, she couldn't hold back. Clarence was just going to have to bear witness to her anger.

"Adam, if the Daughters of the American Revolution wouldn't let Marian perform, you really think they will allow me to grace their precious stage?"

Adam sighed, reaching for her hands, but she pulled them away, too upset at being blindsided to accept his gesture.

"That was six years ago with Marian. Plus, you're Mrs. Adam Clayton Powell Jr. Of course, they'll be honored to have you perform. This is a chance to show the world they've moved forward."

"I don't want to risk humiliation." She sank back against the seat. "This whole spectacle today was too much. And you didn't even give me a chance to speak for myself. You made it sound like I was unhappy at Cafe Society, like I was settling by performing there, when that's the reason people even know my name."

"I'm just trying to help," he said, dismissing her feelings with practiced ease. "I want the best for you."

"I know you do," she replied, her voice heavy with resignation. "But I need to be able to speak for myself, to make my own decisions about my career."

The conversation faded into a tense silence as Clarence pulled into the driveway. Without a word, they stepped out of the car. Hazel slammed the door a bit harder than necessary. Inside the house, she kicked off her shoes with a sharp flick, letting them land wherever. She moved through the living room like a storm—straightening a crooked picture frame that didn't need fixing, flipping a lamp on, then off again. Her breath was measured, too controlled to be natural.

Adam tried to meet her eyes as they prepared for bed, but she refused to look at him. He opened his mouth to speak but thought better of it, letting the charged silence stretch between them. When they finally lay down, the bed felt bigger, the physical space a reflection of the emotional chasm. Hazel stared at the ceiling, her mind racing, while Adam turned onto his side and, within moments, was sound asleep.

The heaviness greeted them the next morning. Hazel moved through the kitchen in a silent rhythm, her silk robe cinched tight around her waist. She didn't hum like she usually did. No idle chatter about her upcoming performances. Just the clink of silverware, the hiss of the percolator, the soft thud of the morning paper hitting the table.

The cook, sensing the mood, moved quietly as well. She placed a steaming cup of coffee and a plate of scrambled eggs and toast in front of Hazel, offering a tight smile before retreating.

Hazel stared at the food but made no move to eat. She wrapped her hands around the coffee cup like it was an anchor.

Across from her, Adam sat stiffly in his chair, still in his shirt-sleeves, trying to break the silence with forced lightness.

"Supposed to be a warm one today," he said, glancing toward the window where the morning sun strained against heavy curtains.

Hazel didn't answer.

He cleared his throat and tried again. "I think the Schaumburg is hosting a new exhibit—Negro poetry and early music manuscripts. Thought we might stop by this weekend."

She lifted her coffee to her lips and sipped again, still without a word.

Adam gave a short, humorless chuckle and pushed his eggs around with his fork. "Guess that's a no."

The sharp trill of the telephone shattered the quiet.

"I'll get it," Adam said quickly, rising from the table.

As he disappeared down the hallway, Hazel finally let her shoulders drop. Her gaze flicked toward the chair he'd left empty, then back to the cooling eggs on her plate.

When Adam reappeared, the way his brow furrowed into a V made her momentarily forget her anger.

"What's going on?" she asked.

"That was Fred E. Hand from Constitution Hall." His eyes blazed.

"And?"

"They didn't know you were a Negro when they agreed to host you."

"And . . . ?"

Adam's shoulders sagged, and for a moment, Hazel saw something in him she rarely did—defeat. "Now that they know," he said slowly, his voice taut with suppressed rage, "they've withdrawn the engagement."

The words struck Hazel like a physical blow. The sting of rejection and blatant racism washed over her in waves. Her voice was brittle when she said, "So, that's it? They just . . . withdrew it?"

Adam nodded, his fists clenching at his sides. "They wouldn't give any other details. Just that they were 'unable to accommodate the engagement.'"

Hazel's mind reeled. "So much for progress," she snapped as all of her anger came barrelling back. "I told you this would happen! And you've already announced to the world that I'm performing there."

Adam eased toward her, his brow smoothing. "I'm sorry. I thought it would be different this time."

His words were not enough to soothe the anger bubbling inside her. "We can't keep pretending that everything will change just because we want it to," she said.

He moved around the counter and rested a hand on her shoulder. His touch brought her no comfort. "This isn't over, sweetheart. We'll make sure they can't ignore you."

Tears of frustration blurred her vision. "I didn't ask to be part of this fight. You put me in the middle of it, and now I'm the one paying the price."

IT HAD ONLY been two weeks, but the DAR's rejection still stung. They had made it clear she wasn't the "right kind" of American woman to represent their so-called heritage. She had tried to let the matter go, focusing on her music and the audiences waiting for her across the country, but Adam was relentless. He'd been barking at anyone who would listen, from local newspapers to Washington insiders. He even wrote to First Lady Bess Truman, reminding her of how Eleanor Roosevelt had resigned from the DAR when they refused to let Marian Anderson perform. Adam urged Mrs. Truman to take a similar stand.

And judging from the string of curses Adam was bellowing from their bedroom, he must've gotten his answer from Mrs. Truman.

Hazel put on her pearl earring, glanced at her reflection in the bathroom mirror, then walked into the bedroom to find her husband pacing in anger.

"What is it?" she asked.

Adam didn't say a word. Just crumpled the piece of paper in his fist and tossed it onto the floor like it had personally offended him.

"This is some high-class foolishness!" Adam exploded. "It's a telegram from Mrs. Truman."

Hazel picked the balled-up paper off the floor. She flattened the creases and read. *My acceptance of the Daughters of the American Revolution's hospitality isn't related to the merits of the issue.* Mrs. Truman did add how she deplored racism, but Hazel guessed not enough to condemn it.

Adam snatched the phone off the receiver with such force it rattled in its cradle. "Get me the White House," he barked to the operator. "Now."

Hazel returned to the bathroom to finish getting dressed.

"This is Congressman Adam Clayton Powell Jr. I need to speak with President Truman," Adam said, his voice carrying through the wall. "Tell him it's urgent." A beat. "I see. So the president doesn't take calls from his own congressmen now?" His voice was tight, the words clipped and heavy with restrained rage. "Private enterprise? That's what you're calling this? Well, you tell President Truman that silence in the face of injustice is complicity." He slammed the phone down hard enough to rattle the lamp on the nightstand.

For the next twenty minutes, the room filled with the mechanical clicks of the rotary dial and the rising pitch of Adam's frustration. One by one, he called colleagues, reporters, anyone who would listen. Each conversation fanned the fire in his chest.

Now dressed, Hazel sat quietly at the piano, hoping music would calm them both. But it was no use. The mood had shifted, and her melody couldn't compete with his fury.

Finally, she rose, grabbed her gloves, and stood near the door.

"Adam." Her voice was calm but firm. "We need to go, or we'll miss the start of the parade."

He was already dialing again. Hazel stepped forward and gently covered his hand. "It'll still be waiting when we get back."

For a moment, he didn't move. Then, reluctantly, he lowered the phone.

"All right," he said, his voice still simmering. "But this isn't over."

"I didn't think it was," she murmured.

Hazel felt drained at the thought of attending the Columbus Day parade. The noise, the crowds along Fifth Avenue, and the relentless press coverage were distractions from the unsettling feeling that her life no longer belonged to her. She felt exhausted and could barely keep her food down. All she wanted to do was sleep.

She tried to push her anxieties aside, focusing instead on her upcoming concert tour: twelve cities in three weeks. She knew she had to be her absolute sharpest, but her husband's feud with the DAR made concentrating difficult.

By the time they arrived in Manhattan, the parade was already in full swing. Marching bands blared patriotic tunes, and flags waved in the autumn breeze. Both of them forced on smiles as they eased into their spots near the front. They marched and waved to the crowds, doing their best to celebrate the day. When the parade ended, the press swarmed them, eager for a comment on the DAR situation. Hazel squared her shoulders, letting her voice rise above the commotion.

"I'm very angry over the incident," she declared firmly. "I don't expect special favors because I am the wife of a congressman, but I am entitled to the same privileges and rights as any other citizen."

For Hazel, that statement was enough. She'd said her piece, but Adam stepped forward, his expression fierce.

"Make sure you write this down," he commanded the reporters. "From now on, Mrs. Truman is the LAST lady."

The crowd went silent, stunned at the disrespect for the president's wife. Reporters froze, their pens poised in midair. Adam's words were a bold challenge to the First Lady herself. Questions erupted, but Adam ignored them, taking Hazel's arm and leading her away.

"We're going to take this to all the press—white and Negro," he said quietly but fiercely as they moved through the crowd back to their car. "We'll rally our supporters, get the media involved, and put pressure on them from every angle. They won't be able to ignore us."

Hazel held her thoughts in. She knew that look in Adam's eyes. Nothing she said right now would matter.

By the next day, Adam had launched a full-blown media campaign. Headlines blared about the "last lady" of the land, and the story quickly became a national debate about this colored man who dared disrespect the First Lady of the United States.

A few days later, Hazel and Adam sat down for lunch before she was to leave for her tour. The housekeeper entered, handing Adam the morning paper.

"Reverend Powell, I thought you might want to see this," she said.

Adam's eyes narrowed as he read the front page, his fingers slowly crushing the paper. Hazel set her coffee cup down and studied her husband. "What is it?"

He shoved the newspaper at her, revealing a headline that made her gasp:

TRUMAN CALLS POWELL A "DAMNED NIGGER PREACHER"

"That bastard," she whispered, shock quickly giving way to anger. "How dare he?"

"He dares because he's the president." Adam stood and began pacing the dining room like a caged lion. "But he doesn't realize those words are fuel to my fire."

The weeks blurred into a patchwork of train rides, stage lights, and headlines. Hazel's tour began in Boston with a packed house and a standing ovation. But behind her radiant smile and graceful bow was a storm gathering. Each night she took to the stage in another city—Philadelphia, Chicago, Detroit—her piano wasn't just an instrument, it was a pulpit. And before her fingers met the keys, her voice rang out clearly over the microphone.

"I stand today because I was rejected—not for my talent, but for my skin. And I will keep speaking out until that changes."

The crowd would react—some clapping with pride, others stiff with discomfort.

Adam joined her when he could, slipping into the wings during her performances. When he wasn't in her dressing room scribbling strategy notes, he was making appearances at churches and town halls, calling out the injustice by name.

"The president may not want to hear from us," he'd say, "but he'll hear us anyway."

Then, while Hazel was on the road in Cincinnati, a telegram arrived at her hotel:

```
CONGRESSMAN POWELL BARRED FROM WHITE HOUSE
FUNCTIONS EFFECTIVE IMMEDIATELY. NO COMMENT FROM
PRESS SECRETARY.
```

She read it three times, the words not fully registering. Barred. As if he were a threat. As if they both were.

When Adam called later that night, she didn't say a word at first. Just held the phone close and listened to him breathe.

"It's retaliation," he said finally, his voice low. "They want to isolate us. Make us think we're alone."

Hazel swallowed hard. "We're not alone."

"No," he said, firmer now. "We've got each other. That's more than most."

She returned to New York for a brief break, but rest wasn't in the cards. Her three-week tour had been extended. In the midst of all of this, she and Adam had bought a brownstone, so that became a war room for the fight.

By day, she stood shoulder to shoulder with Adam in strategy meetings. By night, she walked into smoky concert halls and told her story without flinching.

The backlash followed fast. Some fans wrote in to say she was brave. Others called her ungrateful, divisive. The threats were subtle at first—postmarked letters with no return address. Then came the phone calls, the veiled warnings to keep quiet or risk losing everything. And then the cancelations. Concert promoters who told her she was "too much trouble."

As she prepared for bed, Hazel rubbed her temples, the beginnings of a headache pressing behind her eyes. "It feels like the whole world is against us."

Adam knelt in front of her, took her hand in both of his.

"I know," he said softly. "But we can't stop. This is why we're a power couple. We just have to keep the faith, baby."

If only it were that easy.

CHAPTER 29

November 1945
Detroit, Michigan

The final chord echoed into silence, and for a moment, Hazel stood in the spotlight, her chest rising and falling with the last breath of the song. Then—an eruption.

Applause thundered through the theater, growing louder with each bow she took. People were on their feet, clapping, whistling, some even shouting her name. A bouquet soared through the air and landed at her feet.

She smiled, wide and gracious, but inside, her body begged for rest.

Backstage, the roar of the crowd was muffled behind heavy curtains. Hazel slipped into her dressing room, the adrenaline already beginning to crash. She peeled off her heels, sinking into the armchair in the corner, her legs trembling from fatigue.

"Three more weeks," she whispered to herself, leaning her head back. Her reflection in the mirror looked too pale, her eyes dull beneath the layers of stage makeup. The tour had taken her from Chicago to Kansas City to New York and back again. Sold-out venues. Standing ovations. And yet, the ache of missing home gnawed at her.

The cancelations from last month had turned into a firestorm of support—particularly from colored audiences who now turned out in droves, filling every seat at every concert.

But all that love didn't stop the wear and tear. The mornings came harder. The nausea sharper. The heaviness in her limbs more persistent. She had brushed it off at first—just road fatigue. Too many nights in too many hotel beds. Too many skipped meals. But deep down, she knew something was off.

When her train pulled into Grand Central this morning, Adam had been waiting on the platform in a dark overcoat and fedora, his face tense despite the soft smile he offered.

"You didn't have to come," she'd said, but she was glad he had.

"I'm worried about my wife," he replied simply. "Come on. Let's get you home first."

Now, hours later, Hazel sat in a sterile white room. She pulled her coat tighter around her despite the warmth of the room. Adam sat beside her, his hand resting gently on her knee. Neither of them said much.

A nurse had taken her vitals. Another had drawn blood. She'd filled out forms she couldn't focus on. And still the doctor hadn't returned.

Adam glanced at her, then gently squeezed her knee. "It's going to be okay, honey."

She offered a small nod, but her gaze stayed fixed on the door.

"It's probably just fatigue." His voice was low. "You've been working too hard."

"I know my body, Adam," she whispered. "This . . . this doesn't feel like fatigue. It feels like something's trying to tell me to stop."

He didn't argue. Just looked at her, his face carved with concern, his jaw set tighter than usual.

After a few minutes, the waiting room door opened, and a nurse stepped out, her face a mask of professional calm. "Mr. and Mrs. Powell? Dr. Morgan will see you now."

Adam squeezed her hand as they stood, and Hazel clung to him as they followed the nurse down a narrow hallway. The air was even colder back here, the sterile smell of disinfectant sharper.

The walls in Dr. Morgan's office were lined with medical charts and certificates. He greeted them, gesturing for them to sit. Adam and Hazel settled into the chairs opposite his desk.

"So," he began, his tone gentle, though an underlying serious-ness made her stomach twist. "I reviewed your symptoms and ran a Hogben test—"

"What's that?" Adam asked.

Hazel's eyes widened with a thought she hadn't even considered. "That's the test where they inject my urine into a frog to see if I'm pregnant," she said, not taking her eyes off the doctor.

Adam's shock matched hers. "Pregnant?"

A slow smile spread across the doctor's face. "Yes, and congratulations—you are."

Hazel had imagined all sorts of possibilities to explain the fatigue and nausea that had been coming and going, but she'd never consid-ered that she might be pregnant. It's not like they'd been trying. Her life on the move, the demands of her career—she'd pushed thoughts of a child to the back of her mind.

She looked over at Adam. Slowly, the worry lines smoothed as his eyes filled with a pure, overwhelming joy.

"Hazel . . . we're going to have a baby," Adam whispered, as if he feared speaking too loudly might shatter the moment.

A laugh bubbled up from deep inside her. "A baby," she echoed, the word feeling strange yet wonderful on her tongue.

Adam reached for her hand, holding it tightly between his own, and she saw a swirl of emotions in his eyes—joy, excitement, and a touch of fear.

"I can't believe it," she whispered. "We're going to be parents."

Dr. Morgan gave them a moment to absorb the news. "I know this is a lot to take in," he said. "But everything looks good so far. I'll want to see you regularly to make sure things are progressing well, especially considering your schedule. It's important to take care of yourself, Hazel—get plenty of rest, and don't push yourself too hard."

She nodded, still trying to wrap her head around everything. "Thank you, Dr. Morgan."

As they left the office, Adam's hand stayed firmly in hers. The cold, sterile atmosphere of the clinic had suddenly been replaced by a new warmth. They were going to be a family.

CHAPTER 30

December 1945
Harlem, New York

Alma was in full planning mode. It hadn't even been a week since they'd shared the news of the pregnancy, and her mother had put all Christmas planning on hold and was laser-focused on baby prep. She was already laying out plans for the nursery in their Harlem brownstone, flipping through fabric swatches that she had spread across the coffee table like she was designing a royal suite. "I'm thinking bright yellow," she mused, tapping a sample. "Not that washed-out kind, but a real sunshine yellow. Something warm, inviting. What do you think, sweetheart?"

Hazel barely looked up from her plate, her fork slicing into another piece of chocolate cake. She had eaten two slices already, but her insatiable appetite was a thing of mystery these days. "Sounds good," she said, sliding the moist dessert into her mouth.

Across from her, her mother dabbed a handkerchief to her nose before tucking it into the pocket of her housecoat. A fresh coughing spell rattled her chest, shaking her frail frame. Hazel frowned and studied her mother.

"Mama, are you okay?" Hazel asked, just noticing that her mother looked like she'd lost weight.

"I'm fine." She waved a hand in dismissal. "Just a little cold. Now, where's that catalog? We need to pick out a crib."

Hazel set her fork down. "Mama, maybe you should—"

A sharp knock at the door cut her off.

Her mother pushed up from her chair with a huff of breath, steadying herself before making her way to the door. The cold outside gusted in as she opened it.

Josephine was bundled up in a thick wool coat; her cheeks were flushed pink from the wind. She shook off the cold as she stepped inside, taking in the scene before her.

"Well, well," Josephine declared, eyeing the swatches. "You all redecorating?"

Her mother wasted no time in breaking the news. "Hazel's having a baby!" she announced, beaming despite the slight rasp in her voice.

Josephine's face lit up with joy. "Oh, honey! That's wonderful!" She crossed the room, gripping Hazel's hands before pulling her into a hug.

Hazel smiled, but her gaze flickered to her mother, who had sunk back into the chair, rubbing at her temples with weary fingers.

"Barney was coming up behind me," Josephine said, motioning toward the door just as Barney pounced up the steps, his face ruddy from the cold. Hazel didn't know what to expect. They'd had a long talk the day after she announced that she was leaving the club, but hadn't had much interaction since then.

"Where's my favorite girl?" Barney boomed, stepping inside and shaking the chill from his coat. His eyes landed on Hazel, and her shoulders sank in relief at the fact that everything seemed fine. "Ah! There she is."

"Hazel's having a baby!" Josephine announced.

"My Lord, will you all let me share the news." Hazel laughed.

"We're just so excited," Josephine said, picking up a swatch and holding it up to the light.

"A baby!" Barney clapped his hands together in excitement. "Well, if this isn't the best doggone news I've heard all year! I can see it now—the baby's gonna call me Papa B, or maybe Big Barney. What do you think?"

Hazel let out a short laugh, shaking her head. "Not Big Barney."

"All right, all right, we'll work on it," Barney said, winking. Then his face grew serious.

"Are we okay, you know, with me leaving the nightclub circuit?" she asked, her voice soft. "I'm so—"

"No need for an explanation. I get it. You're a married woman now. And you know I only want the best for you." He flashed a bright smile. "Are you nervous?"

Hazel hesitated before nodding. "A little."

Barney surprised her by taking her hands in his. "Listen, kid, you're gonna be fine. You got this. You're Hazel Scott, for Christ's sake! The only thing stronger than your talent is your will. And a baby? That's just another beautiful thing you're gonna do perfectly."

Hazel swallowed the lump in her throat. Barney's faith in her should've been reassuring, but her body told a different story. The corsets she had once worn with ease now dug into her ribs. Her dresses, tailored to perfection, were suddenly too snug in the bust. And her appetite—Lord, her appetite.

As if on cue, her mother's voice cut through her thoughts as she noticed the empty cake saucer. "But you better watch your eating, Hazel. You know you stress eat."

Hazel frowned, looking down at her stomach, which had grown in just the past few weeks. She had noticed the change—she reached for bread at dinner and craved sweets she never used to. A part of her wanted to brush it off, to argue that she had it under control. But the truth was, she felt different in her own skin.

Josephine must have sensed her hesitation, because she placed a gentle hand on her shoulder. "Don't let her worry you, baby. Your body's changing. That's what it's supposed to do. You just have to listen to it."

Her mother opened her mouth as if to protest but instead turned away, coughing into her handkerchief. The sound was deeper this time.

"Mama, you are not all right," Hazel said, stepping closer.

Alma waved her off with a forced smile. "I told you, it's just a cold."

As the evening wound down and everyone settled into conversation about baby names and the nursery, Hazel couldn't shake the feeling that something was shifting beneath the surface. Her mother's cough lingered in her ears, her own body felt foreign to her, and the life she had carefully built suddenly seemed fragile in a way she had never considered before.

HAZEL SIGHED, SETTING the phone back in its cradle with a shaky breath. She glanced around the nursery, where the baby things she'd picked up earlier that day filled the space. Tiny clothes hung neatly on hangers, soft pastel blankets were folded carefully on the changing table. She'd spent hours at the shops, running her fingers over fabrics and toys, imagining her baby's laughter echoing through the room.

The front door creaked, and a familiar voice called out, "Hazel? You here?"

"In the nursery," Hazel answered.

Billie stepped in, eyeing the room with a curious smile. She looked relaxed in a high-neck blouse and slacks, a cigarette dangling carelessly from her fingers.

"Oops," Billie muttered, glancing down at the cigarette. "Hold on a sec." She darted into the bathroom, and Hazel heard the toilet flush before Billie reappeared. "I may have bad habits, but I'm not about to let my niece or nephew be affected." She paused, examined

Hazel, and lost her smile. "You wanna tell me why you've got a long face, when you should have a permanent smile?"

Hazel sighed eerily. "I'm so tired. And I need Mama here, but she's nowhere to be found. Every time I've called her for the past two weeks, she's made up some excuse. Today she couldn't come over because she has to watch the neighbor's cat! She said she'd be by my side through all of this! I told her don't bother coming when the baby is born!"

Hazel paused her tirade when she noticed Billie, with her head cocked, staring at her.

"Let me guess, you're taking her side," Hazel snapped.

Billie's eyes narrowed, her weight shifting as she folded her arms tight across her chest, her stance sharp with irritation. She let out a dry laugh, full of disbelief, and shook her head. "Lord, Hazel," she said. "You really wanna know why your mama ain't been around? She's laid up with viral pneumonia. Swore me to silence 'cause she didn't want you worryin'."

She paused, then shook her head in disappointment. "Not everything spins around *you*, baby girl. Your mama's sick, and here you are carryin' on like a spoiled child."

Guilt coursed through Hazel. "Pneumonia?"

"Don't worry, she's going to be okay. She just needs to rest and recover. Not be over here decorating."

Hazel blinked back the hot sting of tears that welled in her eyes. "I—I didn't know."

Billie's hard expression relaxed, just a fraction. "I wasn't supposed to tell you, but you needed to hear it," she said, her voice gentler now. "You know your mama. Give her grace. If she's not here, obviously there's a reason."

Hazel nodded. "I'm gonna go call her."

"No, let her rest. I'm here to help, and I charge by the hour," Billie joked.

Together, they worked through the nursery, with Billie filling the air with stories, wit, and laughter. The sharp sting of earlier faded and the room became a space of shared joy. Hazel's spirit felt lighter as Billie held up a small yellow creeper, twirling it in the air with a dramatic flair.

"Would you look at that? The baby ain't even here yet, and she's already dressed better than me!" Billie teased.

Hazel chuckled, taking the garment from her friend and gently placing it in the crib. "I just want this baby to know he's loved. That he has a place in this world," she murmured, more to herself than to Billie.

"You sound like Alma, confident it's a boy." Billie paused. "He'll know, Hazel. With you as his mother, he'll feel that love every single day."

It was just after eight when Billie left. Hazel stood by the crib, staring at the tiny stuffed bear nestled in the corner. With a quiet resolve, she headed down the hall to the telephone.

"Mama," Hazel said when she heard her mother's raspy hello. "I just wanted to tell you that I love you. I know I haven't said it enough, but I do. And I'm sorry for getting upset earlier. I know you'd be here if you could."

Her mother's voice was filled with warmth. "You know I would. And I'll be there as soon as I nip this nasty bug. I can't afford to get my grandson sick. In the meantime, you take care of yourself—and that nursery. I can't wait to see it."

Hazel's smile lifted with the comforting certainty of her mother's love. "You're going to make the best grandmother ever," she said. "No matter if it's a boy or a girl."

"Trust me, it's a boy," her mother replied.

"You just get better so you can spoil *him,* then."

CHAPTER 31

January 1946
White Plains, New York

A snowy haze hung over Harlem. It mirrored the darkness Hazel felt inside. She stood at the window of her White Plains home, one hand resting on her protruding belly, the other tracing lazy circles on the frost-covered pane. The streets outside were blanketed in pristine white and seemed to mock her with their serenity.

It had been five weeks since she'd heard her mother's voice. And three weeks since she'd put her mother in the ground.

At only forty-six, her mother had been stolen from her—gone before she could even say goodbye. One week, Hazel was laughing with her over the phone about nursery colors; the next, she was burying her. The grief clung to her like a heavy winter coat.

"How?" she whispered to the empty room. "How do I do this without you, Mama?"

Her mother had always been her guiding light, her fiercest supporter, and her grounding force. Now, as Hazel faced the twin challenges of marriage and impending motherhood, she felt lost in the dark. Her eyes drifted to the stack of sympathy cards on the side table, their presence a cruel reminder that the world had moved on.

"This is not what your mother would've wanted."

Adam's voice cut through the silence.

Hazel blinked, startled. She hadn't even heard the door open. Just the sound of it slamming behind him, snowflakes tumbling from his overcoat as he stepped into the foyer. He didn't shake them off. He didn't look at her. He just stood there—half in the light, half in the shadow—his words lingering in the air.

Since the funeral, they had been living parallel lives—his filled with schedules, travel, and congressional speeches. Hers filled with silence. And stillness. And the unbearable ache of absence. He threw himself into work. She spent her days in the same room where her mother's perfume still lingered in the walls.

"You think I want to be like this?" she snapped suddenly, startling even herself with the sharpness. She spun to face him. "You think I *planned* to sit here day after day, watching the light disappear from the corners of this house?"

"Hazel, maybe we should just stay at the brownstone."

"Why? It's not like you're ever there," she snapped. "At least here I can feel close to Mama."

His coat was still on, his gloves half off. "Don't start, Hazel. I've had a long day."

Her laughter was sharp, hollow. "A long day. Right. You and your long days. Meanwhile I sit here . . . wondering if I even know how to breathe without her."

She eased onto the sofa, her hand pressed against her back, the weight of her swollen belly making everything feel heavier. "Do you know what it feels like to reach for the phone, to hear something funny and think, *Mama will love this*, only to remember she's not there?"

"Yes, I do know what it feels like, actually," he said pointedly.

Hazel knew his grief over losing his mother was real. But in that moment, she could only focus on herself. "You grieve in motion, Adam. I grieve standing still."

He stepped closer, his brow furrowed. "I'm trying to hold it all together—for you. For us. For the baby."

She flinched. "Don't bring the baby into this."

"But it's *true!*" he snapped. "You're not eating. You're not sleeping. You've stopped playing the piano. I walk into this house, and it feels like a mausoleum. That's not how Mrs. Alma would want us to live."

Hazel fell back against the sofa, his words slicing through her. Her hands went instinctively to her belly.

"I hear her voice in everything," she said. "You think I haven't gone through the 'if onlys'—if only I had brought her to that last doctor sooner, if only I'd canceled my tour, if only I'd done something when I said she looked sick."

Tears rolled down her cheeks. "You want the old Hazel? The strong Hazel? She died with my mother. What's left is the hollow echo."

Adam exhaled, frustration all over his face as he took a seat on the table in front of her. "I married a woman who defied the world, Hazel. Who walked into rooms where they didn't want her and still commanded attention. Who took whatever life threw at her. Where did that woman go?"

"I'm right here," she said, voice cracking. "I'm just . . . buried."

A silence fell between them. He reached into his coat pocket and placed a small blue Tiffany's box on the table. "I thought a diamond bracelet might help," he said quietly. "But maybe I don't know how to reach you anymore."

She didn't move.

"I have to go back to the church." He stood. "Clarence is waiting."

And with that, he turned and left.

Hazel didn't realize she had cried herself to sleep until a knock at the door caused her to sit upright. She glanced over at the clock above the fireplace. She'd been asleep for three hours.

Hazel shuffled to the door and opened it to see Josephine.

"Hey, there," Josephine said, stepping inside and shaking the snow from her coat. "Are you okay? Adam called and suggested I stop by. What's going on?"

"Nothing," Hazel muttered, turning away. "Everything."

Josephine followed her to the couch, sitting beside her and taking her hand. "Oh, sweetie, I'm so sorry I haven't been able to get back here. This weather has just been so bad and . . . well, Alma's loss has just been a hard pill to swallow."

Hazel hesitated, then the words poured out in a rush—the loneliness, the suffocating grief, the widening gap with Adam. "It's like the world just moved on without her," Hazel said, her voice breaking. "Like she didn't matter."

"Oh, Hazel." Josephine pulled her into a hug. "Your mother mattered. She mattered to you, to everyone who knew her. But grief . . . it twists things, makes you feel like you're the only one carrying the weight."

Hazel pulled back, her face etched with pain. "Adam doesn't understand. He just buries himself in work and expects me to 'snap out of it.' How can I? She was my mother."

Josephine nodded solemnly. "I can't pretend to know exactly how you feel, but I do know this: you can't lose the living while mourning the dead. Adam's grieving too, in his own way. He loved Alma, and I'm sure he's still reeling from the loss of Mrs. Powell. And that baby . . ." She placed a hand on Hazel's belly. "That baby needs you, Hazel. Your grief is suffocating to that child. Your mama wouldn't want you to drown in this sorrow. She'd want you to find a way forward."

Hazel bit her lip, tears spilling over. "I'm trying. I really am."

"Life is cruel sometimes, unbearably so," Josephine said gently. "But you are stronger than this. You've faced bigger battles and come out victorious. This? This is just another fight."

Josephine's eyes were gentle. "But you can't do it alone. Let Adam in, even if it's hard. And don't forget, I'm here too."

CHAPTER 32

June 1946

It had taken five months, but the fog was finally starting to lift. Thanks to Adam's unwavering love and moments like this. Adam had secured a table for them at the ritzy Small's Paradise for her birthday, and Hazel had taken extra effort in her appearance to show her gratitude, having the sparkling blue maternity gown she was wearing special-ordered for the evening. From the crystal chandeliers to the ambient lighting to the patrons dressed in their finest postwar evening wear, the night was exactly what Hazel needed.

"They're here." Hazel waved to get Josephine's and George's attention as they entered the restaurant. Josephine looked dazzling in a deep emerald dress, her matching gloves brushing against George's arm, while George wore a crisp charcoal blazer with a silk pocket square.

"If this doesn't prove I love you, nothing does," Adam muttered under his breath, though his expression remained buttery smooth as he gave a casual wave when the Schuylers spotted them.

"Thank you, dear," Hazel whispered. She had contemplated dinner with just Adam, but Josephine had desperately wanted to get the two men together to try and heal their rift. "I just want to enjoy my birthday, so I appreciate you managing civility with George for one evening."

As the Schuylers approached, they could see that George, like Adam, clearly had been forced to come. After a round of air kisses and forced handshakes, they took their seats just as the maître d' appeared holding a microphone.

Adam's eyes sparkled with mischief as he stood and accepted it.

Hazel's stomach fluttered with unease as Adam cleared his throat.

"Ladies and gentlemen," he began, his smile broadening as the chatter dwindled to silence. "I am your congressman, Adam Clayton Powell Jr., and tonight, I've asked this fine establishment to extend a little treat for all of you. Normally, people pay a hefty sum to see this woman perform. But tonight, in honor of her birthday, I present to you Hazel Scott—for free."

Gasps filled the room, followed by murmurs of excitement. Hazel froze, her eyes widening in disbelief.

"Adam," she whispered. "What are you doing? I haven't performed in months!"

He leaned close, his lips brushing her ear. "It's time, sweetheart. You can't keep hiding."

Hazel shook her head, her hand instinctively going to her round belly. "The baby—"

Adam cut her off, speaking into the microphone. "And before you worry, our little one has already given his blessing. He sent me a telegram. Said, 'Daddy, why has Mommy stopped playing?'"

Laughter rippled across the crowd, mingled with sympathetic "awws." Hazel's eyes brimmed with tears as she bit her lip. She felt the mixture of expectation and encouragement throughout the room.

"Go on," Adam said, pointing to the piano. "Show them what Hazel Scott is made of."

Hazel glanced at him, the determination in his eyes reflecting the love that had drawn her to him in the first place. Taking a deep breath, she stood, smoothing her gown. The audience erupted into cheers as she made her way to the grand piano at the center of the room, the spotlight following her every step.

Her fingers hovered over the keys, trembling for just a moment before settling. The room fell silent again, and Hazel closed her eyes, summoning the music buried within her. With the first resonant chord, her fears melted away, replaced by the familiar magic of her art.

As the melody filled the room, Hazel felt the weight of the past months lifting. Her music wove a captivating spell as the room dissolved around her; it was just her and the music, an old friend she hadn't realized how much she missed.

When the final note faded, the restaurant erupted in a standing ovation. Hazel rose, her chest heaving, her cheeks flushed. Adam met her at the piano, pulling her into a tight embrace.

"Happy birthday, darling," he whispered.

"Thank you," she murmured. "For the gift I didn't know I needed."

Hazel soaked in the appreciation as she returned to her seat.

Josephine reached across the table, squeezing Hazel's hand. "That was amazing, Hazel. Motherhood agrees with you on all fronts."

"Thank you."

"Speaking of little ones," she added with a sly smile, "have you two started thinking about names yet?"

Hazel caught the smirk tugging at Adam's lips. It was a question she knew would come eventually, but the thought of naming their child was both thrilling and daunting. "Oh, we've talked," she said, swirling her water glass. "If it's a girl, I'd like to use my mother's name as her middle name. Just the middle name, though. I think children should have their own unique names."

Adam leaned back in his chair, his arms folding across his chest.

"I don't know," he said slowly. "There's something about a namesake. A continuation of legacy. It's tradition."

"Tradition's fine, but I think we can create new traditions too," she replied. "Maybe that's a discussion for when he or she actually gets here." Her tone was playful, but she could tell Adam was serious.

Before he could respond, the waiter approached with their plates, placing the dishes carefully in front of each of them. The rich aroma of roasted chicken and rosemary filled the air.

As they turned their attention back to the table, George raised his glass again. "To new traditions and endless talent," he said with a wink at Hazel.

Hazel lifted her own glass, grateful for the reprieve. "To new traditions," she echoed, though her mind remained on Adam's quiet resistance.

They resumed chatting, and Hazel was pleased with how the evening was going until the topic turned to George's 1931 satirical novel, *Black No More*.

"Well, if I'm being honest," Adam began, setting down his glass of scotch when George brought up the book, "I think the book does a disservice to the Negro race."

George's glass suspended midair. "Obviously, you're in the minority, considering it's been reprinted twice."

"It mocks the struggle," Adam continued, dismissively. "The premise—a scientist turning Negroes white—reduces our fight for equality to absurdity."

George set his glass down, leaned back, and crossed his arms. "And here I thought satire was supposed to provoke thought. Maybe the problem isn't the book but your interpretation."

"Or maybe the book has numerous problems, including the fact that it targets religion, which is the foundation of our community," Adam retorted.

Josephine's hand touched George's arm, a silent plea for restraint. But George was already leaning forward. "I hold both white and Negro churches in contempt," he said, his voice cool. "Both are riddled with conniving preachers exploiting their congregants for personal gain. Christianity has long been a tool of oppression, pro-slavery and pro-racism. I find it laughable that anyone still believes in its moral authority."

"Are you an atheist?" Adam shot back, his tone incredulous.

"I'm a realist," George replied. "And I'm not alone. There's a growing number of young Negroes who see the hypocrisy, who refuse to revere a God who allows lynchings and disenfranchisement."

Hazel's eyes darted between the men. This man had maligned God *and* the Negro race. There would be no saving this conversation now.

George continued, in full defensive mode now. "The book seeks to—"

"The book is trash," Adam declared, cutting him off.

"I'm sure you'll write about it in your newspaper," George said with a smirk. "You'll probably use it to build up your readership. How is *The People's Voice* doing, anyway? Still struggling for subscribers?"

Adam's lips curved into a cold smile. "One, our financials are just fine. Since you're simply a hired freelancer at the *Courier*, you probably aren't privy to their finances. So I can't ask you that same question. And two, you don't have to worry about your book being in our publication because we don't cover garbage."

"Gentlemen," Hazel finally interjected, her voice cutting through the air like a conductor's baton. "The beauty of America is that couples can share a meal despite differing opinions."

Adam shook his head, obviously exasperated with pretending. "When that opinion perpetuates my oppression, I can't cosign it."

Before George could retort, the waiter approached with a cheesecake, a single candle flickering at its center.

"Happy birthday, Mrs. Powell," the waiter said cheerfully, oblivious to the tension.

George stood abruptly. "Happy birthday, Hazel. Enjoy the rest of your night." He turned to Josephine. "Let's go."

Josephine hesitated, her eyes filled with apology. "George, maybe—"

"Now," George snapped, his voice sharp enough to make Hazel wince.

Josephine cast Hazel a sorrowful look, mouthing, "I'm sorry," before following her husband out.

Hazel turned to Adam, anger and embarrassment warring within her. "Adam—"

He raised a hand to stop her. "No, my love. Tonight is about you." He slid the cheesecake in front of her. *"Happy birthday to you . . . happy birthday to you,"* Adam began to sing. His voice was so off-key, so utterly unmusical, that Hazel couldn't help but smile.

"Make a wish, baby," he said as he finished.

Hazel closed her eyes, the glow of the candle warming her face. She wished for a happy, healthy family and the return of her career. When she opened her eyes, Adam was staring at her with a wide grin. "I want to spend every day making all your dreams come true."

CHAPTER 33

July 1946

The soft clicks of Hazel's knitting needles matched the rustle of the newspaper in Adam's hands.

Hazel glanced over the rim of her reading glasses, noting the frustration gathering in her husband's expression. They'd been in a good place since her birthday, and though she was still battling grief, she'd learned to live while grieving.

Hazel resumed knitting the pale yellow blanket, the latest project she'd started in place of the grander dreams she'd once chased.

Adam's brow furrowed as he muttered, "This man has some nerve."

"What's wrong?" she asked.

"Grant Reynolds." Adam spat the name of the man the Republicans had chosen to challenge his congressional seat. Though the election was still four months away, Grant had been trying to goad Adam into a debate. "He thinks he can sway Harlem with his nonsense, dragging our personal life into this mess."

Adam flung the newspaper onto the coffee table with a scowl. Hazel put her knitting aside. "What did Grant say?"

"He's talking about the divisions in the church because of my divorce, how quickly we got married. He's even bringing up the trouble with the DAR and the Trumans, talking about I come with too much controversy. And to top it off, Zora Neale Hurston and Joe Louis are backing him. Of course, George is, too. Him, I get, but Zora and Joe? It's infuriating!"

"Maybe you should consider debating him," she suggested. "Let Harlem see who you really are."

Adam let out a humorless laugh. "Debate him? Grant's offered a thousand-dollar bond for a debate. That shows his desperation, not mine. I'm not stooping to his level. Everyone in Harlem knows what I'm about."

"But, Adam," Hazel started, aiming to reason with him, but he stopped her.

"No." His voice rang with finality. She felt a familiar sting of dismissal; she often sought his input, but he never seemed open to hers. "I won't dignify his ridiculous challenge with a response."

Hazel reached for him, to soothe his anger, but a sudden, sharp pain gripped her abdomen, making her gasp. She clutched her stomach, the pain cutting through her.

Adam was at her side in an instant. "Hazel? What's wrong? Is it the baby?" His mask of composure slipped to reveal the man beneath—the husband, the father-to-be.

"I think . . . I think the baby's coming." Hazel's voice trembled in both fear and anticipation.

Adam's face paled. He called for his driver, who he'd had on twenty-four-hour standby in anticipation of this very moment. "Clarence, get the car ready! We're going to Sydenham!"

At the hospital, a blur of white coats and concerned faces surrounded her, but Hazel felt herself blacking out from the pain. Each contraction tore through her with brutal force.

"You're doing great, Hazel," Adam murmured, gripping her hand. His shaky voice was so unlike his usual confidence. "You're so strong."

She wanted to believe him, but each contraction left her barely holding on. After examining her, the doctor's face was tight with concern when he said, "We need to perform a cesarean, Mrs. Powell. The baby's not positioned right."

Hazel managed a nod, too drained to protest. She just wanted her baby safely delivered.

Adam kissed her head. "I'll be right here in the father's room, waiting to shower you and our baby with kisses!" he called out as they wheeled her away.

The bright lights above her blurred as the procedure began. Time felt elastic, stretching and snapping back as moments passed in a haze of pressure and muted voices. Then, at last, a piercing cry—a sound so pure, so beautiful, Hazel's breath hitched.

"You have a son," the nurse said, handing her the baby.

Hazel exhaled a shaky breath. "A son." A small, tired smile formed at the sight of his fair skin and head full of curly black hair. "Get my husband please."

As if he was waiting on the other side, Adam burst through the door and stopped when he saw her sitting in the bed, holding their baby.

"We have a son," she said.

Adam eased over to her, his hair tucked under a net, a hospital gown swallowing his large frame. His voice brimmed with pride. "Hazel, we did it. We have a son. Adam Clayton Powell III. He'll continue my legacy."

Hazel debated protesting, but when she opened her mouth, what came out was "Yes, he will."

CHAPTER 34

December 1946

Motherhood had been wonderful. And tiring. Everything she dreamed of and nothing she could've imagined. But mothering Skipper, as they called their son, had kept Hazel confined to the house for the past five months. She'd built something safe at home—a cocoon of late-night feedings and soft lullabies. She wasn't ready to let the world back in. But Adam was. He'd soundly won his reelection and took every chance to be out in Harlem. He wanted her back as well. Which was why Hazel was in the back seat of her car—with Billie by her side—heading to church for the Abyssinian Christmas luncheon.

"I can't believe we're drinking on the way to church," Hazel said.

"Jesus turned water into wine, remember? And it's just a taste," Billie replied with a shrug, pouring bourbon into a glass and handing it to Hazel.

Maybe she needed the liquid courage. She took a small sip.

Billie gave her a sideways glance. "Baby, I don't know nothin' 'bout motherhood, but you're too young to have bags under your eyes. You look like you need a few drinks."

Hazel let out a breath, not quite a sigh as she leaned back in the seat. "I am tired. Skipper's my heartbeat. But . . . I'm more than a mother. More than a wife." Hazel had been thinking a lot about that day at Josephine's, when she saw her friend resigned to losing herself. And she was scared that would be her story.

Billie raised a brow. "Then get your behind back on the road. And take Skipper with you. That's what nannies are for. You're no good to that baby if you're miserable. The best thing you can give that child is a happy, whole you."

Hazel opened her mouth to argue but shut it again. Damn Billie for always being right in that infuriating, too-honest way.

Hazel drained the rest of her drink, steeling herself as the car eased to a stop in front of the church. The building loomed like a stone sentinel. Hazel stepped out and pulled her fur coat tighter as if armor could be stitched into mink.

The church doors stood ahead, but Hazel's feet didn't move. Not yet.

"I don't want to be here," she murmured, her eyes lifting to the steeple as if divine intervention might scoop her up and carry her anywhere else. But it wasn't the building that unnerved her—it was what waited inside. The eyes. The expectations. The judgment.

Hazel wore an emerald-green satin dress that hugged her post-maternity curves. Her hair was tucked neatly into a chic bun. But neither of them looked as though they belonged here—especially not Billie, with her tight silver dress and bold red lipstick.

"I don't get it. If you didn't want to come, why are we here?" Billie asked.

"Because my husband requested it."

"Guess that's why my marriages are in the gutter," Billie said dryly. "Because I don't take requests."

"I am the First Lady," she continued. "I've already put off our return for months. Besides, Adam took Skipper ahead to make sure I came."

"So your man has to kidnap your kid to get you to church?" Billie snorted. "Lord have mercy. Let's get this over with so we can find some real communion—bourbon and bitters."

Inside the fellowship hall, red, white, and green decorations dangled from the ceiling like tinsel. A towering Christmas tree twinkled in the corner, its lights blinking in time with the gospel spilling from the speakers. Hazel scanned the crowd—nearly three hundred people laughing, hugging, sipping eggnog, trading gifts.

It was all so warm, so festive.

So suffocating.

"There he is," Billie muttered.

Hazel followed her gaze. Adam was surrounded by a group of women hanging on his every word. One woman, tall and curvaceous in a tight red dress, lingered close to him, her hand resting on his arm, admiration shining in her eyes.

"You see that?" Billie whispered harshly. "Your husband is too friendly with these vultures."

Hazel gritted her teeth. "I see it." She wondered if the red dress woman was who Adam was talking to on the phone last night in a whispered tone. There'd been a lot of that lately, but every time she mentioned it to him, he dismissed her as overreacting. "What am I supposed to do, though? I can't control him or them."

Billie shook her head. "Good Lord. Did marriage kill your spunk? Don't let anyone mess with what's yours."

"What I won't do is squabble with a woman for a man, especially in church, and especially for someone who's supposed to be my husband. That's . . ." Her words trailed off when she spotted an older woman seated nearby, holding Skipper in her lap, feeding him collard greens with her bare hands. Without thinking, Hazel rushed over.

"What are you doing?" Her voice cut through the air.

The woman looked up, startled, the smashed-up greens and cornbread poised near Skipper's mouth. The baby eagerly reached for the food. "I was just feeding him. No harm—"

"No harm?" Hazel snatched Skipper from her lap. "He's a baby! Are you trying to choke him?"

The woman blinked, taken aback. "Honey, back on the plantation, folks fed babies collard greens all the time. They grew up just fine."

Anger surged in Hazel. "Well, you're not on a plantation anymore, are you?" The words came out louder than she intended and bounced off the walls.

A collective gasp followed, and Hazel felt the judgment from every corner of the hall. She glanced around, meeting the shocked stares as Adam appeared beside her.

"What's going on?" he asked.

She clutched her son. "She thinks it's okay to feed my baby without my permission!"

Adam sighed, his expression exasperated. "Don't make such a fuss, Hazel."

Her voice trembled with suppressed rage. "Maybe if you'd been watching him instead of entertaining your fan club, you'd think differently."

Adam's jaw tightened as he stood erect. "Maybe you should take Skipper home."

For a moment, Hazel wanted to scream, to shout, to release every ounce of her frustration. But instead, she grabbed Skipper's bag and slung it over her shoulder.

"Come on, let's blow this joint," Billie whispered.

Hazel happily obliged.

CHAPTER 35

February 1947

Reverend Powell had surprised everyone by remarrying a sweet young woman named Inez Cottrell. That union, and Adam and Hazel's desire to make Skipper's first Christmas memorable, was the only thing that saved the holidays.

They'd fought after the Christmas luncheon and every day thereafter until Reverend Powell introduced Inez, and they called a truce to celebrate with Skipper. Even if the baby wouldn't remember it, they were determined not to spoil his first Christmas with bickering. Now they'd settled into a comfortable existence, and Hazel couldn't help but feel like it was because she'd paused her professional career.

When Hazel wasn't caring for Skipper, she was helping Adam out around the office as he tried to balance politics with his ministry. The task had him more on edge than ever.

Today, however, she had only meant to stop by his office quickly before she and Josephine headed out to do a bit of shopping. But as soon as they stepped into his congressional office at Abyssinian, she was greeted by a whirlwind of disorder, books lying open and papers cascading off the desk in a chaotic flood.

"Doggone it!" Adam was on the telephone, his agitation palpable. "Where is Maxine?" he said, referring to his Harlem secretary. "Sick? Again? Find me somebody now!" He slammed the phone down.

"How can I help?" Hazel asked gently.

He looked up, then without a greeting to her or Josephine, reached for a stack of envelopes and held them out. "Can you take these to the post office? They've got to go out today."

Hazel took them without hesitation. "Of course, Adam."

"Then can you hurry back and help me get this place cleaned up? The NAACP folks are coming here. They've been a thorn in my side all this time, but now that I've been named to chair the Fair Employment Practices Commission, they want to act like we're friends." Adam was on a tangent. "Just go, and when you get back, can you make some fresh coffee too."

"Yes, Adam." Hazel turned to Josephine. "I'm sorry, I'm going to have to take a rain check on shopping."

Josephine was staring at Hazel in shock. "I'll walk out with you," she finally said. As soon as they got outside, Josephine took her arm. "You're following in my footsteps."

Hazel blinked. "What do you mean?"

Josephine sighed. "The footsteps you once said you didn't want. The ones you warned me about when I stayed too long in a man's shadow."

Hazel started to object, but Josephine held up a hand.

"I get it. You're doing what you think a good wife does. So did I. But one day you'll look up and realize your reflection is gone. You've wrapped your whole identity in his orbit, and somewhere in that, you disappeared."

"That's not fair," Hazel said softly, though the weight in her chest said otherwise.

"I didn't say it to be fair. I said it to be honest. I've already lost myself. It's too late for me." Josephine's voice cracked on that last line, but she straightened. "However, it's not too late for you."

Hazel looked down at the envelopes in her hand.

Josephine studied her, then added, "I saw Langston last week. He read me a new line he's working on. I thought of you the moment I heard it." She paused as if trying to recall the words. "'What happens to a dream deferred?'" Josephine recited softly. "'Does it dry up like a raisin in the sun?'"

The words didn't just land—they lodged.

CHAPTER 36

April 1947

Hazel stood at the corner of West Forty-Fourth and Seventh Avenue, the chill of the April wind slipping beneath her coat and tugging at the brim of her hat. She pulled the lapels tighter around her neck, but it wasn't just the cool air that made her uneasy. All around her, the city pulsed with its usual rhythm—horns blaring, footsteps echoing against concrete, voices rising and falling like jazz riffs. But here, as she approached Billie's apartment, the air felt different.

Billie had been trying to see her for months now. Hazel had meant to respond, truly. But between marriage, trying to get back on the road, working on her album, and the constant tug-of-war between her public life and private self, she'd canceled on her friend three times in a row. But after this morning's phone call, Hazel knew she couldn't put Billie off any longer.

Hazel climbed the narrow steps and raised a hand to knock, her knuckles grazing the flaking paint on the door. It opened before she made contact and she found herself face-to-face with a man she had never seen before.

"Hello," she said, her tone was warm but measured.

Before Hazel could respond, Billie's voice rang out from within. "All right, Fletcher. See you later."

"Nice to meet you." Fletcher tipped his hat and stepped around her.

"But we didn't meet," Hazel said looking from the man to Billie, who had appeared in the doorway of the living room, her dark curls pinned back loosely and a silk robe tied casually at her waist.

He just smiled as he walked away. "Ummm, who is Fletcher, and where is Joe?" Hazel asked after he was gone.

Billie's lips curled into a sly smile. "He's just someone I'm seeing."

"In the same house you share with Joe?"

Billie waved a dismissive hand. "Oh, Joe's on his way out the door. Good riddance, too. But Fletcher . . . he's just . . ." Her voice trailed off. "Anyway. I called you over so you could see this."

She reached into a stack of papers on the counter and handed Hazel a single folded sheet. Hazel took the letter and opened it carefully; the government seal from the Federal Bureau of Narcotics was the first thing she noticed.

Miss Billie Holiday,

It has come to our attention that you continue to perform the song "Strange Fruit" in public venues. This song, with its inflammatory content and suggestive imagery, constitutes subversive propaganda and presents a danger to the preservation of law and order.

While we respect the right to artistic expression, when that expression promotes dissent and unrest, it becomes a matter of federal concern. Consider this letter a formal warning. Continued performance of said material will result in further scrutiny and potential action under existing narcotics enforcement authority.

Sincerely,
Harry J. Anslinger, *Commissioner*

Hazel's fingers curled around the page. "Wow."

"Yep. Anslinger has it up his ass for me. He's not even trying to hide it anymore," Billie said, lighting a cigarette. "This has nothing to do with drugs. If I was up there singin' about moonlight and sweet kisses, he wouldn't give a damn what I was shooting. But I sing about *them*—about what they done to us—and suddenly I'm a threat to the nation."

Hazel's eyes scanned the letter again. "'Continued performance will result in further scrutiny.' That's not a warning. That's a leash. He wants to muzzle you."

Billie leaned back, exhaling smoke toward the ceiling. "He can't stop me through the courts, so he's trying to starve me, scare me, lock me up. Just for opening my mouth."

Hazel slammed the letter down on the counter. "This is outrageous. All this . . . because of a song."

"Because of *truth*," Billie corrected her.

Hazel stood, her voice shaking with fury. "Langston always says an artist must be free to choose what he does . . . and never afraid to do what he might choose." She met Billie's eyes, her voice rising. "But how are we supposed to be fearless when the price is everything?"

Billie smiled bitterly. "Langston is right. But The Man makes sure courage costs more than silence."

CHAPTER 37

May 1947

The morning light filtered through the thin curtains and onto the piano as Hazel struck the final chord of her practice. The notes hung in the air like a benediction. She closed her eyes, letting the music seep into her bones. Then the shrill ring of the telephone cut through the peace. Hazel's eyes snapped open. She pushed her sheet music aside, half expecting Adam with some trivial news or another request.

"Haze, it's me." Billie's voice trembled.

Hazel sat up straighter, gripping the receiver. "What's going on?"

"They tried to arrest me." Billie's words tumbled out. "After my show at the Earle Theater last night. I had to run."

"Run?" Hazel's confusion deepened.

"Yeah. I was in Philadelphia for a show. You know I got that letter. Well, now, the fuzz has been tailing me, looking for any excuse to pin me down. Last night, they tried to take me at the hotel in Philly. I barely got out . . . had to drive through a damn blockade. They shot at me, Haze. Shot at me!"

Hazel's pulse hammered in her ears. "They shot at you? Did they hit you? Where are you now?"

"I'm not hurt, but I can't do this anymore," Billie cried. "I'm at the Hotel Grampion in New York. Drove all night. They're going to catch me, Hazel."

"I'm coming to you right now." Hazel's words left her lips before she fully registered them. She was already on her feet, throwing on her coat. Her driver was off, not that she would've had time to wait on him anyway. Her fingers fumbled as she grabbed her keys while Billie gave her the room number. "Just stay there. Don't move. I'll be right there."

Hazel alerted the nanny they'd recently hired, Mrs. Hughes, to let her know she was leaving. The drive to the Grampion blurred by, the usual bustle of the streets reduced to mere noise. She pulled up to the hotel, and took off, half running through the lobby, her heels echoing against the marble floors.

She knocked on Billie's door. The door cracked open. Lady Day, the woman who commanded the stage as though born for it, looked like a shadow of herself. Her eyes were wide, bloodshot, and rimmed with fear.

"Get in." Billie stepped aside, ushering her in before closing the door with trembling hands.

The white dress she wore was dingy and plain. Her hair was mussed like she hadn't slept in days. Stale cigarette smoke clung to the room, but the sharp edge of fear was stronger.

"I can't go on like this, Haze," Billie murmured, her voice breaking as she wrung her hands and paced back and forth. Hazel noticed the syringe and foil packets on the bed. "I've been trying, trying to stay clean. But they're always after me. Everywhere I go, they're there. I'm tired, Haze. I don't know what to do anymore."

Hazel pulled her into a hug and stroked her hair as Billie quivered against her like a frightened child. "We'll figure this out. But you need help. You can't run forever."

Billie pulled back and their eyes met. "I know. But I'm scared. I don't want to go to prison. I don't think I could survive it."

"We won't let it get that far." Hazel's voice was firm, though uncertainty twisted in her gut. "We'll get you to a hospital. A real one this time, where you can get the help you need. We'll leave tonight if we have to."

She reached for Billie's suitcase, already mapping out their escape plan, as a sharp, deafening knock rattled the door. Both women froze, their eyes locking on the door until it burst open.

Men in navy suits and felt fedora hats stormed in. Hazel's stomach lurched as one stepped forward, handcuffs gleaming in his grip. His voice was cold as it sliced through the air.

"Billie Holiday, you're under arrest."

"No!" Hazel threw herself between them, pushing against the weight of their authority. "She needs help, not prison. Please, you can't do this."

Then she saw him. Jimmy Fletcher. The man who had become Billie's friend and, though neither of them would admit it, her lover. What was he doing here? Hazel's eyes slowly went to the badge around his neck.

"You . . . you're with the Feds?" Hazel said in disbelief.

Billie's eyes sparked in shock. "You bastard!" she screamed, lunging at him as the agents restrained her. "You made love to me, comforted me when my mother died. Was it all just a setup?"

Hazel caught the flicker of guilt in Fletcher's eyes, but he quickly shut it down, his face hardening.

"We already got your husband," Fletcher said coldly.

Billie's face crumpled. "You capped Joe?"

"With two ounces of heroin," Fletcher said.

Billie let out a bitter laugh. "Screw you, Jimmy Fletcher. Nabbing Lady Day is a big victory for you, huh?"

"Get her out of here," Fletcher snapped, turning away.

"I promise, Billie!" Hazel shouted after her. "I'll get you out!"

But the door slammed shut, leaving the room in a chilling silence.

The next few days were a blur. Every phone call Hazel made hit a wall; every door she knocked on slammed shut. She reached out to anyone who might help, but no one wanted to be involved in Billie's case. Not even Adam.

Hazel had stormed into Adam's study, her hands clenched at her sides. He was at his desk, flipping through the day's mail, his expression unreadable.

"You need to help her," Hazel demanded.

"That's not your fight."

"She doesn't belong in that place, Adam."

Adam sighed, setting his letters aside. "Sweetheart, I like Billie, but I don't put my name on the line for drug addicts."

Hazel recoiled as if struck. "You can't just dismiss her like that! She needs someone to stand up for her."

"She needs to stand up for herself," Adam countered, his voice colder than she expected. "And you need to focus on your own career instead of trying to save someone who refuses to be saved. Billie has been given chances before, and what does she do? She stumbles right back into the same mess."

Hazel shook her head. "So that's it? You're just going to let them throw her away?"

Adam leaned back in his chair, his gaze steady but firm. "I already did something for her. That incident at Winnette's dress shop? I made sure it didn't make the papers. But that's the problem with Billie. No one holds her accountable. And if you keep trying to pull her out of every hole she digs herself into, one day she'll drag you down with her."

Hazel's jaw tightened. "So you'd rather see her destroyed than help her?"

Adam sighed, running a hand over his face. "I care about Billie, but I care about you more. You have too much to lose, Hazel. You've worked too hard to get where you are. And you know as well as I do that the world is waiting for an excuse to see you fail. Don't give it to them."

Hazel crossed her arms, her breath heavy. "I can't just walk away from her, Adam."

"Then don't." He shrugged. "But don't expect me to jump into the fire with you."

Hazel exhaled sharply, turning away from him. She had promised Billie. And she intended to keep that promise—with or without Adam's help.

It took three days, but she finally tracked Fletcher down outside the FBI office in New York. He didn't try to avoid her.

"How could you do this?" Hazel demanded as he walked toward his car. "Billie cared for you, and she thought you cared for her."

"I'm just doing my job." His tone was flat. But his eyes said this was more than just business.

"Your job?" Hazel said. "She believed you cared about her."

He sighed, glancing away before meeting her gaze again. "I do care about Billie. Didn't mean to, but I do. Honestly, though, this is the only way to save her."

"Save her? From what? From men like you who build her up just to tear her down?"

"From the drugs," he said matter-of-factly. "Her manager, Joe Glaser, is the one who set her up. He told us where to find her and her husband. He thinks prison's the only way she'll get clean."

That betrayal settled in like a sickness. "Glaser?"

Fletcher's voice lowered, almost conspiratorial. "He threw her to the wolves to save his other client, Louis Armstrong, who was also in some trouble. Between you and me, that's what this is really about."

"What's going to happen to her?" Hazel said.

Fletcher shrugged. "Best case, she gets clean in rehab. Worst case, she gets clean in prison."

He looked at her, his expression stern. "Go home, Miss Scott. This isn't your fight. You can't save anyone else. You can only love them as they save themselves."

CHAPTER 38

May 1947
Philadelphia, Pennsylvania

I t seemed as if things had gone from bad to worse. Hazel sat with her hands clenched tight in her lap, watching Billie slumped at the defendant's table. The courthouse at Ninth and Market Street in Philadelphia wasn't far from the Earle Theater, yet it felt like they'd been dragged across an ocean to get here.

Billie wore a plain khaki dress and no makeup. The woman who used to light up stages with her voice looked like a beaten-down and weathered version of herself. Every time she glanced back in Hazel's direction, there was nothing but emptiness in her eyes.

The court proceedings had yet to begin, so Hazel took a moment and leaned forward. "Where's your attorney, Billie?"

Billie's bloodshot, dull eyes met Hazel's. "I don't have one." Her voice sounded like she had been swallowing gravel. "Joe's locked up. Glaser hasn't even checked on me. Nobody will or can help me, Haze."

The defeat in her voice was heartbreaking. She hoped Billie never found out that Glaser was behind her arrest. "No, we'll get you an attorney," she whispered fiercely, hoping to inject some sliver of hope.

But Billie shook her head, her lips pulling into a sad, almost grimacing smile. "It's fine. I've already signed paperwork to waive counsel. I'm just ready for this to be over." She leaned in closer, her voice a mere whisper. "They had to give me a shot of morphine just to walk into this courtroom."

Hazel's breath caught. "Billie, you can't—"

"Haze, it's okay." She paused, her voice a mix of resignation and faint hope. "Maybe this is the best thing that can happen to me. I need help."

Before Hazel could say more, the bailiff shot them a sharp look. "Miss Holiday, turn and face the front," he ordered.

Hazel leaned back, a chill seeping into her bones as the bailiff's voice echoed through the courtroom.

"All rise," he called out as the judge entered. They stood as Judge J. Cullen Ganey took his place at the bench. His silver hair was parted with military precision, every strand locked into place as if even time dared not ruffle it. A thick brow shadowed eyes that gave nothing away—not sympathy, not anger, just a cold, bureaucratic weight.

When he leaned forward, the bench creaked faintly beneath him, but he remained silent for a beat too long. The striped tie at his throat seemed to tighten with each breath he took, but his voice, when it finally came, cut cleanly through the room.

"You may be seated," the judge said. His gaze bored into Billie. "Miss Holiday, it has come to the court's attention that you have waived your right to legal counsel. Is that correct?"

"Yes, Your Honor."

"How do you plead?"

Billie's eyes remained fixed on the floor. "Guilty, Your Honor," she said quietly, then added, "and I'd like to be sent to a hospital."

A brief silence filled the room, and Hazel felt a glimmer of hope.

But the district attorney rose. "Your Honor, if I may . . . This is a serious case involving a drug addict, but Miss Holiday is a professional entertainer of high status." He looked down, referring to his notes. "For the past three years, she's earned nearly a quarter of a million dollars and yet . . . she doesn't have any money."

Hazel's jaw tightened as the prosecutor continued, describing how Billie's pushers charged her exorbitant prices for drugs, robbing her blind while claiming to be her friends.

"She left her mother—God rest her soul—to starve, while she spent hundreds of dollars on narcotics."

At the mention of her mother, Billie's shoulders slumped and Hazel was sure Billie was fighting back tears.

Judge Ganey looked down at Billie, his tone softer but still detached. "Miss Holiday, do you have children?"

"No, Your Honor."

"And your husband? Joe Guy. I understand he was arrested as well?"

"That's what I heard. But we're separated."

"How often do you use? How much do you take at a time?"

The questions came one after another, each one chipping away at her dignity. Hazel gritted her teeth, knowing an attorney would have objected to the invasive questions. But Billie stood there, stoic, accepting every blow.

Finally, Billie raised her head. "Your Honor, they told me if I pled guilty, they'd send me to a hospital."

"Miss Holiday, as moved as I am by your plea, I must note that you've been in the theatrical world for nearly a decade. I find it hard to believe this act of contrition." He paused, his eyes narrowing. "You are being committed as a criminal defendant. You are not being sent to a hospital solely for treatment. You'll receive it, but you stand convicted as a criminal." He leaned back, a finality in his tone. "Therefore, it is the sentence of this court that you undergo imprisonment for a period of one year and one day."

The air rushed out of Hazel's lungs. Billie remained still, her expression blank as the gavel struck. "Court is adjourned." Hazel leaped to her feet, hurrying to Billie's side.

"Billie, I—"

Billie's voice was barely a whisper. "They don't care, Haze." A mist covered her eyes. "People on drugs are sick, but they don't care. Nobody cares. Except you."

Tears stung Hazel's eyes as she reached for Billie, but before she could touch her hand, the bailiff clamped cold metal cuffs around Billie's wrists. The sight of her friend shackled tore at her chest as they led Billie away.

CHAPTER 39

May 1947
Harlem, New York

The May heat prickled Hazel's skin as she waved goodbye to Mrs. Hughes, who balanced Skipper on her hip with practiced ease. If not for the firm grip around his tiny waist, Hazel knew her son would have wriggled free and dashed after them, determined to come along.

"Goodbye, sweetie," she called, blowing kisses through the haze of summer air. Skipper flailed his arms in an enthusiastic wave.

Adam settled beside her in the car, the rustle of the newspaper filling the space between them. The bold headline—"New Labor Law Restricts Union Power—President Truman Opposes!"—stared back at him. Hazel was tempted to ask him about it. He loved when they could have discussions about his work, but they were still at odds over his refusal to help Billie, who had been sent to a women's prison in West Virginia. And beneath that, an even deeper rift simmered—whispers from the beauty salon, murmurs of infidelity that Hazel couldn't shake.

The car jerked slightly as they pulled onto the main road, and Clarence offered an apologetic "Sorry, boss."

Adam nodded, then closed his paper. He sat in silence for a moment, before the sounds of Dinah Washington's "I'll Close My Eyes" filled the car.

"Heaven sends a song through its doors . . . Just as if it seems to know, I'm exclusively yours . . ."

Hazel stiffened. She didn't want to be soothed. But the slow, hollow melody lilted through the vehicle, wrapping around her, and against her will, her shoulders loosened.

Adam used the lyrics as a peace offering. He gently took her hand, then leaned over and kissed her. The taste of mint and tobacco drifted between them.

"I know things have been rough," he sighed, his hand settling over hers, "but can we set everything aside tonight? This is your triumphant return to the stage. Can you please focus on that—and nothing else?"

She exhaled slowly, knowing he wasn't just talking about Billie. He wanted her to forget everything—the accusations, the late-night phone calls he'd taken in hushed tones, the way his eyes flickered with something unreadable whenever she pressed too hard.

"You're right," Hazel said, forcing a smile. "It feels good to be performing again." She added the last part more for herself than for him. Tonight was her first performance since giving birth. She should be ecstatic. She should feel that electric pulse of excitement. But the weight of everything that lingered in her life dimmed her joy.

The car glided toward Manhattan, passing the neon glow of Harlem's late-night haunts.

". . . I'll close my eyes . . . And see you with my heart."

The song ended, leaving behind an aching silence. Hazel turned to Adam, and truly looked at him. He was leaned back against the seat, his eyes closed. She studied him. The fatigue etched into his face ran deeper than she'd noticed before. His skin had taken on a grayish pallor, beads of sweat peppered his forehead.

"Adam?" she asked. He didn't respond as his lips pressed into a thin, grim line.

"Are you okay?"

"It's just a little pain." Adam pressed his fingers to the center of his chest. His voice was steady, but Hazel could see the strain behind his eyes.

"You don't look okay," she said, leaning in.

Adam opened his mouth to speak, but the words didn't come. His jaw clenched. Then, suddenly, he bent forward with a sharp gasp, both hands clutching his chest.

"Adam!" Hazel lurched toward him. A groan escaped from deep in his throat and his body trembled.

"Clarence—take us to the hospital. Now!"

Clarence hit the gas, and the car jolted forward. He weaved through traffic like a madman.

Hazel cradled Adam's upper body as best she could, one hand gripping his, the other stroking his chest in frantic circles. "Breathe, baby. Just stay with me, okay? You're gonna be all right. You hear me?"

But Adam's face had gone pale, a thin sheen of sweat breaking across his brow. His eyes fluttered shut, and Hazel could feel his grip loosening.

"Don't you do this," she cried. "Don't you dare."

Clarence slammed the brakes, and the car skidded to a halt in front of the emergency entrance. He jumped out and raced inside and within seconds, a wave of doctors and nurses surged forward. The back door was yanked open.

"Sir, can you hear me?" A doctor leaned in, pressing fingers to Adam's neck.

They lifted Adam onto a gurney. Hazel scrambled out of the car, nearly stumbling as she followed. "Please take care of him," she pleaded.

Hazel tried to keep up, but the emergency room swallowed him whole, doctors barking orders, machines beeping frantically. And then she was alone in the sterile brightness of the emergency room lobby.

Hazel's knees felt weak as she clutched her hands together to stop them from shaking. She scooped up her gown and sank into one of the hard plastic chairs, staring at the doors through which Adam had vanished.

"Clarence, please call the theater and let them know I won't make it to the concert tonight," Hazel said when he appeared in the doorway.

"Of course." He scurried away.

She fumbled for the hospital phone, her fingers unsteady as she dialed long-distance. Papa Powell was in Chicago at a church convention. The last thing Hazel wanted to do was deliver this message, but he would want to know. "Operator, I need to place a call to Chicago . . ."

She reached Reverend Powell first. Thankfully, he stayed at the same hotel on every visit. "Adam's in the hospital," she said, trying to sound calm. "They think it's his heart. You and Inez should come as soon as you can." Hazel hung up, then called Mrs. Hughes to let her know what was going on. Finally, she settled into the waiting room.

The minutes that followed dragged like hours. Hazel sat, wringing the hem of her coat. Time crawled by, stretching seconds into agonizing minutes.

Hazel swallowed her tears, knowing she had to stay strong. She prayed silently, each minute stretching painfully until, after three long hours, a nurse finally escorted her to his bedside.

"Hey," she whispered. She hoped her tone didn't reveal her fear. Adam's eyes fluttered open; the stubborn fire that defined him was dim, but it was still there.

"Hazel . . ." he rasped. "I'm sorry. Your show . . ."

"Don't worry about that," she said, fighting back tears. "You're going to be okay. That's all that matters."

He tried to smile, but it came off as a grimace. "You should've gone on and performed. I would've still been here when you finished."

"You're talking crazy, Adam." She squeezed his hand. "Just rest. I'm not going anywhere. Your dad and Inez are on their way here from Chicago. They'll be here soon."

Adam nodded weakly, his eyes fluttering shut as sleep overtook him again. His breathing was shallow—each rise and fall of his chest tugged at Hazel's nerves. She sat close, her fingers gently tracing the curve of the hospital blanket.

The door creaked open, and a tall, middle-aged man in a white coat stepped in. Hazel stood instinctively.

"Mrs. Powell, I'm Dr. Liggins. Your husband suffered a severe heart attack. He's stable, for now. But let me be clear—this was a warning shot. Your husband needs rest. Not the kind he pretends to take between speeches, but real, sustained recovery."

Hazel folded her arms, nodding slowly as she whispered prayers of gratitude.

Dr. Liggins looked over at Adam, asleep but visibly unwell. "If he doesn't step away, it won't be a question of *if*—but *when* he collapses again. And next time, he might not make it."

After the doctor left, Hazel watched her husband sleep, until she too closed her eyes.

Later, when he stirred awake, blinking groggily toward her, she met his gaze.

"You need to step away" was all she said.

Adam gave a weary smile. "I can't just—"

"You have to," she cut in. Her voice was soft, but her eyes held no room for debate. "The doctor said it. And I'm saying it. You've given everything to the people. It's time to give something to yourself."

He looked away, his jaw tightening with resistance. But even that required effort he no longer had.

THE NEXT FEW days blurred into each other. Mornings folded into evenings, marked only by the changing rhythms of the hospital—nurses switching shifts, meal trays arriving and being left untouched. Hazel stayed with Adam through it all.

Their conversations shifted. She reminded him of who he was outside of the pulpit, outside of politics. He reminded her why he had pushed so hard.

Adam resisted, of course. It was in his blood. But the toll on his body, the doctor's warnings, and the slow, painful look he caught of himself in the mirror—all of it began to chip away at his pride.

By week's end, he gave in.

With the help of loyal church members and family friends, they packed up their lives. Hazel oversaw the details, coordinating with Mrs. Hughes and making arrangements to relocate not just Adam, but their sense of peace to a new home in Mount Vernon. Though it was only about thirty minutes outside of Harlem, it was an entirely different world.

THE HOUSE SAT nestled among fields and trees, the ocean breeze whispering through tall grasses. It was quiet—not just in sound, but in spirit. A place where no headlines chased them down and no demands were placed on either of them.

Here, in this haven, Adam learned to exhale.

Here, Hazel learned what it meant to love him through stillness.

And together, away from the noise, they began again.

As summer surrendered to autumn, Adam's strength slowly returned. The crisp salt air worked like a balm against Adam's frayed body. Some mornings he walked the entire length of the field behind the house, Hazel at his side.

They thrived in that Westchester County cocoon. The outside world, however, refused to be forgotten. Rumors from Harlem crept in like wind under a door. Adam was resigning. Adam was dying. They heard it all via relayed messages from Reverend Powell.

Hazel did her best to shield her husband. She intercepted phone calls, turned away uninvited visitors, and trained Mrs. Hughes to be just as vigilant. She knew all too well what pressure could do, how quickly concern could turn to expectation, and expectation to demand.

So, when the house phone rang one quiet afternoon, Hazel answered with practiced calm.

"Olphelia?" she said, instantly recognizing the voice.

"I need to speak to Adam," Olphelia snapped. "I've called three times already."

Hazel's fingers tightened around the receiver. "He's resting."

"Well, tell him to stop resting and pick up the phone. Harlem is in turmoil, and people are talking like he's already dead. He needs to speak for himself."

Hazel drew in a slow breath, measured and sharp. "He will. When he's ready. You take care, now."

Hazel hung up before Olphelia could respond.

She returned to the porch. Skipper was playing on the lawn with Mrs. Hughes. Adam was pensively writing on a notepad.

"Ummm, I thought we agreed, no work for six months," she said. That had been hard, putting her career on hold. But if there was ever a time she needed it, it was now.

"Does it count as work if you love it?" He grinned. "Seriously, you know I was working on that community grocery store before the heart attack. Maxine and Deacon Brown have been keeping it going, and I was just jotting down some thoughts."

Hazel eased the notepad from his hands. "And that, my love, is still work." She motioned to the jigsaw puzzle she'd been working on. "Help me finish this puzzle."

"You're shielding me, Hazel," Adam said, a faint smile lifting from the corners of his mouth. "I've been here five months."

"You're on leave from Congress and the church. You need to focus on getting better," she said. "I'll handle the rest. Besides, what was our pact?"

"No work for six months," he said. "This time, we're keeping our promise."

"Exactly. We have to get you healthy and focus on our family."

They settled in the silence, working on the puzzle in tandem until the shrill of the telephone made Hazel rush inside.

"Hazel, darling!" Her agent's voice crackled through the line. "I know you're on vacation, but I've got great news," Isa said. "The government of Trinidad has reached out, and they want you to headline the opening of their new music festival. It's the first time they've ever done it and they want to do a three-week residency with you in conjunction with some of the local universities. The money is . . . well, it's significant."

She had never performed in her hometown, and this would be an amazing opportunity. But as she glanced out at Adam, who still looked frail, she hesitated.

"I can't," she said softly, remembering their agreement. "My husband," she explained, "he's recovering from a heart attack."

A beat passed, then Isa asked, "Is there no one who can care for him? It's only three weeks, and it's Trinidad, darling."

It wasn't like they really needed the money, since Adam was still drawing his congressional salary. Then she thought of Adam, the man who had given so much to Harlem, how she'd gone against him for Broadway. "I don't see how I could make that work," she replied. "Adam needs me more than the stage does."

A long silence filled the line before Isa sighed. "Okay. But don't say no just yet. Sleep on it, then let's chat tomorrow. Just remember, opportunities like this don't come around often."

Hazel hung up and returned to the porch.

"Who was that?" Adam asked.

Hazel debated whether she should share the details of Isa's telephone call. Ultimately, she decided to go ahead and recounted the entire conversation.

"Hazel," he said when she finished, "you've been there for me through everything. It's your time to shine."

His words caught her by surprise. "What?"

"Call her back and tell her you're coming to Trinidad. All of us are."

She stared at her husband, her mouth agape. The heart attack must've really made him reevaluate things. "Are you sure?"

"Absolutely," he replied, squeezing her hand. "It's your time now. I want to see you succeed."

CHAPTER 40

November 1947
Harlem, New York

Adam was returning to church just the way he left—proud and strong, an emperor ready to reclaim his throne. The late autumn breeze nipped at Hazel's cheeks as she adjusted her hat and wrapped her coat more snugly. She stole a glance at Adam, walking beside her with his head held high, as if the heart attack that nearly claimed his life had left no trace. His skin glowed, and his smile was brighter than it had been in months.

For Adam, Abyssinian had always been a refuge where he could draw strength from the people and return it tenfold. But today held extra significance. It was the church's 139th anniversary, and his return after months of recovery was the highlight.

As they approached the building, the crowd outside parted, greeting him with open arms and warm smiles. Hazel even felt welcomed.

"Good to have you back, Reverend Powell," one woman said, clasping her hands as she beamed up at him.

Another man, hat in hand, nodded appreciatively. "Ain't been the same without you, Pastor."

Adam nodded graciously, ever the politician, ever the minister. "It's good to be back," he said, his firm voice softened by gratitude. "The Lord's seen me through."

They made their way inside, not to the sanctuary but to the recreational area. Adam paused in the doorway, his eyes sweeping across the room. Since his absence, the space had been transformed. Tables filled with fresh produce lined the walls, and people moved among them, comparing prices and filling their baskets. A child tugged at her mother's skirt, pointing eagerly at a basket of apples, while a group of older women gathered by a table, marveling at the sight before them. This wasn't just any store. It was Adam's vision realized, a place that sold fruit and vegetables at prices Harlem's people could afford.

Hazel watched as his chest rose with pride. "This," he said softly to her, "is what I dreamed of when I first envisioned this program. People shouldn't have to choose between feeding their families and keeping the lights on."

She scanned the room—the bright yellow lemons piled high, the bags of flour and sugar stacked neatly, the rows of condensed milk. Shoppers moved eagerly from table to table, eyes wide, hands quick to grab deals before they vanished. One man excitedly lifted a can of condensed milk. "Half the price of what they charge at the A&P," he called out. "Reverend Powell, you're a blessing to this community!"

"God bless you, Reverend Powell," added another woman, her hand resting on a cart filled with fresh greens and potatoes. "We couldn't have made it through the week without this."

Adam's smile was wide as he devoured the praise. "It's not just me. It's all of us, together."

He moved through the crowd, shaking hands, patting backs, exchanging kind words. There was a renewed fire in him, but Hazel still felt a ripple of unease. Adam had always been a fighter, but the fight had nearly killed him.

"I love being back here," Adam said, like the sight was food for his soul. "I'm back in shape and ready to fight on all fronts. And I'm not just talking about Congress. I'm going to reassemble my picketers. We need to ensure that every company doing business in Harlem provides jobs for our people."

His eyes flashed with determination, and Hazel took a step toward him.

"Adam, I understand what you're saying, but—"

Before she could finish, a commanding voice sliced through the air. "Adam Clayton Powell Jr.!"

They both turned as a tall, broad-shouldered man strode toward them, his hand outstretched in greeting. Henry Wallace—President Roosevelt's third vice president—had the bearing of a man used to commanding attention. His steel-gray eyes gleamed with intensity behind wire-rimmed glasses, and his thick auburn hair, now streaked with silver, was neatly combed back. He carried himself with a quiet confidence, his three-piece suit impeccably tailored, as if he had stepped straight out of a political poster.

Wallace had caused waves with Negro leaders. Many thought his candidacy would take away votes from Truman, allowing Republicans to capture the White House. But Adam liked that he didn't kowtow to any one party. He was progressive, outspoken, unafraid to challenge the establishment—so it was no surprise to see him here. Standing next to him was a man who looked like he'd rather be anywhere else—pale, stiff in his navy suit, eyes scanning the crowd with thinly veiled discomfort. The kind of assistant who clenched his jaw at the sound of jazz and couldn't understand why a presidential hopeful needed to court votes in Harlem, much less shake hands with Adam Clayton Powell Jr.

Mr. Wallace clapped Adam on the shoulder with the ease of an old friend. "Good to see you, Reverend." Then, turning to Hazel, he offered a perfunctory nod. "Mrs. Powell, just as beautiful in person."

Hazel managed a polite smile, and before she could respond, he turned back to Adam, surveying the area with an approving nod. "I've heard about the great work you're doing here, and I had to see it for myself. This is exactly what Harlem needs."

Adam, clearly pleased, straightened his posture. "We do what we can."

Mr. Wallace wasted no time. "I need a man like you on my team. Come work for me. Help me fight for the people on a national stage."

Hazel cleared her throat. "Adam is still recovering. He's on indefinite leave from Congress. He needs to focus on his health."

The man in the navy suit stepped up. "Now, now, lil' lady, this is menfolk's business."

Hazel's fingers curled into fists at her sides. She opened her mouth, ready to speak her mind, but Mr. Wallace stepped forward.

"Now, Bradley, Mrs. Powell is anything but a lil' lady." Mr. Wallace tipped his hat apologetically at Hazel. "You'll have to excuse my aide here. He's from the South and has some ways we've yet to break."

"He's going to get something broken all right," Hazel said just as Adam stepped forward and placed a hand on her arm.

He spoke matter-of-factly. "Adam Clayton Powell Jr. works only for the people."

"Then our goals align." Mr. Wallace gave a knowing smile. "Hear me out. You're on an indefinite leave. I just need you to be a vocal supporter to your people. And advise me behind the scenes. I know your anti–Jim Crow bill is languishing in Congress. When you get back, I can help you get it passed."

Hazel stepped forward, forcing calm into her voice, though her insides twisted. "As I said, my husband is taking things slow."

This time, Mr. Wallace just laughed as he patted Adam on the back again. "I've seen this man on all fronts. He's a fighter if I've ever seen one."

Hazel wanted to scream, to tell this man not to dangle these offers in front of Adam, not when they were supposed to leave for Trinidad soon. But Mr. Wallace leaned in, lowering his voice as if sharing a secret. "Think about the things we could accomplish together, Adam. Hell, if I didn't already have a running mate, I'd consider you for VP."

Hazel resisted the urge to roll her eyes. Mr. Wallace already had Glen Taylor on his ticket, and they barely let Adam into Congress—there was no way he'd be accepted as second-in-command. But this man knew how to play the game, stroking Adam's ego just enough to make it seem plausible.

"Well, I'm flattered," Adam said, "and I may definitely be interested in working with you on a consulting basis. Let's chat next week."

"Splendid. I'd love for us to dive in before the holidays."

Adam nodded. "We'll talk. But right now, I need to get back to my members."

Mr. Wallace nodded. "Of course. I'll be in touch." He gave Adam a thumbs-up before turning and walking away.

As soon as he was gone, Hazel said, "I know you're not seriously thinking of working with him?"

Adam shrugged as they headed toward the sanctuary. "If he's serious about supporting some of the things I'm doing, I might have to consider it."

While Adam was a pure Democrat, he made no secret that he wasn't loyal to any side. Whoever he believed would best serve Harlem was who he aligned with. "Adam," Hazel said, turning to face him, "you can't take this on. We're supposed to be leaving in a few weeks."

He hesitated, his eyes revealing his conflict. "Yes," he said slowly, "about that . . . I've been gone awhile. Being back here made me realize I can't afford another three weeks away."

"But you're the one who said—"

"Surely you understand." He paused and grinned, throwing her words back in her face. "Opportunities like these don't come along often."

She stared at him in disbelief, and a sinking feeling filled her. They were back in Harlem. Back to reality. And the reality was, she'd be taking the journey to Trinidad without her husband.

CHAPTER 41

January 1948
Port of Spain, Trinidad

The ship eased into the Port of Spain just after dawn, its horn sounding a low, solemn note that rippled across the harbor. Hazel stood at the rail, her gloved hands resting lightly on the polished wood, her eyes fixed on the hazy silhouette of the island ahead. Trinidad. The place of her birth. The place where her first lullabies were sung in calypso and Creole, where memories clung to the palms and the rhythm of the earth still spoke in drums.

Adam had offered to arrange a flight—his diplomatic credentials could've secured seats aboard a British West Indian Airways plane with no issue. But Hazel had declined. She needed the sea. The slow passage gave her space to think, to breathe, to shed the layers of tension that New York had wrapped around her. More than that, it spared her the sideways glances and stiff politeness that often accompanied air travel for Negroes.

As the ship pulled into the dock, the scent of brine and blooming hibiscus drifted up to greet her. Porters shouted and shuffled below, ropes were tossed and tied, crates stamped with customs seals were wheeled across sun-warmed planks.

Hazel descended the gangway, the warm air wrapped around her in a gentle embrace. She paused at the bottom, closed her eyes, and inhaled. Sea salt, ripe fruit, woodsmoke. The scent of home.

It had been ten years since she last set foot on this island. The buildings were lower than she remembered, the palm trees taller, but the rhythm of the place—its pulse—was unchanged.

Behind her, Mrs. Hughes shuffled with Skipper in her arms, the boy's sleepy head resting against her shoulder. He had been restless on the journey, anxious to run and play along the promenade deck of the ocean liner. He'd asked endless questions—about the water, the sky, the people on board, and countless 'whys' about everything. Hazel had answered patiently at first, then with waning energy as the voyage wore on. He was too young to understand the significance of this trip, but Hazel wanted him to see this place, to know it, to carry it with him as a piece of his heritage.

Hazel smiled at the large banner hanging at the entrance: "Sharing our warmth with the world."

"Miss Scott!" a voice called out, breaking her reverie. A customs officer waved her over, his face bright with recognition. Hazel smiled as she approached him. Here, she was both an international star and simply Hazel from Belmont.

"I'm a big fan. Welcome home!" he said excitedly.

The officer escorted Hazel to get their suitcases, and momentary guilt filled her. She had left New York and Adam in the midst of chaos. Over the holidays, Harold Burton, an unqualified opportunist seizing on Adam's illness, had decided to make a play for his congressional seat. A former plumber, Harold had no business in politics, yet Adam's heart condition had left him vulnerable. Hazel had debated staying to make sure he didn't overexert or stress himself.

No, she scolded herself. If anything, she was the one who should be angry. He'd left her in the lurch on a trip he had encouraged her to take.

"Hazel!" Her cousin Joycelyn's voice rang out as soon as she entered the arrivals hall. Hazel looked up to see her waving excitedly, her bright yellow dress fluttering in the breeze.

"Joycie!" Hazel exclaimed, embracing her cousin tightly. Joycie smelled of coconuts and hibiscus, the scent carrying Hazel back to carefree childhood summers spent running barefoot through fields.

"How was your journey?" she asked.

"Long," Hazel sighed.

"You look just like Aunt Alma." Joycie held her at arm's length. "It's uncanny."

"I don't see it, but people used to call us twins," Hazel said.

Joycie laughed, her eyes sparkling. "This must be Skipper," she said, tickling Skipper's cheek as he rested on Mrs. Hughes's shoulder.

Skipper lifted his head groggily, rubbing his eyes before looking around. "Mommy?"

"I'm here, sweetheart." Hazel kissed the top of his curly head.

Joycie beamed. "Oh, he's precious! How old is he now?"

"Almost two."

"Well, he is just the most adorable thing. Come on, let's get out of this heat."

They made their way to Joycie's car. As they drove through the streets of Port of Spain, Hazel marveled at how little had changed. Cyclists wove deftly through traffic, dodging streetcars and trolleys. The scent of roasting cashews and curry wafted through the air, mingling with the distant perfume of frangipani and night-blooming jasmine.

"Everyone is so excited about your concert," Joycie said as she navigated her car around a vendor pushing a wooden cart overflowing with bright red sorrel and fresh coconuts. "Of course, they're trying to get free tickets. I told them everyone must buy, including family!"

Hazel chuckled, savoring the enthusiasm of home. They arrived at Joycie's house, a modest wooden structure painted a cheerful blue, perched on a hill overlooking the sea. The Long family wasn't wealthy, but they were among Trinidad's middle class.

Inside, the cool interior offered refuge from the humidity. Hazel sank into a worn armchair by the window, gratefully accepting a glass of fresh lemonade from Joycie as Mrs. Hughes settled Skipper in a small cot in the guest room. Hazel had made the right decision bringing him here.

That evening, the house filled with family. Laughter and conversation bounced off the walls as cousins, aunts, and uncles squeezed into Joycie's small living room. The scent of fried plantains and rum filled the air, mingling with the upbeat rhythm of calypso music playing from the radio. Hazel accepted hugs, kisses, and endless questions.

"Hazel, girl, you remember me?" A woman with graying hair and a warm smile wrapped her in an enthusiastic hug. "Aunt Clara's daughter, Eudora!"

"Of course!" Hazel lied with a bright smile. "How could I forget?" Eudora laughed heartily, then leaned in closer. "Now, I hate to ask, but . . ."

There it was.

"My son's trying to get into medical school in the States," Eudora continued in a hushed tone. "We could use a little help with a good word from your husband—I hear he's pretty powerful. And also, that tuition, you know, it's steep."

Since Hazel had stopped spending summers here, the family had drifted apart. None of them had even come to her mother's funeral, though Joycie had reached out. But there was no hesitation in asking for money. Hazel nodded, masking her irritation. "I'll see what I can do."

That night, sleep came fitfully, interrupted by the hum of night insects and the occasional laughter from the street below. When the first streaks of morning light filtered through the lace curtains, Hazel forced herself up, stretching stiff limbs before heading to Skipper's room. He was already awake, sitting cross-legged on the bed, as Mrs. Hughes read *The Tale of Peter Rabbit*.

She ran a hand over his soft curls. "Good morning, love. Are you hungry?"

Mrs. Hughes smiled. "We've already had a wonderful breakfast of mashed oatmeal and bananas."

"Sounds yummy. I'll let you finish your book."

Hazel made her way into the kitchen to see if she could find something to eat, other than mashed oatmeal and bananas.

"Hey, I'm going to run some errands," Joycie said, stepping into the kitchen. "You should come with me so you can see how much has changed."

Hazel happily joined her cousin and as they drove through the winding streets of Port of Spain, she leaned against the open window, letting the warm island air caress her face. Children in pressed uniforms hurried along sidewalks, and vendors called out in singsong voices, selling roasted corn and tamarind sweets.

When they turned onto Richmond Street, Hazel's breath caught in her throat. The two-story brick house stood as it had in the black-and-white photographs her mother had kept. Its cast-iron veranda curled around the top floor. Hazel felt nothing—no deep pang of nostalgia, no sudden rush of childhood memories. The house, though tied to her existence, felt foreign.

"Do you remember it?" Joycie asked, tilting her head toward the window.

"Not much," Hazel admitted. "I was too young, I think."

Or maybe I blocked it out, she thought. As the only survivor of her parents' six children, her birthplace was more a symbol of loss than of beginning.

They drove past St. Joseph's Convent School, its grand round arches looming over the street like silent sentinels. "That's where Aunt Alma trained," Joycie reminded her, nodding toward the stately building.

Hazel smiled faintly. "She always said the nuns were strict, but she credited them with her discipline. 'You'll thank me one day, like I did the sisters,'" she said, mocking her mother. "Mama used to tell me that whenever she made me practice piano past the point of exhaustion. And I did. Eventually."

They continued their drive through town, passing the grand, sprawling President's House, its white walls framed by towering palm trees and a manicured lawn. "Grandfather Samuel built that," Joycie said proudly.

"I think I remember Grandma mentioning that," Hazel said. "She always talked about how he was an amateur violinist when he wasn't laying bricks."

As they turned onto a quieter street, Hazel's gaze landed on an old concert hall. "Isn't that where Mama had her concert?"

Joycie nodded. "Yes, it is."

Hazel exhaled slowly. Alma had trained herself through sheer discipline, but when she stepped onto the grand stage in a solo performance, pain shot through her wrists mid-performance, cutting her moment of triumph short. No amount of strengthening exercises, medical attention, or home remedies had helped.

"That's when she started giving piano lessons to the neighborhood kids," Hazel recalled.

"Yeah," Joycie replied, "and that's when they discovered you could play too."

Joycie turned to her. "You should come back more often, you know. This is where it all started."

Hazel hesitated, staring out at the place that had shaped her family long before Harlem ever entered her story. "I know," she said, her voice barely above a whisper.

"Roots matter, Hazel," Joycie said, reaching over to squeeze her hand. "Sometimes you have to come home to remember who you are."

Hazel nodded, feeling a rare sense of peace settle over her. Maybe she would come back. Maybe she needed to.

CHAPTER 42

February 1948

Hazel sat on the veranda of her great-aunt Maud's house. The wooden beams creaked softly in the breeze and the lanterns lining the porch flickered like fireflies. It had been an evening of triumph—her final performance had stirred something deep in her chest, the way only music could. Hazel had felt it in the way the audience held their breath with her, in the way their cheers erupted the moment her fingers left the keys. She had felt it in the eager music students who devoured her every word at the school she visited. She knew she'd lit a musical spark in several children in Trinidad.

Now, in the quiet aftermath of tonight's performance, Hazel watched Skipper twirl through the grass with his cousins, his small feet kicking up dust, his laughter wild and free. The sight of him—of all the children, barefoot and unbothered by time—made something deep in her bones ache. Wasn't this the dream? To see her son bathed in the glow of family, untethered from the weight of the world?

"Joycie, you see this child?" Hazel called over her shoulder toward the kitchen, where her cousin was fussing with a pot of tea. Laughter bubbled from her lips as she thought of the absolute conniption her mother would have had at the sight of her grandson outside in his bare feet. "Skipper thinks he's a whole dance troupe by himself."

Her aunt Maud chuckled from her rocking chair on the front veranda. Her hands were busy shuffling a deck of well-worn playing cards. She wore a floral housedress, its faded blues and yellows soft from years of washing, and her feet were bare against the wood of the porch. A red scarf was wrapped snugly around her head, holding back wisps of gray curls.

"That boy got rhythm in his bones, same as you. You surprised?"

Hazel smiled but said nothing. Maybe she shouldn't have been. America had tried to tell her otherwise, but rhythm—true, gut-born rhythm—could never be taught.

At the wooden table near the veranda's edge, family members gathered, slapping cards down in the middle of a raucous game of all-fours. Voices swirled—Creole, English, laughter blending into an effortless harmony. Hazel slid into an empty chair beside her cousin Miriam, her fingers idly tapping against the table.

"You playing or you watching?" Miriam teased, her dark eyes glinting with mischief.

"Playing," Hazel said with mock seriousness, reaching for the cards. "And winning."

Miriam cackled. "Big talk, Yankee girl."

The game went on, cards slapping against the table, accusations of cheating met with riotous laughter.

Miriam leaned in, lowering her voice as she picked up her next card. "So, cousin, what's the real deal with Billie Holiday?"

Hazel kept her expression even as she glanced at Miriam. "She's getting out soon." Miriam, sensing the steel in Hazel's tone, nodded and let it go.

Across the table, Aunt Maud studied her quietly. It was the same look that preceded every difficult truth her aunt had ever spoken. Sure enough, as the game wound down, her aunt sat back, her eyes sharp and assessing.

"Girl," Maud said, setting her cards down, "what you really want?"

Hazel frowned. "What kind of question is that?"

"The kind that matters," Maud said simply. "You doing all this running—playing music here, touring there, back and forth like a hummingbird. You living the life you want, or just the one that landed in front of you?"

Hazel hesitated. She wanted to say that she had fought for this life. That every choice, every risk, had been hers. But something about the way Maud was watching her made her pause.

"I love what I do," she said at last. "Playing, performing . . . it's who I am."

"That so?" Maud nodded, considering her. "And what else? You want to be a wife? A mother first? A star? Or you think you could be all of them?"

Hazel exhaled. "Why can't I?"

Maud let out a short laugh, shaking her head. "Because something always suffers. And most times, it's the woman."

Hazel paused. "That's not fair."

"It's not about fair, chile. It's about what is." Maud leaned forward, folding her arms on the table. "Your mother had dreams big enough to swallow this whole island. And she passed those dreams on to you." A nostalgic look passed over her face. "She loved you. But she wasn't always there, was she?"

Hazel remembered the loneliness of childhood, the way she had idolized her mother's talent but had never quite known her as a person. She had vowed to be different with Skipper. To be present. But was she?

Maud reached for her hand, squeezing it gently. "You have to decide, Hazel. What's worth more to you? The world clapping for you? Or your son looking for you in a crowd and seeing you there?"

The question hit her like a wave.

The sound of Skipper's laughter drifted through the air. Hazel turned, watching him. His joy was *here*, in this moment. He wasn't looking for her in a crowd tonight. He knew exactly where she was.

She swallowed past the lump in her throat. "Can't I have both?"

Maud let out a long breath, shaking her head with something like sorrow. "It's a delicate dance, niece. You could try."

Hazel's fingers curled against the worn wood of the table.

"Why do men not have to choose?"

"It's just the way of life. And you just have to exist in it. Or you have to fight hard to change it."

Now she wondered if she was chasing the right dream after all.

CHAPTER 43

March 1948
Alderson, West Virginia

The car hummed beneath Hazel as she leaned against its sleek silver frame. Barney stood beside her, a cigarette perched between his fingers. The 1943 Oldsmobile Ninety-Eight, its chrome gleaming like polished silver, turned heads as it sat outside Alderson Federal Prison Camp. But the small crowd gathering there wasn't interested in the car. They were waiting for Billie.

Ten long months had passed since Billie was sentenced, and now, having been a model prisoner, she was being released early.

Mister, her loyal boxer, tugged at his leash, wagging his tail furiously as if he sensed her return. Hazel had gone to pick the dog up at Billie's request.

Adam had opposed Hazel's decision to come to Alderson. After her three weeks in Trinidad, he insisted that her life should exist in neatly organized compartments: wife, musician, public figure. He never understood that her friendships weren't something she could set aside for convenience. Hazel suspected his real concern was how her public support for Billie might affect his political aspirations. She shook the thought away, her eyes fixed on the closed prison gate.

"Can you give us a statement, Miss Scott?" a reporter called out from behind the wire barrier separating the press from the waiting crowd.

Hazel glanced at Barney, who paced a few feet away. The look on his face told her he had nothing to say. "No comment," she answered firmly.

"She's coming soon," Barney muttered, half to himself. Hazel nodded but didn't look away from the gate.

Finally, the gate groaned open.

Billie emerged, her hand over her eyes to block the blinding sunlight. She was thinner, her cheeks hollow, but she walked tall, her back straight and her head held high. A simple navy dress hung loosely on her frame.

Before Hazel could call out, Mister broke free, the leash slipping from her fingers. The dog bolted across the pavement, a blur of fur and energy.

"Mister!" Hazel shouted, her voice drowned by the reporters calling out from the barricade.

Billie spotted the dog just in time. Her face lit up as Mister leaped into her arms, knocking her hat off and nearly making her stumble. She laughed—a sound so pure and joyful that, for a moment, the prison behind her seemed to vanish.

"I missed you too, my love," she murmured, burying her nose in his fur as he licked her face with unrestrained enthusiasm.

The moment didn't last. The reporters broke through the barrier and swarmed, cameras clicking and questions flying.

"Miss Holiday, what's your first move now that you're out?"

"How does it feel to be free?"

Billie's smile faded, her eyes darkening as she clutched Mister closer. "I might just as well have wheeled into Penn Station and had a little get-together with the Associated Press, United Press, and International News Service."

Hazel stepped forward, slipping her arm around Billie. "Come on, Billie. Let's get out of here."

Barney was already by the car, holding the door open. "Welcome home, Billie."

Once inside the Oldsmobile, the noise outside dulled to a faint hum. Billie slumped against the seat, her body trembling with exhaustion and relief. "It felt like I'd never see the outside again," she whispered, closing her eyes.

"But you're here," Hazel said softly, squeezing her hand. "And we'll make sure you're okay."

About thirty minutes into their drive, Barney cleared his throat from the driver's seat, glancing at Billie in the rearview mirror. "Billie, I've been thinking. You know you're always welcome at Cafe Society, but how about a comeback concert? Carnegie Hall?"

Billie's eyes snapped open, narrowing in disbelief. "Carnegie Hall? Are you out of your damn mind, Barney? No one's gonna want to see me after . . . after all this."

"You're wrong," Barney said, handing her a piece of paper over the seat. "Bobby Hackett was supposed to perform in three weeks, but ticket sales are slow. They think you can help with that." Barney wasn't officially Billie's manager, but he was always looking out for her—just like he did Hazel, even though they'd both left him at the club.

Billie stared at the paper. After a long silence, she sighed. "Fine. I need the bread. Let's do it. But when no one shows up, don't say I didn't warn you."

MARCH 27 ARRIVED faster than any of them anticipated. Every ticket to Billie's Carnegie Hall concert sold out within twenty-four hours. It had been nearly a year since Billie graced a stage, but that night, she was a legend reborn.

Backstage, Hazel watched the controlled chaos as the crew prepared for the performance. Billie paced, her hands trembling just enough to betray her nerves. Hazel adjusted the gardenias in her hair. "You're going to knock 'em dead, Billie."

Billie gave a half smile, but doubt filled her eyes. "I hope so."

When the curtains rose, the applause surged. Billie stepped into the spotlight, and for a moment, the world seemed to hold its breath. Then she sang.

Her voice—soft, aching, and powerful—carried through Carnegie Hall, enchanting the audience. Thirty-two songs poured from her soul, and it made Hazel ecstatic to be here to witness it all.

CHAPTER 44

June 1948
Manhattan, New York

The slight chill nipped at Hazel's bare shoulders as she stepped onto the stage of Lewisohn Stadium. Above her, stars pierced the thinning clouds like shy spectators peeking out to witness history. All day, the city had held its breath, willing the rain to stay away. Now, under a deep indigo sky, Hazel stood bathed in moonlight and stage lights, her white organdy gown rippling gently in the breeze. She was really about to perform with the Philharmonic.

She moved toward the piano. Nearly fourteen thousand faces stretched before her. At the podium, conductor Walter Hendl stood poised, baton in hand. His warm gaze met hers, and he gave a small, steadying nod.

Hazel inhaled deeply. Then the music began.

The orchestra swelled behind her, and she folded into the sound, her body attuned to every phrase. Her fingers danced with precision and fire, coaxing life from the piano. The night around her faded until only the music remained.

When the last note dissolved into the night air, a hush blanketed the stadium—just for a heartbeat.

Then came the applause, thundering through the air, crashing like waves against the stage. Hazel blinked, stunned for a moment by the sheer volume of it, then smiled as it washed over her. She turned slightly to see Walter glowing with approval. "Bravo," he mouthed.

Backstage, Hazel's team greeted her with joy and relief. Isa rushed forward. "You were magnificent, Hazel," she said, pulling her into a warm hug.

"Thank you," Hazel replied, her voice tinged with lingering adrenaline. The gown clung uncomfortably to her skin, but she didn't care. Nothing could dampen the high of the evening.

As she walked toward the greenroom, Hazel's thoughts drifted to Adam. An important roll-call vote had kept him in Washington. The pang of disappointment she felt at his absence weighed on her. Tonight had been monumental, and she had wished for him to see her perform, since he'd missed her performances in Trinidad.

When she pushed open the greenroom door, she froze.

Standing in the center of the lushly furnished room was Lee.

But not the Lee she remembered.

The last time she'd seen him, he had been just a boy—lean, restless, carrying the weight of too few dreams and even less direction. His face had been softer then, his jawline still finding its shape.

But the man standing before her was different.

His shoulders were broader, his stance more grounded. His dark hair, once wild and unruly, was now neatly cut. And the sharp angles of his cheekbones more pronounced, his jawline strong and set with quiet confidence. Even his smile—wide and easy as ever—carried a weight it hadn't before, as if life had finally given him something solid to stand on.

He took a step forward, holding out an enormous bouquet of black-red roses. "You were nervous during that first movement, but you settled down and took care of business," he teased.

Hazel rushed forward, pulling him into a tight embrace. Any

residue of anger he might've had over their breakup was gone. "What are you doing here?" Memories of their shared youth surfaced—Lee had always been her biggest cheerleader.

"Your dream was always to perform with the Philharmonic," he replied with sincerity. "Do you think I'd miss this?"

"You remembered?"

"How could I forget? Since we were twelve years old, you've been saying there were three places you always wanted to perform: Carnegie Hall, Lewisohn Stadium, and Constitution Hall," he said, mocking a young girl's voice. "You'll get to all three," he assured her.

"Maybe Carnegie, but Constitution Hall? Racism is alive and well."

"I read about that mess with the DAR," Lee said.

She swatted his arm, unwilling to dwell on old wounds. "I still can't believe you're here. I heard you left Harlem."

"Decided I wanted more than Garrison's Packing House, and since I had nothing keeping me in Harlem"—he shrugged, with a pained wink—"I enrolled at Fisk University. About to graduate."

"Ooooh, a college man."

"Anyway, one of my classmates is studying with Walter Hendl. When I discovered you would be here, I told him I needed a front-row seat," Lee explained.

"Well, I am really happy to see you. My mother-in-law cooked a celebratory dinner. Why don't you join us?"

"I'd love to. But I have an early train."

"My driver can take you home as soon as you're ready. You can ride with me to the dinner and just stay for a bit so we can catch up." Hazel was thrilled when he agreed.

When they arrived at the Powells', the party was in full swing. Inez glided through the room, ensuring everyone was comfortable. Hazel found a divan and got comfortable as Lee immediately began sharing childhood stories with the other guests. She laughed, savoring the warmth of the moment.

Then she saw Adam. He stood in the doorway, a dark expression on his face. His suit was immaculate—deep charcoal with a sharp crease—but travel and stress clung to him like a second skin. His tie was slightly askew, as if he'd yanked it loose mid-thought.

There was a weariness in his eyes that hadn't been there the last time Hazel saw him, something heavier than just fatigue. His usual charisma—the kind that lit up a room on contact—felt dimmed, held at a distance. For a moment, the music and laughter faded into the background as she watched him scan the room, his shoulders squared but his expression guarded, like he wasn't sure if he'd walked into a celebration or a battlefield.

"Adam!" Inez greeted him, surprise evident in her tone. "We didn't know you'd make it."

"Obviously." His sharp gaze was fixed on Hazel and Lee.

Lee stood, extending a hand. "Nice to see you, Congressman Powell." That was just like Lee, to harbor no ill will.

Adam ignored Lee's outstretched hand. "Hazel, let's go." His demand sliced through the celebratory atmosphere.

Hazel stared in shock at his rudeness.

"Adam," Inez interjected, trying to ease the tension, "let me get you a drink. Dinner will be ready in ten minutes."

"I don't want a drink or dinner," Adam snapped. "I want to go home. I'm exhausted."

The room fell silent. Hazel was speechless. Adam's outburst embarrassed her, but more than that, it enraged her.

"Adam, I'm starving," Hazel said, her voice low.

"And I'm ready to go," he repeated, his tone brooking no argument.

Everything in Hazel wanted to shout, *Then leave!* But the room was watching. Adam's demands left her no choice. Gritting her teeth, she grabbed her cloak, swallowed her humiliation, said goodbye to Lee, and followed Adam out into the night.

The car ride home was thick with silence, the kind that smothered the air like heavy wool. Hazel sat stiffly in the passenger seat, her arms crossed as Adam gripped the steering wheel. The tires crunching over the pavement were the only sound between them.

"What the hell was that back there?" Adam finally barked.

Hazel exhaled. "You're acting like you have no class."

"You think I didn't see the way you and Lee were looking at each other?"

"Looking at each other?" Hazel's jaw tightened. She was surprised he even remembered Lee. "Adam, I was being civil to a friend since childhood. You're the one who made a scene."

"Civil? Hazel, that man would take you back in a second if you let him."

"And what does it matter? I married you. What more do you want?"

Adam's lips pressed into a thin line. "I want you to stop always making me look like a damn fool who can't control his wife."

"That's the problem. You want to control me." She huffed, trying to keep from unleashing all the anger bubbling in her chest. "You're impossible," she muttered.

Adam let out a dry laugh, full of disbelief. "I'm impossible? I just watched my wife sit across from a man who's been waiting for me to fail. Do you have any idea how that looks?"

"I know exactly how it looks," Hazel shot back. "It looks like my husband is so insecure he'd rather humiliate me in front of our family and friends than trust his wife."

Adam slammed his palm against the wheel. "You have no idea

what I deal with every damn day, Hazel. The pressure, the politics. I don't need to come home and fight you, too."

"I don't want to fight, Adam." Hazel's voice dropped, her exhaustion seeping through every word. "I wanted one night. One peaceful night where I could just rest on my accomplishments and enjoy the company of friends."

The rest of the drive passed in silence. When they reached their brownstone, Adam got out first, slamming the door behind him. Hazel took a moment, gathering the energy to follow him inside.

The fights didn't stop that night. If anything, that one evening had unleashed years' worth of resentment and conflict.

Days turned into weeks, and every conversation between them became a battlefield. They fought over everything and nothing at all. Hazel's schedule, Adam's absences, her performances, his work. The only time they weren't fighting each other was when they were fighting *for* something—his civil rights bill, his latest push for funding in Harlem, his battle against city corruption. In those moments, they were united, their passion igniting like old times, but as soon as the cause was won or lost, they returned to their corners, both exhausted from the constant war.

After five months of that back-and-forth dance, Hazel found solace the only way she knew how—she went on the road. She hated leaving Skipper, but she felt like leaving was saving herself.

Touring was demanding, but at least it was predictable. The music was hers, the applause hers, the audience hanging on her every note. Onstage, she wasn't the woman locked in a marriage that felt like a prison; she was Hazel Scott, the brilliant pianist, the headliner, the woman who made even the most hardened crowds weep with a single touch of the keys.

But every night, when the curtain fell and the applause faded, loneliness settled deep in her bones. She would return to her hotel room, kick off her heels, and stare at the phone, debating whether to call Adam, recalling their last stilted conversation.

"When are you coming home?"

"I don't know yet."

Silence.

She could hear him sigh, frustrated but unwilling to say what they both knew: Maybe she didn't want to come home. Maybe *he* didn't want her to.

If it hadn't been for Skipper, she'd probably have stayed on the road forever. Mrs. Hughes was taking good care of him, but she knew her son needed her. Even if her husband didn't.

CHAPTER 45

January 1949

Every time she felt herself drifting away, moments like this pulled her back in. Hazel stood in the doorway of their study, watching Adam on the telephone, the glow of the fireplace casting flickering light against his charcoal suit. His voice carried authority as he spoke into the telephone.

"Three dozen white roses, not a stem out of place," he said. "And make sure they're in her dressing room before she arrives. Reserved seating, center stage. I don't care who you have to move—just get it done."

Hazel watched him, mesmerized by his command of the moment. She had seen him like this countless times, orchestrating the world around him with a sharpness that was both intimidating and exhilarating. Tonight was no exception. Though tonight was for her and about her. Adam had poured every ounce of his energy into making this event perfect. Moments like this were why she had a seesaw of emotions regarding her marriage.

This was how he always drew her back in. She forgot the unproven rumors and forgave the incessant fighting. This was why she couldn't stop loving him.

Not only had Adam devoted the entire holidays to her and

Skipper, he'd arranged the ultimate gift. She wasn't performing at Small's Paradise. This was Carnegie Hall.

"You look incredible," he said, placing the phone back on the receiver.

Her velvet gown, a deep burgundy that clung elegantly to her figure, glimmered in the soft light. A fur stole draped over her shoulders, and diamond earrings—also a Christmas gift from Adam—sparkled with every movement.

"And you," she replied, running her fingers along his lapel, "look as dashing as ever."

Adam's expression glowed with the same intensity he had shown during her Cafe Society debut years ago, though tonight, it carried a greater weight.

"I still can't believe you arranged a performance at Carnegie Hall."

"Why not? These are the stages you deserve to be on. Besides, I arranged it, but your talent secured it."

He extended his arm, and Hazel accepted it, allowing herself to be drawn into his world of boundless optimism. "Your Carnegie Hall audience awaits," he said.

Later, as Hazel stepped onto the stage, the lights momentarily blinded her, but soon the sight of the packed hall came into focus. Six thousand faces stared back, waiting for her to transform the night with her music.

She took a seat and inhaled deeply before letting the opening notes of *Caribbean Fête* flow through her. The music surged like a tide, each movement alive with the essence of Carnival—the steel drums, the vibrant streets, the joy of her Trinidadian heritage.

The suite was her secret creation, a bold blend of tradition and swing she had crafted during her time in Trinidad. She played Caribbean tunes for thirty minutes, then shifted seamlessly into classical pieces with precision and grace. Bach. Chopin. Liszt. By the time she struck the last chord, the audience erupted into a roar of appreciation, rising in a standing ovation.

Hazel stepped back from the piano, her breath ragged with exhilaration.

That night at Carnegie Hall stitched something back together—imperfectly, but tightly enough to hold. As the curtain closed behind her, Hazel walked backstage, exhilaration still coursing through her. She found Adam waiting in the wings, his hands outstretched.

"You were . . . magnificent," he said softly.

She stepped into his arms.

And for a while, they found their rhythm again.

The months that followed moved like a montage, moments folded into each other like pages in a well-worn book. In March, Hazel stood in the humid sun of Panama as Adam addressed a crowd of dockworkers in the Canal Zone.

In May, it was his turn to follow her lead. In Montreal, then Toronto, then Quebec, he moved like a shadow just behind the stage curtain, watching her slip into song with grace and precision. After each performance, they shared quiet dinners in unfamiliar cities, trading notes—him on speeches, her on set lists—over candlelight and black coffee. He never tried to steal her spotlight. She didn't try to shrink his mission. Their marriage was complete contentment.

By September, they were in South America—Bogotá, São Paulo, Buenos Aires—each chasing justice through different mediums. She played to crowded concert halls; he met with grassroots organizers, journalists, and church leaders. In hotel lobbies and embassies, they found each other again and again—sometimes with laughter, sometimes with exhaustion, but always with intention.

The world didn't slow down for them. If anything, it spun faster. But for a time, they learned to move with it—*together*. Not as perfect lovers, not without friction, but with shared purpose.

And when the new year came and went, Hazel sat alone one morning, composing in the quiet, and allowed herself to hope.

Not just for the next tour or the next standing ovation.

But for the marriage that, against all odds, still had its rhythm.

CHAPTER 46

September 1949

It had taken Isa a year and a half—months of relentless calls, meetings that went nowhere, and doors slammed in her face—but today, she was striding toward the towering glass façade of the Du-Mont Television Network offices like she had never doubted this moment would come.

Hazel, on the other hand, wasn't so sure. She had been on some of the biggest stages in the country, played for royalty, shared the screen with legends. And yet, the thought of stepping onto this particular stage—a new, uncharted, unpredictable medium—filled her with uneasiness.

Beside her, Isa's heels clicked in perfect rhythm against the pavement. She adjusted her hat, then cast Hazel a quick, reassuring smile that carried a hint of mischief. "You ready?"

Hazel nodded, though the knot in her throat made it hard to speak. "I just can't believe they're serious about offering me my own show."

Isa smirked. "They are. I didn't drag you all the way here for fun. They saw you on *Toast of the Town* and were completely taken with you. They're in love. You said you wanted to be the biggest entertainer in the country, well, this is the last stop to make that happen!"

Her own television show, something no other Negro woman had ever done? The idea thrilled and terrified her in equal measure.

"Every week? A show every week?" she murmured, staring up at the DuMont sign, the enormity of it looming above her like an omen.

Isa placed a steadying hand on Hazel's arm. "Hazel, you've wanted this. You earned this. You've dominated every stage you've touched. This is just another stage—and it's one the whole country will see."

Inside, a young assistant greeted them, her blue eyes wide with nervous energy. "Miss Scott, Mrs. Kloukowsky, they're ready for you." She led them down a gleaming corridor that stretched like a runway. The lights buzzed softly overhead as the scent of fresh ink and warm circuitry filled the air. Hazel felt electricity vibrating through the walls.

"Remember who you are," Isa whispered.

The conference room was large but intimate, its walls lined with bookshelves and framed renderings of studio sets. Three men in immaculate suits rose as they entered, their smiles polite but their eyes cool and measuring. The scent of leather, faint cigar smoke, and ambition clung to the air.

"Miss Scott," said the tallest of the three. None of the men extended their hands to shake hers. "We've followed your career, and your performance on Ed Sullivan's show was simply outstanding."

Hazel nodded, forcing steadiness into her voice despite the whirlwind inside her. "Thank you."

The men gestured for them to sit. The leather chair creaked under Hazel as she settled, her spine straight despite the unease curling at the edges of her confidence.

The youngest of the trio leaned forward, his enthusiasm evident. "As I'm sure Mrs. Kloukowsky has told you, we're launching into television broadcasting, and we want you to host your own show—a fifteen-minute slot, airing every Friday night."

The words rang in Hazel's head like an unfamiliar melody she wasn't sure she could play.

Isa, always poised, leaned in. "You mentioned some unique operational plans. Care to elaborate?"

The third man, shorter but sharp-eyed, interlaced his fingers. "Unlike other networks, we plan to sell advertising to multiple sponsors rather than just one. That means fewer restrictions for producers like Miss Scott and more creative freedom."

Hazel's back straightened. "Television is still unproven," she said carefully. "How do you plan to compete with NBC and CBS?"

The tall man smiled slightly, like he'd been waiting for that question. "Television is the future, Miss Scott. We're counting on groundbreaking talent—like you—to help build that future. No sketches, no variety acts. Just your music and your voice."

The first.

That word followed her everywhere. She had been the first in nightclubs, in concert halls, on film sets where she fought tooth and nail to keep her dignity intact. And now here it was again, pressing against her chest, as heavy as ever.

No sketches, no acts. Just you.

Her voice barely above a whisper, she said, "This means a great deal to me." Then, stronger, "Thank you."

Isa eyed Hazel, measuring her response.

Hazel inhaled deeply.

"Let's do it."

The executives' faces lit up. Contracts were mentioned, details laid out, but Hazel barely heard them. Her mind was already racing ahead, the shape of the show forming in the space between fear and excitement.

Later, outside, Isa hailed a cab, glancing over her shoulder. "Well?"

Hazel looked back at the DuMont sign, its letters bright against the early evening sky.

"I think I'm scared out of my mind," she admitted.

Isa chuckled. "Good. That means you care. But, Hazel," Isa continued, her tone softer, "this is your moment. Television is about to change everything, and you're leading the charge."

A new stage. A new fight.

And this time, the whole world would be watching.

IT TOOK NEARLY five months of planning, but the time was here.

The studio lights dimmed as the countdown for her debut began. *"Five . . . four . . . three . . ."*

Barney, Josephine, Adam, and James sat shoulder to shoulder in the studio's front row. Behind the glass, the director pointed, and the screen flickered to life.

The Hazel Scott Show opened with a soft, shimmering shot of the New York skyline at dusk—the camera panning slowly across glowing rooftops and twinkling lights before cutting to the show's set: an elegant replica of a penthouse terrace, complete with wrought-iron railings, potted palms, and a soft breeze teased by a hidden fan.

Then came the sound—the opening chords of "Tea for Two."

Hazel sat at the baby grand like she was born there, framed in soft lighting that gave her the glow of a woman fully at ease in her element. Her satin gown was the color of champagne. Diamond earrings sparkled beneath her neatly coifed hair.

Her fingers glided across the keys with a lighthearted bounce, her shoulders relaxed, her smile calm but alive. The melody skipped into a playful rhythm, and the camera slowly pushed in, finding her face as she lifted her eyes and spoke directly to the camera.

"Hello, I'm Hazel Scott," she said.

There was no stiffness in her voice, no trace of fear. Just clarity and warmth. As though she'd done it a hundred times before.

She played a medley of American standards and European classics with ease, folding in a spiritual that left even the studio techs in awe. Each transition flowed like water. Her fingers moved with a dancer's grace, but it was the depth behind her notes that held everyone still.

When the final note faded and the camera dissolved into the end credits, the room erupted in applause.

"You're a *natural*," James said when Hazel made her way over to her friends.

"Elegant, brilliant," Barney added, clearly choked up as he dabbed his eyes with a handkerchief.

Josephine's eyes were shining. "You are the very picture of dignity. What *white America* needs to see."

Adam was the last to greet her. He let the moment hang in the air before speaking. "I always knew you'd shine," he said, his face filled with pride. "But this is different. This show will be something special. You've gone out into the world. Now the world comes to *you*."

CHAPTER 47

July 1950

The aroma of fresh coffee drifted between Adam and Hazel as they sat at the breakfast table. The morning sun peeked through the curtains. Adam had his nose buried in *The New York Times*. A photo of helmeted soldiers charging up a hill dominated the spread.

"Paul Robeson has lost all good sense." Adam's voice cut through the quiet as he folded the paper and slapped it flat on the table. "He was speaking at Madison Square Garden, urging Negroes to avoid going to war. Yes, we should fight for freedom here at home, but in this hour of crisis, we need to stand with our nation."

Hazel marveled at how he could shift from radical to patriot in the same breath, adapting to whatever role the moment demanded. She set her coffee cup down. Adam's words swirled around her, but her mind wandered to the stack of letters she had been sorting through—messages from viewers of *The Hazel Scott Show*. They came from across the country, written in elegant cursive or rushed, uneven print. Most were thank-you notes, praising her for bringing poise and dignity to their screens.

You've become a beacon of grace and dignity for Negro women every-where, one letter read.

She traced her fingers over the neatly inked lines. She felt like she was making a tangible difference. Her show wasn't just entertainment; it was a platform, a weapon to reshape perceptions of her people.

But another letter caught her eye. Its typed, cold print stood in stark contrast to the warmth of the others. She pulled it out of the envelope.

You think you're doing something because you're not playing a mammy role, but you're perpetuating the stereotype that colored women are just sexpots. You think your European gowns make you elegant? You are a doll, a toy for white men.

Hazel froze. She read the letter again, the sting sinking deeper each time.

Finally, she couldn't hold it in. "Adam . . ." Her voice faltered. "I got this letter." Her hand trembled slightly as she held up the paper. "This woman says I'm perpetuating stereotypes, that I'm just a . . . doll for white men's entertainment."

Adam dismissed it with a wave of his hand. "You're taking that seriously?"

Her shoulders stiffened. "It's not just this one letter." She held up another letter she'd tossed aside earlier. "They think I'm . . . selling out. That I'm not doing enough for the race."

Adam sighed and leaned back, the chair creaking. "Hazel, we're in the middle of a war with North Korea. Truman's waging a war against Communism. Do you know they arrested W.E.B. Du Bois! He's eighty-three, for Christ's sake, and they threw him in jail for handing out peace petitions." He shook his head. "So, forgive me if I don't have time to worry about whether some stranger doesn't like your dress."

The casual dismissal cut deep. "You think this isn't real for me?"

Adam let out a long sigh. "I didn't say that. I'm just aggravated about this article on Paul. I'd expect more from a member of the Talented Tenth," he added, referencing W.E.B. Du Bois's idea of a college-educated Black elite that would lead the race forward.

Hazel's eyes narrowed. "Can you focus on *this* member of the Talented Tenth?" she said, pointing to herself. "Your wife."

Adam let out a chuckle. "Talent alone doesn't make you part of the Talented Tenth."

She stared at him incredulously before speaking. "What did you just say?"

Adam looked up, clearly regretting his words, but too proud to retract them. "You know what I mean. The educated elite." He shrugged, trying to soften the blow. "You're gifted, Hazel. No one's denying that. But you didn't go to college."

"So because I don't have a degree, I don't qualify? You think Du Bois meant only professors and politicians? Not artists? Not activists who use their platform to speak truth to power?"

"Hazel—"

"I speak seven languages, Adam. I've broken barriers. I've risked everything to fight for what's right, in my own way. But to you, I'm just some girl with a piano and a pretty face."

"That is not what I'm saying," he replied. "This fight—it's political. Strategic. We need leaders who can sit at the table with lawmakers, write policy, influence institutions. That's what Du Bois meant. The Talented Tenth would be the scholars, thinkers, planners—"

"The *respectable* ones," she cut in, bitter. "The ones who went to Hampton or Howard or Morehouse College. Who write editorials and wear three-piece suits. But what about the rest of us, Adam? What about the people onstage, in the pulpit, in the clubs, using their art and voices to reach the ones those boardrooms will never touch? My battlefield looks different. And just because I didn't earn a degree doesn't mean I haven't earned my place."

He pushed his chair back abruptly, the harsh scrape of wood on the floor echoing in the room. "And I'm out there in Washington, fighting real battles! Not worrying about whether some white woman thinks you look too pretty on TV."

Hazel stood, her breath catching in her throat. "Maybe if you cared about the smaller battles, you wouldn't be losing the big ones." She knew he was still angry about his "Powell Amendment" being shot down, which was legislation that he'd introduced that would ban federal funds from being used in segregated institutions.

Her comment stopped him. His jaw tightened and a flicker of pain crossed his face. He snatched his jacket from the chair and shrugged it on with sharp, jerky movements. "I don't have time for this," he muttered, heading for the door.

"Of course you don't," she said quietly, more to herself than to him. The door slammed shut, leaving the room achingly silent.

For a long moment, Hazel sat motionless, staring at the door. Finally, she picked up the letter again.

The words *you are a doll, a toy for white men* burned into her mind. She crumpled the paper and tossed it into the trash.

HAZEL PUSHED THROUGH the heavy doors of DuMont Studios, her heels clicking sharply against the tile floor. The usual bustle of the production crew filled the air—electricians adjusting lights, sound engineers fine-tuning levels, and designers making last-minute tweaks to the set. But none of it could drown out the words still echoing in her mind from five days ago.

You are a doll, a toy for white men . . .

The words had followed her into the studio. She inhaled trying to shake off the lingering doubt. She had a show to run.

"Morning, Miss Scott." The receptionist greeted her with a wide smile, but Hazel only managed a distracted nod as she made her way to the conference room, where the day's production meeting was already underway.

Announcer Gloria Lucas glanced up from her notepad. "Hazel, there you are. We were just going over the lineup for tonight."

Her trumpeter, Max Roach, leaned back in his chair, twirling a drumstick between his fingers. "We were thinking of opening with 'Chopsticks,' jazzed up, of course," he said. "A little fun before we hit the heavy stuff."

Charles Mingus, who played the bass in her band, let out a low chuckle. "Then we slide into 'The Man I Love'—classic, but with a twist. I reworked the arrangement last night. Should give it a new edge."

Hazel set her coffee cup down with a quiet clink, scanning the set list in front of her. Normally, she'd have been thrilled. The show had become a cultural touchstone and was now beamed into living rooms three nights a week. But today, doubt gnawed at her.

"Are you okay?" Gloria asked.

"I took some of the fan mail home to go through. And let's just say it's a little disheartening." Hazel slid into her seat. "Some think I'm not doing enough, others think I'm doing too much."

Charlie exhaled, shaking his head. "That's the price of being visible. You're showing folks something they never thought they'd see—a colored woman with power, with elegance, commanding a national audience. You're changing the world with music. Everyone isn't going to appreciate that."

"I just want it to matter." She sighed.

Max grinned. "It does. And tonight, you're gonna do what you always do and remind them why."

A knock at the door signaled it was time. The floor manager poked his head in. "Hazel, you need to get dressed."

Hazel straightened and met the gazes of her team—Gloria, Max, Charles.

She stood, shoulders back, chin high. "I'll see you on set. Let's give them a show they'll never forget."

CHAPTER 48

August 1950

The humid August air clung to everything like a damp shroud. Hazel had opened all the windows, hoping for a breeze, but the relentless heat refused to budge.

"I'm hot, Mommy," Skipper said, pausing from his toys to wipe sweat from his brow.

Hazel picked up the cool, damp towel she'd been using all afternoon and gently dabbed his forehead.

"I know, my love. Daddy's sending someone to fix the window unit later today," she said. They were one of the few families in Harlem to even own an air-conditioning unit, and the stupid thing wouldn't work.

Mrs. Hughes stepped in. "Come on, Skipper. A cool bath will help."

Grateful for the reprieve, Hazel turned her attention back to a new set list she had been reviewing for her show. She traced the titles with her fingers, mentally preparing for the rhythms and chords ahead. The moment of calm was interrupted by the sharp chime of the doorbell.

When she opened it, Josephine stood on the threshold, her face ashen, her breath uneven. A small pamphlet trembled in her hands.

"Jody?" Hazel stepped aside, ushering her in. "What on earth is the matter?"

Josephine's eyes darted around the room as if expecting someone—or something—to emerge from the shadows. She thrust the pamphlet toward Hazel.

"It's bad," Josephine said.

"What's bad?"

Josephine gestured toward the pamphlet. When Hazel saw the name Counterattack, a nervous jolt shot through her. The publication's infamous *Red Channels* list had been tearing through the entertainment industry, branding artists as Communist sympathizers and ending careers in a single stroke.

Hazel skimmed the pages, her pulse quickening as familiar names leaped off the paper. Paul Robeson. Lena Horne. Then she froze.

"'Hazel Scott,'" she read aloud, her voice tight. "'Communist sympathizer . . . attempting to subvert American citizens via TV, film, and radio.'"

The words struck her like a clenched fist to the gut. Her breath hitched, and her knees buckled as she dropped onto the couch.

"They've named me?" she whispered, her fingers tightening around the pamphlet. A rush of heat flooded her chest as anger and disbelief collided. "They're calling me a Communist? This is madness. I hardly even *speak* on the show—I *play*."

Josephine shook her head, her expression grim. "I don't even think it's about the show. They're saying you're involved in Communist organizations and unions."

"That's a lie."

"I know that." Josephine's mouth twisted. "They're going after anyone whose voice carries. Langston, W.E.B.—they're all in here too. It's open season on Negroes who refuse to stay in their place. They don't care who they ruin."

Before Hazel could say anything more, the front door creaked open. Adam stepped inside. "Hello . . ." His words trailed off as his eyes darted between Hazel's stricken face and Josephine's tear-streaked cheeks.

"What happened?" he asked, setting his briefcase down.

Hazel's hands shook as she held the pamphlet toward him. He scanned the words.

"This is *bullshit*," he growled. "McCarthy and Nixon are treating this like a game. They're throwing names around like dice in an alley."

"People are losing everything, Adam," Josephine said, her voice hollow. "Their jobs, their homes—some have even taken their own lives."

Hazel's spine stiffened, the initial shock giving way to a searing fury. "I don't care about Communism. But I *do* care about justice. About our people's rights. And I'll be damned if I let fear silence me."

Adam exhaled sharply, raking a hand through his hair. "They've been waiting to drag me down, and now they've found the perfect way in."

Hazel's eyes flashed. "*This* isn't about you, Adam."

"The hell it isn't," he shot back. "You being labeled a Commie puts a target on both of our backs."

Hazel wanted to remind him that he was the one who stirred the pot. But he was a man, a powerful man. She was a colored woman and a much easier target.

"I want to testify. Don't they hold hearings?"

"Absolutely not," Adam said with finality.

"So what am I supposed to do?" Hazel asked.

"You stay quiet," Josephine pleaded. "Let your team issue a statement and move on."

Adam nodded, rubbing his temples. "She's right. These hearings aren't about truth. They want a circus. And once they drag you in, Hazel, you don't walk out the same."

Hazel shot up from the couch. "So I say nothing and let them paint me as whatever the hell they want? Let them rewrite my life?" She paced the room, her anger crackling like a live wire. "No. If I stay silent, I *am* guilty in their eyes."

Adam sighed. "You think walking into that chamber will prove anything? You think reason will win against men who've already decided your fate?"

Hazel stopped pacing, her hands curled into fists. "If I don't fight, it tells them they *can* do this. That they can drag our names through the mud, destroy our careers, and we'll just bow our heads like good little Negroes." She lifted her chin. "I *will* testify."

Josephine shook her head. "Hazel, you're walking into a lion's den."

"Then I'll face them with my head held high."

"They'll devour you." Adam's mouth pressed into a hard line, his frustration simmering just below the surface. "Hazel. Think. Once you sit before that committee, there's no undoing it."

She squared her shoulders, her gaze steady. "I'm doing it."

CHAPTER 49

September 1950

The morning air was deceptively cool as Hazel stood before the United States Capitol. She adjusted the collar of her tailored black suit, hoping its simplicity masked the nerves coiled beneath her composed exterior. Modest pearls adorned her neck, and her makeup was understated. Every detail had been chosen to project restraint and respectability.

Beside her, Josephine moved with measured steps, her face drawn with worry. She'd insisted on being by Hazel's side. Ever since news of the hearings broke last month, reporters had been following Hazel, pummeling her with questions, and Josephine had gone into protective mode.

"Are you sure about this?" Josephine asked as they stood in front of the chambers. "Once you step in, there's no going back."

"I'm positive," Hazel replied without hesitation. Even though Adam had made the calls for her to testify and had helped her prepare, Hazel was under no illusion. This was the House Un-American Activities Committee—a room full of men determined to break spirits and ruin lives.

Reporters swarmed them as they ascended the steps, hurling questions like stones.

"Mrs. Powell, are you a Communist?"

"Do you support Soviet sympathizers?"

"How do you respond to being named in *Red Channels*?"

Hazel kept her head high, her expression unyielding. Every flash of a camera and shouted question felt like a jab, but she didn't falter. Part of her wished Adam were by her side, but they had agreed. *This was her fight to lead. And she would.*

The hearing room was stark, cold, and packed to capacity. Hazel took her seat at the table seated at the U-shaped center, facing the twelve white men. Her back never touched the chair's spine. Her fingers clutched the typed statement she had revised again and again in the dark hours of the night.

Behind the committee, a cluster of cameramen adjusted their equipment, the heat of their lights already bearing down on her. Hazel glanced up briefly, not at the cameras, but at the men watching her.

Congressman John S. Wood, the chairman, banged his gavel with unnecessary force. His voice filled the chamber—loud, patronizing, full of Southern drawl.

"This session of the House Un-American Activities Committee is now in order," he announced, his eyes narrowing as they landed on Hazel. "Mrs. Hazel Powell," he began, drawing out her name, "your voluntary appearance before this committee is not customary, but it has been granted as an act of generosity on our part out of respect for our colleague, your husband."

Hazel nodded stiffly, tamping down the indignation bubbling inside her. She knew Adam had threatened to cancel his scheduled campaign speeches if they didn't allow her the chance to be heard, but she needed them to see her on her own merit, not as Adam's wife.

Senator Joseph McCarthy leaned forward, his tone dripping with politeness. "Mrs. Powell," he began, smiling for the cameras, "you've been named as a Communist sympathizer in *Red Channels*. How do you respond to these allegations?"

He spoke as though he were the star of the show, playing to the audience with calculated theatrics. Hazel met his gaze squarely.

"Senator, I am not a Communist," she stated clearly. "I have never been a member of the Communist Party, nor have I ever tried to subvert American citizens. My work has always been about fighting for racial justice and equality."

She unfolded her paper and took a calming breath. "If I may, Mr. Chairman, I have a prepared statement that is rather lengthy. May I read a few highlights, with the understanding that the full statement be included in the committee's records and printed as if it had been read in full?"

Congressman Wood gave a curt nod, though impatience was written across his face.

Hazel straightened her shoulders and began.

"I come before you today not as a defendant, but as a loyal American citizen, a performer, and an artist who has been unjustly accused. I condemn *Red Channels* and Counterattack, challenging their methods, their listings, and their very existence. The accusations against me are baseless and false. Seven of the nine listings are false." That was what outraged her most. She was having to defend her name from unwarranted accusations.

She continued. "I have never even heard of two of the nine listings. Three others, I refused to join. One advertised I was a guest of honor at an event I never attended. One used my name three years after I performed there. Another was a series of benefits for orphaned children. And yet another was an appearance at the behest of my employers. As a performer, you work for hire and rarely know the political affiliations of the organizers or organizations you played for."

The words came steadily, but she felt the room brimming with tension. They wanted her to falter, to give them something incriminating.

When she finished, Congressman McCarthy leaned back, his expression smug. "You have a close relationship with the proprietor of Cafe Society," he said slowly. "A known hotspot for leftist activity. How do you explain that?"

"I explain it by stating the truth," Hazel replied. "Cafe Society is a place where people of all races come together to enjoy music and art. It promotes equality and justice—values central to the American dream. My association with the owner, Barney Josephson, is based on our mutual commitment to these principles."

Unmoved, Congressman McCarthy pressed on, looking at his notes, then back at her. "How did you end up playing at a fundraiser for the Communist-backed city councilman Benjamin Davis?"

"I don't recall how that appearance came about," Hazel said, her voice steady. "Most likely, it was arranged by Mr. Josephson, my employer, who often lent my name and time to events without consulting me."

Congressman Burr Harrison leaned forward, his voice thick with disdain. "Mrs. Powell, is the listing false, or is the information false?"

"The information is false, and the listing is unjustified," Hazel answered firmly.

Congressman Harrison scowled. "I don't agree that it's a false listing," he snapped.

Hazel's temper flared. "It doesn't matter what you agree with. It only matters what is," she countered. She took a deep breath, then calmly added, "Let me put it this way: If you said I had two heads, does that make me have two heads? Does that give *Red Channels* the right to publish that I have two heads?"

The room stiffened. Congressman Harrison flushed red, sputtering, "They make no bones of the fact that they do not evaluate the listings."

"They simply prepare a blacklist," Hazel retorted sharply. "Are we ready to say, in effect, that Communists have taken over the whole country except for a few self-appointed patriotic virgins, such as the gentlemen of Counterattack? I, for one, am not ready to hand over America's entertainment industry to Moscow."

She paused, her voice resonating through the silent room. "Our country needs its artists now more than ever. We cannot let them be written off by the slanders of little and petty men."

The room fell silent as Hazel sat back, her words hanging heavy in the air. The committee members exchanged looks, their faces unreadable. Hazel knew she had given them something to think about, but she doubted their minds would change.

CHAPTER 50

October 1950

H azel stood at the dining room sideboard, absentmindedly stacking dishes from the night before. The remnants of Skipper's schoolwork were still spread across the table—pencil smudges on crumpled paper, an open arithmetic book, a half-eaten apple browning at the edges. She barely registered the task at hand, her movements mechanical.

The bitter aroma of coffee floated in the air, but the cup she had poured for herself sat untouched, its surface now cooled and undisturbed. Across the room, *The Washington Post* lay discarded on the sideboard, the bold headline taunting her: "Hazel Scott Denies Communist Links." Beside it, an unopened issue of the *New York Journal-America* rested ominously, thick with yet another column of names compiled through suspicion and paranoia. She didn't need to read it to know the damage inside.

The sharp chime of the doorbell sliced through the quiet. Hazel flinched. When she opened the door, Barney stood on the other side. No smile, no greeting—just a grim expression and sagging shoulders. In his hands, a thick stack of papers, gripped like they might slip away if he loosened his hold.

"Hazel, I need to speak with you." His voice was heavy, leaving no room for pleasantries. He stepped inside before she could respond.

Hazel closed the door behind him and led him into the living room, where sunlight streamed in through the lace curtains, casting fractured patterns across the rug. Barney didn't sit. Instead, he turned on his heel, exhaling sharply before handing her the top sheet from the pile.

The familiar DuMont Networks letterhead glared up at her. The words beneath it sent a chill down her spine.

"Isa asked me to deliver this," Barney said, his voice tinged with defeat. "She's out of the country. Hazel . . . DuMont is pulling the plug. The sponsors don't want to risk being tied to someone accused of Communism, no matter how baseless the claims."

Hazel's fingers tightened around the paper. The quiet in the room grew thick, pressing against her chest. Then, with slow, deliberate movements, she sat down on the edge of the couch, the letter crinkling in her grip.

She had known things could get bad. But she hadn't anticipated this.

Her show—her hard-earned place in history—was gone.

She swallowed hard, blinking back the sting in her eyes.

"My show is getting canceled?" Her voice came out barely above a whisper. "It's not even eight months old."

Barney nodded. "Yes. I'm sorry."

The shock gave way to a flood of emotions—anger, disbelief, and fear crashing over her like waves. "This makes no sense," she said. "The media has been relentless."

Barney sank into a chair, his own face drawn with exhaustion. "I get it, Hazel. Believe me, I do. My brother Leon was one of the first casualties of this witch hunt. He invoked his Fifth Amendment rights, refused to testify, and ended up with a yearlong prison sentence for contempt."

Hazel began pacing, her hands clenched into fists. "They're trying to destroy me, Barney. My career, my reputation—everything I've worked for." She stopped and turned toward him, her eyes blazing. "And for what? Lies and fear?"

Barney's expression shifted, his sadness giving way to something sharper—hurt. "Hazel," he said quietly, "this isn't just about you. You dragged me into this."

She froze. "I was just answering their question."

"You mentioned my name during your testimony," he said, his voice tight. "Explicitly. They're digging into my venues, scaring off my customers. Everything I've built is at risk. Why would you do that after all I've done for you?"

"They asked me . . . I didn't mean—" Hazel stammered. "Barney, I was answering their questions. I was trying to explain how bookings worked. I never intended for this to happen."

"But it did," he said, his voice breaking slightly. "Now Cafe Society's under siege, and they're coming for me. You may not have meant to hurt me, but you did."

"Barney, I'm sorry," Hazel said, stepping toward him.

Barney shook his head, his jaw tight. "Maybe you're willing to lose everything for the sake of your principles, Hazel, but I'm not." He sighed. "I think it's best that we sever our working relationship."

"Barney, don't say that. We've been through so much together. Don't let this tear us apart."

His eyes were glassy with unshed tears. "I've already spoken with Isa. She'll handle all your bookings from now on. I don't see how we can keep working together."

"No, Barney," Hazel pleaded. He was supposed to be like a father to her. Surely he wasn't about to just walk out of her life. "Please. Don't do this."

"I don't think you understand what you've done," he said. "If I lose everything, it'll be because of you."

A hollow ache settled in her chest as he turned and left. And she knew deep down that she'd seen the last of Barney Josephson.

CHAPTER 51

March 1951

The walls of their bedroom seemed to tighten around Adam's words. Hazel ignored her husband's ranting on the telephone as she sat at the vanity, smoothing the satin of her cobalt-blue gown.

She fastened a diamond earring, watching herself in the mirror—watching and waiting. She'd flinched when Mrs. Hughes announced that the accountant was on the phone. That had been twenty minutes ago. Adam still hadn't returned.

When she finally spotted him in the reflection, she exhaled. At least he was dressed—his tailored tuxedo was cut sharp, his bow tie sat perfectly centered. He looked like he belonged on the cover of *Ebony*. But his scowl told another story.

"Hazel, we need to talk about your spending."

His gaze swept over the bedroom, landing on the mink fur draped across the bed. He moved to the dresser, lifting a diamond necklace between his fingers, the stones winking under the chandelier's light.

"How much jewelry does one person need?"

She barely glanced at him, adjusting her second earring with a delicate touch. "It's fine. That's what accountants are for."

"That's not the point," he snapped. "You act like this money will last forever. Your show has been canceled and yes, you still have a lot of money, but that won't always be the case."

She met his gaze in the mirror. "You're one to talk. Fine suits. Fancy cigars. Exquisite cars. But I buy a few furs, and suddenly, I'm the problem?"

Adam's jaw flexed. "That's different."

"Is it?" She reached for her perfume, dabbing a touch behind each ear before turning to face him fully. "I check my finances regularly. No one's robbing me blind." She sighed. "But what's the point of having a husband if I have to worry about my finances?"

Adam opened his mouth, but she had already turned back to the mirror, applying a final stroke of crimson lipstick. He muttered something under his breath, then spun on his heel, leaving behind the embers of his frustration.

Hazel exhaled sharply. Between trying to recover from the shock of losing her show, worrying about Billie, who had been rumored to have returned to using (though she denied it), and preparing for the gala, a financial discussion was the last thing she needed. Tonight was too important for another fight.

By the time they arrived at the Mayflower Hotel, where she was being honored for her efforts in the fight against segregation, Adam's aggravation had settled into a polished veneer. The moment they stepped onto the red carpet, the night erupted into a symphony of flashbulbs and shouting voices. Hazel had mastered this long ago— how to let the lights love her, how to smile with mystery, how to stand in her power. Adam's arm circled her waist, his smile flawless, his grip a touch too tight.

Then, a voice cut through the commotion. "Mr. Powell, would you mind stepping aside for a moment? We'd like to capture Miss Scott on her own."

Hazel felt the tension ripple through Adam's body before he moved. He stepped aside smoothly, the cameras catching only his polished smile—but Hazel saw the clenched jaw, the narrowed eyes, the quiet storm brewing beneath his calm.

She held her pose as the lights flared again. Thankfully, a soft, commanding voice cut through the noise.

"That's quite enough, gentlemen. We need Miss Scott inside."

Mollie Moon was elegant in a floor-length sapphire gown that shimmered like nightfall, her pearl earrings catching the light. The organizer of tonight's Beaux Arts Ball extended a gloved hand toward Hazel.

"Tonight is about celebrating excellence," she said with a smile. "And your brilliance, Miss Scott, is lighting the way."

Hazel exhaled and followed her inside. The Beaux Arts Ball wasn't just a party. It was the crown jewel of the National Urban League Guild's fundraising season—part costume gala, part political summit, all elegance. Organized by Mollie herself since its founding, the ball brought together Harlem's finest, raising critical funds for the League's education, housing, and civil rights work.

Inside the ballroom, Hazel took in all the elegance in full bloom, justice in sequins, progress in pearls. She and Adam had barely crossed the threshold before Lester Granger, executive director of the Urban League, approached with a broad, genuine smile. His tailored suit was sharp, his eyes thoughtful behind thin glasses.

"You look radiant tonight," he said, taking Hazel's hands in his. "Harlem is proud of you."

Hazel's smile deepened, warmed by the acknowledgment—but behind her, she could still feel Adam's eyes.

Mr. Granger turned to Adam. "Congressman Powell, pleasure to see you."

Adam grasped his hand with practiced ease, his own polished smile slipping into place. They exchanged the usual pleasantries, their words light, yet beneath them, Hazel could feel Adam's energy had shifted.

Mollie handed Hazel a piece of paper. "This is the program for tonight. Just wanted you to quickly review."

Adam leaned in and studied the program, his fingers grazing the small of Hazel's back. The simple act might've been reassuring—if not for the way his grip tightened as he read the program.

"What's my role here?" he asked.

Mollie chuckled lightly, oblivious to the undercurrent in his voice. "Oh, we just need you to make sure Hazel gets to the stage safely in that gorgeous gown." She gestured toward the flowing train of silk pooling at Hazel's feet.

Adam's jaw flexed. "So, I'm just here to make sure she doesn't trip?"

Mollie's smile didn't waver. "It's an important job. Every star needs someone to help them shine."

The words hit—Adam stiffened.

"I'll take you backstage for some more interviews, Miss Scott. Congressman Powell, we'll get you to your seat." Mollie turned, waving over a stunning Puerto Rican woman standing near the entrance. "This is Miss Yvette Flores," Mollie said, her tone light. "She'll make sure you're situated."

Yvette moved toward them. She had the kind of poise that made men straighten their ties, without realizing it. Her skin gleamed under the soft lighting, her long hair cascading down her back. The drape of her dress skimmed her figure just enough to leave an impression.

"This way, Congressman." Her voice was smooth as warmed honey.

Adam hesitated for only a second before following the woman from backstage.

The night moved forward in a blur of handshakes and murmured congratulations, but Hazel couldn't ignore the way Yvette lingered near their table. Her presence was as deliberate as a carefully placed chess piece. She leaned in just a little too close between Adam and Hazel, her perfume heavy in the air.

"Let me know if you need anything, Congressman Powell," she said. Then, in a lower tone, "By the way, I hope I'm not being too forward, but if you're ever looking for an assistant or secretary, I'd love to apply."

Hazel's fingers curled against her palm, the diamond on her ring biting into her skin.

"So she's just going to flirt right in my face?" she muttered when the woman walked away, her hips swaying.

"Don't start," Adam warned, his eyes locked on the stage. His voice was even, but Hazel didn't miss the tension threading through it. "Focus on your moment." He gestured toward the glittering crowd. "Since tonight is all about you."

The words stung, and Hazel wasn't sure if it was the underlying resentment or the way he made it sound like she'd done something wrong by being honored.

Hazel was grateful when Mollie took the stage, that just moved them that much closer to the night being over.

"Ladies and gentlemen, tonight we honor not only a legendary musician but a fearless advocate for justice. In 1948, Miss Scott walked out of a performance at the University of Texas at Austin when they refused to allow Negroes and whites to sit together. And in 1950, in Pasco, Washington, she faced a humiliation our people know all too well. She and a companion were denied service at a diner—because they were Negroes.

"But what did Hazel Scott do?" Mollie paused, her gaze sweeping across the crowd. "She sued. She won. And she gave every penny of that victory to the NAACP."

Applause thundered through the ballroom.

"That case in Washington helped Negroes challenge racial discrimination in Spokane. It inspired civil rights organizations to pressure lawmakers and we believe the state will soon pass the Public Accommodations Act. Her courage made that possible." Mollie's voice was reverent. "We could go on and on about this fearless woman. But instead, let's welcome our honoree—Mrs. Hazel Scott."

As her name rang out, Hazel rose and a wave of applause crashed over her.

Adam reached for her hand, guiding her toward the stage as instructed. His touch was steady, his arm offering support. But when she thanked him publicly, his smile felt forced.

By the time they got home, the dam burst.

"So you're just going to keep an attitude with me all night like I did something wrong?" Hazel dropped her evening bag onto the console table with a sharp *clack*, then turned to face him.

Adam stood near the bar cart, his shoulders tight with frustration as he yanked at his bow tie, ripping it loose with a force that spoke louder than his words.

"Do they even know who I am?" His voice was laced with the bitterness that had been simmering all evening. "I've fought for civil rights, stood on the front lines for our people, and tonight I was just some damn footnote to your fame." He tossed the tie onto the chair, his hands moving to unfasten his cufflinks with quick, jerky motions.

Hazel exhaled. "Adam, tonight wasn't about you," she said. "It was about my work, my contributions."

His laugh was short and humorless. "I *know* what you've done, Hazel." He shook his head, pacing the length of their bedroom. "I've watched you fight, push back, refuse to bend. I *love* that about you."

He gestured toward her, his frustration spilling over. "But don't act like tonight wasn't designed to make me feel small. Your career, your image. What about everything I've sacrificed for the sake of your career?"

She crossed her arms, resisting the urge to throw something—her shoes, a pillow, *something*—just to match the sharp edge of her anger.

"And I haven't sacrificed anything? Do you think it's easy, always being in the public eye, always striving to be perfect? We both made sacrifices, Adam. That's what marriage is," she snapped.

"I felt like a fool tonight," he said.

"I didn't put that program together," she shot back. "I didn't tell them what to say. I just showed up, accepted my award, and tried to enjoy one damn night where I wasn't being questioned about my place in this world."

His jaw tightened, the muscle ticking just beneath the surface. He stepped closer, his voice dropping, but not losing its intensity. "You think I don't see it? The way they look at me now? Like I'm just your husband. The man standing *behind* Hazel Scott."

She sucked in a sharp breath.

"Maybe that's because tonight, you *were*," she said.

The air between them went still.

Adam stared at her, something dark flickering behind his eyes. He scoffed softly, running a hand over his head. "Right." His voice was quieter now, but no less dangerous. "That's just the type of man you want, one who will stand *behind* you."

Hazel was tired of making herself smaller to accommodate his ego. Tired of softening her success just so it wouldn't bruise his pride.

"I don't know how we got here," she muttered, falling into a chair in the corner.

When he finally responded, his voice was hollow. "And yet here we are."

He snatched his keys up and walked out the front and shut the door behind him.

Not slammed.

Just shut.

And somehow that felt worse.

CHAPTER 52

April 1951
Harlem, New York

Billie sauntered into the dimly lit restaurant, her eyes sweeping the room with purpose until they landed on Hazel. Her small, enigmatic smile carried a weight that Hazel couldn't quite place. Something about Billie was different tonight—a heaviness in her expression that contrasted sharply with the lively buzz of the room. At least she looked sober, even if the mischievous glint that usually sparkled in her eyes seemed to have been replaced by something far more somber.

"Hey, Haze," Billie said as she slid into the seat across from Hazel. She looked like the old Billie tonight, her dark hair styled in soft waves, her lips painted a deep scarlet, her nails meticulously manicured.

"Hey, Lady Day," Hazel replied, offering a smile meant to lighten the mood. Billie had called and asked her to meet for dinner, and Hazel was thankful for the opportunity, but this seemed like it was more than a catch-up meeting.

Billie sighed and glanced away, her shoulders slumping slightly. "You know I care about you, Haze. And I try not to meddle in other folks' business, especially when it comes to love."

Hazel frowned, a knot of unease tightening in her stomach. "Okay, what's going on?"

Billie reached into her purse, pulled out a folded newspaper, and slid it across the table. Hazel's eyes zeroed in on the gossip column. There, in black and white, was a photograph of her husband sitting at the Stork Club in his usual sharp suit. A redheaded white woman was leaning in far too close, her hand resting familiarly on Adam's arm.

"That bastard," Hazel hissed, shoving the paper away as though it scorched her fingertips. She grabbed her fur coat from the chair and stood abruptly. "When he gets back from DC—"

Billie reached out, her hand gently wrapping around Hazel's wrist. Sympathy was etched in her eyes. "Hazel, Adam isn't in DC."

Hazel looked at her friend, confused. "What? Yes, he is. He's been there for two weeks."

Billie shook her head slowly, her gaze clouded with concern. "No, Haze. He's been here, staying at a Greenwich Village hotel. Doris Gamser saw him last night."

"Greenwich Village?" Hazel repeated, confusion mixing with anger. "What the hell would he be doing there?"

Billie hesitated. "Doris has seen him there a few weekends now. She said he'll probably be there tonight." Doris was a good friend of Billie's and Hazel was doubtful that she would carry gossip if she hadn't seen it with her own two eyes.

"Tonight?" Hazel's mind raced as she slid back into her seat. Adam had even skipped church this past Sunday because he had pressing matters in DC. "Why would he lie about this?"

"I figured you'd ask." Billie stood and smoothed her dress. "Let's go find out."

They left the restaurant and slid into Billie's Cadillac.

The drive passed in tense silence, Harlem's broad boulevards and brownstones gradually falling away as they headed downtown. By the time they crossed into the Village, the rhythm of the city had changed—quaint town houses and tiny cafés replacing Harlem's jazz clubs and corner stores.

Billie finally pulled up in front of a nondescript building with dark windows and no sign. "Here we are," she announced, cutting the engine.

Hazel squinted at the entrance. "What's this place? It doesn't even have a name."

Billie hesitated. "It's one of those spots people go when they don't want to be seen. Married folks. Public figures. Folks with secrets."

Hazel's stomach tightened. She'd heard of clubs like that—quiet, exclusive, designed for discretion. A place where affairs unfolded under low lights and no one asked questions.

"Adam wouldn't—" she began, but the words died in her throat.

Billie handed her a pair of sunglasses. "Let's go see if Adam would."

Inside, the air was thick with cigarette smoke and soft jazz. Low lights glowed over velvet booths where couples leaned in too close. Hazel scanned the room, her eyes sweeping every shadowed face, heart pounding with the fear of recognition.

Billie stopped suddenly and nodded toward the corner. "Over there."

Hazel followed Billie's gesture. There, in a secluded booth, sat Adam. A drink in his hand, he laughed softly with a different woman from the one in the newspaper—this one a blonde—practically sitting in his lap. She wore a tight black dress, her hand resting on Adam's chest. His arm was draped casually over her shoulder, his face inches from hers.

Hazel's fists clenched. "I'm going to kill him," she hissed, stepping forward.

Billie grabbed her arm, her voice low and firm. "Not here, Haze. Don't make a scene."

Hazel seethed. "So, what am I supposed to do? Just stand here and watch?"

Billie's grip tightened. "No. You needed to see for yourself. Now file this away. When the time comes, use it."

Hazel stared at Adam, his easy laughter slicing through her. Her stomach churned with a mix of rage and heartbreak.

"Harlem's beloved minister," Hazel scowled.

"Harlem turns a blind eye to his mess 'cause they think what he does for the people is more important than what he does to you," Billie said. "He brings jobs, parades, and pride. So when he breaks your heart, they just call it collateral damage."

"How long am I supposed to put up with this?" Hazel whispered.

"Long enough to get an exit plan? Don't pull the trigger until you have one," Billie replied. "You can't afford the negative publicity."

Hazel did not have a plan, but after what she had seen tonight, she definitely needed to get one.

CHAPTER 53

August 1951

The whispers of infidelity had grown into a widening wedge between Hazel and Adam. Their home now felt like a hollow stage where they played the roles of husband and wife without conviction. Even the little quirks she once adored—the way he hummed while shaving, the careful way he folded his newspaper—had become unbearable reminders of the intimacy they had lost.

It had been four months since the incident at the Greenwich Village club. The anger had long since gone, but not the memory. Every detail burned into her mind—the blond woman, the laughter, the casual way he carried on, like he didn't care about being seen. Like he didn't care about her. The humiliation simmered beneath her skin. It had been hard to pretend, but Adam hadn't come home until a week after that night. By then, her fury had been replaced with a resolve to find a way out.

Then, today, on the front page of *The New York Beat*, was yet another photo of Adam with another woman. More disrespect.

Hazel paced the length of the parlor, one hand trailing along the velvet drapes, the other clutching the edge of her robe. She had never asked questions about their finances. First her mother took care of that, then Adam. She performed, he provided. That was their rhythm. But now she needed to get her head out of the sand—*just in case.*

Hazel reached for the telephone, her fingers hovering over the rotary dial before spinning it decisively.

"Louis Jenkins speaking."

"Louis. It's Hazel."

"Hazel. What a surprise. Everything all right?"

She swallowed. "I need to talk about . . . things. Privately."

There was a pause long enough to let them both feel the weight of what wasn't being said.

"I see," he said. "Do you want to come by the office?"

"No," she said quickly. "Not yet. Just tell me—are my accounts I had before my marriage still in my name?" Because she'd made so much money, Hazel was among the few women who were allowed their own bank accounts.

Louis sighed. "Yes, royalties are still directed to you. Your personal account hasn't been touched in months, but it's there."

Hazel nodded slowly, the information settling in her bones. She hadn't made up her mind yet, not entirely. But she was done being blind.

"And the house, the brownstone?" she asked, her voice even. "Are they in his name?"

"Technically? Both. But you'd need legal advice if—"

She cut him off. "Not yet. I just needed to know."

Louis didn't press. "You have my number. Day or night."

She thanked him and hung up, her hand lingering on the receiver. She was still thinking about Louis's words the next day when Adam strolled in. He set his briefcase down with the practiced ease of a man who had no reason to feel guilty.

"Evening." He had the audacity to be warm and cheerful.

Hazel sat rigid at the dining table, before sliding the newspaper across the table. "You just don't give a damn anymore, do you?"

Adam picked up the paper and his eyes scanned the page. A flicker of annoyance crossed his face as he tossed the paper back onto the table. "Hazel, are you really letting some gossip column get to you? You know they're out to twist everything."

"How do you twist a picture?" That's what he had told her the first time *The New York Beat* ran his picture. She'd let it drop then. She wasn't letting it go now.

Hazel didn't even feel rage anymore. Just disgust. "You don't even try to be discreet. You disrespect me openly, parading your conquests around like I'm blind."

"You're making too much of this. It's not what it looks like. It's politics."

"Politics?" Hazel released a pained laugh. "Is that the best you can do?" The words "Greenwich Village club" burned her tongue. But Billie's advice lingered in her mind. *File this away. You need an exit plan.*

"You know this marriage isn't working, right?" she said calmly.

Adam's face paled, and he stopped just as he was removing his jacket. "Don't make any rash decisions."

"The sooner we admit that, the better off we'll be," she said, before getting up and heading to bed.

Adam climbed into bed next to her an hour later but didn't bother trying to kiss her good night.

Hazel stared at the ceiling, tracing invisible patterns in the plaster. She turned onto her side, hoping that shifting positions might trick her body into sleep, but the space beside her felt like an ocean. Adam was snoring softly, his back to her.

Tears burned at the edges of her eyes, but she refused to let them fall.

With a quiet sigh, Hazel threw back the covers.

Barefoot, she padded down the dimly lit hallway toward the living room. She poured herself a glass of scotch, took a sip, then made her way over to the piano. She sat and let her hands rest on the keys, pausing when the diamond on her finger caught the faint glow of the moonlight.

Hazel had been so happy when Adam slid that ring onto her hand. She had twirled it around her fingers, admired the way it sparkled, believing it was a promise of forever. But now all she saw was a ghost of what once was.

Hazel exhaled slowly, her throat tightening. Then, with deliberate slowness, she slid the ring off and set it on the piano.

It left a pale indentation on her finger. For a moment, she stared at her bare hand.

Then she pressed the keys.

The first few notes were soft and hesitant. The melody had been in her mind for days, waiting for her to find the courage to give it breath. She played quietly at first, but the music swelled, refusing to be contained.

It was sorrow and release.

Adam's footsteps interrupted her moments later. "Hazel," he mumbled. "It's four thirty in the morning."

She kept playing. "I know."

"Do you really have to do this now?"

Her fingers never faltered. "Well, Adam, God is giving me this inspiration. Should I tell Him to come back later?" she said over the music.

He exhaled sharply, a sound of frustration and defeat, maybe. Without another word, he turned and shuffled back to the bedroom.

Hazel didn't stop him.

They had lived this moment too many times for it to hold any new meaning. In the morning, they would pretend none of it had happened. At least that had been the story of their life. Hazel was ready for a different ending.

She played until sunrise. By the time Adam reappeared, fully dressed, she had finally tired.

"Skipper is still asleep. I assume you're not going to church," he said.

"No."

He stared at her for a moment, then walked out without another word. Hazel watched him go, relieved that he hadn't pressed the issue. She couldn't bear the thought of sitting in a pew, pretending to be the devoted wife of the honorable Reverend Adam Clayton Powell Jr. Not anymore.

Later, as she sat at the kitchen table attempting to balance her checking account—a futile exercise—she startled at the phone's shrill ring.

"Hazel, darling," came Isa's cheerful voice when Hazel answered. "Sorry to call you on a Sunday, but I have some wonderful news for you. I've secured you a three-week engagement at the Olympia Theatre in Paris," Isa announced. "And working on some promising French film stuff. It will be magnificent, darling. Please tell me that you won't turn this down."

This must be what they meant by an "on-time God." The very thought of leaving for Paris, of all places, sent a thrill through Hazel. The cobblestone streets, bustling cafés, glittering river lights, the distance—it was exactly what she needed.

"That sounds wonderful," Hazel said. "When can I leave?"

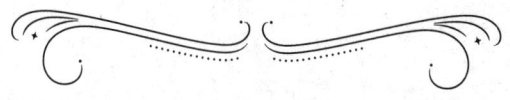

PART
III

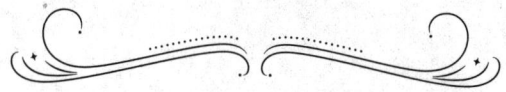

CHAPTER 54

March 1958
Paris, France

For seven years, Hazel had lived the happiness that had eluded her in the States. Paris had become her refuge, where she could live married, yet single. The arrangement between her and Adam had settled into a quiet, unspoken understanding. He roamed the world, moving between Africa, Libya, and Europe, preaching the gospel of Black liberation, making deals, stirring revolution, and indulging in the same philandering that had once broken her heart.

Hazel had long since stopped asking where he was or who he was with. The fury, the betrayal, the hurt—it had burned out, reduced to cold embers she had no desire to reignite. Here, in Paris, she had reclaimed herself. There were no cloying whispers of scandal, no judgmental stares reminding her of what she was supposed to endure as Adam Clayton Powell Jr.'s wife. She was simply Hazel Scott, the pianist, the performer, the woman. And if she chose to let a handsome young Frenchman drape his arm over her shoulder as they strolled along the Champs-Élysées, so be it.

What began as a three-week engagement had stretched into something more permanent, something she could no longer imagine leaving behind. The city had wrapped itself around her. Here she was respected and admired. Her music was celebrated; her presence commanded a room. More importantly, Skipper was with her now.

Having him close had sealed her fate, tethering her to Paris in a way that no contract, no love affair, and certainly no man ever had. She played for him in the evenings, watching as he soaked in the music, his eyes shining with the same appreciation she had once felt as a child when she watched her mother.

Hazel was finally happy. She wasn't sure she'd ever go back to Harlem.

"Hey, fellas," Hazel said, speaking to a group of musicians leaving out of Rupart Studios as she made her way into the modest building tucked into the heart of Montmartre.

"Hey, Hazel, we were wondering if you were coming by today," one of the men said.

"You know it," she said. "Had to get Skipper off. He's going back to New York for *les vacances de Pâques*," she said, then added, "Easter vacation," when the young American looked confused.

"Sorry. Still working on my French," he laughed. "Have a good session, I think there's someone inside waiting on you."

The studio inside was a contradiction—high ceilings and arched windows lent an air of grandeur, but the worn wooden floors, scattered recording equipment, and the faint scent of aged vinyl reminded occupants that music ruled, not appearances. Shelves sagged under the weight of records, and the walls seemed to hum with the echoes of past sessions.

Hazel's first stop was the overflowing bar. She poured herself a glass of brandy, then moved toward the balcony, breaking into a huge smile when she saw James sitting outside. He had moved to Paris before her but had recently left to tend to an ailing relative in the States.

"James Baldwin, when did you get back? And what are you doing here?" she asked.

A cigarette dangled between James's fingers as he leaned back with his feet up on the railing.

"Last week. And I just love being around other artists, so I stopped by the studio."

"Why are you out here by yourself?"

"Been in there shooting the breeze. Came out here to take in some of the night air." James took a long drag from his cigarette. He exhaled slowly, watching the smoke disappear. "Paris is a beauty in an ugly world," he murmured. "Are you loving it?"

Hazel inhaled. In the distance, faint fireworks bloomed like flowers against the dark. "Yes," she said softly. "I finally feel like I've found my way back to music, back to myself. Here, I can breathe. I feel light, unburdened . . . free."

"You sound like a damn greeting card." A sharp voice cut through the moment.

Hazel and James turned in unison.

Billie stood in the doorway. Her mink stole hung off her shoulders. Her skin looked luminous even under the dim glow of the balcony lights. Her eyes, though, still burned with that defiant glint, the same one Hazel had always known—one part mischief, one part warning.

"Oh, my God, Billie!" Hazel rushed forward, pulling her in a tight embrace. The familiar scent of gardenias and whiskey surrounded her.

Billie let out a soft laugh. "Hey, baby," she said, squeezing Hazel before pulling back.

"When did you get in?" Hazel studied her.

"Just now," Billie said, her voice a smoky rasp. She turned toward James, tilting her chin.

"What's shakin', Mr. Baldwin?"

James rose from his chair and pressed a soft kiss to her cheek. "Hello, Lady Day. I can't believe we're all in Paris."

Hazel smiled. Skipper had settled beautifully into his new life as a Parisian—adapting with the ease of someone who had always been meant for more—yet, his absence still hit her like a missing note in a familiar melody. The apartment felt too quiet without him. Having Billie here, at least, would keep her company and dull the sharp ache of missing her son.

Billie drifted toward the balcony railing, peering down at the city unfurling beneath them. Paris stretched out before them—cobblestone streets winding like ribbons, the soft glow of café lanterns flickering. Somewhere near the Place du Tertre, an accordion hummed a melancholy tune, its notes floating into the night like drifting petals.

Billie sighed. "Damn," she whispered. "Ain't she something?"

Hazel nodded, following her gaze. "She really is. You're gonna love it here. For once, I'm not weighed down by expectations. No prying eyes, no whispers behind my back, no one dictating who I should be."

Billie turned and raised an eyebrow, scanning Hazel's loose unkempt hair tucked underneath a wool coppola and the comfortable cotton dress and canvas vest she wore every day. "Yeah, but you're out here living like a Neapolitan fisherman." She laughed.

Hazel let out a small chuckle. Since her European tour had ended, Hazel had been taking life slower. She performed at the world-famous Blue Note in the early years. Now she worked a few gigs until the money stacked up, then retreated into the simple pleasures of Parisian life.

"This is exactly what I love," Hazel said. "My Paris"—she raised her glass in a toast—"is like the very first time you realize you're in love, like the very first time you're kissed."

Billie reached over and took one of James's cigarettes, lit it, and took a long drag. "Well, doesn't that sound like a fairy tale?"

"It's a much better story than what we write in America," James said, standing. He exhaled slowly, as if letting go of a weight. "A Negro man in America is a contradiction—expected to be invisible yet always watched, expected to be grateful yet given nothing. They want us to be proud but punish us if we stand too tall." He shook his head, eyes dark with knowing. "In America, the Negro man fights to prove he is a man. Here, he simply is."

Hazel tilted her head. "And the Negro woman?"

James let out a low chuckle. "She's the strongest of us all. She carries everything—the history, the pain, the men who love her but leave her behind. And yet she still stands, still sings, still loves."

Billie blew a stream of smoke toward the sky. "Damn right."

Hazel swirled the brandy in her glass. James was right. America had written a different story for them. Here, at least, they had the chance to rewrite it.

James flicked his cigarette over the balcony. "Anyway, I'm blowing this joint. Got a book to write and need to let you musicians do your thang."

Hazel smirked. "That book is still giving you hell?"

James sighed, rubbing his forehead. "Hell ain't the word. I've been trying to finish *Another Country* for damn near a decade. I swear, every time I think I have it, it slips through my fingers. It's like trying to hold on to smoke."

Billie leaned back, watching him through narrowed eyes. "That's 'cause you're trying to write the truth, baby. And truth don't like to sit still."

James chuckled, shaking his head. "Perhaps. Or maybe I'm just running from it. I keep thinking about my main character, Rufus, this Negro musician who jumps off the George Washington Bridge, and all the people left picking up the pieces. His white lover. His sister. His friends who think they knew him. But how do you write about that kind of pain without drowning in it?"

"You don't," Hazel said softly. "You just let yourself sink into it until you find the words."

James looked at her, his expression unreadable, then nodded. "Yeah. You might be right." He exhaled, glancing out over the Paris skyline. "Maybe I can get it finished here in Paris."

Hazel raised her glass again. "To Paris, then."

James gave her a small, knowing smile. "To Paris. And to finishing the damn book."

After he left, Hazel noticed a slight tremor in Billie's hands as she flicked ash over the balcony.

"Billie, how are you doing?" Hazel asked.

"Same story, different continent. But don't weep for me." She held out her hand to reveal a glistening diamond on her finger. "Me and Louis got married last month."

Hazel pushed back the words threatening to escape. She'd heard about Billie and Louis McKay, who was rumored to be a mob enforcer. She worried he couldn't be any better than the other men in Billie's life.

Finally, she said, "I'm worried about you, that's all." Hazel took another long swallow of brandy, deciding to forgo any dating advice.

Billie's eyes flashed, and she spun to face Hazel. "And what drink number are you on?" she snapped. "You're one sip away from being a drunk yourself, so don't you judge me. Stop trying to save everybody like you're some kind of saint. Now, let me go get one of those drinks you got."

The outburst left Hazel speechless. Deep down, she knew Billie was right. She had her own problems. Over the years, drinking had become almost as natural as eating.

Hazel followed Billie back inside and was about to continue the conversation when the door to the studio swung open. Greg Harrison, the owner of Rupart, strolled in, his boisterous personality filling the room. Behind him, a young man in a crisp, tailored suit followed, his eyes wide, and eager. He had a guitar slung over his shoulder.

"Whoa, it's not often I have two of America's biggest stars in my studio." Greg grinned. When neither of them said a word, he added, "What's going on?"

Hazel forced a smile. "Nothing."

Billie was already closing off, pouring herself a drink as she slipped back into her armor.

Greg turned to the young man beside him. "Ladies, meet Quincy Jones," he said, gesturing grandly. "He's a new producer in town. Just arrived from the States."

Quincy, who looked like he was barely out of his teens, stepped forward, tipping his hat in an old-fashioned yet effortlessly charming manner. He was tall and lean, with the kind of smooth, unhurried confidence that suggested he had seen just enough of the world to understand it—but not enough to be hardened by it.

His smile was easy. The soft lilt of his voice, touched with the cadence of the South, hinted at a past he might not speak of outright.

There was something calming about him, and for a second, the tension in the room seemed to dissipate.

"I actually had the honor of playing for you in Chicago several years ago, Miss Holiday," Quincy said.

Billie's eyes flickered, and she nodded, though Hazel could tell she didn't remember. Billie had hired local musicians in every city she'd played, so it was plausible. Quincy's gaze lingered on Hazel, and she tilted her head.

"You look familiar," she said.

"We met in Harlem at one of your shows years ago as well. You didn't pay me any mind then, though." He grinned. "Probably because I looked too young."

"And you still do." Greg laughed. "So, how you ladies feel about going out and painting the town?"

Hazel glanced at Billie, but she was already detached, her face a mask of indifference. Hazel's glass felt heavy in her hand, the remnants of brandy turning bitter on her tongue.

"No partying for me," Hazel said, setting the glass down. "Just dropped in for a bit. I'm kind of tired. Think I'll call it a night."

Quincy stepped a little too close. "I can walk you home, if you'd like."

Hazel hesitated but then shrugged, and they left the studio together, walking in silence for a while.

"You know . . ." Quincy finally spoke as they walked toward her apartment on the rue de Miromesnil. "My mother loved to drink. Then one day . . . she just didn't."

Hazel stopped and turned to face him, her voice sharp. "Do I look drunk to you?"

He raised his hands in surrender. "Not at all," he said with a wide smile. "You look . . . beautiful." His words felt genuine, despite the absence of her usual minks and jewelry.

He continued, "But I grew up around every liquor imaginable. I can tell when someone's using a bottle to cover up the cracks."

"I don't need a lecture, Quincy. I'm a grown woman." Hazel folded her arms.

He chuckled softly, his eyes sweeping over her. "That you are."

Hazel smiled slyly, despite herself. "Little boy—"

"Man." Quincy cut her off. "All man. Who appreciates beauty when I see it." He smiled again, disarming her completely. "I'm a great listener. But I'd better get back, or Greg will fire me before I even start." He took her hand and kissed it, his lips warm against her skin. "See you around," he said, before turning and walking back toward the studio.

CHAPTER 55

April 1958

The American Library in Paris carried an air of quiet dignity, the scent of aged paper and rich mahogany weaving through the space. Soft pools of lamplight illuminated the tables, their glow spilling over the neatly lined bookshelves, where shadows curled between the spines. The audience—a mix of expatriates, literary enthusiasts, and curious onlookers—sat in rapt attention as Billie, draped in a clingy violet dress, read aloud from her new memoir, *Lady Sings the Blues.* Her voice carried through the room, wrapping itself around the listeners like a slow-burning melody.

Hazel slipped into the back of the room, careful not to disrupt the moment. Though it released in the States a few months ago, the book had only just made its way to Paris. Hazel had devoured it in a single sitting, the words pulling her into the pages of a life she already knew too well. Yet, as she read, Hazel found that the story danced between truth and embellishment.

From her seat, Hazel studied Billie—the way she swayed ever so slightly, how her fingers trembled against the pages. Her eyes, ringed in dark kohl, were bright yet unfocused, the glassiness betraying more than exhaustion. Hazel had seen Billie in every shade—exultant, broken, untouchable onstage—but this was something else. Her voice slurred at the edges.

The reading ended to thunderous applause. Hands shot into the air as Billie pointed to a woman in the front row.

"You have a question?"

"A comment," the woman corrected her. "Miss Holiday, this book is something else."

Billie chuckled, shifting on her stool. "That about sums it up. But they didn't want my truth at first. Tried to clean me up, make it sound like I grew up in some fancy sorority house and they definitely didn't like what they called my foul mouth."

A gruff voice from the back rang out, edged with amusement. "Your truth wouldn't sound right without the profanity. You got a talent for it."

"Damn skippy," Billie said, drawing laughter from the crowd.

"Was it hard to bare your soul?" someone else asked.

"I've been an open book," Billie said.

She took a few more questions before standing and suddenly announcing, "Okay, I'm done."

A wave of admirers rushed forward, books clutched to their chests, eager for autographs. Billie leaned against the table stacked with crisp, untouched copies, her smile slow and syrupy as she scrawled her name across the title pages.

Hazel hung back until the last eager person had gotten their book signed.

When she finally stepped forward, Billie's face lit up. "Well, if it ain't my girl," she drawled, her smile widening. "Didn't think you'd show."

Billie had been busy with her gig at the Mars Club, and they hadn't spent as much time together as Hazel had hoped.

"I wouldn't miss it," Hazel said, taking her hand in a gentle squeeze. Billie's skin was damp, her pulse thrumming just a little too fast beneath Hazel's fingertips. "You were wonderful."

"Of course I was," Billie said, but the bravado wavered as she tucked a stray curl behind her ear. "I always am. Boring doesn't sell, Hazel. If the truth makes you a legend, you give the people what they want—with a cherry on top."

Hazel laughed. "I'm just glad my name isn't in the book in a bad way."

"I left out your dirt on purpose," Billie murmured, her gaze turning sly. "Didn't want to tangle your good name in my shadows."

"I'm not so sure about a good name anymore."

Billie tilted her head, her eyes heavy-lidded. Hazel noticed smudged lipstick at the corner of her mouth, the sheen of sweat glistening along her brow, the telltale redness in her eyes. "Who decides what's good? The ones telling the story—or the ones brave enough to live it?"

"You're right about that." She paused.

"But really, are you okay?" Hazel's voice was low, careful.

Billie scoffed, waving a dismissive hand. "Don't start. I'm just tired, Hazel. Ain't easy tellin' your whole life to a room full of strangers."

Hazel wanted to believe her. She wanted to pretend Billie's sway was exhaustion, that the slur in her voice was nothing more than the weight of the night. But she knew better.

Before she could press further, Louis approached, wearing a suit that looked like he had slept in it for three days. Hazel had heard that he'd joined Billie in Paris. She'd chalked Billie's distance up to his presence, especially because the few times that Hazel had met Louis over the years, they weren't exactly friendly.

"Billie," he said, ignoring Hazel completely. No surprise. He didn't care for her, and the feeling was mutual. "Is this shindig over?"

Billie shot him a glare. "Seeing as how it started two hours ago, I'd think it was."

"Well, then, let's go." He snapped his fingers as if summoning a dog.

Billie's expression darkened. "Don't you see me talking? I'll leave when I'm ready."

"You're ready now."

"You think you own me, Louis?" Billie hissed, jabbing a finger into his chest. "You think you can run me like you run my money?"

A hush settled over the few people still hanging out in the library.

Louis clenched his jaw. "I'm trying to help keep your wild ass in line."

Billie let out a bitter laugh. "Help? By keepin' me on a leash?" She turned to Hazel suddenly, eyes blazing. "You believe this man? Thinks I can't make a move without his say-so."

Hazel forced a smile, glancing at the onlookers. "Billie, let's just get out of here, all right?"

"I am sick of him," Billie said, plopping down in a chair. "He doesn't tell me what to do."

"Then come with me," Hazel said gently.

Billie's gaze flickered between Hazel and Louis before she let out an exaggerated sigh. "Fine," she grumbled. "But I need a drink." She took a small flask out of her handbag and gulped the liquor down before Hazel could stop her.

"No," Hazel said, reaching for her arm. "You need fresh air."

"You need to change your name to Lady Wasted. You're pathetic," Louis said, spinning and knocking over some of the books as he stomped out the library.

"Come on, Billie. Let me get you home," Hazel said, trying to help her friend to her feet. Billie snatched her arm away, almost toppling over.

"Dammit, Hazel, stop trying to save me," Billie said.

"You sure you can handle her on your own?"

Hazel turned, startled. Quincy leaned against a bookshelf, a book tucked under his arm.

"What are you doing here?" she asked.

Quincy lifted his book. "I read, Hazel. Contrary to what you may think, I'm not all jazz and whiskey."

She sighed as she guided Billie out the library. "You wanna help? Hail us a taxi."

Quincy darted outside. Hazel all but dragged an agitated Billie out. Thankfully, it didn't take long before a taxi pulled up.

As Hazel settled Billie inside, she stole a glance at Quincy. He met her gaze.

"Thanks for your help," Hazel said. "I'm going to get her home."

Quincy peered at Billie, who had opened the flask and had now turned it all the way up to her mouth like she was trying to get every last drop.

"She's got demons," he mumbled.

Hazel exhaled. "Don't we all?"

CHAPTER 56

May 1958

The telephone rang just as Hazel was holding the last note of her scales, letting it settle in the hush of her apartment like the final brushstroke on a masterpiece. She exhaled slowly, savoring the resonance before crossing the room to answer.

"Hazel, darling, it's Isa." Her agent's voice crackled through the receiver, electric with excitement. "I did it. I got you a film. A real role, not just some lounge singer draped over a piano. You're going to be in *Paris Blues*, playing opposite Sidney Poitier, Joanne Woodward, and Paul Newman. A proper dramatic role, Hazel. You'll be Sidney's love interest. This is it. This is the one."

Hazel's breath caught. For a moment, the world stood still, her fingers tightening around the telephone cord. She squeezed her eyes shut. "Isa, you didn't."

"Oh, but I did," Isa crowed triumphantly. "You'll be getting the script in a few days if you say yes."

"Yes," Hazel breathed, then louder, as if the word itself could break open the heavens. "Yes, yes, a thousand yesses!"

An unrestrained laugh bubbled up from her chest, filling the apartment's silence with joy. *Finally.* A role that stretched beyond the piano, beyond smoky lounges and cabaret shadows. A role where she could move, command, *be seen.* And with Sidney Poitier, no less!

She twirled the phone cord around her finger, grounding herself in the moment. "I can't wait to see the script," she said, her voice still laced with disbelief.

She had barely placed the receiver back on its cradle when a knock echoed at the door.

Hazel smoothed her hands over her skirt and pulled it open.

Quincy stood on the threshold, his lean frame relaxed, one brow lifted in amusement. His jacket hung open, the chill of the Parisian evening clinging to him and the scent of tobacco drifting in with him. In one hand, he held a stack of papers; the other rested easily in his pocket.

"You left these at the studio," he said, handing her the sheet music. "Figured you'd need them before rehearsal tomorrow. And before you ask, I'm not a menace. Greg gave me your apartment number. Hope it's fine."

Hazel took the pages, her fingers brushing his. "It's fine." She studied him for a beat. "You didn't have to come all this way."

"Yeah, those three blocks was quite the journey. I probably should stay here tonight and rest." He curved his lips in amusement.

Hazel laughed and shook her head. "You are funny, Mr. Jones."

He studied her for a moment. "You're glowing."

"What?"

"At first, I thought the glow was because I was at your door. But something happened. I can tell." His eyes drifted over her features as if he were reading music written across her skin. "What's got you looking like you swallowed a star?"

She exhaled, then stepped aside for him to enter. "I got a big role in a movie," she said, closing the door behind her.

Quincy's face lit up. "Congratulations! That sounds like a cause to celebrate. I know a place. Let's go!"

Hazel hesitated. "I don't know . . ."

"Come on," he pressed. "Rooftop cinema, stunning view, Paris at night—all the good things." His eyes danced with mischief. "Let's celebrate."

She clutched the sheet music, torn between caution and the pull of the moment. "Quincy, I really shouldn't. I have rehearsal in the morning, and—"

He placed a hand over his heart in mock devastation. "You wound me, Hazel. Turning down an evening of my charming company?"

She laughed despite herself. "You are relentless."

"That I am." He extended his hand, palm up. "Come on. Live a little."

Hazel hesitated for only a breath before sighing in surrender. This moment did deserve a celebration. She reached for her wrap, draping the soft fabric over her shoulders. "Fine. One film. *Then* I'm coming straight home."

"Of course," Quincy said, grinning as he led her out into the night.

THE ROOFTOP WAS tucked away above a quiet Montmartre theater, a secret known only to those who understood the romance of a Parisian evening. A small screen had been propped up against the brick wall, a projector humming as the opening credits of *Funny Face* flickered to life.

Hazel settled into the seat beside Quincy, the city stretching out below them.

"So, tell me about this film of yours," he said, turning to her as previews played on the screen.

Hazel smoothed her hands over her lap, still feeling the thrill of Isa's call. "I'm going to play Sidney Poitier's love interest," she said, her voice lifting with excitement. "Not just a singer they shove onstage between the real action, but a speaking role that's actually part of the story. One of the stars!"

Quincy nodded, his attention fully on her. "That's big, Hazel. They finally see you for more than just your voice."

She looked at him, surprised that he saw through her.

He nudged her elbow. "Let me know if you need a leading man. I can be your . . ." He paused dramatically, searching for the right name. "Your Marlon Brando."

She burst into laughter, shaking her head. "Quincy, please. You are neither brooding enough nor tragic enough."

"That can be arranged," he said, stroking his cheek as he gave her an array of profile views. "All I need is the right lighting."

She swatted at his arm, still laughing.

They turned back to the screen, the film unfolding before them in flickering black and white, Paris captured in a way that felt both dreamlike and tangible. As the music swelled, Hazel let herself relax, the weight of expectation, worry, and exhaustion slipping away.

CHAPTER 57

July 1958

The lights in the club on rue Fontaine glowed softly. A golden sheen lit up the plush velvet chairs. The air buzzed with conversation, a blend of artists, intellectuals, and musicians. Ada "Bricktop" Smith's voice floated through the room, filling it with a rich, smoky tone. Her red curls glimmered like embers in the soft lighting, and she moved from table to table, serenading the crowd.

Across from Hazel, Quincy leaned back in his chair, his dark eyes glinting with youthful fire. Relaxed, he seemed to drink in every detail of the evening, as though trying to absorb it all.

"You know," he said, glancing toward the stage, "this woman's pretty good."

Hazel smiled. "Yeah, my mother used to talk about Bricktop all the time. Said she had pipes that could make angels weep. Called her a force, more than just a singer."

Quincy nodded, his eyes following Bricktop's graceful movements across the room. "She is something else."

As if on cue, Bricktop raised her voice, her lyrics floating toward them:

"Thanks for the memories, of Paris in the spring, the Cole Porter songs we'd sing, of the old Grand Duc and onion soup. And other priceless things."

Quincy chuckled softly. "It's like she's writing our story."

Their eyes met for a brief moment, and Hazel let herself enjoy the warmth of the evening—the wine, the music, the rhythm of their conversation. They'd hung out a few times over the past few months, but it was always with other people from the studio. This was the first time they'd been out alone since their rooftop cinema celebration— not that he hadn't tried.

"How long have you been in Paris?" Quincy asked, breaking the moment.

"Seven years," Hazel replied.

"What about your husband? Adam Clayton Powell Jr., right?"

The word "husband" felt distant, like it belonged to someone else. "Adam and I live separate lives."

Quincy leaned forward, his elbows on the table. "You ever think about leaving him? I mean, for good?"

The question hung in the air between them. Hazel considered her answer. "It's crossed my mind," she admitted. "But it's not that simple."

"Divorce never is . . ." She felt something shift in his tone. But just as quickly, it was gone. Quincy's voice softened, and he watched her for a long beat. A small smirk tugged at the corners of his lips. "Well, if you ever do . . . I'm just sayin'—I'm right here."

Hazel laughed, shaking her head. "You're bold."

"Confident," he corrected, leaning back and lighting a cigarette. "I've always known what I want." He paused, his gaze lowering to his plate as if he was searching for the right words. "I dropped out of Berklee, you know? Left the school to tour. Everyone thought I was crazy. Said Berklee College of Music was the best and I was throwin' my future away, but I knew I needed to be performing music, not studying it. Didn't need a piece of paper to tell me what I could do."

There was fire in his voice, a passion that reminded Hazel of herself when she was starting out. Before politics and gossip columns. Just the music, just the stage.

Quincy's expression darkened. "My mama . . . she went into a sanatorium when I was ten. My father worked so damn much, he barely knew I existed. And my stepmother . . . Let's just say she wasn't exactly warm." A bitter laugh escaped him. "I spent more time on the streets than I did at home."

Hazel's heart clenched. "I'm sorry."

Quincy shook his head. "Don't be. It's what led me to music. One night, I broke into this old building and found a piano sittin' there. Never seen anything so beautiful in my life. Taught myself how to play."

His eyes lit up as he spoke, the same light Hazel had felt in her own eyes. "That's how it started for me. I used to watch the bands, see how they moved, how they commanded respect. It wasn't just about the music—it was about identity, power. And all the girls, too," he added with a wink.

Hazel chuckled, but she understood. There was something about music that transformed people, made them larger than life.

"I saw Ray Charles one night," Quincy continued. "He wasn't but sixteen but still had his own place, his own woman, his own life. And I thought . . . that's what I want. To have control. To be seen. To be more than just some boy from Chicago."

The hunger in his words was unmistakable, and it resonated deeply with Hazel. She reached across the table, her fingers brushing his. "You've got the talent and the passion, Quincy. You'll make it."

Her hand curled around his. "We should make music together someday, Hazel. Real music. The kind that leaves a mark."

The suggestion hung between them. For a brief moment, Hazel allowed herself to imagine it—to be with Quincy, to untether from Adam, from America, from the weight of her past.

But before she could respond, a shadow loomed over their table. Hazel looked up to see Bricktop standing there, hands on her hips. The warm smile she had just moments ago was now replaced with cold fury.

"Hazel Scott," Bricktop said, her voice sharp. "I didn't realize that was you. Might I have a word?"

Hazel exchanged a glance with Quincy, who raised an eyebrow in confusion. She pulled her hand away.

"Of course."

Hazel stood and followed Bricktop toward the back of the club, through double doors, and into the kitchen. The clatter of pots and pans sounded distant as Bricktop spun around to face her.

"As happy as I am to have you in my fine establishment, I must ask, are you still married to Adam Clayton Powell Jr.?" she demanded.

Hazel blinked, caught off guard. "Excuse me?"

"You heard me," Bricktop snapped. "What business do you have flaunting yourself around with that boy out there when you're still married?"

Hazel had heard that Bricktop had a habit of minding everyone else's business and was staunch in her religious beliefs, but was this woman really standing in the kitchen judging her? Heat rushed to her face. "What business is it of yours?"

Bricktop crossed her arms, her glare cutting. "I'm a devout Catholic."

Hazel raised an eyebrow. "Congratulations. I was raised Catholic too."

"And you have obviously abandoned the religion." Bricktop scoffed.

"Lady, this is none of your—"

"I don't condone adultery," Bricktop interrupted. "So you and your little boyfriend need to take all that to another joint. You want to make a fool of yourself? Fine. But you won't do it in my place."

The finality in her voice left no room for argument. Hazel's chest tightened with humiliation. She wanted to defend herself, to tell Bricktop she had no right to speak to her this way, but the words stuck in her throat. She was too ashamed to fight back.

Swallowing the lump in her throat, Hazel nodded stiffly. Without another word, Bricktop brushed past her, leaving her standing in the dim light of the kitchen.

Hazel steadied herself with a deep breath, then walked back to the table where Quincy waited.

He stood as she approached. "You okay?" he asked, concerned.

Hazel didn't answer. She didn't sit. Instead, she grabbed her purse and slipped on her coat. "Let's go."

Quincy looked toward Bricktop, who was standing behind the bar, glaring at them. "All right, if you say so . . ." He patted his pocket, frowning. "Umm . . . can you take care of the bill?"

Hazel froze. Her embarrassment deepened. Of course, this would be how the night ended.

CHAPTER 58

September 1958

Quincy Jones's youthful, reckless insight had seeped into Hazel like a melody she couldn't shake. His laughter lingered long after he was gone. She thought about him every day now. Even today as she walked to the studio, memories of their visit to the Louvre filled her mind. He reminded her of a younger Adam, when they discussed everything from world affairs to music and literature. But unlike Adam, there were no airs, no expectations. He stimulated her intelligence, then turned around and made her laugh. When she was with Quincy, Hazel let herself enjoy him.

He's too young.

You're still married.

The reasons they could never be ran through her mind like the refrain of a song she didn't want to sing.

Hazel pushed the thoughts aside as she stepped into the studio. Musicians were scattered across the small space.

"*Bonjour,* Hazel!" the engineer called from the booth, his face lighting up at the sight of her.

"Let's make some magic," she sang, letting the rhythm of her words dance through the room.

"You rang?"

Quincy's voice filled the air before he even walked in. He stepped out from the back, his brown suit hugging his frame. The lavender tie made his deep-brown eyes gleam.

Everything about him carried a challenge wrapped in charm.

"You look beautiful today, Hazel," he said, his voice smooth.

She glanced up from the piano, arching a brow. "Flattery will get you nowhere, Quincy."

He leaned against the piano, folding his arms across his chest. "Just trying to see how I can get my ivory tickled like those keys."

Hazel froze, mid-chord, and shot him a slow, unimpressed look. "That line might work on those young girls you keep around, but a lady will look at you crazy."

He grinned wider, raising his hands in mock surrender. "Touché, Miss Scott. Touché."

She chuckled and let her fingers dance across the keys, shifting the conversation into the background like white noise. His flirting had become familiar, a melody played in the backdrop of their every interaction.

It was nice—really nice—to be noticed. To have someone remind her she was still a woman, still desirable, still seen.

"Besides," she said, her voice lighter now, "you're thirteen years my junior. I've got shoes older than you."

She would've flashed her wedding ring, but that would have required actually wearing it.

Quincy leaned in slightly, the scent of him—musk, cedar—settling into the space between them. He watched her hands move over the piano, then reached forward, his fingers grazing hers as he pressed a chord she hadn't expected, a harmonic shift that sent a ripple through the melody.

"That," he murmured, tilting his head, "is how you make it sing."

Hazel stilled, absorbing the way the note resonated, how seamlessly it fit—something she hadn't thought to play.

She turned her head toward him, her breath catching just slightly. "You really have an ear for this."

His lips curved, that slow, knowing smile. "I have an ear for a lot of things."

The air between them tightened.

Hazel exhaled, shifting her focus back to the keys. "Let's stick to the music."

But the days passed, and the flirtation deepened. The playful exchanges gave way to something more dangerous—stealing glances, whispered words, touches that lingered too long. Quincy was bold, charming, everything she hadn't had in years. And when he played, when he leaned close to show her something on the keys, his breath warm against her skin, the line between music and romance blurred.

One evening, after a particularly intense recording session, Quincy cornered her in the hallway, his expression serious.

"Hazel," he said quietly, stepping closer, "why are you holding on to a marriage that's already dead? You're the only one showing any restraint. He's always in the papers," he added, not mentioning Adam's name.

She inhaled deeply, steadying herself before she spoke. "I'm not going to divorce Adam for another man," she said, her voice steady. "If I leave him, it'll be for myself. If I get involved with someone else, it will be something I want."

"I don't mean to get under your skin. I just want you to want me like I want you. But I'll wait."

Hazel reached out, touching his arm gently. She wanted to tell him to stop waiting, to say that this was all a fool's game. But the words stuck in her throat.

CHAPTER 59

December 1958

The final night of 1958 wrapped Hazel's Paris apartment in a vibrant, festive energy. She'd made ham hocks and collard greens (not exactly staples in Paris), and her friends had packed her place to bring in the new year downing delicious soul food.

Hazel moved through the room, greeting friends with a kiss on the cheek, pressing a hand to a musician's shoulder, exchanging a knowing glance with a writer in deep conversation. She loved being more than just Adam Clayton Powell Jr.'s wife. In fact, no one in this space gave Adam a second thought.

Her apartment had grown into a sanctuary, a place where Negro artists, expatriates, and dreamers gathered, free from the rigid constraints of back home. No one questioned their presence here, no one demanded their obedience. In Paris, she had stepped out of the shadows and back into the light.

"Hazel, where are the paper towels?" someone called from the kitchen.

"Under the sink," she answered automatically, shaking herself from her thoughts.

From the balcony, the hum of the city stretched beneath her, the laughter of late-night revelers drifting up, mixing with the distant crackle of fireworks over the Seine. She stepped outside, letting the cool air embrace her, and leaned against the railing. The Eiffel Tower glowed in the distance, its lights shimmering against the dark sky.

She exhaled, pressing a hand lightly to her stomach. A little weight had settled on her since she'd moved here, a soft curve where sharp edges had once been. At first, it had bothered her—reminded her of the old expectations. But now? She had decided to let herself be. The weight wasn't just in her body—it was in her peace, her joy. Still, she made a mental note: *I'll get back in shape soon. Maybe tomorrow. Or the next day.*

"So, is that young whippersnapper your muse?"

James joined her on the balcony. He leaned against the railing, glancing back inside at Quincy.

Hazel turned to watch Quincy, who was animated as ever, likely spinning a wild story. "Quincy has a way of making everything seem possible. He's . . . passionate."

James arched a skeptical brow. "Passionate? Is that another word for broke?"

"James!"

"Just spitting facts," he said, smirking. "Look, I came to Paris with forty dollars, so I'm not knocking the guy for being broke. But word around town is you're paying for his studio time."

Hazel rolled her eyes. "He's talented. Sometimes you have to invest in the people you believe in."

James shook his head. "Just be careful, Hazel," he said, his voice lowering. "That kind of talent can burn bright and burn out fast."

Before she could respond, someone called out from inside—champagne glasses already in hand.

"It's almost midnight!" a woman shouted.

As they stepped back inside, the room buzzed with anticipation. Quincy broke away from the group and moved toward Hazel just as the countdown began. He handed her a glass of champagne.

Ten . . . nine . . . eight . . .

She felt the warmth of his hand slip into hers.

Seven . . . six . . .

He smiled, his eyes full of promises she wasn't sure she was ready to accept.

Five . . . four . . .

But in that moment, Hazel let go of the uncertainty.

Three . . . two . . .

She leaned in as the clock struck midnight, and they kissed, surrounded by laughter, music, and the pop of champagne corks. The room erupted in cheers, and for a brief moment, everything felt perfect.

Quincy pulled her closer, whispering something sweet in her ear, but Hazel couldn't shake the echo of James's words.

Be careful.

As the night wore on and the party began to fade, guests trickled out one by one, until it was just Hazel and Quincy, standing on the balcony, looking over the glowing Parisian skyline, the remnants of the celebration still lighting up the night. He moved behind her, wrapping his arms around her from the back.

Hazel knew what was about to happen. She thought of Adam—his betrayals, his broken vows, the loneliness she had carried for too long. She deserved this. She deserved to be held and loved.

Quincy reached for her hand, tracing his fingers along her wrist before pulling her into his arms. No words were needed. The last of the fireworks lit up the sky, and Hazel let herself be consumed by the moment.

Much later, wrapped in the quiet warmth of the early hours, Hazel rested her head against Quincy's bare chest. He brushed a curl from her face, his touch soft, reverent. She closed her eyes, letting herself exist in this stolen pocket of peace. Not only was her body completely relaxed from his exuberant lovemaking, but all of the guilt was gone.

CHAPTER 60

Billie breezed into Hazel's apartment with a stack of magazines tucked under one arm, her fur-lined coat slung over the other. She kicked the door shut behind her.

"You still on that magazine kick?" Hazel teased, shaking her head as she poured two cups of coffee and handed one to Billie, trying to casually assess her sobriety. Grateful to see clear eyes and her usual spark, Hazel settled beside Billie as she flipped through the pile of magazines on the table, her painted nails tapping idly against the glossy pages. She suddenly stopped, lifting the latest issue of *Ebony* with a dramatic gasp.

"'I found God in show business,' huh?" Billie's voice dripped with mockery as she read the headline. "Where is He, Hazel? Because I sure could use Him right about now."

Hazel rolled her eyes. "Very funny."

Billie sank deeper into the sofa, moving slower than she used to, but still every bit the performer, even in repose. Her once-effortless movements now came with a hint of fragility Hazel wasn't used to seeing.

"Where's Skipper?" Billie asked, flipping the pages.

Hazel sighed. "With Adam for Christmas break. He'll be home in a couple of weeks."

Billie gave a slow nod but said nothing. She flipped back through *Ebony* until she found Hazel's interview. She read a bit, then tapped at a photo where Hazel posed in a sleek white gown, her hair sculpted to perfection.

"How does Adam feel about this? You say quite a few things I can see him being upset about."

Hazel stiffened as Adam's voice echoed from their last conversation.

You look like a showgirl, Hazel. Not a preacher's wife. And you're still a preacher's wife.

"Oh, he was livid," Hazel said, rolling her eyes. "Had the nerve to call me an embarrassment when he's the one tangled up in scandals with other women. But I'm the disgrace? Because I dared to look glamorous on a magazine cover?"

Billie scoffed, her eyes darkening with empathy. "Adam can go straight to hell. He's got no right to judge you, not when he's out here parading around with whoever will have him. I saw him on the news last week, bold and brash in that damn trench coat with a pipe hanging out his mouth, looking like some kind of spy."

"He's in campaign mode," Hazel said, shaking her head. "But he's also got tax troubles now. The IRS—the entire system—is coming after him." She exhaled, rubbing at her temple. "He thought he was untouchable, but the government is determined to prove otherwise. And thank God I didn't get pulled into the mess. I didn't have anything to do with all that."

"Consider yourself lucky the government isn't messing with you." Billie closed the magazine. "Because Lord knows, they are relentless. You still haven't filed for divorce?"

Hazel sighed. "He refuses to grant it. Says it's not 'politically advantageous' to be a twice-divorced preacher. Like that matters when he's out here embarrassing himself left and right."

Billie's laughter was mirthless. "And cheating on your wife is?" She shook her head. "No, life is short. We can't keep wasting our lives on people who don't value us."

Something shifted in Billie then. The look in her eyes turned distant, her fingers tightening around her coffee cup. "I dream of getting away sometimes," she murmured. "Away from the drugs, the men, even the music. Somewhere peaceful. A big house in the country, full of stray dogs and kids nobody wants. I'd take them all in; I'd love them. Just . . . peace and happiness. Is that too much to ask?"

The raw vulnerability was touching. Billie never talked like this, not about dreams or things she might never have. But before she could find the words to respond, Billie inhaled sharply and shook off the melancholy, straightening her spine like she was preparing for battle. "Anyway," she said, her usual fire returning. "No room for sadness in Paris. We can't let life kick our ass."

She snatched up another magazine and flipped through it. Her eyes suddenly went wide, her whole body stiffening.

"What is it?" Hazel asked.

"Ummm," Billie began. "What's up with you and Quincy?"

His name brought an instant smile to her face. Hazel leaned back against the sofa. "I'm going to be honest. We're kinda together."

Billie arched an eyebrow, waiting, and Hazel didn't fight the grin tugging at her lips. "It just happened," she continued, fingers tracing absent circles on the rim of her coffee cup. "New Year's Eve. And, Billie . . . it was *magic*." Hazel chuckled, her eyes glinting between amusement and disbelief. "Not just how he touched me, but he didn't look at me like I was Hazel Scott, the woman with a scandalous marriage or a career to rebuild. I was just *me*. And since then . . . I don't know. We've barely spent a moment apart. I don't think I'm in love, but I feel *something*—something deep." She sighed, running a hand through her hair. "And for the first time in a long time, I feel wanted for all the right reasons."

Without a word, Billie slowly turned the magazine she was holding toward Hazel—*Confidential* magazine. And there, in bold, merciless letters:

UP-AND-COMING MUSICIAN QUINCY JONES BRAGS ABOUT SNAGGING THE INFAMOUS HAZEL SCOTT!

Hazel snatched the magazine and read the words on the page. They blurred, then sharpened again, searing into her mind like a brand. Her fingers tightened around the magazine, her pulse hammering against her ribs.

Billie was already on her feet. "Let's go find him."

But Hazel couldn't move. Not yet. The fury was too hot, too all-consuming. She forced herself to breathe, the betrayal thick in her throat.

"He's coming by in a little while," she said.

Billie arched a brow. "Good." She started removing her jewelry.

If Hazel hadn't been so furious, she might've laughed. "No. I need to deal with this alone."

Billie hesitated, her eyes searching Hazel's face. Finally, she sighed, grabbed her coat, and left. The moment the door shut, Hazel threw the magazine onto the coffee table and started pacing, the rage clawing up her spine.

Quincy had made a mistake—a big one.

CHAPTER 61

B reathe, Hazel. Breathe."
For the past two hours, she'd been whispering that mantra, pacing the apartment, clenching and unclenching her fists, trying to tame the fury coiling inside her. But it was no use. The anger was too much. The headline had been bad enough, but it was reading the entire article that sent her over the edge.

The front door creaked open, and she spun around, her pulse pounding. Quincy stepped inside, his easy, lopsided smile in place—until he saw her face. His expression faltered.

"What's wrong?"

Hazel didn't answer. Instead, she snatched the magazine from the coffee table and hurled it at him. The glossy pages struck his chest before fluttering to the floor, scattering like the pieces of her shattered trust.

Quincy froze, caught in the tangled web of his own lies for a moment, his mouth opening and closing with no sound.

"Hazel, I—I don't know what you're talking about—"

"Don't you dare lie to me!" She snatched the magazine back up, jabbing her finger at the damning words. Her voice cracked as she read aloud, "'Quincy Jones was overheard bragging to friends about snagging the famous Hazel Scott and how she's been funding his career.'"

Quincy's hands shot up defensively. "Hazel, listen, it's not like that! I had too much to drink. I didn't know the guy I was talking to was a reporter."

"Are. You. Married?" she demanded.

A beat of silence.

Then, in a voice barely above a whisper, Quincy said, "Yes."

The word sucked all the air from the room.

Hazel staggered back as if he had struck her. When she'd read the third paragraph about his wife, she'd prayed it was a mistake.

"But," he rushed on, "she was my high school sweetheart. She knows the deal."

Hazel let out a bitter laugh, shaking her head. "Oh, she knows the deal?" Her voice dripped with venom. "Well, *I* sure as hell didn't. I don't care about your damn *deal*, Quincy!"

She had promised herself *never again*. Never let herself fall for another married man, never let another liar sweet-talk his way into her life. But here she was, duped and tricked again.

"Y-you're married, too," he finally said.

Her voice was even as she replied. "You knew about Adam. I didn't know about *Mrs.* Jones."

Quincy reached for her, desperation flashing across his face. "Everything I felt for you—everything I *feel* for you—is real."

"Get out." Hazel's voice was low and ragged, trembling from the force of her fury.

Quincy hesitated, his eyes pleading. "Hazel, please, I didn't mean to—I *love* you—"

The words snapped something inside her. A furious, breathless laugh escaped her lips. *Love?* He dared to call this love?

Her hand shot out, grabbing the lamp from the side table. With a guttural cry, she hurled it at him. The ceramic shattered against the wall, missing him by inches.

Quincy stumbled back, his eyes wide with shock. Without another word, he scrambled for the door, yanking it open and disappearing into the Parisian night.

The silence was loud.

Hazel stood, her chest heaving, her hands twitching.

The wreckage of the lamp lay in jagged shards at her feet. The crumpled magazine, the damning words still blaring from the page.

A single tear slipped down her cheek, followed by another, until they fell in earnest. She wiped at them furiously, but it was no use. The truth was too heavy to ignore.

Had it all been for a career boost? A stepping stone? A chance at fame? Or worse—had she been *convenient*?

The apartment echoed with silence, but Hazel's mind roared with unanswered questions.

She paused in the hallway, clutching the back of a chair, her breath catching as a fresh wave of fury surged through her. Her nails dug into the upholstery. Then it passed, leaving behind an emptiness in her chest.

In the kitchen, the floor was cold under her bare feet. She stood for a long time staring at the liquor cabinet, its polished glass reflecting her shadow. Her gaze fell to the half-empty bottle of vodka, its label curling at the edge.

She opened the cabinet slowly. The bottle was heavier than she expected.

Hazel unscrewed the cap, lifted it toward her lips.

And froze.

The scent hit her first—sharp, sterile, like the loneliness she'd once tried to drown. She could almost hear her mother's voice, low and firm: *That's not strength, baby. That's surrender.*

Her arm dropped to her side. Then, with a suddenness that surprised even her, she spun toward the trash bin and hurled the bottle in. It crashed against the metal canister with a hollow clatter, rolling among coffee grounds and yesterday's newspaper.

She leaned on the counter, breathing hard. Her hands were damp—she rubbed them down the sides of her dress as if trying to wipe off the temptation.

"Tea," she muttered. "I'll make tea."

Her movements were stiff as she filled the kettle. The clank of ceramic cups, the hiss of gas beneath the flame—ordinary sounds. Steady sounds. She clung to them like lifelines.

Hazel wrapped her arms around herself and stared out the kitchen window as the kettle began to hum.

Eventually, she drifted off to sleep. By morning, Hazel felt heavy and exhausted, but she pushed herself out of bed. Showering, dressing, and making breakfast became mechanical actions to stave off the flood of emotions threatening to drown her.

She didn't want to go to the studio, but deadlines loomed. Contracts and expectations waited for no one. The music had to go on, even when her heart was breaking.

When Hazel arrived at the studio, the musicians greeted her with sympathetic glances. Their eyes flicked to her and quickly away as if they had already passed around the scandalous magazine.

She kept her head high. "To anyone worried, I'm fine. I'm not going to tear the place up," she said, her tone steady.

That let the air out of the room. She spotted Quincy standing off to the side, regret filling his eyes. He approached her cautiously.

"Hazel, can we talk?"

Hazel sat at the piano, adjusting her sheet music as if he weren't there. "There's nothing to talk about."

Quincy winced. "I'm so sorry. I was stupid, reckless—"

"You were more than that," she interrupted, her voice cold. "You should go into show business. You're a fantastic actor."

"I wasn't acting."

"Go away, Quincy," she said calmly.

His eyes dropped to the floor, and he stepped back. "I understand if you never want to see me again."

Hazel closed her eyes momentarily, gathering the strength to face him one last time. When she opened them, she looked at him with icy clarity. "I don't want to see you, Quincy. Not now. Not ever. As a matter of fact"—she turned to the studio owner, Greg, who was trying to act like he wasn't paying attention—"if he is working here, I'll find somewhere else to go."

Quincy backed away, defeated. "I'm sorry, Hazel. Truly."

Greg eased up to Quincy and handed him his guitar. "Sorry, man. If I gotta choose . . ." He shrugged. "She's Hazel Scott."

CHAPTER 62

February 1959

The script lay open on the coffee table, pages fanned out. Hazel had been curled up on the sofa moments earlier, mouthing lines with quiet intensity, letting herself believe—just for a moment—that this role could be her return. Her redemption.

The phone rang.

She hesitated before reaching for it, her fingers brushing the receiver like it might bite.

"Hello?"

"Hazel, it's Isa. I have some news."

The excitement of the script before her dulled at the tone of her agent's voice.

"Hazel, are you still there?"

She stood now—somehow she had risen without realizing it—rooted in the middle of the living room, the receiver clutched in her hand, its long cord draped across the floor.

"I'm here."

"I don't know how to say this . . ." Isa began. "I know how much this role meant to you, but they decided to give it to a young American dramatic actress. Diahann Carroll."

Hazel blinked hard, the name slicing through the silence. She looked down at the script, the lines she'd marked in pencil already starting to blur. Her mouth went dry.

"I see," she said. Her tone was flat, but her throat burned. "A *real* actress. That's what they said."

Isa didn't answer right away.

Hazel let out a bitter chuckle that barely made it past her lips. "I guess once you've played the priest, you can never play the gangster."

"Hazel . . ." Isa's voice was soft. "I'll keep you posted if anything changes."

The line clicked, and Hazel realized Isa had hung up—or maybe she had.

Hazel lowered the phone, her hands numb. She sat, then collapsed onto the sofa, pressing both hands to her face. The tears came hot and sudden, slipping through her fingers. Her chest rose in shallow gasps as a sob broke loose from deep within her. It echoed off the high ceilings, then disappeared, swallowed by the stillness of the apartment.

Paris Blues was over before it even began.

After she had no tears left, Hazel took a deep breath. She had to pull herself together. Skipper was returning home today.

Hazel busied herself, moving from room to room, straightening the piles of sheet music, adjusting the fresh-cut flowers on the table, setting out a plate for Skipper as if he had never left. The apartment was quiet, save for the occasional sound of traffic from the street below.

Her heart pounded when she finally heard the knock on the door. She rushed to answer it, needing her son like never before. Hazel had barely turned the handle when she saw him.

Adam.

For a moment, she couldn't breathe. He stood in the doorway, his suit crisp, his hat tilted just so—but his face . . . there was something different about him. He looked older and wearier.

"Adam?" Her voice cracked, sharper than she intended. "What are you doing here?"

He didn't answer right away. Instead, he stepped forward, brushing past her and into the apartment, like he had a right to be there.

"I brought our son back," he said, removing his hat and glancing around. His eyes skimmed over the apartment.

Hazel's voice was laced with disbelief. "He was supposed to travel back with Mrs. Hughes."

"Both of them are here. I asked her to take him across the street for gelato so I could surprise you first," he said with the same disarming smile that used to make her weak. "I've been thinking a lot, Hazel."

Hazel shook her head, incredulous. "Thinking?"

Adam stepped toward her, his voice softening as he spoke. "I'm sorry. About everything. The way things have been, the way I hurt you. The things I said . . . I regret so much of it. I miss you," Adam said, reaching out.

But Hazel took a step back.

"You miss me?" Her words were sharp and bitter.

His voice was earnest as he continued, "I know I made mistakes. But I've had time to think about what matters. And it's you and our family. It's always been you."

"Since when?"

"Since I lost you. Since I had to live without you."

His words hung heavy with years of history, hurt, and betrayal. Hazel felt the crack in the walls she had so carefully built around herself. Her resolve wavered.

"You've always known how to say the right things, Adam," she said, her voice barely above a whisper. They had seen each other ten times in seven years. They lived their separate lives, and that was just fine with Hazel. She didn't need him back here, throwing her world into a tailspin. "Words . . . they're not enough. Not anymore."

"I know," he said, stepping closer. "That's why I came here. To show you that I mean it this time. I want us to be together again."

Together again. As if it was that simple. As if he erased years of hurt with sweet words and a charming smile. Hazel laughed bitterly.

"Do you really think it's that easy? That you can just waltz in here and I'll fall back into your arms?"

Adam flinched, but Hazel didn't care.

"I came to Paris to get away from you, Adam. From us. Because I needed to remember who I am without you."

"And who is that?" His gaze was intense, searching. "Who are you without me, Hazel?"

"I am Hazel Scott," she said.

"You're Hazel Scott *Powell*." Adam took another step toward her, so close she felt the heat radiating from his body. "Give us another chance."

Before she could respond, a soft voice called from behind her. "Mom?"

Hazel turned to see Skipper standing in the doorway, beaming. Mrs. Hughes was behind him, her expression suggesting she hadn't thought this was a good idea at all.

She raced to hug her son, and while her arms were wrapped around him, Adam joined in and hugged them both.

Skipper wiggled away from the embrace. "Mom, I'm twelve. Stop treating me like a baby."

Adam looked at her over Skipper's shoulder, his eyes pleading. "Let's just take the next month and see what happens," he said softly. "For Skipper."

"Please, Mom. Please let Dad stay."

Hazel's breath caught. Had they planned this? Her mind raced—flashes of Quincy's smile, Isa's dejected voice on the phone. Heartbreak. Heartache. It was too much.

She looked at Skipper—wide-eyed, hopeful, holding on to something she wasn't sure she could give him. Her chest ached.

For Skipper. Always for Skipper.

Adam's voice returned to her, low and steady: "A boy needs his father, Hazel. I need my family."

"I live here now. Paris is my home."

Adam stepped closer, his voice barely above a whisper. "I'll go back to Harlem for important congressional stuff. But since you're my heart, I'll make Paris my home too."

Hazel didn't answer. Couldn't.

She just reached for Skipper's hand—and didn't let go.

CHAPTER 63

April 1959

Why had she ever believed it could work? Seven weeks. That was all it took for the old Adam to resurface, bringing his familiar brand of hurt with him.

They had walked along the Seine, dined at charming bistros, and talked late into the night. Adam had listened to her fears and frustrations, his apologies heartfelt and his promises convincing. Skipper had been in Heaven. But it was all a farce.

Now, backstage at La Rose Rouge, Hazel fought off the exhaustion that seeped in her bones. Her nerves were raw as she watched the scene unfold before her.

"So you're not the emcee?" A young musician, his saxophone slung over his shoulder, stared at Adam in confusion. His tone was light, too light, for the fragile tension already coiling in the air. "You're in that tux." He pointed to Adam's tuxedo, then motioned around to the informally dressed Parisians in the nightclub.

Before Adam could respond, another young man stepped forward. He carried a horn, his youth practically spilling out of his skin.

"That's Hazel Scott's man," he said with a cruel edge, then motioned to her long champagne mermaid gown. "He probably wore the tux because his wife looks so glamorous and he wanted to look good as her escort."

Adam stiffened beside her, then said through clenched teeth, "I am not her man, nor her escort. I am her husband. A United States congressman."

The musician flushed, embarrassed. "Sorry, Mr. Scott," he mumbled, retreating a few steps.

"I'm going to my seat," Adam snapped, turning on his heel. "Before someone asks me to take their order next."

Hazel wanted to follow him, but the flicker of the lights told her the show was about to start.

She took a deep breath, trying to refocus. The spotlight burned hot against Hazel's skin as she stepped to the microphone. The crowd's energy pulsed but her eyes were locked on Adam. He was seated three rows from the stage, grinning in that familiar, easy way—the one that used to be just for her. But it wasn't her he was leaning toward now. It was a woman ten years younger, thinner, more stylish, laughing too loudly at something he'd said. Her hand brushing his arm like it belonged there.

Not again.

Hazel blinked hard and forced herself to inhale. This stage was sacred—her sanctuary. She could not fall apart here. She stepped forward, gripping the microphone like a lifeline.

"Ladies and gentlemen . . ." Her voice cracked, just slightly, but she swallowed it down and plastered on a smile. "Are you ready for a show?"

The audience erupted in applause. Whistles, claps, shouts of *Hazel, Hazel!* filled the air.

She crossed to the piano, each step heavier than the last. Her fingers hovered over the keys, hesitant, as if they'd forgotten what to do. She pressed the first chord. Too hard. The sound jarred against her ears.

Focus.

She started the melody, trying to anchor herself in the rhythm. But her hands were unsteady. Her mind drifted back to the sight of Adam tilting his head toward the woman, his lips moving close to her ear. Hazel missed a note.

She flinched.

The crowd didn't seem to notice. But she did.

She pushed through the rest of the set, her body playing the part, her voice finding the notes, but her soul was offstage—back in that third row, watching something unravel.

When the final chord rang out, she let it linger longer than usual, stalling. She risked another glance toward the house.

Empty seats.

Adam and the woman were gone.

Hazel's smile faltered, just for a second. She dipped her head in a practiced bow, the applause swelling around her like a storm she no longer felt part of.

HOURS LATER, HAZEL stood at the window in the dark apartment, her breath fogging the glass as she stared down at the street below. And then she saw it. A fiery red Peugeot pulling up. Adam stumbled out, the woman from the club still in the driver's seat. She threw her head back, laughing as Adam leaned over into the car.

Hazel didn't wait. By the time Adam entered, she was at the door. His collar was smeared with lipstick, the scent of alcohol and tobacco danced around him as he stumbled inside.

"I can't believe you." Hazel wasn't even furious. She actually felt numb. "I'm so glad Skipper isn't here to see you like this." Their son had a sleepover at a friend's, thank goodness.

He barely reacted. "I'm tired," he slurred. "I'm going to sleep in his room." He waved her off like she was an inconvenience before disappearing into the bedroom.

Hazel stood frozen in the doorway, watching the back of him retreat down the hallway.

The click of the closing door echoed through the silence like a final verdict.

She didn't cry. Couldn't. Something inside her had turned to ash.

She lingered there, her hand still resting on the frame, as if letting go would make it real. Her chest felt hollow, scraped clean. But underneath, something was shifting.

She began to pace, barefoot across the hardwood, back and forth, the hem of her silk robe fluttering with each sharp turn. Thoughts stormed through her mind, tumbling one over the other.

How did I let this happen again?

She replayed every sacrifice—each lie she had swallowed, every red flag she'd painted white. The promises she'd believed, the laughter she'd held on to.

The more she paced, the more frantic her movements became. Her hands clawed at her hair, twisting it into knots. Her breath came in shallow bursts, and her heart galloped in her chest like it was trying to escape.

The first light of dawn slipped through the curtains in streaks of gray and gold, Hazel hadn't slept. The bottle of sleeping pills sat open on the nightstand, scattered like confetti. They'd done nothing but leave her drowsy and dry-mouthed, her thoughts still sharp enough to wound.

Her head pounded—a dull, relentless throb that made her squint against the soft light. She fumbled for the aspirin bottle, knocking over a glass of water. The pills rattled in her shaking palm. She tossed them back without thinking, without caring.

She rose too fast. The room tilted beneath her, the floor lurching like a ship at sea. She gripped the vanity for balance, her knuckles whitening.

When she finally met her reflection, she gasped.

Her eyes were glassy and red-rimmed. Her lips pale, cracked. Her hair, tangled and wild, clung to her damp forehead.

She barely recognized the woman staring back.

Hazel reached for her lipstick—the French red satin one Adam loved. Her hand trembled as she twisted the tube.

She dragged it across her lips in slow, uneven strokes. Once. Again. And again. Smearing it like war paint. Or maybe like a child coloring outside the lines.

Back and forth. Back and forth.

A mask of control. A symbol of the star she once was. Of the woman she used to be.

But it couldn't cover the unraveling.

Thread by thread. Seam by seam.

Hazel stared at herself and didn't move. There was no audience left. No spotlight. No saving grace.

Just a woman breaking in a quiet room, and no one coming to stop the fall.

HAZEL WOKE TO the sharp scent of antiseptic and the soft beep of machines. Her eyelids fluttered open, and the bright light above her stung her eyes.

"Wh-where am I?" Her throat felt raw.

Mrs. Hughes's face swam into focus beside her, her puffy eyes full of tears. "You're in an American hospital at Neuilly," she said. "Hazel, you were dead on arrival. They barely brought you back."

Dead on arrival?

"They thought you were gone," Mrs. Hughes continued, her voice quivering with tearful gratitude. "The doctor refused to give up. He massaged your heart and pumped you full of adrenaline until you came back to life. Thank God. They've arranged for you to return to the States as soon as you get stabilized." She sounded both relieved and terrified.

But then Mrs. Hughes's voice dropped. "Adam . . ." She whispered the name like it burned her tongue. "He was on the phone with the American embassy, trying to falsify your death certificate. He wanted them to say you died of a ruptured appendix. He didn't want anyone to know . . ."

The door creaked open, and Adam stepped in. He looked worn but determined. He locked eyes with Hazel.

"You're right," he said as Mrs. Hughes looked away like she'd been caught tattling. "I was doing exactly that."

Adam turned to Hazel, his face full of resignation. "Because if something had happened to you, Hazel, I didn't want your legacy to be that you took your own life."

He took her hand. She didn't snatch it back only because she was too weak. "Contrary to how things have been. I love you, Hazel. I can't stand the thought that I played a role in you . . . doing this . . ." His voice faltered. "I want to make things right. I'm taking you back to Mount Vernon. You need rest, and I'll be there. We'll figure this out. Together."

Hazel closed her eyes. She no longer cared.

CHAPTER 64

May 1959
Mount Vernon, New York

The house in Mount Vernon felt like a tomb, despite the sunlight fighting its way through the heavy drapes. Hazel's fingers gripped the worn armrests of the overstuffed recliner where she'd sat for the past hour.

Across the room, Dr. Milton Davis adjusted his silver spectacles, his eyes flickering between Hazel and the notepad balanced on his knee. He scribbled something, his pen moving with clinical precision, as though she were just another patient in a long line. He glanced up, and when he spoke, his tone was cold and detached.

"Let's start from the beginning. Tell me how you're feeling."

Hazel swallowed hard. *How did she feel?* A thick fog swirled in her head, and her once-sharp mind felt like it was wrapped in gauze.

Dr. David Leitelbaum, the family physician, stood by the door. His posture was rigid, his eyes full of concern, but he remained silent.

"Well?" Dr. Davis pressed. The impatience in his tone irritated her.

Hazel glanced at the door, looking for an escape.

Dr. Leitelbaum cleared his throat. "It's important to talk, Hazel. You've been through a lot."

"Talk?" Hazel finally rasped. "What is there to say?" She shifted in the chair, feeling the cold air brush against her skin. "You want me to relive one of the lowest moments of my life?"

Dr. Davis didn't blink. "I want you to confront it. To understand why you're feeling this way."

Because despair had become her constant companion, she wanted to shout. Because the man she married kept tearing her down until nothing of her remained. Because she had poured from her cup, given up pieces of herself for him, for their family, for her friends, until there was nothing left. Because she had been running, trying to outrun the darkness, but it always found her. Because her dreams had died.

But she didn't say any of this.

"Very well, Dr. Davis," Dr. Leitelbaum said defeatedly. "I'll sign off on your recommendation."

Hazel blinked, confused.

Two orderlies, clad in white hospital jackets, entered the room, moving quickly to her sides. Before she could react, they slapped restraints on her arms and pushed her back into the recliner.

"What are you doing?" she demanded.

No one answered as Dr. Davis approached, holding a silver machine in his hands.

"What is that?" Hazel's voice shook with fear as she squirmed, trying to break free.

"Just relax, Hazel. We're trying to help," Dr. Davis said, his voice eerily calm as he held up the contraption that looked like two bowls.

"What is that?" she shouted when he moved the silver contraption closer.

"This will send an electric current to the brain to treat your psychosis," the doctor said.

"I'm not psychotic!" Hazel squirmed, trying to get up, to no avail as one of the orderlies forced a rubber bite block into her mouth. The first jolt of electricity shot through her like fire, seizing her muscles and silencing her. Her teeth clenched; her jaw ached as though it might crack. She wanted to scream, but no sound came—only a low, guttural moan as her body convulsed.

When the shock finally stopped, Dr. Davis studied her, his face impassive. "One more, and amp it up," he finally said.

Hazel's body tensed, preparing for the next wave of agony. She pushed heavy breaths through her nostrils as she struggled to exhale. The second jolt hit her harder, hotter, sharper, like her body was being ripped apart from the inside. Tears stung her eyes, but she held them back.

"That's enough for today," Dr. Davis declared, as though crossing off an item from a to-do list. He nodded at Dr. Leitelbaum, who gave her a pitying smile before they both left.

The pain swelled, drowning out everything else, and then came the darkness. Sweet, terrifying darkness.

When Hazel came to, the room felt colder.

She was no longer in the recliner—someone had moved her to the guest bed. The sheets were tucked too tightly, the pillow beneath her head too firm. She blinked at the morning sun spilling through the lace curtains.

The ache in her body was everywhere. Her limbs were heavy, her mouth dry, her head pulsing. She tried to lift her hand, but even that felt like too much.

A quiet knock at the door, then the soft creak of it opening. A pair of heels clicked across the hardwood, and then a familiar scent—powder and jasmine—rushed toward her.

"Hazel?"

She turned her head slightly. Josephine stood in the doorway, her eyes glossy, her coat still buttoned, her brow furrowed with worry. Behind her, Mrs. Hughes hovered uncomfortably.

"I told her no visitors," Mrs. Hughes muttered. "But she wouldn't leave."

Josephine didn't wait for permission. She crossed the room and sat on the edge of the bed, taking Hazel's limp hand in hers.

"You scared me," she said softly, brushing a strand of hair from Hazel's damp forehead. "I had to come."

Hazel's eyes fluttered. She tried to speak, but her voice was buried somewhere deep beneath the fog.

Josephine pushed down the trembling in her voice. "You know, I've always admired you," she said. "Not just your music, not just that fire you bring to the stage. I admired the woman. The fighter."

Hazel blinked slowly. A tear slipped from the corner of her eye.

"No matter what life threw at you, you fought," Josephine continued, her grip tightening. "Whether it was the music or your marriage—you fought. And you inspired all of us to fight too. So don't you dare stop now. Don't you *dare*."

For a brief, fleeting second, Hazel felt something spark beneath the weight. A flicker of the woman she used to be. She held on to Josephine's gaze, let it anchor her in the moment.

Then—soft footsteps.

Josephine turned as Skipper appeared in the doorway, his shoulders small, his eyes wide and wet.

"Mommy?"

His voice was barely a whisper.

Hazel's heart clenched. He'd stopped calling her Mommy on his twelfth birthday. She wanted to reach for him, but her arms wouldn't lift. Her throat burned as she tried to form words.

Skipper stepped closer, clutching the hem of his shirt. "Are you okay?" he asked, his voice cracking.

Hazel tried to speak, but only air came out. Her baby—her boy—was looking at her like she was broken and he wanted nothing more than to fix her. In that moment, she hated herself for letting him see her like this.

"Please, Mommy," he whispered again. "Please get better."

That did it.

The tears came in a wave—hers and his. Hazel pushed against the mattress, forcing herself upright inch by inch, ignoring the pain in her body and her heart. She opened her arms.

Skipper ran to her.

He folded into her, sobbing quietly into her chest, and she wrapped her arms around him with all the strength she could muster.

"I'm trying, baby . . ." Hazel whispered, her voice hoarse. "I'm trying."

Mrs. Hughes appeared behind Skipper. "Come on. Let's let your mother rest now."

She gently pulled him away, but Skipper's eyes stayed locked on Hazel's until the very last second. When the door closed behind them, the silence returned—but it wasn't as heavy as before.

Hazel let her head rest against the headboard, breathing hard. She closed her eyes.

You're stronger than this.

The voice wasn't Josephine's this time. It was older, deeper—her mother's voice, echoing from the far corner of her childhood.

Hazel opened her eyes again, staring at the ceiling.

"What can I do to help?" Josephine asked.

"Help me get dressed before the doctor gets here."

Josephine quickly obliged, helping Hazel out of the bed. Hazel's legs trembled as she made her way to the bathroom. But each step felt like she was reclaiming a piece of herself.

By the time Dr. Davis arrived, clipboard in hand, ready to

continue his assessments, Hazel was sitting up. Her eyes were sharp, her mind clearer than it had been in the two months since she'd been back in Mount Vernon.

He raised an eyebrow when he saw her sitting in the living room. "Feeling better, I see?"

Hazel met his glare. "Better than you think."

Dr. Davis nodded. "Then the shock treatment was successful." He looked at Josephine. "Will you excuse us?"

"No, she'll be staying," Hazel said.

"That's highly—"

Hazel cut him off. "Dr. Davis, I won't be needing your services anymore."

He froze. "Excuse me?"

"I've spoken to my lawyers," she said, making a mental note to speak to her lawyers. "The treatments stop today. You will not subject me to another round of shock therapy, or any other so-called remedy." She was unflinching.

He narrowed his eyes. "This isn't a decision you can just make on a whim. Your mental health—"

"My mental health is mine to manage, not yours. You work for me, not the other way around. And as of now, you're fired."

The words came out stronger than she expected, and Hazel saw the surprise flicker across his face. He didn't argue. He simply closed his notebook with a snap.

"Very well," he said curtly, standing. "I'll speak with Mr. Powell when he returns on Friday. If you relapse, if you show any signs of instability, we will have the courts intervene."

"Do what you need to do. Just do it from somewhere else," Hazel replied. "You know your way out." She pointed to the door.

Josephine's smile was wide as she left. "She's back."

"For good," Hazel said. "But, Jody, I do need one other thing."

"Of course."

"The doctor said Adam will be home on Friday."

"Yes," Josephine replied.

"Three days. That's more than enough time. Can you call a locksmith, too?"

CHAPTER 65

June 1959
Harlem, New York

Hazel was healing. The shock treatments had left her raw, fragile in ways she couldn't yet put into words, but the fog was lifting. Slowly. Day by day. She'd started to feel like herself again—at least in pieces.

One of the first people she'd reached out to once she found her footing was Billie. Their friendship had been strained, but some bonds ran deeper than time or silence. And Billie had always shown up when Hazel needed her. Now it was Hazel's turn.

Adam hadn't been happy when he returned from Washington last month to find all the locks changed. He'd raged, accused, cajoled—but she hadn't budged. Their marriage had been unraveling for years, thread by bitter thread. This last estrangement had turned ugly, and finally she had the clarity—and the strength—to walk away. For good.

She had welcomed the distraction of someone else's troubles—anything to keep from drowning in her own—but now, sitting in plastic chairs in the cold hallway of Metropolitan Hospital, she realized she'd had no idea just how bad things really were.

Billie was dying.

The sharp scent of antiseptic stung Hazel's nose as she held Billie's hand. Her friend was barely cognizant. She was losing the battle against whatever it was that was ailing her. The doctor barely looked at Billie before snapping orders at a nurse. "Run every test," he barked before disappearing down the hall.

Less than an hour later, the doctor returned, his expression grim, and speaking directly to Hazel, said, "Her liver's failing. Her heart's weak. We'll admit her, but . . ." He let the words hang. He didn't have to finish.

Hazel nodded, swallowing the lump in her throat as they wheeled Billie into a room. She stayed by her side, the days blurring together in a haze. Billie's eyes fluttered open occasionally, her lips moving as if to speak, sometimes humming a fragmented tune.

On the third day, just as Hazel dared to hope, the fragile peace shattered.

A nurse entered, her soft-soled shoes whispering against the tile. She adjusted the IV drip, then hesitated, her gaze falling to the nightstand. Slowly, she lifted a crumpled tissue from the Kleenex box, revealing a small packet of heroin beneath it.

Hazel's heart sank. She had been at Billie's side daily—except yesterday, when she'd stepped away to check on Skipper.

The nurse rushed out, and moments later, heavy footsteps thundered down the hallway. Security and two uniformed officers stormed into the room as if responding to a violent criminal.

Billie groaned and rolled her eyes. "What the hell now?"

The lead officer, a tall man with a square jaw, stepped forward. "Miss Holiday, we've received a report of narcotics found in your room. You are under arrest for possession."

Billie's eyes narrowed, her hands trembling on the bed. "Possession? Are you out of your mind? I'm in a damn hospital. I don't possess anything."

The officer ignored her protests, motioning to his partner, who approached with handcuffs. Hazel stepped between them. "This is absurd! She's hooked up to machines—how could she smuggle anything in?"

The officer's cold glare met hers. "Step aside, ma'am."

"This is harassment!" Hazel protested. "She's sick. Addiction is an illness. The city just launched a program to treat it like one. Where's your humanity?"

The officer smirked. "This isn't her first offense. The law doesn't care how famous she is."

Billie stared at the fluorescent lights, her voice laced with defiance despite her exhaustion. "Do what you gotta do. I don't even care anymore."

They placed a guard outside her room and handed Hazel a paper detailing new visitation restrictions. Anger and helplessness warred within her as she watched Billie reduced to a prisoner in her hospital bed.

Days dragged on. Hazel stayed at Billie's side, holding her hand as nurses whispered about an arraignment in the hospital. Billie's health deteriorated visibly. One afternoon, she murmured, "They're gonna drag me outta here in chains, Haze. I can feel it."

"Don't say that," Hazel whispered, her grip tightening on Billie's frail hand. "You're stronger than this."

Billie turned to her, her eyes glassy and tired. "They don't want me strong. They want me gone."

Hazel blinked back tears. She couldn't argue. Billie had fought her entire life—against addiction, against racism, against a world that punished her for her brilliance. Now, it seemed, the fight was nearing its end.

HAZEL STEPPED INTO Billie's hospital room, her eyes immediately falling on the crumpled newspaper lying on the bedside table. The bold headline detailed Billie's arrest and public humiliation—

shackled to her hospital bed like a criminal while her body fought for survival. A wave of anger swept over Hazel.

"Who even brought this in here?" Hazel snapped, pointing at the offending newspaper. She crossed to the table, snatched up the paper, and crumpled it further before tossing it into the trash.

Billie, propped up weakly in the bed, turned her hollow gaze toward Hazel. Her cheeks were gaunt, her beauty diminished by exhaustion but not erased. The metal cuff glinted on her wrist as it chained her to the bedpost. Despite her condition, she managed a faint, sardonic smile.

"Hey, Haze," Billie rasped. "I would wave, but . . ." She gestured weakly to the handcuff, letting her arm fall back to the bed.

Hazel's fury deepened. She stormed out of the room, hunting down the nearest officer stationed in the hallway. Her voice was low but fierce. "This is cruel and unnecessary. Billie Holiday is not a threat to anyone. She's sick, dying even. What kind of person keeps a dying woman in chains?"

The officer shifted uncomfortably under Hazel's glare. "It's procedure, ma'am. Orders from higher up."

"Then override those orders," Hazel countered. "Or I will call every journalist, every lawyer, and every activist I know to expose this inhumanity."

The officer hesitated but finally said, "Hold on." He walked down the hall and used the phone. Hazel stood defiantly, keeping her glare on him to let him know she meant business. Relief fluttered inside her when he hung up and said, "I'll remove them."

Within minutes, the cuffs were off, and Billie offered her a tired smile. "That's my Haze. Always fighting the good fight."

Hazel sat down by the bed and took Billie's hand, now free from its shackle but still frail and cold. Her fingers closed gently around it. "No one should be treated like this, Billie. Least of all you."

That brought a faint smile to Billie's face. She took a deep breath like she needed to refill her lungs with oxygen, then pointed toward the trash can. "What'd they say about me this time? Another headline about the 'fallen jazz star'?"

Hazel shook her head. "It doesn't matter."

Billie let out a bitter laugh that turned into a rattling cough. When she finally spoke, her voice was hoarse. "It's not like I don't know what they're saying. They've been doing this for years—watching me fall, enjoying every second of it. But this . . ." She paused, her voice cracking. "This feels different. Like they're circling, waiting for me to go under for good."

"You're stronger than they think. You've always been a fighter." Hazel tried to force a smile, but it wouldn't come.

Billie's lips curled into a faint smile. "A fighter? Not anymore, Haze. The gigs are gone, the money's gone. Even Louis . . ." She shook her head, her voice breaking. "He's the one who brought the heroin to the hospital. Probably called the coppers, too. Crazy thing is, I didn't even use it." She released a hollow laugh. "Only 'cause I didn't have the strength to shoot up. But it's fine. I don't have anything left to fight for anyway."

"Yes you do," Hazel said firmly. "You'll get better."

Billie's bitter smile returned. "Always the optimist, my little sister. Well, the good news is my heart and liver have stabilized. The bad news? The doctors found another kidney infection." She hesitated before adding softly, "James came to see me earlier. Said I should move to a private hospital. But the doc said I'm too fragile for another relocation."

Hazel blinked back tears. "You're going to get through this. You've made it through worse."

Billie's voice was barely audible as she spoke. "A priest is coming later . . . to give me last rites."

Hazel's composure cracked, but she quickly wiped her eyes, her hand tightening around Billie's.

"Not yet," Hazel whispered. "It's not time yet."

The room fell into silence, the steady beeping of monitors and the distant shuffle of nurses the only sounds. Finally, it was time for the thing she'd been regretting most since she arrived this morning—she had to leave.

Hazel smoothed the hospital sheets around Billie, trying to ease the growing ache in her chest. "Listen, tomorrow is Skipper's birthday so I may not be able to come by until much later."

Billie's lips curved into the faintest of smiles, though her eyes remained closed. "Of course. You've got to be there for your boy." Her breath rattled as she inhaled. "Kiss him for me, will you? Tell him . . . tell him I'm sorry I couldn't be there to sing for him."

Hazel nodded, her throat tight. The thought of leaving Billie felt like tearing herself apart, but she forced herself to speak. "I will. But I'll be back later, okay? You hang in there for me."

Billie's eyes fluttered open, more lucid than they'd been in days, though the effort seemed to drain her. "I'll be here when you get back," she said weakly but with quiet determination. The fear behind her words, however, was unmistakable.

Hazel bent down and kissed Billie's clammy forehead. "I'll be back soon," she said softly. But as she turned and walked out the door, each step heavier than the last, she couldn't shake the nagging fear that this goodbye might be the last.

CHAPTER 66

June 1960

It had been nearly a year since the world lost one of its greatest voices—and Hazel lost one of her closest friends. She knew Billie was smiling in Heaven, cheering her on for the other thing she'd lost—Adam. Or maybe she hadn't lost him. She'd just finally let him go.

Yes, Billie would have been proud to know that the woman who had allowed herself to drown in sorrow and silence was gone. In her place stood someone stronger. Bent, yes. But not broken.

Hazel had returned to the stage, first cautiously, then with fire—starring in a Harlem revival of *Porgy and Bess*, then a string of triumphant solo concerts across Europe. Now she was back in the States, carving a new chapter with an old friend.

Langston stood at the center of the Westport Playhouse stage, his *Tambourines to Glory* script in hand. His foot tapped steadily against the wooden floor as his eyes darted across the page. Dressed in his usual loose-fitting brown jacket, a scarf wrapped around his neck, and a beret tilted just so, he paced, occasionally muttering notes to himself.

The hush of the theater was broken only by the rustling of paper and the rhythmic beat of Langston's worn soles on the stage floor.

Hazel sat at the edge of the stage, a tambourine resting limply in her lap. She twirled it absently, watching Langston with a mix of admiration and exhaustion.

"You rewrite every time I start to get a feel for the scene," she teased, her voice echoing slightly in the quiet house.

Langston looked up, his face breaking into a smile that crinkled the corners of his eyes. "You bring new meaning to the words, Hazel. I can't help myself." He waved the script. "You've got me seeing the lines in ways I never imagined."

She chuckled. "You say that now, but you're going to rewrite act two again tomorrow, aren't you?"

"Probably."

The past few weeks had been a whirlwind of rewrites, lighting cues, missed marks, and divine chaos. And yet, Hazel wouldn't have traded it for anything. Not now. Not after what she'd been through.

"Just make sure Nipsey keeps his tongue to himself next time," Hazel muttered, giving the tambourine a sharp jingle. Nipsey Russell, her costar, had been delivering his lines with his trademark charm, but yesterday, he'd crossed a line when he'd stuck his tongue in her mouth during a kiss on stage. "If he tries that stunt again . . ."

Langston laughed, though a touch of seriousness crept into his expression. "I'll talk to him. You know how he is—a bit of mischief, that's all."

"Mischief is one thing," she said, setting the tambourine down. "This is something else. He knows better."

Langston nodded, understanding without pushing further. He knew how much Hazel valued the play. *Tambourines to Glory* was something special, and despite the constant flux of the production, she was determined to see it succeed. And honestly, she was grateful to be back at work.

Hazel's thoughts drifted from the theater to Adam—and to the meeting she was already late for. Facing him lately felt like walking through quicksand, each step heavier than the last. She stretched her back and stood.

"I have to go," she said, grabbing her bag. "Meeting with the attorney."

Langston gave her a sympathetic nod. "Go on and show them who you are!"

She managed a small smile. "I'm just glad it's almost over." With one last look at the stage, she left the theater.

BY THE TIME Hazel entered the mediation room, the tension in the air was already thick. Adam sat at the head of the table, his fingers tapping an impatient rhythm. The election had him running nonstop, his twenty-six-city campaign tour consuming his time and focus. And what energy he had left was spent battling ongoing tax charges.

Hazel's lawyer, Vincent Robinson, sat across from Adam, calm and composed as he flipped through documents. Beside Adam, his attorney shifted uncomfortably, adjusting his ill-fitting jacket.

"You're late," Adam snapped, irritation clear in his voice.

"Rehearsal ran over," Hazel replied evenly, taking her seat. She placed a folder of paperwork on the table. "I received another tax bill—this one for eleven thousand dollars, for unpaid federal income taxes. Years 1949 through 1955."

Adam glanced at the documents, his expression unreadable. His lawyer stiffened, glancing sideways at his client.

"This is separate from your tax trial," Hazel continued. "They've filed a lien against the Mount Vernon house, the property on Seventeenth Street—everything. All of this needs to be handled by your team."

Adam leaned back in his chair, crossing his arms. "She's being vindictive," he said, speaking to his lawyer as though Hazel wasn't in the room. "Because she thinks I'm involved with my employee."

Hazel laughed sharply, the sound cutting through the room. "Mr. Powell and his affairs, while numerous, are of no interest to me anymore." It was no surprise Adam had hired Yvette Flores to work in his office, and Hazel would have bet money that the Puerto Rican beauty was also in his bed.

Vincent cleared his throat, trying to redirect the conversation. "We're here to resolve the terms of the divorce," he said, "not personal grievances."

Hazel leaned forward, locking eyes with Adam. "I've been more than fair. I've kept this out of the press, asked for no financial settlement, no alimony. All I've asked is that you support our son and cover the costs of the divorce. That's it."

Adam's fingers drummed faster against the table, his jaw tightening. "I'm in the middle of a campaign. These US attorneys have waged a political witch hunt against me. I don't have time for this."

She refused to let his dismissal slide. "And I don't have time to wait. I need to move on. This needs to end." Her divorce filing had been met with opposition: Adam wouldn't agree to any of her terms, which was why they were now in mediation.

Adam's frustration morphed into something that looked almost like recognition. He studied her for a moment, realizing she was serious this time.

"I can't pay the legal fees for this divorce," she said, her tone unwavering. "You're reluctant to support your son financially, as if you're trying to punish him for our relationship, and I've had enough. It's over. I promise you, you don't want to tangle with me. I'm not the same woman."

For once, Adam didn't argue. He exhaled slowly, his shoulders dropping slightly.

Hazel's lawyer raised an eyebrow, but Hazel already knew the battle was over.

"I'll grant the divorce," Adam said, his voice quiet but firm. "You can have full custody of Skipper. Just don't ever try to keep him from me."

Hazel kept her composure. "You know I would never do that. You may be a horrible husband, but you are a wonderful father." Rising from her chair, she gathered her papers. "This was never about winning. It was about doing what's best for our son."

Adam didn't respond, only watched her leave. As Hazel stepped into the brisk evening air, she felt the weight of the past few years lift. She felt totally free.

CHAPTER 67

December 1960

Hazel sliced through the array of vegetables with deliberate focus. She savored the simple joy of preparing dinner. Years ago, an insurance agent had forbidden her from cooking, afraid she might injure the hands that brought music to life. Now the mundane task of chopping onions felt like freedom.

"Mom! Come quick! Dad's on TV!" Skipper's excited voice pierced her moment of peace.

Hazel wiped her hands on a dish towel and hurried to the living room, where her son was perched on the edge of the sofa. His wide eyes fixed on the television, and his finger pointed toward the screen. Adam was addressing a jubilant crowd. Beside him stood Yvette Flores.

The reporter's voice cut through the applause. "Congressman Adam Clayton Powell Jr. is celebrating his reelection tonight."

"He won!" Skipper said.

Hazel was actually happy about that. No one fought harder for Harlem than Adam. It was why they gave him a pass on his bad behavior.

Adam's voice boomed, full of energy as he took the podium. "Thank you, Harlem! But that's not the only thing worth celebrating tonight." He pulled Yvette close. "We were married last week," he announced, to cheers from the crowd. "And we're expecting our first child together. If it's a boy, he'll carry the name Adam Clayton Powell IV."

Hazel froze, her breath catching. Her hands trembled slightly as she hit the knob to turn off the TV. The room fell into silence, broken only by her shaky exhale.

She turned to her son, who sat just as stunned. "Mom? Dad's having another son? And he's naming him Adam, too?"

Hazel swallowed hard, blinking away the sting behind her eyes. She forced herself to exhale and sat beside him, taking his hands gently in hers. She smoothed his fingers between her own, grounding herself in the warmth of his palms. Skipper was growing into a confident young man, but she could see the hurt in his eyes.

"Sweetheart," she said, keeping her voice steady. "You're unique. There's only one you, and that's what makes you so special. You're my Skipper, and nothing can ever change that."

His lip quivered for a moment before he nodded slowly, still working through the weight of the news.

"Tell you what," she said, squeezing his hand. "How about a game of chess before dinner?"

His face brightened a little. "I guess."

"I have to redeem that loss last time when you lucked up and beat me," she said, already moving to the hall closet where they kept the game boards.

They sat at the dining table, the chessboard between them. The clink of white and black pieces against the board filled the room, breaking up the silence that had felt so heavy just moments ago. Skipper played with determination, his brows knitting in concentration every time he calculated a move. Hazel let herself relax into the rhythm of the game, laughing softly when he caught her in a double-jump.

"Checkmate!" He grinned.

She placed a hand over her heart, feigning devastation. "You got me good, Skipper. I might never recover."

He laughed, and for a little while, that was enough.

After two games (and Skipper's triumphant win streak), she ruffled his curls and said, "All right, champ, go wash up. Dinner will be ready soon."

Skipper, still grinning, hopped up and made his way toward the bathroom. Hazel watched him go, a small smile playing on her lips before she turned back toward the stack of mail on the table.

She flipped through the usual bills and advertisements, her fingers moving automatically—until a yellowed envelope caught her eye.

She picked it up carefully, feeling the faint crinkle beneath her fingertips. The return address was faded, nearly smudged beyond recognition, but she was able to make it out: *The Daughters of the American Revolution*. Hazel's mind flashed back to 1945, to the sting of being banned from performing at Constitution Hall simply because of her race.

With steady hands, she opened the envelope and unfolded the parchment inside. The header at the top read: "From the desk of Mrs. Julius Y. Talmadge."

The words blurred for a moment before she focused on the text.

Dear Mrs. Powell, I am writing to you personally to offer an apology for the injustice you experienced in 1945 when the Daughters of the American Revolution did not allow you to perform at Constitution Hall. It was wrong, and it is a decision that has weighed heavily on our organization.

Hazel's breath hitched and her grip on the letter tightened.

. . . Barriers are being broken, and it is my hope that we can right some of the wrongs from the past. I have watched your illustrious career from afar and have been moved by your undeniable grace, talent, and perseverance. It would be a great honor if you would accept our invitation to perform at Constitution Hall for our 70th anniversary celebration. The doors that were once closed to you are now open, and I believe your presence would be a powerful symbol of how far we have come. Please consider it.

The letter closed with a looping signature: *Mrs. Julius Y. Talmadge.*

Hazel sank into the chair by the table, the letter resting in her lap. The irony struck her like a well-timed chord—moments ago, she'd been blindsided by Adam's public display, a wound reopened. And now this letter arrived like a balm, an acknowledgment of her worth beyond any man's shadow.

After years of exile in Paris, blacklists, and battles in her personal life, she felt a rare sense of vindication. They wanted her back—not out of obligation, but because they saw her for who she was and what she'd done for the country.

She set the letter aside and stared out the window, where the late afternoon sunlight bathed the room in gold. Life, she realized, had a strange way of opening doors at just the right moment.

CHAPTER 68

The greenroom at Constitution Hall hummed with distant voices, but inside, Hazel found a quiet sanctuary. She sat still, her fingers trailing over the velvet armrest of her chair. The mirror reflected her poised figure: a bright yellow satin gown that hugged her form, framed by the flickering lightbulbs overhead that haloed her like a star yet to rise.

Tonight was monumental. A long-denied dream was finally within reach.

Hazel took a slow breath, steadying herself. *This isn't just for me,* she thought, casting a glance toward Skipper, who sat quietly in the corner with a book in hand. His presence was calming. This was for him too—for the better life she'd fought to build.

She looked up to see Josephine enter. "Hello, my dear friend. Philippa and I are so excited about tonight. She's already in our seats."

"Thank you both for being here. And thanks for watching Skipper."

She hugged him. "Oh, I'm the lucky one to have such a dapper escort for the evening. You ready?" she asked.

Skipper closed his book, his face lit up with pride. "Yes, ma'am."

He stood and walked over to her. "Mom, you're going to be amazing. I know it," he said.

Hazel adjusted his tie, then pressed a kiss to his forehead, a surge of emotion sweeping through her. "Thank you, sweetheart. Having you here means everything to me."

As they exited, a stern-looking white woman stepped in. She was as stiff as her pale suit, a woman who carried herself as though the weight of history rested on her shoulders. "Mrs. Powell," she began, her voice cool, "I am Mrs. Julius Y. Talmadge."

"Oh," Hazel said with a genuine smile. "It's a pleasure to meet you in person."

"I wanted to thank you for accepting our invitation. Tonight is significant for all of us. And given the way you were treated before, well . . . words can't describe how honored we are that you are joining us."

"And thank you for allowing the audience to be integrated. I know that was not an easy decision," Hazel said. She'd been sure they'd rescind the invitation when she made that request.

Mrs. Talmadge's smile was tight, a brief curve of the lips. "It is a step forward. Hopefully, a step in the right direction. I look forward to your performance. There is a reporter here, and I'll show him in on my way out." With a curt nod, she turned and left, signaling for Hans J. Massaquoi to enter.

The reporter from *Ebony* entered, full of youthful energy and eager ambition. Hazel greeted him with a warm smile and gestured for him to sit.

"Miss Scott, thank you for making time," he began, pulling a notebook from his pocket. "I know how significant tonight is, both personally and historically."

Hazel poured herself a cup of hot tea. "It's a culmination of years of struggle and resilience. But it's more than just history—it's about breaking barriers for those who come after. Tea?"

"No, thank you." Hans looked at his notes. "Your opening act is definitely breaking barriers. When I heard about that, I thought it was magnificent for you to share the stage." He waited for a second while she took a seat. "But I know I only have a few minutes, so let me jump right in. Your career has been nothing short of ground-breaking, and tonight feels like a full-circle moment. Do you see it that way?"

"Absolutely." Hazel's voice was steady, but a flicker of emotion stirred behind her words. "Constitution Hall represents more than a venue. It's a battleground where I once faced rejection. Returning here isn't just about music—it's about claiming space."

"Though you have lived your life publicly, I understand you're actually a private person," he said.

Hazel smiled faintly, her eyes darkening with thoughts of the past. "Privacy is a luxury I've learned to guard fiercely. After living in the public eye—first as Adam's wife, then as a woman carving her own path—I had to reclaim what was left of it."

"I understand. But, if I may, I have to ask. Your ex-husband, Congressman Powell, has been through some highly publicized battles."

Hazel held up her hand, cutting him off gently but firmly. "Let's be clear, Mr. Massaquoi: Adam and I have parted ways. I won't contribute to the spectacle of his legal or political battles. There's enough noise out there without my voice adding to it."

Hans nodded. "Of course. How did your time in Paris shape you?"

A smile tugged at Hazel's lips. "Paris was everything I needed—an escape, a refuge. In Paris, I wasn't just a woman of color. I was an artist, free to explore my creativity without the weight of the world pressing down on me."

He jotted something down, clearly absorbed. "And your music? Did Paris influence your sound?"

"It made me fearless," she confessed. "I experimented with different sounds, fused classical with jazz in ways I hadn't before. That freedom gave me a new kind of confidence."

Hans paused, tapping his pen against the pad. "It sounds like Paris was a healing time for you."

"It was," she agreed, her voice carrying a quiet nostalgia. "But as much as I loved Paris, I can't turn my back on the fight here in America. There's still so much work to be done, and I want to be part of that change."

Hans leaned forward, his voice softer now as he pulled out a photograph. It was an old one—Adam, Skipper, and Hazel in a family photo, perfectly staged.

"This is what the world remembers," Hans said. "But we both know pictures don't tell the whole story."

Hazel took the photo, her fingers brushing the glossy surface. "People see the smiles and think they know what happiness looks like," she said softly. "But there were moments when my spirit was at its lowest, and it felt like the public envied a life that was breaking me down."

Hans's eyes dropped, absorbing her words. "You've been through so much, Hazel. Yet, here you are. What's next for you?"

She paused, reflecting on the years that had shaped her. "I'm at a crossroads," she said, returning the photo to him. "I have my health, my son, my music. I don't know what's next, but whatever it is, I'll face it with the same dedication I've always given my craft."

"And your love life?" Hans asked, a teasing smile tugging at his lips.

Hazel chuckled, glancing down at her hands. "I've loved, I've lost, and I'm better for it. What matters now is that I've learned to love myself."

Hans's smile widened. "That's a strength not everyone finds."

"There were times when I wanted to give up," she admitted. "But being a Negro woman in America teaches you resilience. You learn to focus on the good, even when it's hard. Life has a way of circling back. Today is my triumphant homecoming."

"Five minutes, Miss Scott," a stagehand called through the door.

Hans stood, offering his hand. "Thank you. This was an honor."

"The honor's mine."

Hazel walked to the back of the stage and peered through the curtains. Her eyes landed on her opening act, the talented and beautiful Nina Simone, the young woman she'd met at Cafe Society twenty-three years ago. She was onstage, pouring her soul into her performance.

Nina's power and presence were undeniable. Hazel had never imagined she'd play a role in Nina's career, but knowing she had opened a door for Nina to shine in that moment filled Hazel with immeasurable joy.

As Nina finished her set, the applause thundered through the hall. She came backstage, her eyes alight with gratitude. "That was amazing. Who knew those words you told me that day in Cafe Society would lead me here," Nina said, pulling Hazel into a warm embrace. "They've guided me all these years. Thank you for suggesting I open for you tonight."

Hazel smiled, her heart swelling. "You've earned this place." She watched Nina turn, her back straight as she gave one final grateful smile and stepped aside.

Now it was her turn. Hazel walked onto the stage, the applause overwhelming her. The spotlight swallowed her whole, and as she settled in front of the piano, she glanced at Skipper, blowing him a kiss. His face glowed with pride.

Her fingers brushed the cool keys, and the first note rang out. The audience fell silent, the air vibrating with the weight of history, of struggle, and of triumph. Each note felt like a prayer, each chord a declaration of resilience. The music wrapped around her, filling the spaces where words fell short.

When the final note hung in the air, the audience erupted into a standing ovation. Hazel stood, her chest rising and falling with the enormity of it all. She bowed deeply, her gaze fixed on her son, who was still clapping, tears in his eyes. His face was locked on hers, his applause the loudest of all. This was for him. This was for them. For the future.

In that moment, Hazel knew she had reclaimed her stage, her legacy, and her power. She was changing the world—one note at a time.

HISTORICAL NOTES

Writing *With Love from Harlem* was a labor of both love and discovery. I spent years researching Hazel Scott's extraordinary life—poring over letters, articles, archival footage, personal papers, and her own unpublished autobiography. Most of the scenes and moments in this book are grounded in real-life details. The rest? That's where fiction steps in to fill the gaps and, sometimes, to rewrite history the way I wish it had played out.

Like many people, I knew of Billie Holiday and Sarah Vaughan. But imagine my surprise when I stumbled down a rabbit hole and discovered that in addition to those two legends, there was Hazel Scott—a woman who, in her prime, was arguably bigger than both, conquering platforms in all avenues of entertainment. Hazel was a concert pianist, a movie star, a civil rights warrior, and at one time one of the most famous Black women in America. And yet . . . she's been all but erased from history. That erasure fascinated—and frankly, infuriated—me, and it made me determined to bring her story back to light.

If you're like me, you love getting lost in the story, but there's a part that wonders what's fact, and what's creative retelling. Let me tell you some of the biggest in this book.

The story opens with Hazel's dazzling double piano performance. That wasn't something I invented—Hazel actually did that move in the film *The Heat's On* with Mae West. I chose to open with her performing it at Cafe Society because it perfectly captures her boldness and brilliance, and I wanted readers to feel her power right away.

You'll also notice Nina Simone appearing in the opening and closing chapters. In real life, Hazel and Nina were indeed friends. In fact, Nina credited Hazel with helping her early career. However, they didn't meet at Cafe Society in 1943—Nina was only ten years old then and unlikely to have been anywhere near a nightclub. Still, I wanted to highlight Hazel's deep influence on generations of artists, so I took creative license to frame their connection in a symbolic way.

Also, while there were other so-called "integrated" clubs in Harlem at the time—places like the Cotton Club—those clubs were integrated only onstage. Black and white performers could share the bill, but the audience was segregated. Cafe Society was revolutionary because it was the first truly integrated nightclub in New York, allowing Black and white patrons to sit together and enjoy the music. That distinction was critical to Hazel's story and activism.

A few other historical clarifications:

Hazel never publicly named the boyfriend I fictionalized as Lee in this novel. She did have a special guy in her life whom she was dating when she met Adam, but she was very particular in her personal papers about not naming him. So here, he is a complete invention to help round out her personal story. There are a few other fictional people, some of whom were never named by Hazel and others (like her family in Trinidad) who were created to enhance her story. Speaking of Trinidad, while Hazel was proud of her heritage, and they certainly were proud of her, there is no documentation that she ever returned there to perform. For the sake of condensing characters, I also gave promotions to people in Hazel's life, e.g., her agent Isa (whose name is actually Isabelle, but I didn't want readers to confuse her with Adam's first wife).

There's also no evidence that Hazel was at the center of the Harlem Riots, though she was an outspoken activist throughout her life.

Another creative liberty I took was Hazel's Broadway offer. The very well-known producer, Richard Rodgers did not offer Hazel a Broadway role in *Carousel*, though I loved imagining what could have been.

One figure who especially fascinated me during my research was Josephine Cogdell Schuyler. Josephine—writer, artist, and mother of renowned composer and prodigy Philippa Schuyler—was a white woman from Texas who defied her own family and social norms by marrying George Schuyler, a Black journalist and intellectual. Historical records show that she and Hazel were indeed acquaintances, but I chose to embellish their friendship in the novel. I imagined their bond as one forged through shared passions: a love for the arts and a fierce commitment to activism. While their closeness is fictionalized here, their mutual fight for justice and equality, art and activism, made it easy to believe their lives would have crossed in meaningful ways.

You'll notice a significant time jump between parts two and three—the seven years Hazel spent in Paris. In reality, she moved to Paris twice: first in 1951, and again in 1957. But for the sake of narrative clarity and pace, I made the decision to creatively condense the timeline.

During those seven "missing" years, Hazel and Adam traveled the world together, fighting for justice across continents—from Haiti to Sierra Leone. While the impact they left on the world was profound, I chose to focus this story on their time in Europe, where both their romance and political awakenings took new shape.

And speaking of Adam Clayton Powell Jr.—how do you tell the story of a man who *was* Harlem? A man who was bold, visionary, and tireless in his fight for Black empowerment, yet also deeply flawed? I wanted to honor all the good Adam did—from his groundbreaking work in Congress to his transformative leadership in Harlem. But I also felt it was essential to portray the full man: charismatic, complicated, sometimes selfish and reckless. Because that's the truth of who he was. And Hazel's story can't be told without also telling his.

(And yes, they really did call him "Lord and Master"—a nickname that says a lot about both his charm and his ego.)

I thought I knew Billie Holiday's story, but digging deeper revealed the emotional layers she carried and the quiet strength behind her voice. Her friendship with Hazel stretched over years. Though there are no records placing Hazel at Billie's side when she died, their bond was real and resonant.

And finally—the biggest creation of my imagination? Hazel's homecoming to Constitution Hall. In truth, the Daughters of the American Revolution never invited her back. That's a travesty. But given the opportunity to rewrite history, I did what any storyteller would do: I used the power of the pen to create what *should* have been.

As a journalist, I thrive on delivering facts and uncovering truths. But as an author, I love tapping into my imagination to explore the untold stories and emotional truths behind the headlines. Historical fiction gives me the best of both worlds: the chance to honor real people and events, while also filling in the spaces history left blank. My hope is that *With Love From Harlem* not only entertains, but inspires readers to dig deeper into Hazel Scott's life—and to remember a woman who, against all odds, dared to shine.

ACKNOWLEDGMENTS

After writing about Hattie McDaniel (in *The Queen of Sugar Hill*), I knew there were countless other unsung sheroes whose stories had been erased from history. I went on a quest to find them—and that journey led me to Hazel Scott. I had heard her name before, but it wasn't until I watched Alicia Keys pay homage to her that I began to truly *see* Hazel. The depth of her story, her artistry, her boldness—it captivated me. And so began my journey to tell it. And what a journey it has been.

As a journalist, I'm used to living in the world of facts. Only facts. So writing historical fiction challenged me in ways I wasn't prepared for. I struggled with balancing truth and imagination—trying to remain faithful to history while also giving myself the freedom to fill in the emotional and narrative gaps. A huge shout-out to one of my best friends, Victoria Christopher Murray, who must've screamed at me 7,343 times: "You are not writing a news article!" (She wasn't wrong.) Thank you for helping me with my book in the midst of writing your own.

This book took sweat, tears, and a whole lot of letting go— especially of the towering mountain of research I often became lost in. But in the end, I'm proud of what emerged.

I'm usually hesitant to start thanking people for fear of leaving someone out—but so many of you were instrumental in bringing this story to life, and acknowledging your love and support is the very least I can do.

I begin with my editor, Ariana Sinclair, who believed in this story, worked with me, and smiled even when I know she was frustrated with me—I am so lucky to have had you help me shape this book into the beauty that it is. My agent, Liza Dawson (and her magnificent team, especially Meg Blackstone, who helped shape the early version of this story), thank you, thank you, thank you. We went through several versions to get here. I'm so glad to have you on this journey with me. And to the entire William Morrow team, I'm ready to make you proud!

To my husband, Jeff—thank you for listening to no fewer than six different versions of chapter one with a smile on your face. Your never-ending support means everything.

To my children—Mya, Morgan, Myles, and my bonus son, Jordun—thank you for asking (repeatedly) when I was going to finish this book and return to the land of the living. I love you more than words can say.

To my blood sister, Tanisha, and my sisterfriends—Kim, Kristie, Clemelia, Jaimi, and Raquelle—thank you for your patience and grace as I pulled out my laptop in the middle of our Vegas girls' trip or over Sunday brunch. Y'all held me down. To Pat—for our endless Hazel conversations over happy hour and for always being the one to "keep it real." And to Renee and Tiffany—thank you for being there every step of the way. And of course, I'd be remiss if I didn't extend a mountain of gratitude to Marie Benedict, who opened my eyes to telling herstories and encouraged me in this genre.

To my sorority sisters and literary forces, Casey Kelly and Dr. Tammy, founder of *The Personal Librarian* Historical Book Club—thank you for your never-ending support. A thousand thank-yous won't ever be enough.

To the book clubs, libraries, influencers, and readers who've championed my work—please know that I see you, I appreciate you, and I'm eternally grateful.

This one's for Hazel. And for every bold, brilliant woman whose story deserves to be told. I hope you enjoy!

ABOUT THE AUTHOR

As a nationally bestselling author and award-winning journalist, RESHONDA TATE has the credentials and the passion to bring stories to life. A highly sought-after motivational speaker and poet, Re-Shonda is a three-time nominee and previous winner of the NAACP Image Award for Outstanding Literary Work. She has received a plethora of distinguished awards and honors for her journalism, fiction, and poetry, including an induction into the Arkansas Black Hall of Fame and the Texas Literary Hall of Fame. Two of her novels have been made into television movies.

Read more from bestselling author

ReShonda Tate

Bestselling author ReShonda Tate presents a
fascinating fictional portrait of Hattie McDaniel, one of
Hollywood's most prolific but woefully underappreciated stars

"This beautifully written novel is a brilliant portrayal of a conflicted woman struggling to
find her place in a world that didn't accept her. Definitely a must-read."

—VICTORIA CHRISTOPHER MURRAY,
New York Times bestselling author of *The First Ladies* and *The Personal Librarian*